THE CELLINI MASTERPIECE

THE CELLINI MASTERPIECE

Raymond John

iUniverse, Inc.
New York Lincoln Shanghai

THE CELLINI MASTERPIECE

iUniverse, Inc.

For information address:
iUniverse, Inc.
2021 Pine Lake Road, Suite 100
Lincoln, NE 68512
www.iuniverse.com

ISBN: 0-595-32805-9 (pbk)
ISBN: 0-595-66688-4 (cloth)

Printed in the United States of America

This book is dedicated to the memory of WB Frank Ronich, a lost treasure that, alas, can never be recovered. Though not an avid reader, Frank enriched the lives of everyone who knew him with his infectious laugh, boundless energy, generosity and understated intellect. May his journey through the undiscovered country provide as much delight to those he meets there as his presence did to those he left behind. Rest in Peace, Frank.

ACKNOWLEDGMENTS

Writing *The Cellini Masterpiece* has been a trip, as they say, or perhaps a Homeric voyage. It began 35+ years ago when, as a graduate student, I put together a European history course and my Malta stamp collection and birthed the idea. My advisor, Dr. David W. Noble from the University of Minnesota Department of History, provided early encouragement and has looked at draft after draft as we both became grayer.

Several friends have brought unique insights and have been lavishly patient with my rewrites. Tom Kendall of Evanston, IL, was my earliest mentor. Mike Chapin of St. Paul has an accountant's eagle eye for problems of continuity and tiny grammatical glitches. Most of all, I want to thank my right hand, Jack Kollodge of Minneapolis, whose ear for the music of language and mind-reader's understanding of my intent has made my task manageable if not always enjoyable. My greatest fan has always been my greatly beloved wife, Evelyn. Every writer, scratch that, *everyone,* should have such a mate. The world would be a much better place if they did.

I also wish to thank members of the Minnesota Writer's Workshop, particularly Herb Montgomery and Rex Pickett, who have offered criticism, both positive and "constructive."

I am especially indebted to three Maltese friends, Charlie Fiott, Tony Abela-Medici and Joseph Bugeja, for their help. Charlie Fiott's books have provided me with vital information about Maltese villages. I encountered Dr. Abela-Medici, the coroner of Malta, on the Internet. We later met in person. He has donated many hours guiding me about the island and correcting my descriptions of the island and people. Joey Bugeja has generously allowed me inexpensive quarters while I was on the island doing my research. His guesthouse, renamed the Bellestrado, is the setting for many scenes in the story and Josefina is named in his honor.

During the long gestation of the *Masterpiece*, I have read countless books, articles, and Internet citations on Malta, cryptography, Benvenuto Cellini, the Sixteenth Century, the Knights of St. John, the history of Islam, and other topics. Cellini's *Autobiography* is required reading for anyone who finds this story interesting. It is a rip-snorting adventure story for all time and one of the best books ever written about the creation of art.

Other sources include *The Great Siege*, by Ernle Bradford, a riveting account of that pivotal historical event. His *Siege-Malta, 1940–1943* does an equally good job with the island's second great siege during WWII. Though dated, Maturin M. Ballou's 19th Century travel book, *The Story of Malta,* is still easy to find and well worth reading. Paul Fregosi's superlative history, *Jihad,* provided the intriguing details about Suleiman's motives for conducting the Great Siege. Two other recommended volumes on Islamic history are Bernard Lewis' *The Arabs in History* and John Esposito's *Unholy War: Terror in the Name of Islam.* The history of codes and cryptographers comes to life vividly in *The Code Book* by Simon Singh. Rev. Rodney Wilmoth's *Reflections* includes the amusing story about the corpulent Raynald the Third of Belgium, also known as Crassas. Finally, *The Realm of Prester John* by Robert Silverberg was an invaluable source on the Prester John legend and an enjoyable read, as well.

The Cellini Masterpiece is a work of fiction. As far as I know, Rick Olsen isn't a real person. Neither, regrettably, are Caterina Borg, Josefina Grech, or any of the other characters that people the novel. Benvenuto Cellini and Suleiman the Magnificent were very real, of course, but their motives and actions…well, who knows? Furthermore, the Malta landscape in the story is both factual and fanciful. The geography of Golden Bay and the history and use of Hal Far airfield are two examples of poetic license.

W. Somerset Maugham must have had Malta in mind when he wrote in *The Moon and Sixpence*—

I have an idea that some men are born out of their due place. Accident has cast them amid certain surroundings, but they have always a nostalgia for a home they know not…Sometimes a man hits upon a place to which he mysteriously feels that he belongs. Here is the home he sought, and he will settle amid scenes that he has never seen before, among men he has never known, as though they were familiar to him from his birth. Here at last he finds rest.

—Raymond John, Minneapolis, July 2004

CHAPTER 1

▼

Saturday
12:30 AM

The lights of Malta International Airport came into view, and Rick Olsen pressed his face against the window to take it all in. Somewhere down there his brother and his brother's discovery were waiting for him. Who could ever have dreamed that a drawing for a major unknown work by Benvenuto Cellini would show up in a tiny bookshop in Florence?

As the Air Malta 727 banked for its final approach, Rick took a last look at the Penguin edition of Cellini's *Autobiography* before stowing it in his briefcase. The cover showed a full-color photo of the *Salari*, the spectacular saltcellar Cellini crafted for Francis the First of France. It was the only authenticated work of the noted goldsmith and on display in the Austrian National Museum until its theft in May of 2003. The 60 million-dollar market value was meaningless. It was priceless.

Now there was a second such work. Or at least there had been. Stef had researched the name on the drawing and contacted the present-day descendant only to learn that the work had been lost during the Second World War. For anyone else, that's where it would have ended. Not with Stef. He would search until his dying day to find it.

The jet whined to a stop with a catchy polka blaring from its loudspeakers. As passengers crowded into the aisle, the doors of the plane opened with a grating sound. The horde started forward. After retrieving his laptop from under the seat in front of him, Rick got to his feet. Even bent forward, his six-two frame nearly touched the ceiling. A female passenger stopped to give him room to get into the aisle. He thanked her, retrieved his bag from the overhead compartment and hurried out.

A cool wind blew in his face. As the line of passengers entered the building, a woman in a black skirt and blue sweater pointed him to Lane 4. At his departure from Minneapolis, an ex-Army security guard gave him VIP treatment through the boarding area. At Malta International he was just another visitor to be processed.

The agent looked at his passport. "US citizen, I see. Your occupation?"

Not wanting to say "prairie restorer," Rick answered, "Farmer."

"How long will you be in Malta, sir?"

"A week or two. I'm on vacation."

"Then you may be here for Independence Day. It's a week from Sunday and I'm sure you'll enjoy it. Have a pleasant stay."

Beyond the immigration checkpoint, several signs pointed to the duty-free shop where he located the Black Bush Irish Whiskey. Stef and he would have a festive time with it while Stef told about his discovery and his visit with Lorenzo, the present-day Cornacchia whose family name was on the drawing.

As Rick stood in line waiting to pay, he casually turned to look back at a young man standing three places behind him, holding a carton of cigarettes. Rick had felt his eyes boring into the back of his head. As he turned, the youth quickly looked away. Far too quickly. Rick felt a twinge of concern and he made a note of him. Twenties. Thin. Thick black hair and a prominent nose. Probably an Arab.

He quickly forgot about the man as he made his purchase and started toward customs. As he waited in line he again turned. The young man was now two places back with passport and cigarettes in hand. The customs agent nodded and Rick passed through the door into the lobby. Several people holding signs with names in English, Italian, Maltese and Arabic peered at him, but Stef wasn't anywhere to be seen. Where are you, man?

Tired of standing he found a bench in the most central area and took out his CD player. Seconds later the soothing fluid gold strains of Leontyne Price singing *O Mio Babbino Caro* began to work its magic. Then it ended and he spent the next ten minutes searching the crowd and getting more and more edgy. Before long everyone was gone and the lump in his throat had turned into genuine heartburn.

He got to his feet.

Three men stood together near one of the doors, covertly sharing a cigarette. One noticed Rick and raised a finger. "Taxi?"

"Maybe. I'm waiting for someone but he hasn't shown up. Did any of you bring a large man with red hair and a beard here?"

The cabbies looked at each other and shook their heads.

"He's staying at the San Antwan in Sliema. How much is the fare?"

"Only six pounds," one cabby said, pinching off the lit end of his cigarette and slipping the butt into his shirt pocket. "Let me take your bags."

Seventeen dollars? He had never spent that much for a fare anywhere in Italy. "How far to the hotel?"

The cabby looked puzzled. "Perhaps seven kilometers. Why?"

"Six pounds sounds like a lot of money. I think I'll look around some more."

The man threw up his hands and turned back to his group. As Rick walked away he heard laughter and he caught them throwing derisive looks in his direction. Screw them. There had to be others.

He was right, although his first thought was that the cab was a runt-sized World War II aircraft that had been converted into an automobile. He could imagine the orange machine barreling down the road on six cylinders straining to get airborne, hood panels rattling wildly, and mud flaps moving up and down like wing elevators. The aviator stood with one leg braced against the side of the cab, curiously American-looking in jeans and tee shirt and a baseball cap pulled down over the eyes. To his disappointment, the aircraft was only a 1937 Chevrolet sedan.

"Where to?" the aviator asked.

He looked up in surprise. The voice was low and surprisingly sexy, like the young Lauren Bacall. Her height, which would be tall for most Mediterranean men, surprised him, too.

"The San Antwan, in Sliema."

"Get in," she said, opening the back door for him. As she turned he could see wisps of long hair coming out from under the cap and well-proportioned bulges under the tee shirt. Beguiled, he asked, "Where did you get the great car?"

"*Tarbija*? I rebuilt him myself. He's my baby."

He was stunned. A woman who can rebuild a car? I think I'm in love. He was about to abandon himself to his infatuation and climb into the back seat when he remembered the question of price. "How much is the fare?" he asked.

"They charge six pounds inside, but I'll make it five. It's on my way home."

His dream shattered. "You cabbies must see us coming a mile away, don't you? That's more than double what they charge in Italy. Isn't there bus service?"

"Not directly from the airport. And they stopped running at 22:00."

"Probably because you pay them off," he said angrily. "Well, I'm not going for it. I'll rent a car, thank you."

An irksome smile crept onto her face. "Have you ever driven in Malta before?" she asked. The tone of voice annoyed him even more.

"Of course," he lied.

When she asked, "At night?" he was sure she was taunting him and he ended the conversation with "Yes, thank you. Now please excuse me."

"I sure hope you know what you're doing," she said.

That tore it! Furious, he turned on his heel and walked away. He wouldn't ride with her if it meant he had to walk to his hotel.

He was still steaming when he got back to the rental desks. The Hertz and Avis stands were empty, but a man in a green sweater was still at his desk. "Excuse me," Rick said.

"Yes?"

"I need a favor. My brother was supposed to meet me here but he didn't show up. Would you call please call the San Antwan and see if he left a message? His name is Stefan Olsen."

The attendant set his pen on top of his paperwork and picked up his phone. "I'll be happy to, sir."

"Thanks," Rick said.

After an extended silence the attendant said, "They say he's registered at the hotel but he left earlier and hasn't come back."

What could have happened to him? Rick wondered. "Would you see if they have a reservation for me? My name is Richard Olsen."

The clerk spoke again. "Yes. You're in the same room as your brother."

"This is crazy," Rick said in a worried voice. Had something happened to Stef on his way to the airport? "I've got to get to the hotel. What would a week's rental cost me?"

"Do you have a reservation?"

Rick rolled his eyes. "No. But surely you must have a car left you can rent me."

"Oh yes. We have a Camry that you can have for a week for one hundred and seventy lira," he pronounced it ee-ra.

"I don't want to sound rude but are there any other rental agencies that might have a lower rate?"

"Several. Island Rentals is probably the cheapest. Would you like me to call them for you?"

Rick thought that was nice. "Yes. Thanks."

After several rings the clerk shook his head. "No answer. It's strange. I haven't seen Mario Agius for quite a while. He almost always comes in at least once or twice a day."

"Looks like I'll take the Camry," Rick said with a sigh.

Once again he felt he was signing his life away. Passport. Credit card. Driver's license. "Do you have another major credit card, sir? We require two."

Mumbling under his breath, he laid his American Express on the counter. "I've got a sperm donor's card, too. Would you like to see it?"

"No, thank you," the clerk said, without changing expression. "Do you wish to purchase additional insurance? I would recommend it. It only costs ten lira per week."

Remembering how people drive in Italy, he nodded his head.

The clerk scratched something on his receipt. "Here are your keys. You'll find the car in space 11. If you have any problems with it, or get in an accident, be sure to call the number on the key ring. We will send someone out in ten minutes or less. You're aware that we drive on the left in Malta, aren't you?"

"Yes. Of all the things you had to save from the British, I would have thought you could have come up with something more useful."

"Very true, sir," the agent said. "Here's your keys and rental agreement. Keep the contract with you in the car. The parking lot is through that door."

Rick scooped up the keys and started away. As he stepped out he realized how remote and quiet the area was compared to the rest of the airport. The Hertz section was first, stretching around the side of the building. Next came Avis. Continuing on he saw a lonely dark blue sedan.

Quickly stowing his belongings in the trunk, he moved around to the left side of the vehicle. It wasn't until he opened the door that he saw the steering wheel on the other side. Just as he unlocked the driver's door a dark figure jumped out from the shadows. Rick countered by springing forward toward his attacker. But before he could reach him he was jumped from behind.

He reacted instinctively, bending forward and throwing the second attacker over his shoulder. The man landed flat on his back on the asphalt. The first man backed away. The second made no effort to move, either too scared or out cold. Rick caught a look at the prostrate attacker. It was the young man behind him in Duty-Free.

The first assailant, shorter and much stockier, pulled a knife from his pocket. A blade glinted in the light as it swung open. Switchblade. Crouching, the man inched forward. Rick bent forward and moved around the other side of the car.

Switchblade stopped next to his junior partner, said something, then started forward again. Rick kept the car between them until the man leaped onto the hood of the car. Adrenaline pumping, Rick backed away. When Junior sat up, Rick caught him on the point of his chin with a karate kick. As the young man dropped back to the ground, unconscious, Switchblade jumped off the hood and lunged at him.

To hell with this, Rick thought, taking off at full throttle.

He knew he could outrun Switchblade. His pursuer must have realized it, too, because he chased him for another twenty yards, then gave up. Much too easily, Rick thought. When the lights went on in his rental car he realized why. His attackers weren't after him. They wanted his luggage.

Though unsure what to do, he turned and ran back toward the car. It screeched off, leaving him alone in the middle of the deserted lot. Taillights quickly became tiny red dots in the distance, then disappeared. He threw his hands up in disgust. Everything was gone including the Black Bush. In another hour he probably would be naked and lying in a ditch.

Then he had an even more chilling thought. The attack could have been a random mugging but it could also explain Stef's absence. He said he had been feeling uneasy ever since his meeting with Cornacchia. If Stef had met with foul play and his assailants had his computer, they would have known Rick's flight and arrival time.

Belongings didn't matter. The only thing that mattered was to find Stef.

A glare of headlights coming toward him sent him at full run in the opposite direction until a familiar voice stopped him in his tracks. "Are you still sure you wouldn't like a ride?"

With a resigned shrug, he turned and meekly walked toward the orange cab. "It looks as if I don't have any choice," he mumbled. "I'm glad to see you. What brought you back?"

"Maternal instinct," she said pertly. "What happened?"

"Two men were waiting for me. They stole my rental car and all my belongings."

"Oh no. Did they get your money and passport, too?"

"No. Luckily I still have them."

"Good. I'm Caterina Borg," she said. "Some people call me Cat. I had to make sure you were all right. Fare or not, I wouldn't leave you stranded here by yourself."

"Thanks," he croaked, the lump in his throat making it hard to talk. "I'm Rick Olsen." He settled deeply into the seat as she started away. How he loved the soft prickles of the old velvet seats against the palms of his hands. He barely had time to notice. Still wary from his misadventures, he asked, "Where are you taking me?"

"To the police, of course. To report the theft."

"Of course," Rick echoed with little enthusiasm.

"I'm surprised they attacked you at the airport. That doesn't happen very often."

"I wondered about the same thing. Maybe they were after the car."

"I don't think so," she said. "This is a small island and it isn't as easy to dispose of a stolen car as it is in the rest of Europe. They must have thought you were carrying something more valuable."

"All I had with me was my briefcase, cell phone, computer and clothes."

"Then I have no idea. What brings you to Malta?"

"My brother sent me an e-mail asking me to come. He said he needed my help."

"And you just dropped everything and flew here?" she asked.

Rick was surprised at the note of admiration in her voice. "Of course. Wouldn't anyone?"

She stopped in front of a stone building. Gudja police station was less than a half mile from the airport. It appeared to be closed but the door opened when he pulled on it. They found a young man seated at a desk. The officer jumped to his feet and touched his cap in salute. "Good evening," the man said in English. "What can I do for you?"

Rick cut to the chase and explained how he was ambushed at the airport. The man listened, asked a few questions, and then handed him a form. "This is your case number. My name is Paul Fenech."

Rick took the paper. "Very efficient. Would you contact the rental company for me? I rented the car from National."

As they left the building, Rick asked, "Why did he ask me the color of Junior's passport?"

"It helps to identify nationality," Caterina said. "You said you noticed his passport was green when he was line. That's the color the Arab countries use. Do you want to go to the San Antwan?"

"I'm not sure if that's such a good idea. Whoever jumped me at the airport must have broken into my briefcase by now, so they'll know I have a reservation there. Can you recommend another place?"

"Yes!" she said. "The Bellestrado Guest House on Ghar id-Dud in Sliema. It's anything but four-star, but Auntie Josefina will be delighted to put you up. You'd be especially welcome if the thieves had taken your money."

"I'm afraid I don't understand."

"Helping people in misfortune is her mission in life," she said brightly. "Mine too. I was born on March 25th, the birthday of Catherine of Siena, so my parents took that to be a divine omen. They even got a special dispensation so I could be baptized in Siena because they were sure I would be like her. St. Catherine spent her whole life assisting the poor, serving the sick, and comforting afflicted prisoners."

"But the saintly Catherine also spent most of her life covered with sores and died a virgin."

She broke into laughter. "How did you know that?"

"I've studied Church history from the time I was a freshman in college. I always wondered if what we Lutherans were taught about you Catholics was true."

"And…?"

"I still don't know. It all depends on what books you read. But getting back to my financial situation, I have more than enough to pay for the room and the fare, too."

"Then we better get going. The pub closes in another hour. So does the hotel."

"I'm in your hands," Rick said. "What got you interested in cars?"

"*Ziju*, Uncle Peter, used to be a cab driver and I loved to help him work on it. Later I learned why girls are always so much more tied down than boys were—boys had cars. I always made sure I had one, too." As she said it, she pulled into the traffic lane and hit the accelerator. Rick shuddered. Glowing graffiti on walls and signs along the way made the ride seem like a spin through a funhouse. Even more frightening was her apparent inability to chose a lane and stay in it. At last he felt he had to say something. "Aren't we going a bit fast?"

"No. We all drive like this."

"On both sides of the road?"

"Of course. Haven't you ever heard? In some countries people drive on the left, in some they drive on the right. On Malta we drive in the shade."

It was hard to laugh with his heart in his throat, but Rick managed a chuckle. She didn't slow down appreciably when they reached urban streets, whizzing between parked cars at forty miles per hour down a path so narrow that if he so much as put a fingernail out of the window it would have been immediately torn off. Most of the time he kept his eyes closed. When he did look, the streets seemed to be an endless succession of doors and projecting balconies. After a while Caterina slowed and parked on a dimly lit thoroughfare. "Here we are," she said brightly. A short walk brought them to a raised patio with a table and chairs sitting in front of an open door.

"We have to go in this way," she said. "*Zija* will be working at the bar."

The sign on the street read The Leprechaun Pub. It looked cheery in its yellow light. Tall mirrors advertised Hopleaf and Cisk beer and scores of pictures on the walls showed happy-looking patrons seated at the various tables in the bar. Two heavy-set men nodded at them as they stepped inside and one tilted a glass in Rick's direction. A young, dark-complexioned man who appeared to be too young to drink liquor sat with a coffee cup in front of him watching television. As they passed he looked away from the television set and smiled.

Thinking he had wandered into the Maltese version of Cheers, Rick held up a hand in greeting. He was half-disappointed when he wasn't greeted with "Norm." A large, ruddy man, who wore his remaining hair in a crewcut, caught Caterina by the wrist. "I see you've got another one," he said with a Scottish burr. "And where did you find this one?"

The question seemed a bit offensive and Rick was about to say something when Caterina spoke first. "At the airport. Now mind your own business, Angus."

Angus let go of her and offered a hand and a beery grin to Rick. "I meant no disrespect, lad. She's always bringing someone in off the street. If it isn't an Arab fresh off the boat, it's some poor tourist she rescued from the airport. Where are you from?"

"Minnesota. It's right in the middle of the country on the Canadian border. What do you recommend?"

"Chisk," Angus said, even though the label read 'Cisk.' "Caterina, bring this man a beer."

"Make it a Black Bush on the rocks," Rick corrected. He already missed his stolen Irish Whiskey.

"You should know better than to drink alcohol at this time of night when you've been travelling," she replied. "It isn't good for you. Have a Kinnie instead."

Rick frowned. "Orange soda," Angus whispered.

"I don't want pop, thank you," he said. "If you don't have Bush I'll take a beer. What kind of bartender are you?"

She didn't reply but lifted the lid on an old metal cooler and pulled out a bottle. Once again Rick noticed her lissome figure and now that she had taken off her cap he caught a look at her long dark hair. After opening the bottle she laid the bottle and a glass on a small circular tray.

Rick nodded and turned his attention to the television at the other end of the bar. It was tuned to CNN. A string of captions indicated that an unidentified American electronics firm had donated two remote vehicle-disabling systems to police in London and Birmingham. Instead of chasing runaway criminals the police could use the equipment to bring the runaway's automobile to a standstill by shorting out the vehicle's electronic system using an electromagnetic pulse. Nikola Tesla's Death Ray strikes again, thought Rick. Kevin would love this.

My god, yes. Kevin. He would have to call him and tell him to stop forwarding his e-mail. And contact the cell phone service provider, too. International coverage was expensive.

As he waited for his drink, Rick caught sight of a woman sitting by herself at one of the side tables. She smiled and crooked a finger at him. Too surprised to ignore her, he waved "ta" to Angus and walked to her table. It wasn't until he got closer that he noticed that her dress was just high enough to cover her nipples and low enough to hide her pudenda. He had to avert his eyes when she uncrossed her legs. "Sit down and talk to me," she said in a husky voice.

Caterina appeared behind him. "Don't! Mind your manners, Anna."

Having had more than enough of Caterina's bossiness, Rick sat. "Is this my drink?" he asked.

Caterina set the glass on the table. "Yes. Don't say I didn't warn you," she said in a disgusted voice.

The remark could have been directed to either of them, but Rick was sure it was aimed at him. Anna opened the top of a cigarette box and pulled out one of the four remaining. Rick picked the lighter off the table and flipped the wheel. She covered his hand with hers as he lit the cigarette, then refused to let go. Now that Caterina had left the scene, he began to feel uneasy. The woman was older than he originally suspected, most likely middle forties. Her heavily made-up cat eyes impaled him. She took the cigarette out of her mouth to exhale and Rick noticed that the filter was stained deep rose.

"Aren't you going to drink your drink?" Anna asked.

"Good idea," Rick said, grateful for something to do. He took a swallow and puckered. It tasted like bitter orange juice. "I thought you were bringing beer," he said, loud enough that everyone in the bar could hear. Everyone looked at him except Caterina, who continued to wash dishes. He started to get up. Anna put her hand on his leg to restrain him. He was now trapped hand and leg. Anna bent forward to reach for her drink, pressing her cleavage against the back of his hand as she did. She was an octopus and he was being sucked in. Amazingly, no one else in the bar paid any attention to either of them. He desperately wanted to call out for Caterina again but decided he couldn't live with himself if he did. Anna slid across the seat until her thigh touched his.

Squirming uncomfortably he asked, "What do you do for a living?"

She stretched toward him to whisper in his ear. "Make love." As she said it she removed her hand from his leg and took his freed hand, moving it slowly and inexorably toward her legs that were now separated. The skirt retreated another quarter inch up her legs.

Utterly revulsed, he nearly jumped to the ceiling when a gruff voice behind him shouted, "Stop that!" A matron in a brown dress and apron hovered over him with hands on hips and eyes flaming.

"Sorry," he said.

Ignoring him, the woman bent forward and threw a murderous look at Anna. The frightened prostitute squeaked and wiggled as far away as she could go. Fearing for his own safety, Rick tried to slip around the spectre. She refused to move. Trapped, he collapsed into his seat with a sickly smile.

The matron took three steps backward. "Come here," she said to Rick.

"Henh." As he stood, Caterina stepped around the end of the bar to join them. "*Zija*, this is Rick. I told him he could stay here."

Judging by *Zija's* look, Rick wasn't sure he was welcome. After a last scalding glare at Anna, she turned to him with a smile. In a surprisingly gentle voice she said, "I'm Josefina Grech. How long will you be staying?"

Before he could answer, Caterina answered for him. "At least for tonight. I'll take him to the main police station in Floriana tomorrow morning. He can decide for himself where he wants to stay after that."

"It's been a busy night," Josefina purred. "But we always have room for someone in distress. Follow me."

As he started away, he turned and waved at Caterina. "Good night," he said.

"Sleep tight," she echoed, waving back with her left hand. Remembering his initial reaction to her, he was more than a little disappointed to see the large diamond she wore. "I'll see you in the morning."

He followed *Zija* to a cluttered lobby where a desk stood next to a polished stone spiral staircase that meandered upward. An open register stood on the counter. He scribbled his name.

"I'll need your passport, too," *Zija* said.

His nose wrinkled at a slightly sour smell that hung in the air. After putting his passport into a wall safe the woman came out to join him. "I think we're in luck," she said. "The elevator is working now. It wasn't an hour ago."

Something above them rattled and a red light beamed from the metal plate. The light flickered, then promptly went out. As it did, he heard a second bump.

"I guess we're going to have to walk after all," Zija said. "Follow me."

With her wide hips, she moved with the easy assurance of a drill sergeant as they climbed the three flights of winding steps to the fourth floor. At the top she turned around and asked, "How are you doing?"

"Just fine," he puffed. Even though he was in good shape, the heat and the climb had him laboring for breath. "This way," she said, starting down a darkened hallway. He could just make out a white doorway from the light that came from the lobby.

At last she stopped. "Here we are," she said in a cheerful voice. She set a squarish key into the lock and turned the handle. The door opened and a blast of hot air hit him in the face. Home sweet home, he thought ruefully.

"It's close in here," she said. "I'll open the window in the bathroom. If you turn on the fan, it should be more comfortable."

She disappeared into the bathroom and quickly returned. "The fan is the second switch. You're welcome here, but we do have rules. Breakfast is from eight to nine o'clock in the morning. No sooner and definitely no later. I close the kitchen promptly at nine. No smoking, alcohol, or women in the rooms. That includes Anna. I don't think she'll bother you, but if she comes knocking on your door, tell her to go away."

For a moment he thought he was back in ROTC. "Yes, Ma'am," he said smartly.

She finished by handing him a 2-litre bottle of water. "Use this to drink and brush your teeth. We don't drink the water from the tap."

After she left Rick took a closer look at his room.

Yellowish light from outside was the first thing that caught his attention. The window in the bedroom was to his right and covered by a curtain that looked like a pair of bloomers with a serious wedgie. The window itself was open and looked out over an adjacent building's rooftop garden that ended no more than ten feet below. Memories of his adventure at the airport took over. He closed the window, locked it and pulled the curtains. Next stop was the bathroom to wipe his face with a damp towel.

As he left the bathroom he felt the breeze from the fan at the center of the room. With it quietly thumping away, the room came close to being comfortable. It seemed cooler still when he stripped and crawled onto his bed. After turning off the light he collapsed from exhaustion.

As soon as he did, a familiar high-pitched whine told him he wasn't alone.

Oh, no. I didn't need to come six thousand miles to find mosquitoes. He armed himself with a tour brochure from his night table and went on a search-and-destroy mission. After nailing two, he convinced himself he had got rid of the pests. As he was about to go back to bed he remembered the open window in the bathroom. He took a deep breath of outside air before sliding the bolt tightly into place. With a sigh he turned off the light and stumbled back to bed.

Sheer exhaustion took over; and he dropped off to sleep. Some time later something woke him. Furious, his fingers fumbled for the brochure he used as a fly swatter. He was about to turn on the lights when he realized it wasn't mosquitoes that had awakened him. A scratching sound came from his bathroom.

Great. Rats.

Light flitted on the wall by the bathroom door. This was no rat. Someone was trying to get in.

C H A P T E R   2

▼

Saturday
2:22 AM
?

Stefan Olsen hung like an immense over-ripe Provolone in a butcher shop. Wooden slats sandwiched him front and back, making it impossible to take a normal breath. All the while he wondered if he would suffocate from his own weight pressing against his lungs. Sometimes he even wished he would. Naked and face down with his hands tied behind his back and his right hand laying inertly against his butt, all he could do was move the fingers of his left hand to endlessly caress the stone wall beside him. The bare rock was his only solace against the all-enveloping heat and the ulcers that were starting to form beneath his beard from the constant flow of perspiration. Worse was the charleyhorse that gripped him from his left ankle to his crotch. Even when the muscles weren't tied up in a knot, the leg was a painful nuisance, causing discomfort in the groin when he relaxed it and let it dangle, and unbearable muscle fatigue when he tried to pull it up and keep his legs together. But the worst agony of all was the hunger pains. "Food," he shouted in a voice barely louder than a whisper.

Silence was his answer.

How long had he been here? Though it seemed like an eternity, it probably was only a few days. After his captors had kidnapped him, they had blindfolded him and brought him to his dungeon. Then the four conspirators stripped him and hoisted him into the crib. From that time on they left him alone except to question him or to change the urine-soaked towel beneath him or clean away his offal. Otherwise they could never bear to come within twenty feet of him.

Hours, maybe days ago, one of his four captors had turned on the lights long enough to hold out a crust of bread in his palm. He had lapped it out of his hand like a spaniel retrieving a biscuit. A little later someone had thrust a straw into his mouth and given him a few sips of water, enough to allow him to get the bread down. Otherwise he was in the ancient Jewish idea of hell. Eternally alone, voiceless and aware, stranded in darkness, unable to move, feel, or taste with only the faint sounds of celebration in the distance to intensify his sorrow.

"Per la merci di dio," he said before he bit his tongue.

For once he hoped they hadn't heard him. He didn't want them to find out he knew Italian because he wanted them to continue to feel they could talk freely around him. That was how he had learned that Friday was the deadline to find the drawing before something important happened on Sunday.

A mutter of voices, but the door remained closed.

His sensation-deprived hearing was now sharp enough that he could almost make out the words they were saying even if he didn't understand them. In his present condition he reveled in every syllable, every flash of light; and the faint scent of incense coming from deep within the stones had become necessary to his survival. Occasionally he thought he could hear other sounds, but they came from a great distance. Once he was sure he heard music.

He tensed as a door opened and he heard the sound of breathing.

"Food?" Stef asked.

"Not yet," a familiar voice said. "I have some questions first."

"Screw you. You can torture me until hell freezes over and I'll never tell you where I put the drawing. You'll never find it."

"No. But your brother is here. He'll find it for us."

Unable to control himself, Stef sobbed. Rick was his only hope. Impossible as it seemed, he had to avoid the kidnappers and find the Shield of God. And he had less than a week to do it.

Heart pounding, Rick groped for a telephone. The only one he had seen was the small payphone in the hallway. He had two choices. Run or face whoever was trying to break into his room.

He made up his mind quickly. The element of surprise was with him. Even if the intruder were armed, he wouldn't be expecting anyone to be wide-awake and waiting for him. Unmindful that he was still nude, Rick grabbed a shoe and silently started toward the bathroom door.

It was ajar, and as he came closer to it, he could see bright light leaking out from inside. Though bursting with tension, he moved with cat-like stealth to the door. Without a sound he dropped to his knees to look through the keyhole. Beyond, a flashlight glared through the window. Reflected beams made the vest and chin of the would-be intruder glow with an eerie yellow light. Though seething in anger, Rick watched in fascination as the figure skillfully attached a large suction cup to the pane and began cutting through the glass to get at the lock.

Even after the intruder covered the glasscutter with a cloth to muffle the noise, the pane still screeched audibly in complaint. Seconds later a circular piece of the window disappeared and a hand reached through for the latch.

Forgetting his nakedness, Rick threw the door open and rushed for the window. The intruder's eyes widened in surprise. Before he could pull his vulnerable hand back Rick grabbed it and dove for the floor. As the burglar's mouth opened in a cry of pain Rick recognized the terrified face. It was Junior from duty-free!

Everything went black as Junior dropped the light. He loosed a terrified stream of Arabic as he struggled to free his hand from Rick's grip.

"Help!" Rick shouted. "Someone call the police." His voice fell hollowly and no one answered his cries.

Holding on with one hand, Rick grabbed for the lightswitch with the other. When the lights came on he caught sight of the straps that crossed the young man's chest and continued over his shoulders. Someone on the roof was trying to haul him up. Rick's grip tightened. "Stop struggling," Rick shouted as bright blood spurted from Junior's wrist. "You'll lose your hand."

Junior screamed out in Arabic and the rope went slack. His trapped hand now was all that was keeping him from falling to the courtyard below and he must have realized that, too.

"What do you want," Rick demanded. "Tell me or I'll let go."

"The drawing!" the terror-stricken man shouted.

"I don't have it."

Junior's eyes fixed on Rick's; slowly the blood-soaked hand began to slip away. "Grab the glass!" Rick shouted. "I'll try to open the window for you."

Fingers clawed desperately for a grip but slipped on the slick pane. As Rick made a last grab for the young man's hand, Junior screamed and fell backwards.

Oh my God, Rick muttered thrusting his head out the window.

The night lay silent and Junior was nowhere in sight. Though barely able to control his movements, Rick turned on the light to find he was spattered crimson from forehead to the tops of his feet, and his hands looked as if he were wearing matching gloves.

The tremors continued unabated as he stood under the showerhead and turned on the faucet. Water sputtered weakly from the tap but soon a gentle envelope of water comforted him as it washed away the gore. Red specks on his legs melted into smeary streaks and the gloves faded from crimson to pink. Soon, only the dark rings under his fingernails remained and they soon disappeared down the drain.

Toweling himself as he went, he hastened back to the bed for his clothes.

The hallway was empty. The only light came from beneath the door of the room next to him and he attacked it with both fists. "Please help," he shouted. "Someone is hurt and needs help."

No one came to the door. Rick cursed and streaked toward the elevator. After a jab at the call button he heard a sound of gears meshing. Then total silence. Shouting obscenities he dashed down the staircase to find that the front door was locked.

What did Zija Josefina expect her guests to do if there were a fire? Wait for her to show up and let them out?

Poised to smash the window, he remembered the pay phones and he rushed for the stairway. Covering four steps at a stride, he reached the first landing. A telephone hung on the wall and he snatched the receiver off the hook. He got a dial tone, but the buttons didn't seem to work. Then he realized why. All calls, including emergency ones, required a 20c deposit. If the young man were still alive, Rick was his only hope.

As he began to search for a way to the courtyard, his thoughts turned to how the would-be burglars knew he was at the Bellestrado. The most obvious answer was painful. The women who had taken him in had also betrayed him. His fingers fumbled for the slim metal lockpick in his wallet. It was awarded to him at the completion of his Special Warfare training with the Navy Seals and he had carried it with him ever since. He never expected to have to use it.

The door swung forward as he unlocked it, engulfing him in the pungent aroma of spices. Even in the dark he saw tables and a glass door in front of him. Reaching it he caught sight of a moonlit enclosure beyond. Another few deft turns with the pick opened the door to the courtyard.

As he stepped through he thought of the body lying under his bathroom window and remembered the look of terror—he would never forget it.

The moon had become a tiny fringe of light in the heavens and was nearly completely covered by a smudgy cloud. Lighting a match he saw Junior's crumpled body lying ten feet away, face up. Two matches later he finished going through the young man's pockets. No wallet. Just a few coins and a piece of paper crumpled up in his jeans. As the fourth match reached flesh, Rick caught sight of the stomach pack around the young man's middle. In it he found a hard leather case. He stuffed everything into his pockets and turned back toward the door.

Before he could move he heard a chud by his feet and felt something sharp hit an unprotected ankle. "Ow."

What the hell was that?

He heard a similar sound and felt a spray of rock chips against his pants legs. My God. Someone's shooting at me!

Backing tightly against the wall, he bent his head back to search the roof. The darkness and quiet were impenetrable. Seconds later, a spray of dirt hit him on his head and shoulders. The rifleman had a flash-suppresser as well as a silencer. And he was moving. If the gunmen had a nightscope he would continue to fire the entire time. The courtyard was a perfect box. With no protection the best Rick could do was move to where the gunman would have the most difficult shot.

The moon broke through the clouds, lighting up the courtyard and he flattened against the wall. By premonition or by chance, he moved sideways. Something crashed into the wall where he had been standing. Without thinking, Rick crumpled to the ground. Playing dead was dangerous but for the moment it beat waiting for the gunman to get lucky and hit him on the fly like a target in a video game.

He vented a silent thank you as the moon disappeared again.

Heart pumping noisily in his ears, he waited. A knowledgeable sniper would shoot again to make sure he was dead, but silence reigned. Then another shot rang out and stone chips sprayed as something barely missed his left leg. Then silence. As the moon peeked out from the clouds again, a rope dropped next to where he lay. He watched transfixed as fifty feet above him a figure got on and started down. As it did, the coy moon once again disappeared behind its cloud.

Rick counted seconds until he was sure the gunman had come down far enough to be vulnerable, then jumped to his feet and grabbed the rope. Like a child playing spider-on-a-string in a schoolyard, he pulled it from side to side, then whipped it to send tremors to the top. He had the upper hand. Even if the gunman were holding the weapon, he would need both hands to keep from falling off. With grim satisfaction, he fed out slack and hauled it in with all his strength to send a gigantic whipcrack to the top. "Drop the rifle," Rick called.

A heartbeat later, the moon again reappeared, outlining the gunman who was aiming with one hand and holding on to the rope with the other. Another shot rang out.

"Bad move, chump," Rick shouted, giving the rope an even more violent shake.

The rope went slack and the man screamed as he came hurtling downward. At the last moment, Rick jumped back to get out of the way. The rifle struck the ground with a dull thud. An instant later, the gunman landed on top of it.

He gasped and went silent.

Warrior now fully in control, Rick turned the body over. Switchblade lay as motionless as Junior. Landing on the rifle must have broken a rib and the force of the fall had driven it into his heart. The gunman's pockets yielded a wallet and a handful of bullets. Rick dropped the match and slipped the cache into his own pocket. Lighting another match, he bent forward to get a better look at Switchblade. The man was about Rick's age, probably in his early thirties, but that was about all he could tell from half of a face. Fighting off nausea he gathered up the rifle and held the scope against his eye. It seemed to be undamaged.

Weapon in hand he returned to the hotel. When he reached his room he tore off the bloodied undergarments, and gathered his shirt off the chair where he had left it. After taking another minute to wash the blood off his face and shoes he left the room.

As he passed the gate that separated the pub from the hotel, he caught sight of a half-filled bottle of Black Bush standing on a shelf behind the bar.

"What the hell. They owe me."

Without a thought that the gate might be alarmed, he unlocked it and pushed it aside. He snatched the bottle and headed toward the front door of the hotel. With a gunt of satisfaction he heaved the rifle butt through the front door window. An alarm shrieked behind him as he coolly stepped into the street.

CHAPTER 3

▼

Saturday
3:12 AM
Sliema

He had barely taken two steps when a kaleidoscope of blue lights began to ricochet off the stone buildings surrounding him. Terrified, he slipped the whiskey bottle under his shirt and moved down the street toward a darkened doorway. The lights continued to chase him until he ducked inside. He was greeted by Inky blackness and the suffocating odor of dust. Shielding his mouth and nose with his hand he took three deep breaths to clear his head.

How much more would he have to endure before the night ended? A grilling at the local police station? Being abducted and led away to join Stef? Nothing would surprise him. One thing was sure. He would never forget the colorless scenario that played out under the light of the moon.

He also knew that before long the police would come looking for him.

Almost as he thought of it, the sound of approaching footsteps set his heart pounding.

Already?

The footfalls got louder and he clutched the rifle more tightly, readying himself to use it as a club to strike out at the blinding glare of a flashlight in his eyes. But the footfalls moved on without hesitation. As they receded into silence the pounding heartbeat in his ears and forehead slowed and finally disappeared.

Just someone out for a late night walk.

His grip on the rifle loosened and perspiration unglued its wooden stock from his palms. About to step into the street he realized that the weapon was as deadly now as it had been when it was pointed at him. On Malta the penalty for possession of firearms was ten years of imprisonment. He also knew he couldn't leave it behind. Like the lockpick, it was a weapon, and essential for his survival.

Groping around in the dusty blackness, his fingers met plastic. It was a trash bag. Holding his hand over his nose he emptied it. The rifle slid in with room to spare and he put the Black Bush in with it, too.

Screwing up his courage he peered out. Blue lights still dashed across the buildings, but the police cars themselves were out of sight. Just two steps out of his hiding place he realized he had a serious choice to make. Straight ahead a hundred yards farther down the street a nearly full moon lit an uneasy mid-September sea. To the left, a dark side street seemed to stretch on endlessly between sleeping shops.

The waterfront won.

His first obstacle was the street corner lit by several lights with clusters of three globular bulbs. Even though the clock across the street said it was past three o'clock in the morning, a middle-aged couple sat on plastic chairs along the waterfront and three teenaged boys stood with their backs to him puffing illicit cigarettes. No one seemed to notice him.

Muttering a prayer, Rick crossed to the promenade that stretched the length of Sliema's western waterfront. A strong wind blew in from the southeast, sending the tide crashing onto the shore in great white-capped swells. All the kiosks and food wagons were dark, but an insistent wind tugged at the tied-down canvases of the umbrellas, making their fringes flutter in helpless protest. A wall stretched as far as he could see, turning seaward at the base of an honest-to-gosh fortress fully lit by strong searchlights.

He walked toward it and found a closed-off stairway leading to the sea. Without thinking, he ducked between the obstructing pipes. Three steps down, his foot dangled over air. Even in the dim light from the street lamps he could see that the steps had disappeared, leaving a nasty drop to he knew not what.

The whole damned island is trying to do me in!

Climbing onto the metal railing, he tightroped down to the base of the stairwell.

At the bottom he found himself on smooth rock crisscrossed with narrow, thin fissures, too straight to have been made by nature. He could also see ponds of water glistening in the moonlight, and some hundred yards ahead, the footings of a seafront restaurant. He headed toward them and felt the wind subside as he reached the shelter of the overhanging timbers. Shivering, he laid the rifle down. Seated with his back to the wind and his head resting against the wooden prop, he fished the Irish whiskey out of the bag and pulled the cork. As always, he sniffed the open bottle before drinking. It went down with a satin touch. He savored the taste before taking another sip. By the third his fear and anger subsided and he could think objectively.

The drawing. That's what the young man had said he was after. Why did they think he had it? Though he first thought the attack at the airport was a random mugging, the second attack proved it wasn't. The invasion at the Bellestrado was planned and required specific information. Caterina and Aunt Josefina were the most obvious suspects. And *Zija* had opened the bathroom window to boot.

The thought that either woman might be involved brought an unusual sense of loss. Even in the short time he had known Caterina he had felt a definite chemistry between them. The Chev was only a very small part of the attraction. She owned the spotlight. Long, sleek and independent with a perfect pair of unblinking green eyes she was the perfect embodiment of a cat and her nickname fit her perfectly. But she was also a consummate actress. He had actually been touched by her apparent concern for him. Josefina's, too.

He pushed the cork back into the bottle and stretched out. Ever so slowly weariness and the gentle fog of the alcohol clouded his thoughts, leaving only the gentle tickle of the wind on his face and the sound of the surf pounding like the slow beat of an enormous heart. As he closed his eyes even those sensations melted away and he wondered why he had never before realized how comfortable rock could be.

$$* \qquad * \qquad * \qquad *$$

He was being marched up a gangplank. With each step, the very ground vibrated and echoed under his feet and water slapped at his toes and wetted his ankles. He was being shaken from side to side as the support under his feet rose and fell before him. Even with the iron grip of the men at his sides to support him, being blindfolded terrified him and he struggled desperately to take it off. The restraints became tighter as the footing leveled. But the floor still rocked under his feet. Why were they taking him on a boat?

"Easy," a voice said. It was the main captor, the one who spoke to him. "We're almost there."

Stef took two more stiff-legged steps forward and found his feet on solid footing. His guides turned him to the right. "This way."

He stumbled on until he was told to stop. "Sit."

He lowered himself onto something solid. The floor rolled gently under his feet. Something in the depths of his stomach started to move, too. Though they had bathed him and given him clothes, he still hadn't been fed.

"Relax," the voice said with transparently phony friendliness. "Have some wine."

"Wine?" he said. His belly shook as he broke out laughing. "The last time you gave me wine I told you to get stuffed and you hit me."

"That was a long time ago. All is forgiven."

A friendly hand squeezed his shoulder. Seconds later a straw rested against his lips. Almost against his will he sucked. Happily it only took a couple of deep pulls before the room began to spin. A couple more and he couldn't ask for the food he so desperately needed.

Someone grabbed his left arm and held it in a vise grip. He cried out as he felt a sting. A nasty wasp sting. It was like the one he had gotten when he was on a family picnic. His whole arm had swollen up and his father had to take him to a hospital.

"Don't sting me again," he said. "I don't want to go to the hospital." Certainly the wasp couldn't have understood him. He hardly understood himself. His voice was becoming slurred and echoed like he was talking from a barrel.

"Tell me and I won't sting you again," the wasp said. "Tell me where the drawing is."

"Drawing?" said a strange voice that came from somewhere in his throat. "What drawing?"

"The one you found in Florence," the wasp said angrily. "Where is it?"

Stef broke out laughing. "Oh that. It's with Queen Mab, of course. Queen Mab. Only she won't tell."

The wasp's voice continued to repeat the question. After a while Stef didn't care if he stung him again. So tired he could barely speak, he mumbled, "It's with Queen Mab, I tell you. Ask her."

As his mind started to get lost in the darkness he was pulled to his feet.

"Come on," said the voice called Pawlu. "You're going back to your cell."

✳   ✳   ✳   ✳

7:02 AM

Something nudged his foot.

Rick shielded his eyes then opened them. What he saw terrified him. A towering black-clad police officer looked down at him. "Good morning," the man said.

The voice was friendly but the eyes weren't. Neither was the nightstick he held in his hand. "Did you have a nice sleep?"

"Henh," Rick said, pulling himself into a sitting position. The bottle of Black Bush still sat next to him. And so did the plastic bag. "I came down to do some fishing and I made the mistake of bringing my bottle with me. I guess I must have had a tad too much to drink."

"Fishing isn't allowed here," the officer said in a less than friendly voice. He gestured at the bag. "What kind of gear do you have."

Certain that he would be asked to show what was in the bag, Rick had fight to keep a tremor out of his voice. "Surf-fishing," he said.

The policeman turned his attention to the whiskey bottle. "Alcoholic beverages aren't allowed here, either. Do you have any identification?"

"Just my driver's license. My passport is locked in the hotel safe."

"Which hotel is that?"

Rick swallowed. "The San Antwan. I just got in yesterday." He got to his knees. As he put his hand into his pocket to pull out his wallet he realized that it was wedged against the shooter's billfold and he didn't know which was which without looking. As he fumbled, he felt the stiff lockpick under the leather of his billfold. Breathing a sigh of relief he took out his wallet and removed the driver's license with a steady hand.

The man barely looked at it. "What time did you come to the beach?"

"Ten thirty or eleven o'clock," Rick said. "I walked from the hotel." His heart skipped a beat as the officer nudged the bag with his toe. It skipped another when he caught sight of a streetvendor watching them. Witness or not, he wouldn't be arrested without a fight.

"That's a long walk," the policeman said. As he toed the bag again, Rick readied to strike. Even though armed with a nightstick, the man couldn't swing it quickly enough to fend off Rick's attack.

"Heavy," the officer said, prodding the bag with his nightstick.

Certain he had no choice, Rick took a deep breath and glanced up at the street vendor. Just as he was about to strike, the man stepped backward. "Did you hear a disturbance during the night? It would have been early in the morning?"

"I'm afraid I didn't hear a thing," Rick said, flashing him a sickly grin. "The bottle was unopened when I got here."

The man nodded. "I wish I could afford to drink that," he said. With that he slipped the nightstick into its carrier. "Just be a little more careful with it from now on. Most of us wouldn't bother you, but some wouldn't be able to resist the opportunity to steal a wallet if someone made it so easy for them."

"I appreciate that," Rick said. "I promise you, it won't happen again."

He nearly fainted in relief as the officer turned and walked away. After the man was out of sight, Rick got to his feet. A building that looked like public toilets stood a short distance away with open doors.

The first stop inside was the trash bin. Grimacing, he dropped the whiskey bottle in with the paper towels. Settled into the closest stall, he laid the plastic bag on the floor and emptied his pockets on the floor. He began with the gunman's wallet.

According to the driver's license, Switchblade was a thirty-five-year-old Maltese national named Michael Attard. The wallet contained a few coins and banknotes, and, after pocketing them, Rick started on the cards. One was for a disbursing officer for the Bank of Valletta. Another, a membership card for the Hamrun Hunting Club.

Finding the rest of no interest he threw the wallet into the bag with the rifle. The handful of bullets followed. Junior's ring, inscribed with what looked like Arabic characters amid the red flecks, disappeared into his pocket.

The stomach pack was empty except for a black leather case and two pieces of rubber tubing. Inside the case he found a hypodermic syringe. Liquid squirted out of the needle when he pushed on the plunger. He shuddered to imagine what was in it. But the pack could come in handy, he decided.

The last item was a piece of paper which turned out to be a receipt from the freighter Sanaa for passage from Tripoli to Valletta dated 3 September in the name of Ibrahim il-Selim. On the reverse he found a penciled note 208869339. A phone number? He would find out for sure later.

Finished, he flushed the toilet and got to his feet. He returned to a deserted waterfront and followed the shoreline until he came to a stairway beside the fortress. At street level the streetvendor was arranging loaves of bread on his cart. Rick used one of the gunman's bills to buy a bag of oranges, a cup of coffee and a loaf of bread. After taking a wary look around he sat down on a bench and spread the food on his napkins. The bread had a crispy crust and was soft inside, and the oranges were juicy with half-orange and half-purple flesh. He quickly devoured the oranges and drank the coffee but could only eat half of the bread. He decided to give the pigeons a treat and broke it into several pieces. Feathers flew as a dozen birds fought each other for the largest chunks.

"How do I get to the San Antwan?"

"Up that street," the vendor replied. "Take a left at Manoel Dimich. The hotel is on the right side."

A ten-minute walk brought him to his destination. He didn't like it. The lobby seemed unnaturally dark and his skin crawled at the sound of his feet thudding on the stone steps leading to the front desk.

A man with sharp features and long canines awaited. When he saw Rick he flashed a lupine smile. "Yes sir?"

"My name is Richard Olsen. I had a reservation for last night but my plans changed unexpectedly."

"Ah yes, Mr. Olsen," the man said enthusiastically. "I'm happy to see you. We were worried when you didn't show up. But no harm done. Your brother already paid for the room. Leonard will show you there."

Rick's ears pricked. Before he could respond, the clerk rang a bell and a second man appeared at the desk. This one had the beady eyes of a rattlesnake.

"218," the desk clerk said.

"Sorry," Rick said hastily. "I can't check in right now. If you'll call his room, I'll have him meet me here."

"Mr. Olsen isn't in," the clerk answered too quickly. "He actually left last night and called early this morning to find out if you had checked in yet. He said he'll be back sometime this afternoon or tomorrow morning at the latest."

"Actually I think I know where I can find him," Rick said, taking two steps back from the counter.

The men looked at each other before the desk clerk spoke. "Can I tell him where you've gone if he calls."

"Tell him I've gone to Co-spikwa," Rick said, using a name he had seen in the tour book. "We talked about meeting there. I'll take one of your cards with me."

His heart raced as the bellhop took a step in his direction.

Not again.

If the man had intended to try to stop him, he relented. Rick turned and left, feeling the men's eyes on his back as he walked out the door. He had no doubts what would have happened if he checked in.

A passing horse-drawn cab stopped for him. A few blocks later he got out. Even though he was almost certain Stef wasn't in the room, he had to be sure.

The city of Sliema was busily shaking off the torpor of the night. A woman appeared with a broom to sweep the sidewalk in front of her house and a greengrocer laid a large basket of potatoes on the wooden display racks. Rick slowly meandered back in the direction he had come, keeping a wary eye on the pedestrians as he went. Despite his uneasiness he met nothing more threatening than the angry barks of an unleashed Yorkshire Terrier who resolutely stood in his path and lunged at his heels as he passed.

A short walk brought him to a street that ran parallel to Manoel Dimich and he turned to start up the hill.

He was in luck. An apartment complex under construction broke the solid line of buildings along the street and provided an alley toward the hotel. Somewhere near, a jackhammer rat-tatted away, but no workers were in sight. Rick carefully picked his way between the huge blocks of stone and the holes in the ground next to a four-story building. Scars on its stone surface suggested that the demolished structure had been built flush against it. Now that it was gone, a wooden door had reappeared.

Its large keyhole was an enticing target. The lock mechanism was sluggish but a few deft movements with his pick set it free. Crossing his fingers that the door hadn't been barricaded from the inside, he pushed. It scraped forward and stopped. Something immovable was in the way.

Digging his feet into the ground he shoved against the door with his full weight but it refused to budge. The opening was just big enough to let his shoulders through so he exhaled and wiggled through the rest of the way.

Crates of varying sizes filled the room. Groping his way between them he saw a sliver of light on the floor ahead of him. A doorway. After unburdening himself of the rifle, he opened it. A stairway led upwards and he followed it to a door marked with a numeral 2. A short walk brought him to 218 where he stopped, unsure what to do next. The only way to find out if Stef was inside was to walk into a trap.

A sound from inside sent him to his knees. Eye to keyhole he saw a man sitting in a chair cuddling a nine-millimeter handgun in his lap.

So it *was* a trap. He hurried back to the storeroom to gather up the rifle and left the building. On Dom Minich Street he found a coffee shop that was open.

"Can you tell me the way to the closest Internet café that would be open?" Rick asked.

"There's one on the Strand but it doesn't open until 9:30", said the storekeeper. "The one in Valetta opens at 8. You can catch the bus right out front."

Sure that it couldn't be all that far, Rick decided to walk.

The waterfront was now alive with tourists. And construction workers in trucks as well. Less than a block away the sidewalk ended in a wooden wall. Workmen wearing hardhats pushed wheelbarrows and toted bags of concrete over their shoulders. Moving closer to investigate, he saw a large Volvo pickup with a load of rebar and steel rods pull up to the deliveries gate and honk. An immense pair of wooden doors swung open and the pickup drove through. Through the open gate he saw the forms for concrete footings. Judging from the spacing and the total area of the construction site, some sort of skyscraper was under construction. A large green sign on the side of the fence read *Dukessa Kostruzzjoni*.

As he continued on, traffic got heavier. He kept an especially sharp eye out for the orange Chevrolet. If Caterina Borg really were a cabby, she wouldn't be that hard to find.

And find her he would. He owed it to her. But one question bothered him. If someone were lying in wait at the San Antwan, why would they jump him at the airport? So far he had only thought of what had happened to him in terms of an elaborate plot. But he was a wild card himself. How could anyone else have known he would rent a car when he didn't himself? On the other hand, if Caterina or Josefina didn't alert the ruffians that he was staying at the Bellestrado, how did they find out?

The road along the waterfront fractured into three parts. About to ask a passerby for directions, he noticed a bus approaching and he flagged it down. It turned out to be a good choice because the vehicle made several turns between the waterfront and inland streets and he realized he would never have found his way on foot.

As he rode, the waterfront itself changed. Moorings for tugs and commercial sightseeing boats gave way to clusters of smaller, privately owned craft like speedboats and blue and white fishing boats sporting the eye of Horus on their bows. According to a sign on a nearby building, this was the city of Msida. A short time later the bus reached a wide double boulevard with trees and gardens. The traffic got more congested and so did the walkways. He also became aware of the smell of food.

He had read in his tour book that on Malta all buses run to Valletta. The route map looked like an inverted seashell with rays spreading out to cover the island. The hub was Triton Fountain outside the gates of Valletta. As he neared it, Rick was sure that most of the buses really *were* there, parked nose to tail around the fountain in huge concentric circles like long yellow and white animals resting at a watering hole.

People were everywhere, getting on or off buses, pressing up to concession stands lured by the perfumes of sausage, fennel seed and coffee, or sitting on benches. The street leading to the gates of the city was lined with concession stands. It would have been enjoyable under most circumstances.

After a quick look at the masks, noisemakers and gaudy costume jewelry for the upcoming Independence Day holiday and the huge crepe-paper dragons and

Vikings he determined it was time to get rid of the rifle. An ice cream seller, slouching with chin in hand, looked up when Rick approached.

"Can you tell me where I can find a storage locker?" Rick asked.

"Public toilets," the man said, not bothering to remove his chin from his hand. With his size and expression he looked like Bluto from the Popeye cartoons and seemed to have the same disposition. "Right behind me. How about some ice cream?"

Rick took a step back. "Not now, thanks. Maybe later." After searching among thick overhanging branches he found a doorway and stairs descending into a cavern that resembled a World War II air raid shelter and smelled like a cattle barn. A 20-watt bulb illuminated a series of lockers. Though more than a little dubious of security, he set the bag into a locker, deposited an octagonal fifty pence piece into the slot and turned the key. The coin dropped with a clank and the key came free.

Back on the street Rick stopped a teen-aged boy for directions to the Internet Café.

"It's at the YMCA on Merchant Street," the youth said. "Make a right turn at the first intersection when you get inside the city. It's the next street over."

The bridge into the city was crowded and an open-air market made Merchant Street nearly impassable. The YMCA Building was an old brownstone-fronted building. A sign at the front door pointed to the Café.

A banner on the door read Welcome to the YMCA International Conference on Hunger and Poverty. The Café, with its Internet connections, obviously was the communication center and teeming with young people. At first he was puzzled when he couldn't see any computers. Then he saw them. They were on a balcony that was crowded to overflowing.

"Can I use one of the computers?" he asked.

"Yes. Wait fifteen minutes. Everyone will be going to a meeting then."

He ordered a coffee and sat. As the waitress had said, a quarter of an hour later everyone left in a mass exodus. Gathering up his cup he followed the waitress up a captain's stairway. He sat at one of the machines and she logged him on.

The connection was slow, but before long Kevin MacIntyre's nightmarish home page appeared. A total sci-fi freak, Kevin had decorated his page with some of the most lurid, verging on pornographic, aliens he could find from poster books. One, a green lizard-man, held a sign welcoming the visitor to the Triskar web page along with the company's slogan. "'Cogito ergo sum.' Descartes. 'Coito ergo sum,' MacIntyre." How many of Kevin's customers realized that the scoundrel had turned 'I think therefore I am' into 'I screw therefore I am,' just by removing one letter?

He logged on and went to his e-mail, wondering if he had anything from Stef. His mailbox was jammed with 128 messages. With the slow connection he gave up long before he had sifted through less than a quarter of them. Leaving the machine in disgust he returned to the front counter.

"Are there any phones around where I can call the US?" he asked.

"Inside the main building," the woman answered. "There's a phone in the lobby, but you'll have to get a phone card to use it. They sell them at the desk."

After buying several cards to make sure he had enough time, Rick called Kevin. A sleepy voice answered, "Triskar."

"Sorry for waking you, Bud, but my mailbox is full. Would you mind going through it for me and see if there's anything new from Stef?"

Kevin groaned. "Okay. Look again in ten minutes."

Rick was about to return to the café when he remembered the receipt with the telephone number that was in Junior's pocket. Dialing it, a man's voice answered, "Hamrun hunter's club."

"Excuse me," Rick said in Italian. "I must have the wrong number."

The voice quickly switched to Italian. "No. No. Are you a hunter?"

"*Si*," Rick said.

"Then come to our meeting here on Wednesday night. It's important. This time the government has gone too far. Too far."

Rick asked for the address and wrote it on the paper with the telephone number. "*Grazi*. I'll be there."

CHAPTER 4

▼

Saturday
8:57 AM
Valletta

Another call to Kevin confirmed no new messages. The only person Rick knew for sure that Stef had met was Lorenzo Cornacchia. He was certain he could find information about him in the National Library.

A short walk down Republic Street brought him to a square where men and women sat reading newspapers and sipping cappuccinos under umbrella-shaded tables. Rick flagged down a waiter who pointed toward a building beyond the sea of umbrellas.

As he stepped inside, he caught a familiar scent. Books. More than six centuries of knowledge. Rick was no bibliophile but the smell was so intoxicating he was sure he had died and gone to heaven.

An elderly man sat at the front desk. "Good morning. Can I help you?"

"Yes. Do you have any English language books about the Maltese nobility?"

"That would be the Balzan. May I have your driver's license or passport please?"

Rick gave him a hard look. "Why?"

"It's a very valuable book," the clerk said. "You'll get your identification back when you're done with it."

"I don't have either with me. I'll be sitting right here."

"I don't know…"

"Okay," Rick said. With a shrug he got to his feet. The clerk motioned for him to sit. "Leo, would you get the Balzan, please."

A second man, at least as old as the first, nodded. He tottered off and soon returned carrying a folio-sized book. "Here it is."

The librarian took out a card. "Please sign here."

Rick did. The book was thick and relatively new. As he turned the pages he found a notecard marker with the name "Cornacchia" in large letters. Rick got a thrill. Stef's writing!

Pulse pounding, he turned to the bookmark and found a drawing of the Cornacchia coat of arms: a shield divided diagonally with a crow holding an olive branch against a red background and a red castle against a black background. A ribbon at the bottom read: *Cosi Forma il Signore*? What hath God wrought, indeed.

He made a quick sketch of the drawing and turned to the narrative. The family's history began with Tomaso Cornacchia, who was thought to have come from Sicily in 1090 aboard a ship laden with young olive trees. Over the centuries the trees died, but the boat became the basis of the Cornacchia shipping empire. Tomaso also brought the title of Duke with him. Neither the church nor the Norman overseers disputed his claim.

There followed several pages on Tomaso's descendants, but the first major entry dealt with Bartolomeo Julius, born 1510, died? Was Bartolemeo like Ambrose Bierce and no one knew where or when he died? Bartolomeo wasn't Italian, but Rick found him a quintessential example of the powerful Italian merchant class that arose a century before. Besides increasing the family wealth by shrewd business tactics, he married into a powerful merchant family. He was a renowned alchemist and world traveler. Most interesting to Rick, Bartolomeo was tried and convicted of heresy by Pope Pius IV, then pardoned after promising to devote the rest of his life to the service of Christ. Rick was fascinated. From the date, he was certain that Bartolomeo was the Cornacchia who commissioned Cellini's work.

Paging ahead he came to the present Duke, Lorenzo, who was born in 1943. Although several pages were devoted to him, the only significant information was that he owned Black Dolphin Shipping, one of the world's largest and most lucrative shipping businesses.

Rick finished with a frown. It didn't make sense. The drawing was unquestionably valuable but not worth the risk Cornacchia would be taking by kidnapping Stef. There had to be more to the story.

As he handed the book back to the librarian, he asked, "Do you have any clippings about the Cornacchia family?"

The old man snapped to attention. "You mean the Cor-na-kias. Oh, yes indeed."

The man's enthusiasm was puzzling. He led Rick to a chair. "Please sit down. Oh, Leo."

Seconds later the librarian arose and walked into another room. Suspicious, Rick watched him talking on the telephone. Rick returned to his seat when Leo reappeared carrying three legal-size folders, each tightly tied with black ribbons.

"Here you are," he said.

The first article, dated 12 April 1912 dealt with Lorenzo's father, Alessandro, on his assumption of the title of Duke. The British had accepted his claim to the title and he was immediately inducted into the *Universitat.* Did that mean University? Rick made a note of the word and moved on.

Skipping over several articles written in Maltese, he came to a 1922 *Malta Times* article. At the official ceremonies celebrating the advent of Maltese self-government under British rule, the Duke addressed the cheering crowds in Italian and Maltese, pointedly avoiding English. A panoramic photo showed the ceremonies being held in the square in front of the library.

Unfortunately for the Maltese, self-government didn't last long. In an article dated December 1935, the duke excoriated the British for ending the experiment. According to the reporter, the question of whether English or Italian would be the official language had doomed the project from the start.

Rick quickly thumbed through society columns dealing with poetry readings and costumed balls and stopped when he saw an account of a chamber concert held at *Borgiswed,* the Cornacchia family estate in Notabile. Rick made another note. He guessed that *Borgiswed* was a Maltese word. But Notabile was Italian and meant 'notable.' Why?

He asked the librarian, who replied. "The Knights called Mdina the Notable City. They had their own names for most of our places. We still use them interchangeably."

Rick nodded thanks and went back to the clippings. In August 1926 Duke Alessandro Cornacchia invited the newly empowered Benito Mussolini to join him at his home. Though il Duce was unable to accept, he indicated he would welcome a future invitation.

Other articles chronicled Cornacchia's growing involvement with Italy, through participation in shared cultural events and soccer games. Interesting, but not very useful.

The next page appeared to have something torn out. Pulse quickening, he made a note of the reference. *Malta Daily Observer,* June 8, 1942. A hand-written note in pen read, "The Duke's Challenge." Had Stef removed it?

The last piece was an article from *The Malta Times*, dated two days later, reporting the discovery of the Duke's body in his burned-out car. The Duke had left the family estate at the height of a German air raid. As he approached Valletta he drove into a bomb crater a short distance from Porte des Bombes. The automobile flipped over and trapped him inside. Then it caught fire and he died in the inferno. *Sic Transit Gloria Cornacchia.*

As he finished, the librarian asked, "Are you done with this?"

"Yes. Where's the wc?"

The man pointed to a hallway. "Down that way."

The restroom was cramped and unpleasant-smelling. The wire holder for what had been a urinal deodorizer was empty and now simply acted as a deflector. Before Rick could move to the other stall, another man preempted him, standing shoulder-to-shoulder in an area scarcely large enough for one person. The man was several inches shorter than Rick, and considerably heavier, wearing a blue suit and plain black shoes. Uneasy, Rick held his ground. He flushed, and the other man did, too. Neither made any attempt to leave.

What the hell is this, anyway? Bladder wars?

The bizarre confrontation ended with the arrival of Leo. The man at the urinal turned sideways and stepped back. As he did, a rumpled piece of paper fell onto the floor. Rick picked it up. Opening it, he saw in big block letters the words, "We have your brother. Do not contact the police."

Rick tried to follow him, but couldn't get around Leo in time. As he looked down the empty hallway he knew one thing for sure. Neither Caterina Borg nor Josefina Grech was involved. Only the librarians knew he was here; asking about the Cornacchia family had set the events in motion.

The librarian was waiting for him by the table when he returned. "Here's the next folder," he said. Rick's eyes opened wide when he saw his cell phone sitting on top of his notepad.

"Where did this come from?" he demanded.

"I have no idea," the librarian replied. "I never saw it before."

Skin atingle, Rick sat down and opened the next folder. The top article, dated 1963, announced that Father Louis Santorini had published his doctoral dissertation on Bartolomeo Cornacchia. Tense fingers quickly scratched a note.

He took a cursory skim through a pad of articles about the present Cornacchia.

A noise behind him made him jump, but it was only Leo arranging books on a bookcase. Barely able to concentrate, he dug nervously through the rest of the pile until he came to a picture of a stunning young woman. She was smiling primly with every hair in place. But a look at the eyes and the mouth told the real story. She should have been photographed with wisps of hair criss-crossing her face, her eyes burning like live coals, and sensuous lips half open in invitation. She was a promise of unimaginable pleasure and danger. How many men would have risked anything to gain the favor of such a marvelous creature? Apparently Lorenzo Cornacchia had been willing. Marija Cornacchia was his wife.

Rick felt a shiver of fear as one of his fellow patrons, a college-aged man, stood up and handed his files back to the librarian. That left only one other person, a woman. His sensors sampled the atmosphere but could detect no immediate danger.

The next article pictured Cornacchia standing on the deck of a boat. The text read, "Lorenzo Cornacchia on the *Fahal* at Manoel Island." The darkly handsome face was long and gaunt, with aquiline cheekbones. Dark eyes glittered out at the camera, and his hair was a white halo. After a furtive glance around the room, Rick tore the picture out of the album.

His cell phone rang. Frozen in place, Rick's heart measured the seconds until it rang again.

"You can't use that in here," the librarian said.

Rick jumped to his feet. Making a grab for his notepad, he hurried through the door to the top of the stairs. He took a look down the dark passage to see if anyone was coming before answering on the fifth ring.

"Hello."

"Good morning, Mr. Olsen," a voice said, with a bare trace of an accent.

Rick found a space next to the door and backed against the wall. The stone felt like ice. In a menacing voice he said, "Who is this?"

"A friend of your brother's. He's very sorry he couldn't meet you last night."

"I'm sure he is. Let me talk to him."

"Unfortunately that isn't possible now. He's indisposed. You'll have to wait until a little later. I see you've found your phone. I'm sure you're happy to get it back."

Before Rick could answer, his stallmate from the WC appeared at the top of the stairs. As he saw Rick, he reached for his jacket pocket. Rick leaped forward, catching him in the midsection. Frightened, the man got to his feet and ran down the stairs.

A second man appeared, and knocked Rick aside, taking the stairs two steps at a time. Rick watched both disappear through the front door. Not only did Cornacchia want the drawing, but for some reason he wanted *Rick*, too.

When he gathered up his phone, he was surprised to find his caller was still at the other end. "Your friends botched the job," Rick said. "They just ran out the door."

"Maybe we'll have better luck next time. I'll see that you talk to your brother later today."

The phone went dead.

Before stepping outside, Rick looked over the routes available to him. The outdoor restaurant was packed but the umbrellas blocked his view of the diners. Fortunately that worked both ways. No one could see him, either.

With that in mind, he fell in behind a taller man carrying a briefcase and followed him to St. John's Street where horse-drawn *carrozzin* waited for fares.

Should he take one? He immediately decided against it. Half running, he turned the next corner and ducked inside the first building.

He counted to 500 before stepping back out to continue on his way. At the moment he was torn between contacting Father Santorini, the expert on Bartolomeo Cornacchia, and doing something to change his appearance. On Malta, a six-foot-two man with flaming red hair made him easy to see and difficult to forget. With his blunt Scandinavian features and full red cheeks he could also pass for a number of other nationalities.

Walking down the street he stopped at a tiny building with a telephone call box. After looking up the number in the phone book, he inserted a phone card into the slot and dialed. A woman answered. "One minute, please," she said. "Father Santorini!" she bellowed. *"Telefon!"*

"*Iva?*" said a quiet voice.

"Good morning, Father. This is Richard Olsen. I apologize for intruding on your privacy, but I'm a scholar doing research and I need some information about Bartolomeo Cornacchia. I was hoping I could arrange to speak to you."

"How strange you should call," the man said. "Did you say your name is Olsen?"

Rick scowled. "Yes. Why?"

"Another Mr. Olsen called me about Bartolomeo just a few days ago. He made an appointment to see me but I never heard from him again."

Rick's pulse quickened. "Was it Stefan Olsen?"

"Yes. Is he a relative?"

"He's my brother! When was he supposed to meet with you?"

"Last Thursday afternoon. I trust nothing has happened to him."

"I'm sure he's fine," Rick said in a reassuring voice. "Something must have come up. When did he call you?"

"Wednesday afternoon."

"Did he tell you where you could reach him?"

"No, but I think he was calling from Sliema. He asked for directions from there."

Rick could hardly believe his luck. Sliema was a big area, but a postage stamp compared to the whole island. "Did he say if he would be taking a bus?"

"No. He asked for directions so I think he was planning to drive."

Rick's pulse raced at this second major revelation, more important than the first. "You have no idea how helpful this is. How soon can I meet with you?"

"Tomorrow? Anytime after noon. I'll be saying Mass until then."

"One o'clock then. Which bus do I take?"

"It's the same one that goes to Mdina. Just ask the driver where to get off. I look forward to meeting you."

Rick hung up elated. Stef liked to drive. He hated public transportation because of his size. If he rented a car, the rental slip would tell where he was actually staying. With a wary look around, Rick started away.

As he was walking, he came upon a woman looking at rings in a jewelry store window. An Arab man stood next to her, clearly bored by the whole thing.

She glanced in Rick's direction and he recognized her immediately. It was Marija Cornacchia! She lowered her eyes and opened her lips slightly. He immediately thought of a black widow spider.

He smiled back.

With eyes riveted on his chest and shoulders, she took several steps in his direction before whirling about to face an assortment of bracelets in a window. He caught a whiff of musky perfume and she turned her head to look back at him again. Then, like a wild animal savoring its prey, she opened her mouth and slowly licked her lips before gesturing to her companion.

Transfixed, Rick followed her with his eyes until she disappeared.

CHAPTER 5

▼

Saturday
10:16 AM
Valletta

After Marija Cornacchia's departure he shook himself back to reality and continued on to the Chez Paris. Women sat reading magazines under metal helmets and ammonia poisoned the air. A middle-aged woman wearing a plastic apron broke away from a patron and came over to him.

"Styling?" she asked in English.

Rick shook his head as if he didn't understand. "*Ancora?*" he said. Again?

This time she asked in Italian. "*Taglio dei capelli?*"

"No," Rick said with a blush. "*Tintore.*"

"Don't be embarrassed," the woman continued in Italian. "Many men dye their hair. I'm Annabelle Muscat. I'll be done in ten minutes. You can wait over there."

Rick rummaged through the pile of women's magazines on a low table until he uncovered several copies of *Malta Today*. One issue was devoted exclusively to Black Dolphin Shipping, Cornacchia's company. Reading quickly, he learned that Black Dolphin had increased trade with Libya and Tunisia by more than 400 percent in one year, making five times as many stops in Tripoli and Tunis as it did the year before. The article also noted that Malta now was only slightly behind Liberia in the number of international shipping freighters flying its flag.

Another article reported on the construction of a skyscraper in Sliema, to be the new world headquarters for the Black Dolphin Lines as well as a commercial center for the entire Mediterranean. At forty stories, the skyscraper would be one of the tallest structures in Europe. Rick was sure this was the construction site he passed on his walk to Valletta. Why was Black Dolphin building a relay tower when they could go to satellite for a much lower cost?

Annabelle appeared. "You can take the magazine with you. What color?"

"Red-brown," he replied. "I need to rent a car. Do you have any idea which of the agencies would be the cheapest?"

"I have no idea but Sin-THEE-ya might know. Her sister works for a travel agency. While we're waiting for the color to set I'll ask her."

He was wiping his hair with a towel when Cynthia came to talk to him. Barely out of her teens, she was plump and wore a diamond in the left side of her nose. "My sister says Island Rentals is reasonable."

Rick felt a jolt of excitement. That was the name the clerk had mentioned at the airport. "Thanks," he said.

"Give me the towel", Annabelle said. "I'll finish with the hair dryer."

As she worked, he watched a captioned CNN report about increasing tension in the Middle East. In with the usual plethora of misspellings was the message that radical members of Islamic Justice were promising another torrent of raids and assassinations in the Mideast within a month. The group's suspected present location was western Libya. Right under Qadaffi's nose and less than 300 miles away.

"We're done," she said. "I'll give you a mirror."

He nodded approvingly at his new hair. Not bad. Now reddish-brown and much darker, it still had a hint of the original color.

"Good job," he said. He handed Annabelle a two-pound note. "That's your tip. How much do I owe you?"

11:44 AM

His hair was still damp when he crawled inside a phone booth on Merchant Street. His hand shook in anticipation as he dialed the number for Island Rentals.

After four rings, a woman answered.

"Mario Agius, please," he said.

"Mr. Agius isn't available. This is his answering service. I'll have him call you. May I have your number?"

"It's not that easy to reach me. I'll call back later," Rick said.

Disappointed, he wandered around until he found a tourist shop where he bought a backpack, an extra-large tube of zinc oxide and a bright red hat with the word Malta stitched on it in script. He flicked ointment liberally on his nose and rubbed some more on his cheeks and neck.

Sufficiently camouflaged he made his next stop at a jeweler's where he bought a tiny screwdriver. He made another at an electronics shop on Merchant Street to buy two batteries for his cell phone.

As he walked he realized he was moving upward at a steep angle. Before long the street turned into steps. An open gate beckoned and he stepped through. He had chanced upon a garden at the top of the city's bastions.

It was a very pretty, private place with bougainvillea, hibiscus and silver-leafed fig trees. As he sat down on a bench, a brisk wind sliced through the humid sky, but the dark clouds that hovered over the city refused to move. Far below, Grand Harbour was a licorice sea flecked with bits of whipped cream. With each gust, silver leaves flashed on the olive tree next to where he was sitting.

Spreading out a handkerchief and laying it on the bench, he used the jeweler's screwdriver to work loose the screws on his cell phone. The sheath on the back of the phone came free, and an untidy tangle of wiring jumped out.

His heart took a leap when he saw the grayish glob under the wiring.

Sweat stung his eyes as he pried the mass loose with the screwdriver. Plastique! Two ounces worth or so. His fingers followed the red and black wires leading to a tiny disc imbedded in the glob. Detonator. He took a deep breath before yanking the wires free, then sighed in relief.

Not bad. If he got too close to something the bad guys didn't want him to find, all they had to do was push a button. He bundled up the pieces in his handkerchief and got to his feet. His first stop would be the locker to ditch the explosive. Then he would pay a visit to the American Embassy. Someone had to learn about what was happening.

CHAPTER 6

▼

11:03 PM
?

For the first time in his captivity Stef welcomed the darkness of his cell. It left him free to think. Pleasurable as it might be, plotting revenge would ultimately get him nowhere. He had to escape. But how? Even if he could free his hands and get out of the crib he had nowhere to go. And his only weapon was a passive one: he knew where the drawing was hidden. His survival depended on keeping its whereabouts secret. But keeping it secret put Rick in danger. Either way he lost.

There had to be another way.

*   *   *   *

The crowd had thinned out at City Gate and Rick was surprised to see a diminutive woman wearing a blue-striped smock at Bluto's stand. Her smile made her as approachable as the man was forbidding.

"Ice cream?" she asked.

"Thanks, but it's a little too early for that."

"I've got pistachio," she said sweetly. "It won't fill you up."

Beguiled, Rick took out a coin and laid it on the counter. "Can you tell me where to find the American Embassy?"

"It's the next street over," she said, pointing beyond the circle of buses. "On St. Anne. You can't miss it. It's surrounded by barbwire."

"I can understand why," he said. "I hear that an Arab got killed breaking into a hotel at Sliema last night," he said as he unwrapped the ice cream bar. "Did you hear anything about it?"

She made a face. "No, but it doesn't surprise me. It was probably a Libyan. I wish they'd stay home where they belong. They're constantly marrying our girls to get Maltese citizenship, and after they have children they take the boys back to North Africa. The poor women only have two choices. They can either go with them and become part of their harem, or they can stay here and see their children taken away from them. And now the North African Arabs are coming by the boatload."

Bluto suddenly reappeared. "Bye," Rick said, making a quick exit.

He found the embassy without difficulty. Two Marines with M-16 rifles patrolled behind a barbed wire fence. Rick stopped and one of the marines approached him.

"Yes, sir?" he asked in a business-like tone.

"I'm an American citizen and my passport was stolen," Rick said.

"Any other ID?"

Rick handed him his driver's license. After both of the Marines examined it, they let him in. The one with sergeant stripes led him into the building. The embassy was from the 'thirties, with marble floors and mirror-reflective walls. "Walk down the hall to the left. You'll have to make a report and apply for another one."

"I need to talk to the station chief," Rick said in a low voice.

The sergeant answered with an icy look. "Station chief? Who are you?"

Rick took out his red military ID card.

"This card has expired," the Marine said suspiciously.

"I was a reserve captain in Military Intelligence," Rick said.

The Marine gave him another hard look. Finally he gave the card back and said, "Come with me," in an unfriendly voice. He pointed Rick toward the door of an ornate nickel-plated elevator and pushed a button.

The third-floor receptionist was a youngish woman with impossibly red hair and globby gold earrings ensconced behind a kidney-shaped desk. She lifted a telephone receiver and seconds later a tall man in a light-khaki colored suit appeared. The hard lines of his face and his unsmiling grey eyes made the room seem several degrees colder. "Who's this?" the man asked.

"Tell him what you told me," the sergeant said.

Rick shook his head. Walking to the desk he wrote 'bugged' on a sheet of paper and handed it and his cell phone to the tall man. The man pushed a button on a desk and another man, this one in a short-sleeved shirt, appeared carrying something that resembled a Geiger counter. As he passed the instrument over the phone, a red light came on. The second man took the phone and left the room.

"Let's talk about this in my office," the tall man said. He walked behind his desk and said, "My name is Bob Carpenter," without offering his hand. "Sit down."

Rick sat.

"I understand you were in Army Intelligence."

"As a reservist. I was trained in combat intelligence and psychological operations. My tour ended a year before Nine-Eleven but I volunteered for another year when it happened."

"What unit were you with?"

"The four-eighty-third Psychological Operations Company at Fort Snelling. I did my annual training at the Pentagon. My specialty was the Middle East."

"Do you speak Arabic?"

"Enough to get me in trouble."

"What brings you to Malta?" Carpenter asked.

"My brother found a valuable drawing in Florence and he came here to investigate. I came to help him. Someone was waiting for me at the airport and mugged me."

"Do you have any idea why?"

"They wanted the drawing my brother found."

"You may as well tell me the whole story," Carpenter said.

Rick went through Stef's discovery of the drawing and his activities after he found it. When he said "Cornacchia," Carpenter's eyes widened. "Do you know the name?" Rick asked.

"I'm familiar with it," the agent said. "Go on."

"That was the last time I talked to Stef. I got three e-mails from him. In the first one he told me he was coming here. He knew that if he called, I would have told him to stay in Florence and finish his research. The second one said that since he had visited Cornacchia he suspected he was being followed and had a feeling he was in danger. He asked me to come and I did."

"And the last one?"

"He was registered at the San Antwan. I'm sure it didn't come from him."

"What's this about your cell phone?"

Rick went on to explain his adventures, beginning with the close calls at the airport and the hotel. Carpenter listened carefully, nodding at appropriate times. After Rick finished, the agent said, "That's quite a story. I can understand why you think Cornacchia is involved."

"I'm glad that you agree. What can you tell me about him?"

"Let's just say we have crossed swords on occasion. Even so I can't imagine he would ever involve himself in a kidnapping."

"I can't either. That's why I can't help but think that there's something more than money or antiques involved here."

Carpenter nodded. "There isn't much more I can say at this time. Just ask around. You'll be able to come up as much as I know on your own. You'll find his wife Marija interesting, too."

"She certainly is," Rick said.

The agent got to his feet. "I'll see if your phone is ready yet." Almost as an afterthought he took a card out of his shirtpocket and handed it to Rick. "You can call me at the bottom number twenty-four hours of the day. Let me know if you learn any more."

Even though Rick thought that the information highway seemed to only run in one direction, he nodded. At that moment the agent who had taken the phone entered the office. "Good as new," he said.

Rick slipped it into his pocket. "Thanks. Do you know where Cornacchia keeps his yacht?"

"He has a slip at Manoel Island. It's a five-minute bus ride between Valletta and Sliema."

Rick nodded. As he was about to leave he remembered the card with the number for the Hunters Club. "I found this in the dead Arab's pocket," he said. "It may be nothing, but I called it. There's going to be a meeting on Wednesday night."

"I'll look into it," Carpenter said. At that moment the Marine sergeant appeared in the office.

"Sergeant White will escort you from the building," Carpenter said.

As Rick stepped out, he put himself on full alert and decided to take a different route back to the buses. A passing black car with a blue light on top made him cringe. Sometime soon he would have to clear himself with the police. If only he could find a way to do it without jeopardizing Stef.

He came to a large open area, with tents interspersed among a field of large circular stones. From a distance it could have been a variant of the oriental game of Go. The stones puzzled him. Why were they there? Intrigued, he knelt next to one of them. Running his finger along the base, he discovered it was neatly sealed against the limestone surface with cement. All the others seemed to be, too. He heard a scratching sound and turned. A large pigeon took a step in his direction, gave him an inquisitive look, then flew off.

"He was hoping you had something better than popcorn," a voice said from behind. "I told him he should work for a living."

"You're right," Rick said with a grin. He turned to find an ageless man wearing shorts and argyle socks. "What is this place?"

"It's called the Granary. The Knights used to store grain here so it wouldn't spoil. It's much cooler underground."

"Smart idea. How long have they been sealed?"

"As long as I can remember. They're supposed to be full of poisonous gases."

Rick took a cab to the Marina. Forests of tall masts reached above the buildings, and a single dock stretched for hundreds of yards toward the sea. Most of the watercraft were sailboats, some were motorized. All were expensive. Surprisingly, the marina was almost devoid of human life.

He looked up at the sound of a high-pitched screech. A barefoot young man with walnut-colored skin was using a wire wheel to remove paint from a hull.

"Morning," Rick shouted.

The screech stilled and the chips stopped flying. Squinting with curiosity, the young man stared up at him.

"Do you know which one is the Cornacchia yacht?" Rick asked.

After wiping his mouth with an arm the youth answered. "The *Fahal?* The slip is down that way but the boat isn't here today. Why do you ask?"

"I've got a delivery to make. When was the last time you saw it?"

"Yesterday. It's most likely at Golden Bay. The Duke only leaves it here when it needs work or when he doesn't intend to use it for a while."

"I can't go all the way out there. Which one is his slip?"

"See that yellow pail?" the youth asked, pointing toward a wire-fence enclosed area some 40 yards away. Rick nodded. "That's it."

He found the handle securely padlocked from inside. All he could see beyond was the yellow pail, a heavy coil of rope and two fifty-gallon gasoline tanks. The pail, which had the necks of two green bottles protruding over the top, was just out of reach.

He returned to the young man who was still busily scraping. "Suppose I could borrow your mop for a second?"

"Maybe. Why do you need it?"

"I'll leave the delivery in the pail and tell them where to look. I can't reach it."

The man shrugged an assent. "Go ahead."

Rick returned to the gate and pushed the mop handle through the fence. After a few stabs it caught the wire handle of the pail. He brought the pail close, tipped it over, and used the mop handle to sift through the contents.

Other than the two wine bottles and three sandwich wrappers, there wasn't much to see. He upended the pail and pushed it away. A very small bottle glinted in the sun. He maneuvered it close enough that he could reach under the gate to retrieve it.

It was an empty medical ampoule labeled in Arabic. It seemed a strange find in a bucket of trash. He guessed Bob Carpenter would be able to find out what it was. But first it was off to Golden Bay.

The cab was climbing. The island tilted from west to east divided by an enormous escarpment called the Victoria lines, and Golden Harbor was on the northwestern side. He had hoped to see something of the countryside but found instead an endless succession of storefront businesses in the towns and, in the countryside, wall after wall of stones hung with drooping pads of reddish prickly pears. The little vegetation visible was brown and shriveled. The walls made perfect sense to him. Long ago Malta was lush and green. Thousands of years of erosion had left it a rock. The only way to preserve topsoil was to build a wall around it. But even in exposed areas flowers continued to grow during the winter and spring. And small copses of trees still were in evidence. He found himself wanting to step in and give the harried plant life a hand.

As they drove, he noticed that every sign was spray-painted with electric purples and greens. Gangs? Certainly not on Malta. "What's the story about the road signs?" he asked.

The cabby made a disgusted face. "It's hunters. The symbols are supposed to lead them to the protest meetings."

"I've heard about them," Rick said. "How far is Golden Bay?"

"Only about ten minutes from here."

Rick smiled. Like England, Malta didn't measure distance in miles or meters but in minutes.

At last the driver pulled into a large parking lot and stopped. "Here we are," he said. "The beach is that way."

"Thanks," Rick said, handing him a banknote.

He stood in a half-filled parking lot with a restaurant to his right, and the beach down the hill with its blue water, hot sand and a bright circle of refreshment wagons. As he walked toward the sea he discovered the beach was part of a much larger area. To the left, a sizable green expanse of ground cover and wild plants stretched off to form a rough peninsula. The rocky outcropping extended into the sea like a finger from a hand. Far below a one-story building and dock lay among rugged rocks. But his attention was riveted on the miniature oil tanker bobbing in the center of the harbor. It had to be the *Fahal,* Cornacchia's ship.

Even though he had an unobstructed view of the boat, he cursed himself for not bringing the telescopic sight from the rifle.

He decided that the rocky outcropping would provide a better vantagepoint.

After leveling off at about two-thirds up the hill, the path gradually worked its way down to the spit of land. The closer he got to it, the more surprised he became. It was solid rock jutting into the sea. But instead of being at the same level as rock around it, it soared at least ten feet above ground level. Any hopes he had of following it out into the sea disappeared as he came face to face with a rocky overhang.

Disappointed, he turned around to start back toward Golden Bay. The sound of voices coming from on top of the rock stopped him in his tracks. Carefully making his way down the steep side of the path toward the other side of the formation, he met a man wearing a safety helmet and a padded vest coming down a ladder from on top of the rock.

"What's going on?" Rick asked.

The man pulled an empty cigarette holder from his mouth then reached inside of his coveralls for a blaze green flier. He handed it to Rick. "We're building the *fougasse* for the Independence Day celebration. This entire area is off-limits but you can get a good view from there," he pointed to the hill behind them. "On Sunday there'll be bleachers there for the celebration."

Intrigued, Rick decided to climb the hill for a better look.

The view was stunning. The small group that had already gathered to watch must have thought so, too. The whole rocky peninsula was clearly in view and everyone's eyes were riveted on the workmen. Rick took close notice of the recently dug trench at the front of the outcropping and the piles of wood at the edges. More importantly, he got a clear view of the yacht. When he came back that night with the scope, this is where he would set up to watch.

A bit footsore, he made his way back to the restaurant. "What do you have that's good, cold and wet?" he asked the waitress.

"Kinnie. It's an orange drink we make on the island."

That was what Caterina had tried to foist on him at the pub. He didn't want it then but now it sounded good. "Kinnie it is. Tell me about the *Fougasse*," he said.

"From what I hear, the Knights didn't have enough cannons to protect all the landing places so they dug holes in the rock and filled them with gunpowder and laid rocks and sticks on top of it. When the pirates or Turks came…boom."

"And I suppose the most gnarly person in the village got to light it."

"You're right," she said with a laugh. "I'll get you your drink." Rick stretched and leaned back into his chair.

He still had a long day ahead of him.

CHAPTER 7

▼

Saturday, 3:33 PM
Floriana

Rick had just stepped off the bus when he was startled by the sound of his cell phone. He quickly moved behind the vehicle and answered.

The room, partially lit by a gas lantern, showed little more than a large door ahead of him, three bare stone walls and a smaller door behind. Pawlu, who was wearing a mask, approached.

Stef shuddered, wondering how the man would react to the loss of two of his confederates. If he was angry, he hid it well.

"Awake?" Pawlu asked in a muffled voice. "I have good news for you. Your brother is on the phone. Say hello and tell him you're all right. If you say anything else..."

"No need to threaten me. I know. Give me the phone."

Pawlu thrust it next to his face.

"Rick?" The receiver was too far away from his ear, but he could hear his brother's voice in the background. "Yes," he said excitedly. "It's me. I'm not hurt."

Rick said something else. "I can't say anymore," Stef said. "They won't let me."

More conversation and Stef turned to Pawlu.

"What's the matter?" Pawlu asked, pushing the mute button.

"He says he can't be sure it's really me. There's only one way to convince him. Did you ever watch Star Trek?"

"The television show?" Pawlu asked suspiciously. Stef nodded. "What about it?"

"My brother and I always watched it when we were growing up. I was Kirk and he was Spock. Whenever we were on the phone I'd say... Turn the phone back on."

Pawlu hesitated. "No tricks."

"No tricks," Stef said.

Pawlu pushed a button and held it next to Stef's face. Grinning broadly, Stef said, "Kirk out."

Rick nearly laughed out loud but caught himself as a familiar voice said, "Greetings, Mr. Olsen, I wanted you to have a chance to talk to your brother. I hope you're satisfied that it's really him."

"Yes," Rick said. More than satisfied. Stef had just told him something.

"I see that you found the modifications we made to your phone. It doesn't matter. We can trace you anyway. Cell phones can be triangulated."

Rick wondered how he knew that. "Is that so? I sure hope you're not mistreating Stef. I wouldn't want to be in your shoes if you are. You already know I can play rough."

"There's no need for hostility," the caller said evenly. "You can rest assured he's being well-tended. As a matter of fact, I like your brother very much. I admire his spirit and I'll miss him when we will have to let him go. As soon as we have the drawing he will be returned to you."

Rick pursed his lips at the final confirmation that the airport and attempted break-in were related to Stef's disappearance. "Assuming I have it, how soon would we need to complete the transaction?" Rick asked.

"Immediately."

"Impossible. I wouldn't be able to get it for at least five days to a week."

"Unacceptable," the caller snapped. "If we can't complete the sale within three days, we will have to withdraw the offer. I'm sure you understand the implications."

"I'll see what I can do."

"Please do. I will say goodbye to your brother for you."

In his excitement, Rick almost missed seeing an orange Chev parked on the perimeter near the refreshment stands. When he did notice it, he could hardly believe his eyes. It stood empty, with all the windows open. As he walked closer he saw the keys dangling in the ignition switch.

"Why hello, Tarbija," he said. "Where's your lovely owner?"

Without waiting for an answer he made a beeline for the steps to the storage locker. Even blind from the sun, he easily made his way to the bottom by following the railing. A quick trip to the locker secured the rifle. How he hoped that the cab would still be there when he returned.

It was. But a quick look quickly defeated any hopes for a quick and easy strike.

The cab was parked too close to the refreshment stands for covert action. And he couldn't very well use the rifle without being seen by scores of onlookers. He saw a tree strategically located across the street from the kiosks and some ten feet from the car. When she showed up, he would jump into the cab next to her.

It turned out to be a pleasant interlude. He was close enough to the Independence Day floats that he could hear the wind rustling the crepe paper. And the seemingly endless stream of humanity passing in front of him reminded him how nice his stay could be if it weren't for Stef's situation. Savory odors from the kiosks also reminded him how hungry he was. As the minutes passed and he had still not caught sight of Caterina Borg, he began to wonder when she would be back.

It turned out to be far sooner than he expected. He felt something poke him in his back. "Hello," he said. "Is that a gun?"

"Yes," said Caterina Borg. "What do you think you're doing?"

"Waiting for you, of course. Where did you come from?"

"I never was more than twenty meters from the car. I stopped to get a milk shake and saw your every move. What's that?" she asked, gesturing toward the plastic bag in the back seat.

"The rifle I took from one of the gents who tried to break into my room. I shook him off the rope."

"Give it to me," she said.

He handed it to her. "What do we do now?" he asked.

"After I put this in the trunk, we're going to walk over to the police station and you're going to turn yourself in for questioning."

"I can't," Rick said, stopping in his tracks. "Stef has been kidnapped and the kidnappers say they'll kill him if I contact the police."

She frowned. "Then we'll have to use another entrance. When did you hear from them?"

"This morning," Rick said, handing her the note. "They returned my phone while I was at the library," he said. "What if the police arrest me?"

"You should have thought of that when you ran away," she replied.

He turned to face her. "I didn't know what else to do. I thought you told the intruders where I was staying."

She glared. "That's the stupidest thing you've said yet. Why did you think that?"

"Simple logic," Rick said evenly. "No one knew I was staying at the Bellestrado except you and Zija. How else could they have found out if one of you didn't tell them?"

"Du-uh. They probably followed us from the airport."

"Fine. So how did they know which room I was in?"

"I don't like to sound unkind but you probably could figure that out for yourself if you think about it. But I'll give you a hint. What time did we get to the hotel?"

"Some time after one. So what?"

Rolling her eyes she said, "So how many other guests would have been up at that hour?"

He controlled the urge to slap his forehead but he couldn't keep from turning beet-red in embarrassment. "Of course. My light must have been the only one on in the hotel."

"Bravo. Do you want more?" she asked.

"By all means," he said. "I'm sure I'll hear it anyway."

She ignored the sarcasm and continued. "If I'm arranging to have someone go through your room while you're in it, I'd want to make sure you were sound asleep when they did, wouldn't I? Otherwise you might wake up and spoil my plans."

"As I did."

"As you did. Every bartender has something they can mix into their drinks to put their customers to sleep, right?"

Rick stifled a laugh. "Must be. It's in all the old movies and crime novels."

Either missing the point or ignoring him, she continued without a reaction. "Did I give you anything to drink?"

"Just a Kinnie. You wouldn't let me have alcohol."

"There you are. If I knew someone were coming later to search your room, why didn't I give you whiskey and put something in it to make sure you'd be asleep? And why would they have to break in from the roof? I could have searched the room myself."

Rick didn't know which he wanted to do more, kiss her or give himself a dope slap, but he did neither. "You win. I'm glad my first impression of you was right. I was sure you really wanted to help me when you picked me up at the airport. Thanks again."

Her face softened into a smile. "You're welcome. Now follow me."

4:44 PM

After putting the rifle in the trunk of her car she led him around the block to a recessed sidewalk that led to a door without a handle. When she knocked, a man in civilian clothes holding a soft drink can in his hand answered. "You can't come in this way," he said.

"We know," Caterina said. "This man needs to speak to Inspector Micallef and he can't go in the main entrance."

"I'll see if I can find him."

After the man left, Rick asked, "How do you know Inspector Micallef is the one who wants to see me?"

"He left his card with us at the hotel. And I know him. I've had dealings with him in the past."

"I see," Rick said. "When were you in America?"

She seemed startled by the non sequitur. "I lived in Canada for three years and went to Queen's College in Toronto for two of them. How did you know that?"

"Your English. Either you've been to America or you watch too much MTV."

The door opened and a short and stocky man wearing a blue suit held the door open.

"This is Richard Olsen," Caterina said. With that she turned around and left.

The Inspector gave Rick a steely look. "Mr. Olsen! So nice to see you. A much belated pleasure, to be sure. Come with me."

From the tone, Rick was sure he was being led off to a torture chamber, but a short trip down a hall brought them to a well-lighted office. An invisible curtain of tobacco smoke hung in the air. He also noticed an odor of sweaty wool and over-ripe apples. Overhead, a large fan gently stirred this interesting mixture.

"Please have a seat," Micallef said pointing to a chair in front of his desk.

"I would rather stand, if you don't mind."

"As you wish." After an intolerable silence, the officer shook his head. "Do you have any idea how much trouble you are in?"

"I can guess."

Micallef continued in a louder voice. "How could you have acted the way you did? To begin with, the police report you left at Gudja says you were registered at the San Antwan Hotel, yet you never went there."

"For good reason," Rick said. "My reservation was in my briefcase. Whoever jumped me would know where I was going. Caterina Borg recommended the Bellestrado and I followed her suggestion."

"I see. More to the point, why did you run away from the Bellestrado leaving two bodies under your window?"

Rick started to answer but Micallef cut him off. "And why did you wait until now to contact us? If the evidence weren't so strong that the dead men were trying to break into your room, I would arrest you for first degree murder."

Micallef was frightening as he trembled in fury. This was no cool professional. The man was either genuinely trying to hold back an explosion or he was doing an excellent job pretending that he was.

"You're right. But if I had done anything wrong, why am I turning myself in now? I'm sorry I ran away but what happened at the Bellestrado was anything but murder, I assure you. One of the men tried to break into my room then fell. When I went into the courtyard to try to help him the other one tried to shoot me. If I hadn't shaken him off the rope, he would have succeeded."

A new expression, one that Rick didn't like, appeared on the Inspector's face. "You say he *shot* at you?"

"Several times. I got a look at his rifle in the moonlight while he was coming down the rope."

"How strange," Micallef said, sounding as if he smelled blood. "We didn't find a rifle. Did you take it?"

"No," Rick said, feeling the bottom fall out of his stomach. How could I be so stupid?

Micallef pressed on. "What do you suppose could have become of it?"

"I have no idea. Maybe it's still in the courtyard and you overlooked it. All I know is that I left the hotel as quickly as I could."

"The rifle is important," Micallef said. "I'll send someone over to look for it immediately." With that he lifted the receiver and pushed a button on his phone. As he spoke he kept his piercing eyes on Rick. Finally he was done. "Did you touch either of the bodies?"

"No," Rick said, looking Micallef in the eye as he said it. "Why?"

"We didn't find anything in their pockets. Do you have any idea why they were trying to break into your room?"

"They wanted the drawing my brother found in Florence." Though hesitant, Rick told him about Stef's discovery.

"It must be very valuable indeed," the Inspector said dryly. "Now please explain why you didn't contact us immediately after what happened at the hotel."

"At the time I didn't have any coins for the pay phone. Where I come from, emergency calls are free. Even if I did have the money, I didn't trust anyone. The way I saw it, everyone on the island was out to get me. Including the police."

Micallef leaned forward and put his hands on the table in front of him. As he did, Rick noticed a heavy signet ring with the letter 'A' inside a seven-pointed star against a ruby background. It looked vaguely familiar. The Inspector came so close that Rick could smell the tobacco on his breath. "Why did you wait more than fourteen hours to contact us?"

Rick backed away. "The kidnappers said they would kill my brother if I did."

Micallef glowered. "Do you have any proof for what you're saying about your brother's kidnapping?"

"Just this note," Rick said, holding it out to him. "Someone passed it to me in the National Library. They gave my cell phone back to me, too." He took the phone out of his pocket and laid it on the table next to the note. "I just spoke to the kidnappers a little more than an hour ago. You've seen the report about how I was attacked and robbed at the airport, haven't you?"

"Yes," Micallef said curtly. He took a pair of tweezers from a desk drawer and used them to pick up the paper. After dropping it into a plastic evidence bag he turned back to Rick. "I don't expect we'll find any useful prints but we'll try. I will of course look into your brother's disappearance. When did he arrive here?"

"Last Wednesday. He came by the airfoil from Sicily."

"What was his reason for his visit?"

"I have no idea."

Micallef paused. "Did you have an address for him here?"

"The San Antwan Hotel in Sliema. I was supposed to join him there."

Micallef fingered through the index of a plastic Rolodex, then picked up his phone. "What's his name?"

Rick told him, tensing as the Inspector threw him a suspicious look. "Stefan Olsen. He's a guest registered in your hotel."

Now Micallef was glaring. "Are you sure?" After a pause he said, "Thanks," and hung up. "They say there's no one there by that name."

Rick snorted. Why didn't that surprise him? "Check with the agent at the National Car Rental booth at the airport. He talked to someone at the hotel last night. They told him that Stef was waiting for me."

"We will. In the meantime, do you have any proof he ever actually arrived here?"

"I got a phonecall and two e-mails from him. I'd show them to you except my computer was stolen at the airport and the hard copies were in my briefcase."

The Inspector looked at him in silence for a moment. "Quite frankly, I don't believe a word you said and if it were up to me, I would lock you up and throw away the key for your high-handedness. Since I can't do that, I'm placing you under arrest for leaving the scene of a crime and for withholding evidence."

Rick's world crumbled. He was about to ask to see a lawyer when Micallef said, "I'll see that you have someone to represent you. My assistant will take over from here."

Seconds later an inevitable young man in black wool entered the room. "This way," he said. The first stop was at a PC monitor with an identification form on the screen. Whatever happened to the typewriter and triplicate forms? Rick wondered as he answered the questions.

When they finished the officer printed two copies and handed one to Rick. "Your attorney will want this." Fingerprinting was done the old-fashioned way with ink and paper. The last time Rick was fingerprinted was when he renewed his security clearance; the unit clerk did it with a computer and a finger-pad.

Inspector Micallef appeared, seething mad. "I'll take over, Michael. Thanks." What's eating him? Rick wondered.

"You're free to leave," the Inspector said in an angry voice. "Once again Miss Caterina Borg has intruded where she doesn't belong. You're released into her custody."

A black-uniformed officer escorted Rick back to the door where Caterina awaited him. Her appearance stunned him. Gone were the jeans and tee shirt, replaced by a fetching print dress. No longer an overgrown tomboy, Caterina Borg was obviously a very attractive young woman. "My guardian angel," he said. "Thanks for bailing me out."

"I didn't have any choice," she said evenly. "I see you survived your ordeal."

"Barely. They were just about to lead me to my cell when you came along. Why did he release me to you?"

She cocked her head. "He knows he can trust me. Father Modiglio and I have taken custody of refugees the police have arrested many times in the past. Most of them were simply passengers on the freighters from Libya who got caught entering without papers. Illegal immigrants are coming by the boatloads and it's become a national problem." A wry smile came to her face. "Does Malta seem like a Promised Land to you?"

"Not really. Why do they come here?"

"We're close and we have economic and social ties with Libya. So lots of other North Africans come here from Tripoli and Tunisia. The ones on the freighters usually come to get medical treatment or try to get on another freighter for Sicily. If they intend to stay they're usually coming to join family members who are already here."

"Where did you go after you brought me in?"

"Back to the Bellestrado. I knew I had to return the rifle before the police arrived. I didn't realize they would show up five minutes after I got done. I found a spot where they could have overlooked it the first time. I'm sure they must wonder how it got so far away from the bodies."

Rick wanted to kiss her. "You really are my guardian angel. Actually, it doesn't really matter where they found it. Inspector Micallef couldn't be any more suspicious of me than he already is. What about my fingerprints?"

"What fingerprints?" she asked with a sly smile. "There aren't any. I rubbed the bag over the whole rifle, so all they'll find is dust. There was more than enough of that in the bag to do the job."

"I'm speechless. Unfortunately I don't see how I can find my brother if I have to take you along with me every step of the way."

"Find a way. There's no alternative except to go back to jail."

"Are you going to keep me at gunpoint?"

She smiled. "That wasn't a gun."

"I didn't think so. But you have a business to tend to and I can't very well ride along with you while you're driving your fares. I couldn't afford the time, anyway."

"The fares can wait a day or two. You don't seem to be able to do very well on your own so you need me. I don't intend to let you out of my sight until this is over."

The words suggested intriguing possibilities until he again noticed her engagement ring. "And what is your fiancé going to have to say about the arrangement?" he asked.

"He knows about my work and approves of it. He would realize you were no different from the other unfortunates I've helped in the past."

How true. Right now he desperately needed an ally. Especially one who knew the island.

As they reached the cab he slid into the front seat and said, "I have an idea. Let me hire you as my personal chauffeur at whatever your average daily take would be. That way you won't be missing income and it will make me feel a lot better."

"That would be a hundred pounds a day. Are you sure you can afford that?"

"A steal," he said.

"A deal," she said, shaking his hand. "Where to?"

"First of all, somewhere where I can buy some surgical gloves. I intend to visit Cornacchia's yacht tonight and I don't want to leave fingerprints."

"That's easy enough. Where else?"

"How about a car rental agency?"

She threw him a sharp look. "Why?"

"We need a new set of wheels. I don't want to broadcast our every move riding in this relic, charming as it is."

"I suppose you're right," she said. From the wistfulness in her voice he knew that if she ever had to choose between the Chev and the man in her life, the man would lose out. "There's an agency in Gzira that's only a few stops away from the Bellestrado. When we get to the hotel I'll make us something to eat. Will cheese, wine and bread be enough for you?"

"You must have read my mind. That's exactly what I would have ordered if we went to a restaurant."

She smiled, but not at him. "You must drive people crazy. When are you going to stop your line of bull?"

"When I'm eighty?" he said with a smile. It immediately disappeared as he noticed another car behind them start at the same time. Watching it in the rear-view mirror he said, "Slow down."

She slowed to a crawl, acting as if she were looking for a parking space. The Honda slowed also, followed for a second or two, then passed them. Rick tried to get a look at the driver, but couldn't see through the tinted glass.

"Drive around the block once. He may be waiting for us."

She circled the block at a snail crawl, ignoring the angry honks from motorists. When they got back to where they started, she asked, "Can we go now?"

His eyes made one last circuit before he spoke.

"I think so. It's probably nothing, but if it's one of the kidnapper's agents, he may not need to follow us. Everyone must know your cab. Once he realizes I'm with you, sooner or later he'll head for the Bellestrado."

"I sure hope you're wrong," she said.

*   *   *   *

Stef took a deep breath. Pain and exertion had brought him to the edge of victory. His left hand was numb and soaked with blood and sweat but now only the meat of his thumb stood in the way of his freedom from his bonds. But as hard as he tried he couldn't dislocate his fingers to gain the leeway he needed. The nylon cord, now well past the first knuckle on his little finger, refused to move any farther.

Steeling himself, he made one last pull. The pain in his right hand became excruciating, but he could not move the left.

No, his mind screamed. No! Every muscle ached and his body-stench made him gag. Tears poured from his eyes as physical agony and frustration overcame him. Sobs turned to wails. In his despair he didn't feel the rope slip backwards ever so slightly toward his wrist on his right hand. And with the numbness in his left hand he didn't notice the bonds' unrelenting grip slacken, either. Vomiting white foam, he made one last defiant pull.

To his astonishment his left hand pulled free.

Stunned, he slipped further down into the crib, struggling for breath. Using his hands to pull himself on his side, he lay gasping.

How long before Pawlu returned?

Fighting off exhaustion, he got to his feet.

He waited for the waves of vertigo to pass before he scrambled out of his coffin. Rubbery legs buckled under him as his feet hit the floor. Instead of trying to stand, he crawled forward on all fours until his head banged against a wall.

Good.

He got to his feet and set his right hand against the stone. Even though he had been blindfolded when they took him to the boat, he knew they had walked him to the right. Ten steps brought him to a door. He fumbled in the darkness until he found a latch. It moved up and down but the door didn't budge.

Afraid he would attract attention, but seeing no other way out, he backed up and ran against the barrier. He collided with a loud thump and fell backwards.

He had but one option left.

Crawling on all fours, he found himself at the door Pawlu and company used. Here goes, he thought. His heart beat faster as he found the doorknob. Before he could turn it the door opened and a bright light assaulted his eyes. As he raised his hands to cover them, he heard Pawlu's voice.

"Congratulations, my friend," his captor said. "I had no idea you could get free."

CHAPTER 8

▼

Saturday
6:00 PM
Gzira

As Rick waited, several Arabs passed by him. Most of the men wore jeans and
short-sleeved shirts, and the women cotton dresses with scarves across their faces.
Suddenly he caught the strains of an evocative middle-eastern piece with flutes
and drums and a male voice chanting in time with the instruments. Nodding his
head to the music he punched in Kevin MacIntyre's speed-dial number.

"Triskar," Kevin said in a muffled voice. Rick had caught him with his mouth
full.

"How's Arthur?" Rick demanded without identifying himself. Arthur was his
cat and soulmate.

"Fine. He's been asking about you. He demands that you come home immediately."

"Tell him I'll be back as soon as I can," Rick said, continuing to listen to the
music with one ear until it faded into the distance. "I need information and I
know someone who would be willing to pay a case of Black Bush for it."

"A case? Planning to heist the crown jewels?"

"Something more important. Lorenzo Cornacchia's company is called Black
Dolphin Shipping. It has a big web site and a security lock. I need all you can
find about finances, cargo movements. Everything. And I need it last week."

"You may be in luck. We were able to install the new lines sooner than I
expected so I'll have a little extra time. A lot will depend on what kind of security
Cornacchia has."

"Do the best you can," Rick said.

Caterina showed up as he fingered the call end button. "The car will be wait-ing for us. We can pick it up when we need it."

Tarbija confidently crawled down the narrow alleyway and finally came to a stop behind the Bellestrado. After locking the doors, Caterina threw open the trunk and removed a light canvas tarp. They spread it over the top of the vehicle. She lashed it in place with bungee cords attached to the front and rear bumpers, talking to it continuously as she did. Finally, after giving a fender a consoling pat she led him to the door. As they stepped in, Rick was greeted by a strong scent of spices from a galley a few feet away.

"Does your aunt have a computer?" Rick asked. "I think I know where I can find some more information about Lorenzo Cornacchia."

"She does and you're welcome to use it. I'd help you but she just changed all the passwords. Someone was trying to get into her business files."

Rick snapped to attention. "What do you mean?"

"She has a website to advertise the hotel. She was having problems with her computer and took it in for repairs. While it was in the shop the repairman found a worm in her system that would allow someone to use her computer as if it were their own."

His alarm bell clanged louder. "When was this?"

"Two weeks ago."

"Does she have any idea what they were after?" Rick asked.

"No. The tech thought it might be credit card numbers. Luckily, all she keeps in the computer are the guest registry and the hotel's financial records."

Rick was still considering what Caterina said as they entered the pub. When Josefina Grech saw him she rushed out from behind the bar to wring his hand. "Are you all right?" she asked. "I've been so worried about you."

"Never better," he said.

"Rick needs to use the computer," Caterina said. "I'll cover the bar for you."

"Come with me," she said, taking him so firmly by the arm that for a moment he thought he was back with the Malta police. She swung up a gate at the right side of the hotel desk and stepped through. With the turn of a key the top of the desk rolled back to expose a computer tower and monitor.

"Nice," Rick said. "Pentium Three?"

"Two. 500 megahertz." He watched approvingly as her fingers flew over the keyboard and clicked on the mouse. Seconds later she stood up. "It's all yours."

"Caterina told me about the worm in your computer. Have you noticed any changes in your files?"

"No. I think the repairman is right that they were after credit card numbers so I haven't been too worried."

She stood and pushed the chair back for him. "Just shut the machine down and turn it off when you're done. I'll lock it up."

He looked up as Caterina passed him. Three minutes later he returned to the pub.

"You don't look very happy," said Josefina.

"A total waste of time."

"You'll feel better after you've eaten," Josefina said, patting his hand. "Caterina is getting something for you. She said you should wait here."

Rick nodded. A quick scan of the bar revealed a mostly new cast of characters. With the exception of Anna, that is. A heavy-set man had her by the hand. Two other males stood behind him leaning over his shoulder. Rick could guess what the conversation was about. Negotiating a group rate, no doubt.

A young man carrying a coffee cup approached the bar; his eyes fixed on a page from a gilt-edged book. Rick recognized him. He had been watching TV the first night.

"Hello," said Rick.

Startled, the youth looked up. "Oh, h-hello," he stammered. "P-please excuse m-me." With that he set the cup on the counter and rushed back to his table without another glance in Rick's direction.

Though puzzled by the reaction, Rick turned his attention to the rest of the cast. The other denizens were unfamiliar. One was about five-three or five-four with jet-black hair pomaded and pulled straight back. He raised his glass in salute, showing off pearl-white teeth as he did. Next to him was a burly man seated at the bar. Rick prided himself on his physique but the man put him to shame. Muscles was also a serious drinker, too intent on his beer to notice anything except the inside of his glass.

"Come over here, Rick" Josefina called, gesturing at a stool and setting a foaming glass on the bar. "The drinks are free as long as you stay here."

That seemed to catch Muscles' attention. "How do you rate?" he asked.

Rick bent toward him and whispered in a conspiratorial tone, "It's my half for helping her rob the bank. I held the door open for her while she made her escape."

"My God," Muscles said. "Another American. I thought I was the only one on the island. Where are you from?"

"Minneapolis. Are you from New York?"

"Jersey. I'm working in the shipyards. One of the conveyors we sold hasn't been working right and the company sent me to fix it. You here on vacation?"

"Not anymore. Are you working for the Cornacchia company?"

The man gave Rick a suspicious look. "If that means Black Dolphin Shipping I am. Why do you ask?"

"I may need to touch base with you later. How much longer will you be around?"

"It looks like at least another week." He held out a hand. "I'm Manny O'Toole."

"Rick Olsen." As he said it he felt his hand being engulfed in a vice. Finally, fearing for the appendage, he said, "Jeez, I better drink my beer. It's getting warm."

O'Toole let go. "I'd buy you a round except that yours is already paid for."

Rick took it to mean that he should ask Josefina for a free beer for O'Toole. "I'd buy you one, too, except my money isn't any good here."

"Ha-aahaha," O'Toole brayed, slapping Rick on the back. "You're all right. Glad to meet you."

"The pleasure is all mine. Where are you staying?" Rick asked.

"Down the street. It's called the Preluna."

The yeasty camaraderie ended when Caterina gestured at him from the hall-way. "Should I bring my beer?" Rick asked.

"You can if you want to," she said. "I don't know how well it will go with the wine."

Rick handed the glass to O'Toole. "Here. Have one on me. I never touched it."

"Hey. Thanks," O'Toole said, beaming. Rick waved at him. As he left, Rick remembered the closing line from *Casablanca*. This could be the beginning of a beautiful friendship.

Seven tables with red and white oilcloth covers awaited him in the dining area. Caterina had set the wine bottle, a basket full of bread and a plate of cheese on it. Like the bread he bought on the street, it had a hard crust and a soft marrow. "This is wonderful," he said. "How did you know I was crazy about bread?"

"I didn't." She pointed at a plate. "Have some cheese, too."

"Bread is fine," Rick said, grabbing three pieces. Then he remembered his manners and flushed. "Henh."

She smiled. "Relax and enjoy yourself. By the way, you can expect a lot of food as long as you're around Josefina. She's the world's best cook and she'll browbeat you to eat."

"She won't have to browbeat me. I love to eat almost as much as my brother does. I'm just more active."

She buttered a piece of bread for herself and nibbled at it. "Who's the muscle-bound animal at the bar?"

"His name is Manny O'Toole and he's working at Black Dolphin. He may come in handy some time. That's a nice ring. Who's the lucky fellow?"

"Andrew Xuereb," she said with obvious pride. "He's the chief of accounting with Tal-Lvant Bank. He'll be president some day."

Rick broke out laughing. "You're marrying an accountant?"

She glared at him. "What's so funny about that?"

"Nothing. But I would never guess that an accountant would be your type."

Beet red, she put her hands in her lap and turned away from him. "You have no idea what my type is, so kindly keep your comments to yourself," she said.

He sighed. "Right. Since you're already taken, I guess there's always Anna."

Caterina's eyes flashed. "Don't be ridiculous. Anna is a prostitute."

"I had no idea," he said in mock surprise. "That reminds me, why did you and Josefina squelch our little flirtation the other night?"

She flushed again. "Anna is only supposed to deal with the locals."

"Really? Why's that?"

"It's a long story but the simple answer is we would get in trouble with the tourist board otherwise. She must have got a little drunk and forgot."

"Hold on," Rick said with a scowl. "I didn't get the impression she was trying to drum up business. Things were just starting to get interesting when Zija stepped in."

"Anna knows the rules. And I think Zija was especially upset with her because she thought she was trying to take away what little money you had left."

It sounded a bit patronizing but Rick he appreciated the thought. "You didn't seem very pleased with her, either. Were you jealous?"

Once again a touch of color came to her cheeks. "Of course not. You're free to consort with anyone you want to. Anna included. If you want, I'll even put in a good word for you."

"Do that," Rick said. "Who's the young scholar?"

"A student at University. Josefina has him do odd jobs to make a little money."

Rick remembered the ampoule he found at the marina. Pointing at the Arabic inscription he asked, "Would he know what the inscription means?"

"I can read Arabic," she said. "It's Sodium Pentobarbital. Where did you find it?"

"At the marina. Stef's kidnappers must have used it to get him to talk. By the way, would you happen to have a pair of binoculars? We'll need them when we go back to Golden Bay."

"I don't, but Zija does."

"Zija does what?" Josefina said, suddenly appearing in the doorway.

"Have binoculars," Caterina replied. "He wants to know if we can borrow them."

"Yes, but you'll have to cover the bar until I find them."

The seats at the bar were taken so Rick found a table. Anna was gone, apparently with her suitors. The young Arab sat at a back corner table reading. Manny O'Toole was at the bar with Caterina standing like a cornered animal with her back against the liquor cabinet. Rick came to her rescue. O'Toole saw him and raised an empty glass in salute. Caterina moved close to Rick for protection. "I'm glad you're here," she whispered. "Stay near me."

"With pleasure," he whispered back. "Did Manny make a pass at you?"

She turned red. "Yes. And he nearly connected. With my butt. Zija should throw him out."

"Not a good idea. I may need him later. Just relax."

Taking her by the hand, he said, "Manny, I guess I didn't get a chance to introduce my fiancée. Caterina, this is my new friend Manny O'Toole."

"Fiancée?" the Irishman said, turning crimson. "Sorry, I had no idea." Docilely extending his hand he said, "Glad to meet you, Caterina," in a quiet voice.

Though hesitant, she took it. "Same to you, Mr. O'Toole."

Rick seized the opportunity and put his arm around Caterina's waist. She squirmed for a moment but didn't move away. He enjoyed the curious electricity where the skin of his arm was in contact with her dress. The moment ended when one of the customers called out with an empty beer glass in his hand. Caterina deftly wiggled free and moved to the tap.

The young Arab appeared at the bar with his empty coffee cup and set it on the bar.

"Back for more?" Rick asked.

This time he was greeted with a shy grin. "I d-drink t-too much c-coffee, b-but I n-need it to s-stay awake."

"I understand you're a student."

"Yes. I-I am from B-Bengasi and I'm st-studying ar-archeology at the U-university of Malta. I'm st-staying here until I can get a r-room closer to the c-campus."

"Students from North Africa come to Malta all the time," Caterina said. "It's part of the cultural exchange program and they get the same benefits we natives do. The archeology program is popular because the students get to work on the Neolithic ruins with knowledgeable archaeologists."

"I'm w-working on M-Mnajdra temple," the Arab said. "V-vandals damaged it a few y-years ago, and I'm h-helping to repair it."

When Rick introduced himself, the young Arab shyly offered his hand. "I-I am Yu-Yusef Mansoor. It is an a-honor t-to meet you."

Josefina returned a short time later carrying a black carrying case on a strap. "These are my husband's. He used to use them when he went to the Marsa race track on Saturdays," she said. "I nearly divorced him when I found out how much they cost, so be careful with them."

As Rick and Caterina started away, O'Toole grinned broadly and lifted his glass in salute. "To the happy couple," he said.

6:42

Before leaving, Rick used the phone in the hotel lobby to call Island Rentals and again got the answering service. "I've been trying all day to reach Mr. Agius," he said. "Are you sure you don't have a number where you can contact him?"

The woman sounded worried. "I wish I did. Mr. Agius didn't leave word where he could be reached."

"When did he last pick up his messages?"

After a hesitation the woman said, "It's been four days."

"And he runs a car rental company? Where's his office located?"

"Just outside the city of Marsaxlokk," she said.

Rick remembered the name from his tourbook. It was in the southeast part of the island, the mouth of the whale that was Malta. "Thanks," he said. Turning to Caterina he said, "We're going to Marsa-schlock."

"Fine," she said in an angry voice.

"Is there something wrong?"

"As a matter of fact there is. I appreciate your saving me from Mr. O'Toole but I don't understand why it was necessary to put your arm around me that way."

He grinned at her. "We had to put on a good show, didn't we?"

"I should have slapped your face."

"Why didn't you?"

"I...I didn't want to create a scene. But from now on, you're going to have to stop...bothering...me or I'll have to take you back to Inspector Micallef."

The grin got bigger. "Then you're going to have to stop being so darned adorable," he said.

"What did I just say?"

Her voice wasn't as sharp as he expected. "Mff, mff, mff," he said, covering his mouth with his hand. She didn't say anything more, but her unhappy look spoke volumes. "Okay. I apologize. Please forgive me."

She didn't answer and sat in stony silence as he told her the rest of Stef's story. Although she nodded and asked questions at appropriate times, she had little to say on her own. He finally gave up. *For Pete's sake, you'd think I tried to rape her.*

Twenty minutes later they reached Marsaxlokk and found themselves in a massive traffic jam. The men and women who were pushing wheeled racks of white tee shirts up the incline from the waterside were parked three-deep around the waterfront. Still others loaded small wooden boxes into vans. On the docks, men and women were busily striking tents and taking down canopies. Caterina seemed to forget her anger. "Here we are," she said brightly.

"Busy place," Rick said.

"Especially now," she replied. "The market is closing for the day. We won't be able to drive for a while so I'll find a place to park." As they crawled along she said, "I'm really worried that Mario hasn't picked up his messages. I pray nothing has happened to him. I've known him for years."

"The rental car clerk said that he delivers to the airport. How does he get home?"

"He brings the paper work with him to the airport. His wife used to follow him and they'd drive back together. After his wife died he's had to take a cab back home after he delivers his rentals."

Rick looked amazed. "You're kidding. With what you people charge for fares, how could he make any money that way?"

"We cabbies all like him so we only charge him for the gas. By the way, you're right about the fares. They are too high. But if you tell anyone else I said so, I'll deny it."

It was good to see her smile again, Rick thought. It lit up her whole face.

"It's too bad we're not using Tarbija," she said. "I could have parked on a sidewalk and we wouldn't have to walk so far."

"Wouldn't the police tow it away?"

"No. He's never in anyone's way." She smiled wistfully. "I love to come here. Especially after the vendors leave, so the boats and the nets are the only things by the water. Then the village still looks the same as it did when I was a child. There aren't too many places left where the top of the church steeple is still the highest point in town."

"I like it, too. Do you ever come here with Andrew?"

She eyed him suspiciously. "Why do you ask that?"

"Just curious."

"This isn't his kind of place. We spend most of our time in Valletta and Sliema or Paceville. Sometimes we go to the casino at Dragonara Palace, and he's taken me to Rome, too. He's very cosmopolitan." She broke off and threw him a sharp look. "I don't want you to mention him anymore."

"Okay," Rick said defensively. "I won't."

8:02 PM

They arrived at a shack on a parking lot just on the eastern outskirts of town. "Here we are," she said. The building looked empty and the only vehicle in the lot was a red Honda convertible with a note stuck under the windshield wiper. Caterina pulled it out and read it. "'No one here when we returned the car. Put keys through post slot in door. Please charge our Visa card. The Chamberlains.'"

"This isn't good," Rick said with a worried frown. "If Agius intended to be away from his business for an extended time, he wouldn't have rented out a car that needed to be returned while he was gone."

With a sick feeling he slipped the note back under the wiper. He didn't feel any happier when he found the door to the office locked. A quick look through the window told him nothing. It was too dark to see anything. Unwilling to give up, they walked around to the back of the building. All they found was an empty trash barrel. He made a mental note to find out when trash was collected. It could give him an additional clue to how long Agius had been away.

"We're not going to find out anything more here," he said. "Do you know where he lives?"

"Yes. I've taken him to his house. He lives in town but he has a farm in the country."

"Let's start with his house."

No one was at home. After a bewildering ride on a narrow road between look-alike residences, stone townhouses suddenly gave way to rock walls and Rick realized they were on a country lane. A farmer appeared from behind one of them, pushing a wheelbarrow of carrots.

Caterina stopped the car next to a stone wall. "This is it," she said. "I wonder why the gate is open."

Caterina got out and Rick followed her into the field. Rows of what may have been the tops of beets stood withered in the field.

"I don't like this," Caterina said. "No one has been caring for these plants."

"I thought you said Agius runs a car rental agency. How can he farm, too?"

"His wife tended the farm when she was alive. Now he keeps his cars and business records at Island Rentals, but he's still spends most of his time here. I think he wants to be as busy as possible so he doesn't think about how lonely he is."

"What's that?" he asked, pointing toward a domed cairn made out of stone.

"It's called a *Girna*," she replied. "Farmers use them to keep animals and store equipment."

"Let's take a look," said Rick. He took two steps forward before his right foot slipped out from under him and he found himself sitting on the ground.

"Ohmygod," Caterina screamed. "Are you all right?"

"I'm fine," Rick said as he got to his feet. He reached down to pick up what he had stepped on. It was a small-gauge shotgun shell. There were three of them within inches of each other.

"Is Agius a hunter?"

"No. He told me he hates guns. He loves animals too much."

Rick sniffed the shell, then put it in his pocket. It had been there for at least a few days because the sharp burnt powder odor was starting to fade.

As they got closer to the cairn, an overwhelming sweetish stench had them reaching for their noses. "Go back to the car," Rick said.

"You too. We don't belong here."

"I'll be with you in a minute."

She turned back. He waited until she was through the gate before starting toward the cairn. The stench got worse with each step. Finally he had to take off his shirt to cover his nose. Stooping under the doorway, he peered inside the structure.

The first thing he noticed was an iron pry bar. The second was barely visible by the light that was fast fading from the evening sky. A brown boot nearly covered by blue denim lay on the floor. After grabbing the bar he hurried back to the car.

"What's the matter?" Caterina asked.

"There's a body in the *girna*. It must be Agius."

She took a cell phone out of her purse and began to punch in numbers. Rick grabbed it out of her hand.

"Stop that!" she said. "We have to notify the police."

"Not until I've had a chance to go through the files at Island Rentals. If he rented a car to Stef, there has to be a record with his address on it. I want to see if I can find it before the police get involved. We'll need a flashlight."

"There's one in the glove compartment," she said. "I can't believe I'm letting you do this."

"I'm a bad influence."

She parked next to the returned car. "The car is too new to be Mario's," she said. "But in the dark no one will know the difference."

He got the pry bar out of the trunk. "Stay here. If anyone shows up, take off."

"Absolutely not," she said. "You're in my custody and if you get caught, I'll get into trouble anyway."

They both pulled on their rubber gloves. Rick's were tight but he was able to slip his fingers up to his knuckles without splitting the latex. "Ready?"

"As ready as I'll be," Caterina said in a dubious voice.

Carefully pushing the bar between the door and jamb, Rick leaned against it with his full weight. The doorframe broke with a crack.

They darted inside and closed the door. Even in the dark he could see that all the file drawers were open, and manila folders and the contents covered the floor. If Stef's rental contract were here, it was the proverbial needle in the haystack.

Headlights slowly passed by outside the building to cast a moving streak of light on the wall behind them. "Down!" he said, pushing her to the floor.

The light whizzed over them without slowing. As he lay next to her with his arm across her back he could smell her shampoo and feel her heart beat faster. Then they were again in darkness and they exhaled in unison. "We have to get out of here fast," he said. "You hold the flashlight and I'll get the papers."

"If we're going to look for a needle in a haystack we may as well take the haystack with us," she replied.

"You're right." He handed her a pile and gathered up the rest for himself. Caterina cautiously opened the door. They both breathed a sigh of relief when they got to the car. "Are we done for the night?" she asked.

"We've only started. I want to take a look at Cornacchia's yacht."

CHAPTER 9

▼

Saturday
10:33 PM
On the Road

Once again Rick's heart was in his throat as Caterina barreled down the narrow road that led to Ghain-Tuffieha and Golden Bay. "Look at all these lights," she said in an angry voice. "This was all farmland when I was a girl. I used to ride my horses here. Now it's nothing but townhouses. It makes me sick every time I come this way."

"I sympathize," he replied. "That's why I restore prairie. Tell me what you know about Lorenzo Cornacchia."

"I'm sure I don't know much more than what you saw in the clippings," she replied. "I don't agree with him on many things, but I do with his land-use policy. The developers will turn the island into a single city if they have their way."

"Can you think of anything that isn't in his official biography or the newspapers?"

"Hmm. Well, did you know he's an expert chess player? He's turned part of his garden into a chessboard and he has children in costumes representing the pieces."

"I play chess, too. I nearly won the state championship three years ago."

"Way cool," she said. "Did you know Cornacchia is an artist? He donated one of his sculptures to the government. Melita. It's in the parliamentary hall."

"Honey?"

"Yes," she said, chuckling. "And the name is appropriate. Malta used to be known for its honey and there were beehives all over the islands. You can still find some on Gozo."

"So what does the sculpture look like?"

Her smile widened into a grin. "That's the other reason why the name fits. It's a beautiful naked woman with gossamer wings holding a flower she's licking with her tongue. Most people think that wife MARR-e-YAH modeled for it; the unkind ones say it was the only time Lorenzo ever saw her naked."

"What a waste," he said. "I saw her at a shopping mall yesterday morning. She smiled at me."

"Don't let it go to your head. She smiles at every man."

"Just smiles?" Rick asked.

"No," she said in a conspiratorial tone. "There have been rumors about her for years but she tends to be pretty discreet."

"Anything about a present boyfriend?"

"There's a little gossip about an Arab who's been working at their estate in Mdina for the last month. You're not thinking of making moves on her, are you? She's way too rich for your blood."

"No. My heart belongs to another," he said with a laugh.

That brought a silence that lasted until they reached the parking lot at Golden Bay. "Nothing here," Rick said.

"I saw a turnoff a few meters back." She quickly found it and they followed a narrow road for several hundred yards. Driving with the windows open, they listened to crickets serenade each other then occasionally stop their songs as the car drove past. At last they came to a tarpaulin with the end of a two-by-four sticking out from under it. "This must be the place," Rick said.

He got out to walk to the steep edge of the hill, now clearly evident in the light of the moon. As he stood at the edge, tiny stones clattered over the decline just a few inches beneath his feet. Below, *il-Karraba* was a miniature mountain jutting into the water. A hundred yards away, lights from Cornacchia's yacht reflected off the water. Rick thought of F. Scott Fitzgerald's view of East Egg at the beginning of *The Great Gatsby*. Lights shone through the windows in the ship's cabin.

"Someone's aboard," Rick said. "We may as well bring the blankets over. We could be in for a long wait."

"Do you think Stef is on the boat?"

"He could be. I'm pretty sure he was last night. I can't imagine any other reason why there would be an empty ampoule in Cornacchia's garbage can at the marina."

"What are you going to do if he is?" she asked.

"Depends. It they leave by car we'll follow them. If they move the boat, about the best we can do is see which way they're heading and try to guess where they're going."

His first sweep with the binoculars covered il-Karraba. A red light blinked at the far end of the outcropping. Lit by a strange red glow, the *fougasse* showed up as a pit with kegs and piles of rock around the edges. It was altogether a crude and nasty weapon.

The yacht was clearly in view. Light beamed through three of the windows at amidships and men stood at fore and aft. Sentries? The man aft was leaning against the cabin smoking a cigarette while the other paced around nervously.

Rick kept watch on the windows, wondering if he could catch a shadow or some hint of what was going on inside. Finally he said, "Let's see if we can get a closer look."

They drove back to the parking lot, then followed the downward path he had traversed earlier in the day. It wasn't an easy walk then. Now, with only a full moon to light their way, they clung to each other and walked with tiny steps. At last they arrived at his earlier vantagepoint. A quick look through the binoculars told him the view from the hill was much clearer.

"Let's go back," he said with a sigh.

By the time they arrived the sentry at the fore end of the boat had gone inside and the one remaining seemed to be killing time by pulling unremittingly on cigarettes and dipping the end of a rope into the water.

Rick lowered the glasses to wipe at his eyes with his hand.

"You must be tired," she said. "Do you want to take a rest and let me watch for a while?"

"Yes. And thanks for the offer. Just wake me up if anything changes."

"Promise," she said.

He stretched out on his side on the blanket and gazed at the stars. As he rolled over on his back he caught her looking at him. With a smile he dropped off to sleep.

11:44

He awoke with Caterina poking him. "Quick," she said, handing the binoculars to him. "Some men are coming out of the ship's cabin."

Rick took the glasses and peered intently through the lenses. Yes. Three. One he recognized immediately. Lorenzo Cornacchia. The second man was much older, with a white mane of hair. The third was younger by many years, with thinning black hair and a mustache. The three spoke animatedly to each other.

The conversation ended when Cornacchia stepped between the younger and older man. Shortly thereafter, they all got into a large rowboat with an outboard motor and were ferried back to shore.

"Recognize any of them?" Rick asked.

"I think the old man is Cardinal Vella."

"And I know Cornacchia," Rick said. "Do you have any idea who the third one could be?"

"No. I never saw him before."

Rick watched in bemusement until the trio was at the dock. Cornacchia and Vella disappeared into the building at the edge of the water. The third man waited outside. Minutes later, another boat appeared and the third man boarded it. An outboard motor started and the boat quickly disappeared from sight as it headed toward the sea. "What do you suppose that was all about?" he said.

Ten minutes later the Stallion was dark. And so was the house on the beach. Two sedans drove away in the glow of their headlights. When the vehicles' taillights disappeared, Rick said, "It's time for me to go down and take a closer look."

"Back to the parking lot?" Caterina asked as they got into the car.

"Unless you've got a better idea."

"I think I can find the road down to the house. It must be closer than going all the way back to the restaurant."

"Go for it."

Without much difficulty she found an unmarked road some two hundred yards from where they had turned off. "I think this is it," she said.

"Turn off the headlights."

Luckily they didn't need them. The moon was shining brightly and they had nothing to obstruct their view of the building below them. The closer they came the more convinced he became that the house was empty. He also noticed a rough path that went down to the water. "Stop here," he said.

She did. "This is too steep. There must be a safer way down."

"I'll be fine as long as I have light. Coming back may be another story. I'll need the blanket."

He bent low to keep his balance as he went. The path down was steep, but rocks provided a rude stairway. He still was surprised at how far it was to the harbor. Finally he reached water's edge and stripped, ending with putting on the rubber gloves. After carefully wrapping his clothes in the blanket, he stuck an exploratory big toe into the water. Not too cold. He waded in to his waist, then began to swim.

Powerful arms pulled him forward through the still waters. The boat didn't appear to be very far away, but after five minutes of swimming it didn't seem any closer. He stopped and floated, resting and catching his wind. Swimming took all his energy. An eternity later, he was close enough to the boat to hear the water wash against the stern.

Searching for signs of life, he circled the boat once, moving slowly to avoid making sounds or telltale ripples. Nothing. Everything was dark and quiet. On sudden inspiration, he moved closer and tapped against the hull hoping Stef might answer. Continued silence was his only reply. He tapped again, waited, then moved on. At last he returned to his starting point.

So far he had found nothing and he was tired of swimming. He had hoped to find a line to make his way to the deck, but someone had secured the boat well. The only path on board was up the mooring line.

The moon cooperated by disappearing and the boat barely moved as he started up. His two hundred-plus pounds were more than offset by the weight of the boat. As he reached over the top to climb aboard, the moon returned in all its glory. He waited for it to duck behind some clouds again, but it refused to coop-erate. Finally, tired of waiting, he decided to board in full view. It wasn't much of a risk. He was sure everyone had left long ago.

Reaching the deck took all his strength and he stood gasping for breath for a few seconds before he started his exploration. As he moved forward he wondered what sort of alarm system Cornacchia had on the boat. All the man really needed to do was to protect the doors and windows. Covering the deck would be expen-sive and mostly unnecessary. When he reached the door to the hold he quietly called, "Stef? Can you hear me?"

At first he thought he heard a rustle from inside. Pressing his ear to the door he waited for more. Nothing.

What had he expected to find? Stef waiting for him beyond the first door, and they'd swim away into the darkness together? He hadn't even considered what he would do if Stef were actually there. They certainly wouldn't swim back together. Stef couldn't swim a stroke.

Angry, Rick threw caution to the wind and walked the complete length of the boat, rapping on each of the windows as he went.

No answers from within or calls to halt from an alerted guard answered his call. He had wasted his time and energy. It was nothing more than a big effing empty boat and he had a long swim back to shore.

As he flexed to dive he noticed a light go on in front of the house on the beach. Oh shit. Did I set off an alarm?

Dropping to his hands and knees, he circled to the starboard side of the boat, all the time keeping an eye on what was happening on shore. He could make out a single person getting into the rowboat that was tied to the dock. But the activity was leisurely, not what would be expected if the man were responding to an alarm.

Eyes tightly shut, he listened to the measured splashes of oars plying the water. As the boat came closer, Rick could see that the boatman was alone.

One on one I'll take my chances.

The boat disappeared as it pulled up next to the bow. Rick silently moved to a new vantagepoint. Two metal hooks appeared from over the side and gripped the deck. Rick tensed, waiting. A head appeared, cigarette glowing, and then the rest of the body. Seconds ticked by. The newcomer finished with the cigarette and tossed it into the water. He took another from a pack in his shirt pocket. A match flared briefly to illuminate an olive face with a black mustache. The acrid odor of the smoke reached Rick even though he was nearly forty feet away.

As the cigarette glowed bright orange for a second time, Rick took a deep breath in relief. He hadn't been discovered.

The boatman took two more puffs and tossed the cigarette butt overboard. Then, he took out a keyring and opened the door to the cabin. A second later all the lights on the boat flashed on and off and a buzzer sounded. The lights and noises stopped and Rick thanked providence that he hadn't set the alarm off himself.

Convinced he was safe, he moved forward, his bare feet silent on the wooden deck. Light poured out from the open door and he stopped before reaching it. The upper deck was only a few feet over his head. It would be safer to have the boatman come out to him than to go inside.

Moving as quickly and silently as he could, he circled back around the whole boat to the ladder that was hanging from the deck. He let himself down and grabbed one of the oars from the rowboat, then returned to the stern and climbed to the upper deck. His toes squeaked against the painted surface as he walked. Following the light brought him directly over the door. Bending forward to hammer on the door, he shouted in Italian, "Hey buddy, come here. Quick."

That brought sounds of haste from below. The man's head appeared. Rick brought down the oar and the man crumpled. "Sorry, buddy. Couldn't be helped."

After relieving the stricken man of his keys and revolver, Rick threw him over his shoulder, walked to the ladder and carried him down to the rowboat. Careful to remove the second oar, he untied the craft and let it drift free. Without oars, the man wouldn't pose a threat even if he awoke while Rick was aboard the boat.

The *Stallion* was Rick's.

Inside he found a passageway with several doors on either side. Straight ahead was the bridge with its huge spoked wheel. It was an antique, a beautiful mahogany relic from centuries past. Rick gave it an affectionate pat, then turned his attention to a pile of charts on a stand next to the Captain's chair. He felt a thrill of pleasure when he realized they were all for Libya and the port of Tripoli. The top one was marked with an X for a point on the coastline some ten miles southwest of Tripoli. Rick wrote down the chart number and traced its location on a piece of overlay paper, drawing the longitude and latitude lines to pinpoint it.

His next task was to find something to keep the paper dry on his swim back. The empty 2-liter plastic soda bottle with a screwtop lid lying in a wastebasket was just what he needed.

Now for the cabins.

The first, just aft of the bridge, was the largest.

"Stef?" Rick called before opening the door. No answer and he stepped inside. Cornacchia's stateroom, undoubtedly. It had a sizable liquor stand, a private bathroom, and a large bed. With its spartan lack of female traces, Rick was sure that Cornacchia spent most of his time there alone.

The bookshelves on either side of the bed held a selection of novels, several by Robert Ludlum and Tom Clancy. All of the books were marked with pieces of paper. One was a scrap from the *Malta Times* dated less than six months ago. Other books included Cellini's *Autobiography* with the dust jacket marking the section on the construction of the Perseus; another his Treatise on Goldsmithing. One item that seemed out of place was a 'sixties edition of the *National Geographic*. Paging through it he found an article about "Li Schetti," a yearly festival held in Calatafimi in Sicily. A picture showed ranks of what seemed to be members of the Corleone family; men dressed in black suits, ties and hats, with white vests on parade. Each formally dressed man held a double-barreled shotgun in his hand. The festival celebrated Garibaldi's victory over Bourbon troops on May 15, 1860 using a handful of redshirts.

Altogether it looked like a blueprint for treason. From what Rick had been learning about Cornacchia, it didn't surprise him. He gave the room a final once-over and moved on.

The second cabin was much smaller and smelled of perfume. Marija Cornacchia slept in a single bed and read *Barron's* and the *Wall Street Journal* as well as *The Economist*. He found several issues on the shelves and on the stand next to her bed. Opening the drawer, he discovered a vibrator hidden under several issues of *Playgirl*. The computer monitor on the table suggested Marija was as serious about her work as she was about her pleasure. With an amused smile, he noticed a curtain covered what appeared to be a mirror directly across from the foot of the bed. It proved to be a high-definition television set and a top-of-the-line Sony stereo and sound system. The lady certainly had good taste.

He was about to leave when he stepped on two heavy cables that mysteriously disappeared into a wall that separated the room from the hallway. Sliding a door aside, he found a control panel with a curious assortment of switches and knobs. He wasn't sure but it looked very much like a communications center. Marija definitely was the queen bee. Did she provide the computer security for Black Dolphin, too?

The next cabin was little more than a crackerbox, with a single bed and table. As he turned to leave, he stepped something white lying on the floor. It was a cotton ball, sodden with petroleum jelly. He found two more cotton balls in the wastebasket. One smelled of denatured alcohol and the other had a large red spot that looked like blood. On impulse he took the one with the red stain out of the basket. More important was the pad lying on the table. The top sheet was blank but he could see indentations. He tore off the page then headed back into the passageway to see what lay behind the last door.

He found a funnel, a lantern, a dirty rag and a coil of light rope as well as large roll of silvery duct tape. Storage cabinet. He fingered the handle of a lantern, then closed the door.

The next problem was how to get his booty back to the shore without it getting wet. He rummaged through galley drawers until he found a large carving knife. Piercing the soda bottle with the tip, he cut it half way, then opened it up far enough to stash the papers. He wrapped the cotton balls inside individual pieces of paper. A strip of duct tape from the closet was sufficient to seal the bottle. It would float as long as the seal held and he was sure that would give him more than enough time to get back to shore.

Time to go. Or almost, anyway. He had to cover his trail before he left.

First he gathered up the opened bottles and filled them to the top with water. He then threw them into the sea, cringing at the waste of expensive liquor. He went back into the cabins and went through the closets, throwing clothes on the floor, then turned all the drawers upside down. The break-in would look like a burglary or an act of vandalism rather than a recon mission.

The swim back was easier than the one to the boat. He moved along smoothly, pushing the plastic bottle ahead of him. As he swam, he passed the rowboat with the unconscious man drifting lazily towards il-Karraba. Rick wondered how long it would be before the poor sod inside it came to.

Five minutes later, he waded ashore some ten feet from where he had stashed the blanket and clothes. The moon shone brightly above. In hopes that Caterina was watching him through the binoculars, he faced toward the hill and dried himself thoroughly before putting on his clothes. He was soon back on the road where he started.

1:48 AM

Caterina was waiting for him. "I saw what you did to that poor man on the boat," she said in an accusing voice. "You could have killed him."

"It couldn't be helped. I didn't like having to do it, but I didn't have you with me to suggest another way." As he said it he thought it sounded like a putdown. "No offense intended."

"None taken. I don't know what else you could have done, either. Did you find anything interesting?"

Rick held up the bottle. "We'll have to open it to see what we've got."

"Can it wait until tomorrow? I can barely keep my eyes open."

"Me either. Why don't we stay here and sleep under the stars?"

"Sorry. Zija will be making breakfast for us in the morning. She'd be worried if we didn't show up."

They gathered up the blankets and binoculars and returned to the car. When the engine started with the turn of the key, Caterina made a pouting face and said, "New cars are all the same. So efficient and no personality. I miss my Tarbija. He has a mind of his own. I had to add turn signals and seat belts, but otherwise he's just the same way he was when he was born."

"I noticed that. Where did you find, uh, him?"

"In a field near Zebbug. He had been neglected for years. I had to regrind his valves and find him some missing parts. It took more than a year to put him back together. He came all the way here from Detroit."

"Where did you get the parts?" he asked.

"I bought them over the Internet. The shipping cost more than a thousand pounds alone. But he's worth every penny of it."

Listening to her loving tone, Rick wished he were the Chev. "You did a great job."

"He was lonely sitting in that field all by himself all those years. He needed a friend. I bet he misses me now." Every word dripped with accusation and it was all aimed at him. As if to emphasize the point, she turned on the radio. Loud. His ears were assaulted by a disco beat. "Aren't there any classical stations?" he asked.

"Yes, but you can forget it. They don't play the 1812 Overture at this time of night. Anything less would put me to sleep."

They passed a road sign sprayed with purple and green glow paint. The green mark looked like an arrow. The purple distinctly denoted the numerals 2 and 0.

"Looks like the bird hunters have been busy," he said.

"You're right," she said, "how do you know about them?"

"A cabby told me. Hunting sounds like a national obsession."

"It is and I wish the hunters all would just go off somewhere and shoot at each other instead of the birds. The government is afraid to try to control them because there are so many of them. Do you remember what the Arab boy said about Mnajdra?"

"Yes. The travel book I read said they're supposed to be some of the most important Neolithic ruins in the world."

"That's right. Vandals tried to level the stones that are standing. They also left spray paint all over, too."

"Hunters?" Rick asked.

"They're the most likely suspects."

"And it sounds suspiciously like Cornacchia has some tie-in with their organization."

"I understand he contributes a lot of money to them." She paused. "Why do you suppose Cornacchia and Vella were meeting anyone at this time of night?"

"I have no idea," replied Rick. "But they were up to no good. I'm sure of that."

"Did you know that Cardinal Vella fought for the Republicans during the Spanish Civil War? He was only twelve years old when it started."

"Really. When did he join the priesthood?"

"Just after the Second World War. He was one of Alessandro Cornacchia's closest friends."

"Did he sympathize with the Italians, too?"

"Yes."

"That seems a little strange," Rick said. "He was fighting with the Communists in Spain."

"He saw Mussolini as a patriot and a liberator. A lot of other people on the island did too. Especially if they had Italian roots or sympathies."

Rick frowned. "It's still pretty remarkable that he was able to become a cardinal."

"All was forgiven after the war. He didn't actually become a Cardinal until just a few years ago. He was the archbishop before that. Did you ever hear of Publius?"

"I've heard of several Publiuses. Which one do you mean?"

"The first head of the Maltese church. When St. Paul was shipwrecked here, he converted the people and made Publius the leader. There's been an Archbishop of Malta ever since."

"So why is Vella a Cardinal?"

She laughed. "The Pope gave him the title to make him feel better after the government took away his powers in the 1970s. Until then the church used to be more powerful than the government."

"And Vella didn't like it?"

"He was furious. And he's been feuding with the government ever since."

Conversation ended and they rode in silence for a while listening to the irrepressible beat of disco. The mood changed sharply with Harry Chapin's "Cat's in the Cradle." Rick squirmed uncomfortably. He always reacted emotionally to it. Caterina looked at him when he coughed. "Are you okay?"

"Just thinking about Stef," he said.

"You must be very close to your brother, aren't you?"

He turned and found her regarding him earnestly. "I look out for him," he said.

"I know that. But why?"

"Because he won't do it himself. He puts people off, but he's one of the brightest people I know. The trouble is he's still a kid and he'll always be one if he lives to be a hundred."

Caterina made a sour face. "He should be looking out for himself, not depending on you."

"He doesn't even realize that he is. As for looking out for himself, he's been doing that since he was six years old. Nobody can help him or tell him anything. He started buying his own books and toys when he was eight and washing his own clothes when he was ten. He's never let anyone hug him."

Caterina looked at him. "Except you?"

"Especially not me."

"What do you get out of this relationship?"

"He lets me into his world. It's quite a place and a real privilege, believe me."

Chapin wound down and the song ended with, "We'll have a real good time, then, Dad. We'll have a real good time, then." In the silence that followed, Rick once again wondered whether Stef would have turned out differently if their father had spent some time with him, had listened when he babbled on about Stegosauruses, or bothered to take him fishing once in a while. The only time they ever spent together was on family vacations and picnics. Without realizing it, Rick had assumed the role of father himself. It was a hard job for someone only three years older than the son was.

"Doesn't your father like Stef?"

Rick squirmed. "Didn't. Father died seven years ago of lung cancer. He tolerated me because I behaved and didn't ask much of him. Stef was the annoying fat kid with the big mouth."

"I'm glad I didn't know your father. I would have hated him. What did he do for a living? Infect lab animals with cancer cells?"

"No, actually he was a top-echelon executive with an international food corporation. He was head of the accounting division."

Caterina gasped. "You're just making that up," she said angrily.

"It would be pretty good if I were, but it happens to be true."

"You're not suggesting that all accountants are like that, are you?"

"Absolutely not. Nearly every accountant I've met has been a fine, upstanding person and a good parent. My father was, too. In his own way."

"You really have a mean streak, did you know that?"

"No. But thanks for telling me. I thought I was just stating a fact."

They reached the Bellestrado and Caterina found her alleyway and turned. Once they were inside, the walls closed inexorably in on them. Just when the passage seemed the narrowest she sped up slightly and continued on.

"What are you doing?" he asked in horror. "You'll ruin the car."

She stopped inches away from the Chev. "Relax. I know what I'm doing. Here's where we get out."

"How? We'll never be able to get the doors open."

"Try it," she said.

To his amazement, the car door opened cleanly. Even though he couldn't see a thing, he groped ahead until he literally ran into her. "What took you so long?" she asked.

"I stopped for coffee along the way," he said.

She laughed and took his arm. "You go in first."

"You've already got the door open?" he asked. As he said it he again caught the pungent aroma of spices coming from the galley.

"This way." They took a few steps forward until Caterina stopped. He heard the click of a light switch but the room remained dark. "Power's out; happens all the time," she said. "It's all right. We can still find our way to our room."

"In the dark?"

"Trust me."

She started forward again, then stopped. "Don't move," she whispered.

"What's the matter?"

"Someone's at the front door. Probably just a tourist looking for a place to stay. They come at all hours."

The knocking became louder, escalating quickly to thumping and rattling. "If he keeps that up, he'll set off the burglar alarm," Caterina said.

After another round of heavy hammering, the would-be guest gave up and Caterina started forward again with him a step behind. His foot suddenly banged into a step and he grabbed for the railing to keep his balance.

"Here's the stairs," she said.

Rick snorted. "I figured that out for myself. Why couldn't you have given me a little warning?"

"Sorry. They were closer than I realized. Are you okay?" she asked.

"Peachy," Rick said under his breath.

They climbed until the stairs were gone. Then Caterina veered sharply to the right. "This way."

A key rattled in a lock, a door creaked open. "Here we are," she said. "Your bed is just inside the door on the right against the wall." He patted with his free hand until he located it.

"Uh, and where are you sleeping?"

"There's another bed down from yours."

"You're staying here with me?"

"Stop panting. Josefina only had one vacant room. I'm locking the door, by the way. Just in case you get any ideas about running away. You're still in my custody."

"If I wanted to escape, I could have done it at il-Karraba."

"I suppose that's true enough," she said. She surprised him by taking his arm. How could she see that well in the dark? "The bathroom is this way. There's not much in your way. Watch out for the wardrobe, otherwise you have a clear path."

He shuffled forward until he heard a door open. "Here's the toilet," Caterina said, letting him locate it with his hand. "The shower is here." He found it a short distance away. "Let me know when you're done."

That said, she left and shut the door. Rick fumbled out of his clothes and laid them on the commode. Groping for the spigot, his fingers met a handle. Pipes rattled and water dribbled on him. It felt good but the hardness of the water left his skin feeling sticky. The feeling didn't go away, even after he dried himself and wrapped the towel around his midsection.

"I'm done," he said. He inched along to the left until he ran into a wall. Following the wall hand over hand, he bumped his shin against Caterina's bed. "Good work," she said. "You're almost there."

As he lowered himself onto the bed, he was surprised to hear *Lucia di Lammermoor* playing in the distance. Melodic strains drifted in through an open window and the shade glowed orange from an outside light in the garden of the building next door.

He pulled the towel around him and walked to the window. Moving the shade aside, he peered out into the night. The patioed garden he had noticed his first night lay twenty feet below. Beyond the garden, light streamed out from an open door. He stretched from side to side, trying to see who was listening to opera at this time of night, but no one was in sight. Happy for the company of the music, he settled into bed and listened. The rattle of pipes temporarily drowned out the music but a short time later the noises stopped. A door opened and he heard the pad of footsteps. He listened for the creak of bedsprings. The thought of her lying inches away made him squirm. Caterina's ESP was working perfectly. "I hope you're not a sleepwalker. I'm an expert at karate."

"You've got nothing to worry about," he mumbled.

He floated on the music and drifted off. Sometime later he awoke with a start with someone yanking at his foot. Startled, he jumped into a crouch, poised to defend himself. "Who's there?" he asked, menacingly.

"Me," she said in a tiny voice. "Come here. Something's crawling on my neck."

"You woke me up for that? Take care of it yourself. Better yet, call Andrew."

"Get over here this instant," she snapped, "or I'll make you wish you had."

Rubbing an eye with his fist he asked, "What do you expect me to do?"

"Use your imagination. Just get it off of me, now."

He got up and guided himself by patting along the bedrail until it met warm flesh.

"That's my arm," she said, taking his hand. She held it firmly and guided it to the base of her neck. When something squirmed under his palm he recoiled in fear. "My God," he said. "What is that thing? It's huge."

She strangled a scream. "Get it off of me! Now!"

"Hand me your towel. I don't want to crush it with my bare hand."

"Absolutely not," she said.

Gritting his teeth, he lowered his hand and closed his fist. Something crackled, leaving him with an unpleasant sticky mass on his palm and fingers. "You're safe."

"Thank you. Now go back to bed."

"Aren't you the bossy one? Thanks to you I need to wash my hands." He inched along the edge of her bed and continued on until his head banged into something solid and he fell to the floor with a thud.

"Ohmygod. Are you all right?" Caterina screamed.

Before he could answer her fingers encircled his arm to help him to his feet. "It's my fault," she said. "I should have warned you I shut the bathroom door. Stay there. I'll wet my towel for you and clean you off."

She brushed against his hip as she walked past and he realized it was bare skin. What's more, it seemed warm. Water ran. Then she deftly returned to his side.

The wet towel moved gently over his face. "You really have all the luck, don't you?" she asked, softly.

Before he could answer, warm lips briefly touched his forehead, and were quickly gone. "Don't get the wrong idea," she said. "That's just to make it feel better."

"That does it, all right," he said, aching to embrace her.

She patted the dry part of the towel against his face. "Hold out your hands."

She washed each finger one at a time, then the palms. "Put your hand on my shoulder," she said. "It's back to bed. Your bed. Alone."

He grasped her bare clavicle and once again she guided him through the darkness. "You can let go of me now," she said. "This is where I get off."

As he got into bed he knew he was facing a sleepless night. Damn Cornacchia. Damn Andrew. Damn Caterina and damn Stef.

Someone sat down on the bed "Are you asleep?" Caterina whispered.

"No. I don't think I'll get much sleep tonight."

"Because of me?" she asked.

"Partially. I'll be thinking about Stef and Cornacchia, too."

"Do you ever think of the men who tried to come in your room?"

"If you're asking how does it feel to have killed someone I can tell you its terrible. I'll never forget it, no matter how much I'll want to. I'll always be playing defense attorney for them in my mind. They did what they did because of their backgrounds or because they're poor and needed the money."

"I don't know if it helps much, but I understand," Caterina said.

"As long as we're playing Truth or Dare, do you ever have second thoughts about Andrew, especially since you've met me?"

She vented a derisive laugh. "I can't believe your ego. I'm engaged to Andrew and that means I'm going to marry him." She paused. "I know I shouldn't have kissed you. I really don't know why I did it except you seem to bring out the mother in me."

"That's not quite the relationship I'm looking for with you, but it'll do for a start."

"It's not a start," she said firmly, "and I already told you, there isn't going to be a relationship. Stop driving yourself crazy about something you can't change. You'll make things so much easier for both of us if you do."

"Fine. I came here to find Stef and that's what I intend to do."

CHAPTER 10

▼

Sunday
7:46 AM
Sliema

He awoke to find that Caterina had usurped the bathroom. The door was shut and water running. Minutes later she emerged wrapped in towels. She hurried to the table next to her bed, grabbed her purse and dashed back to the bathroom. As she did he saw what might have been embarrassment on her face.

He slipped into his trousers and whiled the time reading a copy of the same travel brochure he used as a mosquito-swatter the first night he spent at the Bellestrado. She emerged fifteen minutes later, fully dressed, with her eyes fixed firmly on the floor. "You can use the bathroom now," she said quietly. "I'll call the police about Mario Agius while you're getting ready."

After a quick shower he hurried down to the kitchen. He could hardly wait to examine the papers he had found on the *Stallion*. The overlay could tell a lot about what Cornacchia was up to and the paper he found in the other wardroom might help to lead him to Stef. If he had been injected with pentobarbital, his captors may have jotted down what he said. And if the blood type on the cotton ball were A-negative, he would have overwhelming physical evidence that Stef had been there.

Josefina was busily at work in the galley. Beaming, she laid a basket of bread on the table in front of them. "Did you two have a good sleep?" she asked.

"The beds are very comfortable," Rick said. Caterina's blush made him ecstatic.

"They're twin beds, but we sometimes slide them together for couples," Josefina said. As she spoke, Rick watched Caterina from the corner of his eye. The look of embarrassment was gone. She now looked furious. "That's enough," she said sharply. "Both of you."

Josefina frowned and looked over at Rick. He shrugged. She gingerly set the bread on the table and moved away. "Coffee or tea?"

"Tea," Rick said. "Coffee," said Caterina in an icy voice.

Once Josefina was out of earshot, Caterina leaned forward and hissed. "What's the matter with you? Why did you make her think I slept with you?"

"I did no such thing," he said.

"You're the one who brought up the beds."

"What else was I supposed to say?" he asked.

"You're impossible."

"I don't know what made me think of this, but Marija keeps a huge dildo by her bed."

A fleeting smile momentarily lifted the corners of her mouth. "Don't try to change the subject."

"I'm not trying to change the subject." She glared at him and he gave up. "Okay, I am trying to change the subject. Now what do you know about Marija?"

"It's my impression that she'll sleep with anyone if it's to her advantage. She hates men. Her father sold her to his employer when she was fourteen years old."

She nodded at his shocked look. "It's true. Her mother died when Marija was eight and her father worked as a gardener for a wealthy businessman. The owner noticed Marija; she already was very beautiful at fourteen. He told her father that he wanted to hire Marija to do errands and that he would pay her the same wages he was paying him. Everyone was sure that her father knew what was happening, but he agreed to it anyway because she was turning the money over to him. Before long she was working late at night. Then she didn't come home on the weekends. From what I hear, the father was happy with the arrangement. His girlfriend had moved in with him."

"Most of the time the pimp only takes half the earnings," Rick said in disgust. "Wasn't this boss married? Wasn't anyone in the office suspicious?"

"The employer was married, but it wasn't difficult to arrange accommodations, especially when Marija's father had no objections. From what I understand, the employer's wife knew what was happening, too, but she never did anything about it."

"I can understand why Marija has a low opinion of men," Rick said.

"To be honest, it wasn't all bad. She was well taken care of and got to go to a good school. And she learned a lot about how to run a business from him."

"And probably how to handle people, too," he said angrily.

After breakfast, Caterina went to the car and brought in the blankets and the plastic bottle with the items he had lifted from the *Stallion*.

Rick set the bottle on the table and removed the duct tape from the plastic. A distinct mist clouded the inside of the bottle, but the papers were dry. He took a quick look at the first paper and set it aside. "What's that?" Caterina asked.

"It's an overlay for a naval chart. I'll have someone take a look at it today."

He picked up the second paper and held it against the light. Indentations from the last thing written on the pad clearly scored the surface. "Pencil?"

Caterina opened her purse and shook out a stub. As he rubbed the edge of the lead lightly across the paper, two words came into view with a question mark after it. "Do you know what it says?" he asked, handing it to her.

"I know the first word. 'Regina' is the Maltese word for Queen. The second one looks like M A B." She spelled out the letters.

Rick's eyes widened. "Queen Mab? Are you sure?"

"See for yourself. Isn't Queen Mab mentioned in Shakespeare?"

"Yes. In *Romeo and Juliet*. Would you ask Zija to fire up the computer for me? We can look it up on the Internet."

A visit to Google brought up ten pages of references. Wading past several relating to Shelley's poem, he found an article regarding Mercutio's speech. "Queen Mab was queen of the fairies," Rick said. "What did you say Cornacchia's statue of Melita looked like?"

"A nude woman with wings. You don't think...?"

"Absolutely. Didn't you say the statue is in Valletta?"

"In the Parliament Building. It's right by the National Library."

A seagull with a crust of bread in its mouth ran between Rick's feet like an errant terrier as they arrived at the ferry dock ten minutes later. Caught off guard, Rick nearly tripped over it. Caterina laughed and reproved him when he chucked a soda can at it. As they boarded, she said, "I think you'll get the best view topside."

"Topside? I'm impressed. You sound like a real sailor."

"Would it surprise you very much if I were?" she asked testily.

"Nothing about you could surprise me," Rick said. Though it was meant to be a compliment, his tone had a noticeable edge to it.

"For your information I used to sail on Lake Erie every weekend when I lived in Toronto. A man I knew had a forty-foot sloop and we took turns navigating and crewing. That's crewing with a 'c'. It's the only thing about the place I miss."

"Just the two of you?"

"Yes. And yes, I was romantically involved with him. Not that it's any of your business." She sat down on a bench, making sure she stayed a good foot away from him. He took a deep breath. The smell of diesel oil, grease and rope took him back to his childhood on Lake Minnetonka.

"Are you still mad at me?" he asked.

"Yes."

"You know you're not being fair. I think Zija understood and didn't get the wrong idea."

"Well, thanks to you, that's changed."

Rick rolled his eyes. "Clinton was right. If people think you're having an affair, you might as well go ahead and do it."

Though it was said in jest she lit into him, eyes flashing. "Listen here," she said, in a loud voice, "we are not going to have sex. Get that idea out of your head right now. We're not even going to hold hands. I love Andrew and nothing can change that. Maybe I should just take you back to Inspector Micallef now, as much as I would like to help you find your brother."

"You said that before and I think it's wonderful, even if I don't really understand."

"I really like you. You're a caretaker and I find that irresistible in a man," she said in a much softer voice. "I doubt there are very many people who would drop everything and fly off to Europe the way you did."

"You make me sound pretty special."

"You are. Very. And if I weren't in love with Andrew, things might be different."

"Thanks, but close but no cigar doesn't make me feel any better. It just makes me mad as hell."

Caterina shook her head. "Sorry. As you Americans say, get over it."

"I already have," he said, surprised at how convincing he sounded.

9:30 AM

The House of Representatives was inside the President's Palace, a building surrounding a large open square with trees and benches a short distance away from the National Library. Rick paid for the tickets and they started up the stairway.

They were surrounded by magnificent oil paintings at every step. *Melita* stood just beyond the top of the stairs.

Whatever else Cornacchia was, he was a master artisan. The female body was there in detail. From the delicate veins in the feet to the pupils in the eyes, he had caught nuances that were beyond the capability of most metalworkers. The voluptuous curves and the savage expression left Rick flabbergasted. The tongue, now probing the petals of a flower, symbolized sensuality. And it was lethal.

"Stop drooling," Caterina said in a disgusted voice. "You're making the floor wet."

"Instead of making cute remarks, help me find where Stef hid the drawing," he snapped.

They quickly found out that there were precious few possibilities and the statue itself offered none. He could find no crevices big enough to hide anything as large as a drawing. The rug they were standing on offered the best possibilities. But it was so heavy Rick could only lift the corners. No joy. In desperation he examined the back of a nearby painting and set it back in place with a disgusted look. Caterina even got on her knees to look under a bench.

"I give up," she said, brushing off her hands.

Rick shook his head in disgust. "Let's go. I need to call the embassy."

Instead of taking Rick into his office, Carpenter led him down a hall to another area. "We need a more private place to talk," he said.

"You're not suggesting this place is bugged, are you?"

"No, but it's better to be safe than sorry."

A Marine corporal in a sharply pressed uniform saluted and punched a keypad to unlock a windowless door. They stepped in. A Tchaikovsky waltz played gently in the background. The walls were lined with plain-steel bookcases filled with reams of paperbound government documents, hardbound texts including the Janes' volumes of equipment and ordnance, and several atlases. The walls were lined with soundproof tiles and a long table with computer monitors and keyboards stood in the middle of the room.

Carpenter pointed toward a chair. "Sit down. What do you have?"

"You can start with this," Rick said handing him the shotgun shell. "My driver and I went to Marsaxlokk last night to inspect a car rental agency my brother may have used. We found three shells and one body. Mario Agius."

Carpenter rolled the shell around in his hand. "Do you have any idea why he got shot?"

"Probably because he wouldn't cooperate. Someone tore up his office. I think they were looking for Stef's rental receipt." Rick paused. "Oh, take a look at this." He handed him a manila envelope. "It's an overlay for a map of Libya. The spot looks to be about 25 miles from Tripoli."

The agent studied it. "Interesting. Where did you get it?"

"I found it on Cornacchia's yacht." He grinned at Carpenter's look. "I boarded it last night." Rick went on to chronicle the trip to Golden Bay and his surveillance of the yacht. When he got to the description of the meeting, the agent stopped him. "What did this third man look like?"

"He looked like an Arab. He had thinning black hair, and a mustache. He reminded me of King Hussein of Jordan before he got sick. All I can say for sure is that he was quite a bit shorter than Vella."

"Anything more helpful?"

Rick tried to call up a mental image of the three men arguing. "Sorry. Nothing stands out."

Carpenter got out of his chair. "Stay where you are," he said. Stepping over to a computer he typed something as he was standing. "I checked and your TS clearance is still good. Come over here."

The red, white and blue logo of the Department of Defense stood proudly on the screen. The agent pulled down a menu and clicked. Ten different outlines of heads appeared on the screen. "Which one looks the closest?" he asked.

Rick studied them and pointed at the third one, a round one. Carpenter clicked on the image. A box in the lower left corner read 488. The screen went black for a second. Then ten different outlines of the same head but with different eyes appeared.

Rick balked. "Hey. Give me a break. He was more than two hundred yards away."

"I know. Pick one."

One, showing wideset eyes, seemed to be the closest. Rick watched as the box changed to 343 matches. Another click summoned ten images with the same eyes but different noses. Rick pointed to an image with a short wide one, Carpenter clicked and now the box read 274. The mouths cut the number to 160 and adding a mustache reduced it to 130. "Looks like most of them must have mustaches," Carpenter said.

After the new set of images appeared Rick shook his head. "What am I looking at?"

"I can't tell you that. Study them."

Ten faces stared back as Rick moved closer to the screen. "Actually, I think this one is the closest. I don't know why, though." The match-counter read 96.

"We're almost done," Carpenter said. Once again the screen blacked out for an instant. "This is ridiculous," Rick said. He changed his mind as what at first looked like ten identical images slowly resolved themselves to a choice between two. Rick shook his head and pointed at them. "I don't know. Could be either," he said.

"Try them both," Carpenter said, clicking on number one. Fifteen mini-photos appeared on the screen. "These are thumbnails," he said, rising to his feet. "Clicking on them enlarges them. Take your time going through them."

Rick anxiously looked at his watch and saw that it was already past ten o'clock. "I don't have an awful lot of time."

"This whole process shouldn't take more than another fifteen minutes, tops. And I don't think I have to tell you how important it is. You know yourself that since nine-eleven and the Middle-East wars, anything involving terrorism is top priority."

Rick nodded. Minutes later he said, "I've finished this group. I hope I don't sound like a bigot, but they sure all look the same to me."

"But none of them quite fill the bill, huh? Okay. Let's try again."

The agent went to the "back" screen-index. The last rogue's gallery of ten appeared. Rick pointed and Carpenter clicked. Another set of photos appeared. On the third screen of suspects Rick found what he was looking for. "That's him!" he said.

Carpenter leaned over his shoulder. "Are you sure?"

"As sure as I can be," Rick replied.

"Good," Carpenter said, minimizing the computer screen. "You're free to go."

Rick stared at him in perplexity. "That's it?"

"That's it."

"Then how about doing something for me." He handed the agent the cotton balls. "Could you have someone run a blood-type on them?"

"Fair enough. Just be sure to stay away from Black Dolphin shipping and Cornacchia's estate. He'll be under constant surveillance from now on. Understand?"

The tone of voice made Rick swallow. "I understand."

CHAPTER 11

▼

Sunday
11:18 AM
Sliema

A large plastic bag half-filled with yellow and white papers sat on the kitchen floor at the Bellestrado. Rick ruefully tossed another into it. "So much for the rental receipts," he said. "Stef's kidnappers must have found it."

"Don't give up," Caterina said. "The fact they were looking for it is reason to be hopeful. Why don't you take a break and get something from the bar."

"Good idea. Can I bring you something, too?"

"No, thank you," she said. "I'll fix myself some tea."

"Try burdock and thistle some time. I drink it all the time."

She cocked her head at him. "You amaze me."

In the pub, a short man with a long white handlebar mustache stood behind the bar washing glasses. "Hello," he said. "You must be Richard Olsen. I'm Peter Grech, Josefina's husband. What do you want to drink?"

"Cisk," Rick said. He had wanted to try the beer from the first time he heard about it. "Where's Josefina?"

"She went to church. She and Caterina usually go to nine o'clock Mass. That's when I come in to work. I have a bad back and I can't drive cab anymore. I tend bar a few hours a week."

"So now Caterina is driving for you."

"I gave her my license. It's been in the family for nearly a hundred years."

Rick nodded. "I see. You're a lucky man to be married to Josefina. She's a wonderful person."

"She thinks highly of you, too," Grech said, handing him a foaming glass. "She's generous to a fault but I'm afraid her generosity will soon be pushed to the limit."

"Why is that?" asked Rick.

"Another boatload of North Africans landed last night. More than two hundred this time. They were heading for Sicily and their boat began to sink so they came to Malta instead. There's already so many of them that it's taking the entire police and military budget to take care of them."

Rick looked puzzled. "Where do you keep them?"

"We have two resettlement camps, one in Qrendi and the other at Verdala Barracks. We keep the dangerous ones in a compound at the police station at Floriana. They're all overcrowded but we haven't had the time or the money to start another one."

"Do any of them come to the Bellestrado?"

"No. Josefina won't take in anyone who doesn't come by passenger ship and she only lets them stay a day or two. If she can't locate relatives or find them a home she sends them back home. The boat people don't have anywhere to go and there's too many of them to take in. But her church has been helping them by providing meals."

"I see," Rick said. He liked the beer. Feeling a tickle on his mouth he wiped foam away with the back of his hand. "Her generosity shames me. So does Caterina's."

"Yes. They're very much alike even though Josefina isn't that closely related to her. Josefina is her great-aunt. Caterina's parents went to Sicily for an anniversary trip when she was five. A storm came up and they drowned so we raised her. We never had any children of our own."

"Then you both did a wonderful job," Rick said. "Thanks for the beer."

In the kitchen a teapot whistled in the galley. "Your uncle was telling me about the boat people," he said to Caterina. "You mentioned them before but I had no idea it was such a problem."

"It is," she said, quietly. "Unfortunately there isn't much that we can do about it."

Rick looked at the bag of forms. "Any ideas what we should do next?"

"Maybe," she said. "We have a law in our country that rental contracts have to be in the car at all times. Why would anyone ransack the rental office when they could have gotten all the information they needed from the car?"

"I see," he said, feeling excitement building. "Something must have happened to the car before or during the time Stef was kidnapped."

"Right. And the most likely things that could have happened to it were either that it was stolen…"

"Or it got towed away! Brilliant. Do you know where the towers take the cars?"

Caterina nodded. "I know them all well. I visited every one of them when I was rebuilding *Tarbija*. You have a meeting with Father Santorini in an hour. If we hurry I can get you to a bus and I'll meet you at Rabat when you're done."

The bus arrived in Rabat at two minutes before one. Rick remembered that Rabat means suburb in Arabic and the name was appropriate: the town had swarms of unmarked townhouses on nameless streets.

He headed toward a steeple and the nearby greengrocer told him Santorini's house was next to he church. Santorini, who was sitting on his doorstep, nimbly got to his feet. As he did, his narrow cassock easily fell back into place. His smile was cordial, but it reinforced the lines around his eyes. Rick guessed they probably came from being closeted with Thomas Aquinas for too many years. A full head of snow-white hair and relatively smooth skin on his face and neck suggested he was in his early seventies. "Mr. Olsen?"

"That's me," Rick replied. Santorini gestured toward a gate. In a perfect British accent he said, "Come this way, please. If you don't mind sitting outside, there's a lovely breeze blowing. And the hibiscus are very fragrant this year."

Chains creaked as they sat down on a wooden swing. "So you're interested in Bartolomeo Cornacchia," Santorini said. "What do you want to know about him?"

"As much as you can tell me."

"I really doubt that you would want to know *that* much," Santorini said amiably. "I wrote my doctoral dissertation on him back in 1961 after Alessandro Cornacchia's widow, Ag-ga-ta, donated his papers to the University library. It was an enormous project. I spent the first three months of my research transcribing his diary. The whole thing was written in code."

Rick's ears pricked. "Code? What kind of code?"

"Mostly simple substitution cipher. Some of your newspapers use it for puzzles now because they're so easy to solve. But it was quite safe at the time because letter frequency analysis hadn't been invented yet."

Rick was surprised at the man's knowledge. "Do you know why he used code?"

"Probably for many reasons," Santorini said with a chuckle. "He was brilliant and ruthless, and as a merchant he needed to keep his records of his transactions secret. And he also had been accused of practicing the black arts. If so he certainly didn't want to leave incriminating evidence lying around. You may have read he was convicted of heresy."

"I understand he wrote a book on alchemy," Rick said. "Did he ever mention anything about it in his writings?"

"The *Definitus Mallorum?*"

Rick's eyes widened. *The Definitive Hammer?* "How could you have known that? The book and the name were suppressed by the papacy."

"Bartolomeo mentions it himself."

Rick's eyes widened in disbelief. "Incredible. He must have been aware that someone might be able to figure out his cipher. I'm sure the Venetian code breakers could have done it."

"Undoubtedly. How do you know about them?"

"I was doing my doctoral dissertation on them. I got to know quite a bit about the history of cryptography in the process."

"Very good," Santorini said, sounding impressed. "And you're right. Bartolomeo *was* afraid of being found out. That's probably the reason he put the name in the form of a riddle." He opened the book, paged through it and started to read. Not knowing the language, Rick listened for a while and then shook his head. "What does it mean?"

"The words are Maltese but it's a word puzzle. I'm sure you've seen them. In your language it would be similar to 'My first is in gold, but not in log. My second is in green, but not in grown.' And so on. You just have to figure out the letter that's been deleted or changed. The word 'log' is an anagram of 'gold' without the letter 'd.' 'Grown' isn't an exact anagram, but the missing 'Es' tell the story."

Rick nodded. "Very prudent. If the church ever seized his diary, they couldn't use it against him. I understand Pius IV intended to burn him at the stake. Why didn't he?"

"The Duke admitted his guilt, tearfully recanted and begged for his life. He said he didn't want his soul to go to hell and he promised to spend the rest of his life serving the church. Since Bartolomeo was rich and influential and offered a significant donation to the church, the pope spared him."

Money talked. A peasant woman never would have stood a chance. "And did he devote his life to serving the church?"

The priest laughed. "At least to all appearances."

"I see that he has a question mark for his date of death. Does that mean he had learned the secrets of eternal life?"

Santorini chuckled. "You must be referring to the fact he was an alchemist. No. I'm sure he must have died but his date of death is unknown. He disappeared in early 1566. After he did, no one ever heard from him again."

Conversation lapsed as a welcome breeze blew against their faces. A small helicopter appeared in the northern sky and quickly disappeared from view. It was out of sight before they heard the sound of its motors. "That isn't the Gozo shuttle is it?" Rick asked.

"No. The shuttle is much bigger. It must be one of our military craft. Would you care for some lemonade?"

"I'd love some," Rick said. He followed the priest around a well-tended garden. As they passed it, a butterfly flew by going in the opposite direction, tasting the geraniums with its feet. Something similar was called a Rusty Dusty in the Olsen brothers' collection.

Inside, Santorini pulled two tumblers out of a tiny cabinet. Setting them on a counter, he poured from a pitcher in his refrigerator and handed a glass to Rick. "I'm afraid I don't have any ice," the priest said.

"I'm sure it will be fine without it," Rick replied. As they walked back to the garden, he said, "You said he used simple substitution codes. Were there other types?"

"Just one. The priest paged through the book. "Yes," he said. "Here it is."

Rick discovered half a page full of paired letters. "It's a Polybius Square," he said. "The two letters refer to the row and position. Did you ever play battleship?"

"Years ago."

"Actually you solve it just as if it's a simple substitution code. The frequencies are the same."

"I never thought of that," Santorini said.

"Could I get a copy of this?" Rick asked. He could hardly wait to go to work on it.

"Of course. There's a copying machine in the rectory. I'll make one for you before you leave."

"Did you find anything else unusual in the diary?"

"Not for a businessman. The Duke seemed to be especially fascinated with the prices of the cargo he imported. Spices in particular. He sometimes devoted whole pages to individual transactions. In those days a skilled merchant could buy pepper in the Malabar Islands for mere pennies and sell it in Europe for hundreds of dollars."

"Every businessman is entitled to a one-percent profit," Rick said in disgust.

Santorini smiled at the sarcasm. "Indeed. But to be fair, he also had to risk loss of the ship and cargo to pirates or bad weather so he understandably didn't want to have a big cost in the cargo. He also had to pay a sizable royalty to the Knights to be able to operate his ships. Still, all in all, I'll have to agree he did very well for himself. He kept most of his money, too. He even kept track of how much he spent in the brothels so the prostitutes couldn't overcharge him if he ever went back to any of them."

Rick frowned. If Bartolomeo were that cautious with his money, why did he hire Cellini to design a work for him? The cost of the drawing alone would have been significant. The completed work, astronomical. "Can you tell me any more about the *Definitus Mallorum*?"

"Nothing concrete. But I do have a hunch about its origin. Bartolomeo traveled all over the world to study alchemy. After he got a Baccalaureate in natural science from the University of London in 1527, he spent the next fifteen years traveling. Mostly in Europe, but he also visited Palestine, Egypt and China." He paused dramatically. "Later on he went to Ethiopia, too."

Rick's eyes widened. "Really. What did he do there?"

"He didn't say. He went there in 1543 and stayed more than a year even though he never mentioned the trip in his diary. He was fortunate he wasn't forced to stay longer. The Ethiopian kings at the time didn't always let visitors leave."

Hearing the words alchemy and Ethiopia used together created a strange resonance in Rick's mind but he didn't understand why. "Do you have any idea why he went there?"

"It could have been for several reasons," Santorini said with a twinkle in his eye. "He may have been looking for King Solomon's mines or the Ark of the Covenant."

Rick took Santorini's humor good-naturedly. "Or maybe he was looking for Prester John's kingdom of gold," he said with a laugh.

Santorini's mouth opened. "I don't know why you said that, but joking or not, I think you're absolutely right. Bartolomeo saw the visit as a way to make money."

"I don't see how. That was a long and expensive trip."

"He may originally have had some vain hopes that the legend was true. When he found out it wasn't he must have decided to make his money the same way most alchemists of the day made their profits," Santorini said, pausing for effect. "By selling the secrets."

Rick sighed. "They were like magicians, weren't they? They started out believing in their craft and ended up charlatans, preying on the gullible."

Santorini nodded in agreement.

"And he wrote about the so-called secrets he learned there in the *Definitus Mallorum*?"

Santorini nodded and Rick looked puzzled. "But why did he wait so long? He wrote the book more than twenty years after he came back from Ethiopia."

Santorini smiled. "You should have been on my doctoral committee," he said. "Bartolomeo was a very shrewd man. If he had written it immediately after he got back, it would have just become another book about alchemy and could easily have been ignored. But in those twenty years he put all his effort into his shipping and spice trade. The result was almost unimaginable wealth. Some people couldn't believe that it all came from business. They were sure that some, if not most, of it must have come from some other source."

Rick's smile was almost as big as Santorini's. "By waiting and making no claims for it, he made sure he would have customers ready to buy his book at whatever price he asked for it." He stopped. "Hold it. There's still a problem of credibility. Why would his customers think he would be willing to share his secrets? Wouldn't they realize he would want to keep that kind of information to himself?"

"Absolutely," Santorini said, laughing aloud. "And that's the most ingenious part of the whole scheme. He could claim that the book wasn't meant for the general public, that it was a scholarly work intended only for the monasteries and universities where the knowledge would be put to use for the benefit of all mankind instead of the greedy few. That's why he could charge so much for it. Selling a copy was a breach of ethics."

"Which he didn't have," Rick said, clapping his hands in excitement. "Wonderful." Bartolomeo was every bit as devious as Cellini had been. What a great pair they must have made.

His smile didn't last long. Was Cellini's work a hoax, too? If so, everything that happened after Stef found the drawing was tragic and unnecessary. He suddenly found himself pleased that the church had seized the book and ruined Bartolomeo's plans.

"Did you find any evidence that Bartolomeo dealt with Benvenuto Cellini?"

The priest answered with a curious look. "Cellini? Not that I'm aware of, but it wouldn't be out of the question. They were contemporaries and Bartolomeo would have had the means to retain him. I can't imagine why he would have done it, though."

"You said that he was under suspicion by the church. What better way to prove that he was fulfilling his obligation to do good and serve Christ?"

"That's true, but why hasn't anyone heard about it?"

"Good question. I'm more puzzled than ever but thanks for your help."

"You're very welcome. I'll have to tell Agatha about your visit," Santorini said.

Gulp! "No, please don't. At least not yet. Are you still in contact with the family?"

"Not directly with Lorenzo, but I talk to Agatha from time to time. I got to know her quite well while I was doing my research. She absolutely hates my book and thinks everything I said about Bartolomeo is a lie, but we still get together to visit now and then. She's eighty-seven years old and doesn't get much company."

"I had no idea she was still alive. Is she still on the island?"

"Yes, but I really can't say anything more about her. She's a very private person and would be angry with me for even mentioning her name."

Rick walked back to the bus stop deep in thought. Caterina was waiting for him. "Did you find out anything important?" she asked.

"Yes. Bartolomeo was as big a scalawag as Cellini. Any luck finding Mario's car?"

"No, I've eliminated two of the towing companies. There's still half a dozen left."

"Let's try the ones for Sliema and the University first," Rick said.

2:29 PM

The service in Sliema was quickly eliminated from consideration. The operator knew Mario Agius and would have called him immediately if any of his cars showed up. The next stop, Seguna's Towing Service, was less than a mile away from the University of Malta. A man sat half asleep in a lawn chair and wasn't interested in conversation once he knew they weren't customers. "You'll have to look for yourself," he said without opening his eyes. "The most recent day is at the front and they go back from there. The dates are on the windshields."

As they walked, Rick began to think that it was a hospital or morgue for sick cars. Many had their hoods up with vital fluids leaking out from beneath them. Green was radiator coolant, dark red transmission fluid, and inky black brake fluid. Caterina patted them consolingly as they passed.

"These cars must have been here a long time," Rick said. "How long do they keep them and what happens to them if the owners don't come to pick them up?"

"They hold auctions every month. Any car that isn't picked up within ninety days can be sold. I attended some of them myself when I was rebuilding *Tarbija*. Sometimes they go for just a few pounds and the scrap iron dealers buy them. Nobody even wants these for scrap, the poor babies."

"If Mario Agius was killed four days ago, the car would have to have been towed on the 11th or earlier," he said. They threaded their way between a Peugeot and a beat-up Mercedes to the next row back.

"Mario's cars are at least four years old and have yellow stickers on the left front bumper," Caterina said.

They each took a row. Rick had just finished the first when she called out. "Come here. I think this is it."

The car was a blue '94 Volkswagen Jetta with a dent in the driver's door and a large yellow and red sticker on the front left bumper. "It's locked," she said.

"If I can get the trunk open I think I can get in through the back seat," Rick said. The lockpick didn't seem to work. "You don't have a screwdriver do you?"

"No. Did you try pushing the release button?"

He pushed the button on the lock and the trunk popped up. Red-faced, he leaned against the rear wall and pushed. The back seat slid aside to reveal a narrow opening. "You go," he whispered. "You're smaller than I am."

"No way. I'm not going to give you an opportunity to look up my dress."

He threw her a disgusted look. "I'll go around to the front of the car and wait for you to unlock the door." Seconds later her head appeared over the front seat and her fingers pulled up the lock. "Good work," he said, opening the glove compartment.

Empty.

"I'm not too surprised the paper's not here," Rick said sadly. "I'm sure Stef's captors must have come up with the same idea. They would have found it themselves."

"Don't be such a pessimist," Caterina said thrusting her hand into the passenger's seat. She uttered a little cry of triumph as she pulled it out grasping a rumpled piece of yellow paper.

"You're incredible," he exclaimed. Without thinking he planted a kiss on her forehead. "Stef has a room at the Hotel San Roque in Sliema."

CHAPTER 12

▼

Sunday
3:36 PM
Sliema

They stopped in front of a stone building surrounded by a black metal fence. Gilt letters spelled "Hotel San Roque" on the gate.

"Do you want me to go in with you?" Caterina asked.

"You can if you want to, but I'm supposed to be moving into Stef's room. We don't want the desk clerk to think we're a *menage au trois*, do we?"

She snorted and he took off for the entrance alone. Inside, a middle-aged man with thick glasses sat on a stool behind the desk. "Yes, sir," the clerk said.

"Good afternoon. Do you have a Stefan Olsen registered here?"

"Yes, but he's not in."

Heart leaping, Rick laid his passport on the desk. "I'm his brother," he said. "I'm moving in with him."

The clerk barely glanced at the passport. "I'm sorry but that isn't possible.'

Puzzled, Rick said, "I'm really his brother. See how the name is spelled?"

"I don't doubt that you are, sir," the clerk said. "But he owes us thirty pounds. Until it's paid, no one can go in."

Rick laid two banknotes on the counter. "Sorry. That's my fault. I was supposed to have arrived several days ago but got delayed."

The clerk fingered the bills. Finally he said, "Your staying here will cost an additional twenty pounds."

Another banknote appeared on the counter. The clerk gathered it up and put it into the cash register. "Where has your brother been? We've been worried about him."

"He's been staying on a farm in Gozo," Rick said.

"Then I'm sure he's having a good time," said the clerk. "Do you have baggage?"

"It should arrive tomorrow on the catamaran from Sicily."

The man led Rick down a hallway and up a flight of stairs. "Here it is," the clerk said.

Anticipation mounted. When the lights came on, the first thing Rick saw was Stef's duffel bag sitting in a corner next to the bed. With heart leaping, he handed the clerk a fifty-cent coin and shut the door.

What treasures awaited him? He opened the duffel bag and found that it had never been unpacked. Leaving his clothes in his bag was one of Stef's favorite tricks. He tended to wear the same outfits over and over, and he didn't go below the top layer until he didn't have any choice. The full bag was a good sign. Stef's captors would have emptied it or taken it with them if they had found it.

Stef must have considered the room shamefully extravagant because it had a double bed, a television set with remote, a quiet overhead fan, and a cabinet refrigerator. Curious, Rick opened the refrigerator. He found a small wedge of cheese and half a bottle of Evian water. Sure Stef had left them there, he took the cheese and filled a glass with the water before he began his inspection.

He started with the desk. All the drawers were empty and the newspapers and magazines on top of it were weeks old. With a shrug he went to work on the bed, taking the mattress off and inspecting the bedsteads. Still nothing.

After reassembling the bed, Rick sat on it and took out his cell phone. Kevin answered on the third ring. "What's going on, bud?"

"Some good news. I just found Stef's room."

"Great. How about Stef?"

"He's being held in a church, somewhere. The kidnappers contacted me today. Stef must have told them that the only way I would know that it was really he was if he said 'Kirk out.' Kirk is the Scottish word for church."

"Fantastic. How many churches are there on Malta?"

"Not more than ten thousand," Rick said, laughing. "They seem to be on every street corner. He's going to have to be more specific the next time. Have you made any progress on Cornacchia's files?"

"I just got started. I'll let you know when I find out anything. He's got a fairly secure system, but his MIS chief seems to be a bit inexperienced. What's going on with you?"

"Caterina, the woman who's driving for me, has an aunt who runs a hotel in Sliema. She said someone put a worm into the hotel's computer."

"Really? Didn't she have a virus guard?"

"I have no idea. I'll have to ask her."

"Does she have any idea what the hacker was after?"

"She seems to think they were after credit card numbers. I told her there's no way to tell for sure until she notices something different about her files."

"You're absolutely right," Kevin said. "Anything else I can do for you?"

"Not now. Take good care of Arthur for me."

Rick hung up and finished his inspection of the room. Nothing. He wasn't surprised. Stef would never hide anything so valuable where it could easily be found.

Opening the door to the hallway he saw what looked like an endless corridor of closed doors, all the same and unnumbered. He followed the hallway until he came to one that was open a crack and he went in.

What immediately caught his attention was the bathtub. He hadn't seen one since he came to Malta, and for good reason. A bath was a terrible extravagance considering the shortage of water on the island. Even more unusual than the tub was the large framed poster on the wall opposite the sink.

A cherubic female with a bow over her shoulder was leaning against a fence watching a couple kiss in the moonlight. The style was Art Deco or possibly Art Nouveau. If genuine, it would have been worth quite a bit of money if it weren't so badly stained. His tourbook said that Malta was full of antiques. Rick wondered where the poster had come from and why the management had let it get so stained, or hung it in the humid bathroom. Or was it in such lousy condition before they found it? It was even signed. Morgan.

Returning to the room, he was about to go out the door with the duffel bag when he remembered the desk clerk. Afraid that the man might get suspicious if he saw him leaving with it, Rick opened the window and pushed the bag out on the fire escape. He carried it down the flight of stairs and dropped it to the ground, then hurried back through the room and down the stairway.

"I'll be back in a little while," he told the desk clerk.

Caterina made fists when she saw the bag. "Great work."

Rick threw the bag into the trunk. "Let's go back to the Bellestrado."

Feeling like a geologist revealing another strata of deposits, Rick unrolled a rolled-up pair of jeans and dropped them on the kitchen floor.

Caterina shook her head. "Look at these clothes. I should wash them for him."

"I'm sure they're clean. He never put anything away dirty."

"But they're all wrinkled," she said.

"He doesn't mind wrinkled. I paid a hundred dollars for this," he said, gesturing at an unopened shirt bag. "He's never even worn it."

"Clean or not, I'll wash them and hang them up for him. He'll have a whole wardrobe waiting for him when we find him."

Rick smiled wanly, touched by Caterina's generosity and confidence. Did Andrew have the slightest idea how lucky he was to have won her heart? "That's nice of you. I'm sure he'll appreciate it." The last of the garments appeared from the bag. "We'll need a clothes basket to carry all of this," he said.

"Not much of a pay-off for all the work, is it?" she said with a sympathetic look.

"Not much," he echoed. He was disappointed even though he didn't know what he expected to find. "I suppose you might as well wash the bag, too."

As he turned it inside out he heard a rustle of paper. Something was inside the flaps of the bag at the bottom!

Excitement growing, he turned the bag upside down. The bottom of the bag was roughly square and as he ran his fingers along the seams at the bottom he discovered that one side was open. He reached inside and pulled. The whole flap came out. "Yee-hah!" he said, holding up a spiral-bound notebook.

"What is it?"

"Stef's diary. Come take a look."

She stood beside him as he paged through it. "How can you read his handwriting?"

"It takes a lot of practice," Rick said. "Stef has to write quickly to keep up with his thoughts." He paged through the book. "Listen to this. 'Must see Alessandro's papers in University archives. Aegis Dei lost 6/7/42.'"

"The Shield of God?" Caterina said.

"That sounds like it could have been Cellini's work. I'd be more interested in learning how Stef came across the words. And the date it was lost is interesting, too. It was just two days before Alessandro was killed during an air raid." He looked up at her. "I'll be reading through the night so you can take the rest of the day off if you want to."

"What about Stef's clothes?"

"Wash them if you want, or leave them," he said. "Either way I'm sure Stef won't need them for a while yet."

"If you're sure you can get along without me, I'll put the clothes in the washer and take you up on your offer. Josefina can dry them for me. I know Andrew will be happy to see me."

Rick flinched. She started away but stopped before she reached the door. "Give me your phone," she said. He did and she pushed some buttons before handing it back to him. "I just put my cellular number in the memory. If you need me for anything, call."

"I will. Stay as long as you like. Just be back by tomorrow morning."

She colored. "I'll be back tonight, thank you."

It was his turn to color. "Sorry. Have a good time."

5:18 PM

Stretched out full-length on the newly made bed, with the bedroom window open and the music-lover next door playing a Verdi piece that he couldn't place, Rick decided life was good.

The diary had been through some difficult times. Its blue front cover now was badly wrinkled and the back flap missing. Stef had written XVI to indicate volume sixteen of his personal journal begun at age six.

Opening it at random he read: August 18th—*Research going very well. Just went through the last years of Cellini's life from 1563 to his death in 1578. Mind sharp until the very end although age and the ravages of syphilis had long since overtaken his body. Found letter, dated August 1564, demanding prompt payment for the 5,000 gold florins ($50,000?) Cellini had lost in gold speculation the previous year. Still no record of how Cellini was able to repay the debt. I'm more and more certain the money came from a large commission.*

August 19th—Found note to Signor Alberto Castalanti, explaining why Cellini was firing the man's son, Guido. Guido, though a promising worker, got caught helping himself to some loose change and bric-a-brac around the artist's house. It takes a thief to catch a thief. How did the drawing get into Finelli's bookshop?

Rick wondered the same thing, but thought he knew the answer. Whoever bought the drawing was a collector. The wife wasn't and could see no reason why her husband was wasting money buying worthless drawings. Husband dies, wife contacts antiques dealer and finds that the drawings are indeed worthless. Drawing is passed on from generation to generation until it ends up in a pile of worthless paper in a bookseller's shop. Enter Stef.

August 24th—Went through the last bundle of Cellini's papers. The very last a receipt for a doctor's visit, a prescription for Angelwort and Cassia and a fee for cauterization. What a sad end to such an adventurous life.

A sudden blare from music-lover interrupted his concentration. Rick loved music as much as the next person did, but enough was enough. He walked to the window to close it. Looking out, he was suddenly back to his first night in the hotel. How did his attackers get on the roof?

The stairway ended just a few feet above his head at a locked door. He walked back to the elevator and pushed the call button. With a click and a grumble the ancient lift hauled itself up to his floor. Once he was aboard it lurched downward two feet, caught itself, then crawled back down to the ground floor to stop with a thump. As he opened the door he heard the sound of voices from the pub. Every table was full and Josefina frantically poured beer behind the bar. The room was so noisy that it drowned out the sound coming from the TV set.

"Hi," she shouted. "Do you want something to drink?"

"No, but I need some information."

"Come back here where we can talk," she said, taking him by the wrist and pulling him behind the bar with her. He had to speak right into her ear to be heard. "How do you get on the roof?"

"The door is at the top of the stairway. The key is hanging by the front desk."

"Couldn't someone come in off the street and take it?"

Josefina shook her head. "No. I keep the hotel door locked when I'm in the pub. Only the guests can come in that way. Everyone else has to come through here."

"How did the men who tried to break into my room get to the roof?"

"They must have used a fire escape. They're at the front and back of the building."

"Are either of them close to the room I was in that night?"

"Your room is about halfway between them." A patron raised an empty beer glass. "Excuse me," she said. When she came back, Rick said, "Do you know if the police went up to the roof?"

"I think so."

"Do you mind if I take a look for myself?"

"Of course not," she said. "Just lock the door and put the key back when you're done."

Black asphalt crunched under his feet as he stepped out and he had to straighten a mop handle leaning against the edge of the roof to move on.

The building was a square doughnut with a courtyard in the middle. Although the courtyard cut down the total area available for rooms it allowed for cross-ventilation and may have been used as a garden at one time. One side of the building looked out over Ghar-id-Dud Street and the front door of the hotel and pub. To the left he saw music-lover's rooftop garden. Beyond it lay the Strand and Marsamxett Creek, the enormous harbor between Sliema and Valletta. The view was impressive and the presence of a lawn table with ashtray and cigarette butts meant that people occasionally came up to see the sights.

Sidling along the railing and watching the rooftop garden as he went, he located the same view he had seen from his room as he shut the window to keep out the mosquitoes. Bending over the edge to be sure, he saw the top of the frame of the window below him. He straightened up and turned to face the other railing where the rope would have been. He felt a sense of foreboding as he crossed to take a closer look. At first glance he could see no sign that the shooter had ever been there and his hopes took a nosedive.

His feeling of anxiety grew as he squatted next to the courtyard railing to look for marks where the shooter had anchored the rope. A fresh scratch and heavy nick in the railing confirmed the location, but horizontal streaks in the dust on the roof's surface just below it meant the police had been over the area with a broom. He sighed. Whatever slim chance he had to find something on his own seemed to have disappeared entirely.

He braced himself to get to his feet. As he did he noticed a small gray object lying flat against the railing inside the metal molding. Carefully working it loose using a coin he discovered that it was the back of a wide paper match. The other side was white with the words 'il-Qarnita Pub, Msida' printed on it. He could hardly wait to ask Caterina what she knew about it.

After tucking his find into his wallet, he got to his feet and completed the circuit of the roof, thoroughly investigating the outer and inner perimeter.

Reaching the third side of the outside square he saw the dark shape of the shrouded Chevrolet in the alley behind the hotel. From the fourth, he looked down at the roofs of the adjacent buildings. Deciding he had seen enough, he went back inside.

He was still reading Stef's journal when Caterina knocked on his door at ten-thirty. "I see you survived without me," she said.

"Barely. Did you have a good time with Andrew?"

"Very. We walked the entire distance of the Strand."

"Maybe I saw you." He handed her the match. "I found this on the roof. Have you ever heard of the *Qarnita* Pub?"

"Of course! That's where il-*Sequ* has his office. He's the biggest crime boss on the island." She noticed his puzzled look and continued. "*Sequ* is his nickname. It means eagle. His real name is George Bezzina and I visit him at least once a week."

"You're on close terms with a crime boss?"

She smiled. "Don't be shocked. We exchange information to and from the people who work for him. He knows that I know he's a criminal but it's to both of our advantage to work together."

"What do you mean?" asked Rick.

"It's a way for the immigrant families to keep in contact. Father Modiglio and I regularly squeeze donations out of him. It's really enjoyable because we know how much he hates it."

The arrangement made a certain amount of sense, Rick decided.

"Congratulations on finding the match, by the way," Caterina said. "The police would be mortified if they ever found out they overlooked it."

"Don't tell them, then," Rick said.

Her sharp look surprised him. "What do you mean?"

"Just kidding. Are you sure we want to stay at the Bellestrado tonight? The room in the San Roque is much bigger and nicer."

"If it doesn't have two beds, you'll have to sleep on the floor. If we stay here, we'll each have our own rooms."

"Oh," Rick said, feeling deflated. For a moment he seriously considered sleeping on the floor to be in the same room with her. "Okay."

"I know that tone. If you were hoping for a repeat of last night, you can forget it. It's separate rooms from now on."

Rick remembered his conversation with Kevin. "I meant to ask you. Does Zija have virus protection on her computer."

"Yes. She bought a new version in February. Why?"

"I wonder how the worm got into her computer. The newest anti-virus programs scan e-mails. Does she ever let any of the guests use the machine?"

"I wouldn't be surprised if she did. Ask her yourself."

Rick lay on his bed reading Stef's diary for an hour after Caterina returned to the hotel. He had the window open, but music-lover didn't have his player working and the room seemed desolate. Not even mosquitoes to keep him company. Where was Stef? Trapped in a church somewhere? If so, someone in the clergy or the church laity had to be in with his kidnappers.

As he turned off the light and stretched out, he heard the shower turn on in Caterina's room. It wasn't until after she turned the shower off that he was able to fall asleep.

CHAPTER 13

▼

Monday
7AM
Sliema

Rick got up early the next morning and went back to reading Stef's journal. At eight o'clock he knocked on Caterina's door. A sleepy voice answered.

"Good morning," he said. "I'm going down for breakfast. See you there."

A young couple was in the kitchen and the TV on the wall was tuned to CNN. As Rick exchanged nods with them, Josefina laid a basket of bread in front of him and without a word started to walk away. "Is anything wrong?" he asked.

She turned to him with a sad look. "I just heard that we took in another boatload of North Africans this morning. It was overloaded and capsized before it got here. Thirty people drowned and now the army has more than a hundred new mouths to feed."

"Your husband said that your church has been providing meals."

"Our parish feeds nine hundred a day and nearly every other church on the islands is helping. We simply can't keep up."

"I don't understand why your government keeps them here," Rick said. "Why don't they simply return them to North Africa?"

Josefina sat down across from him. "It isn't that simple. The Libyan and Tunisian governments don't want them either. The refugees are from all over North Africa and most of them have no real national identity. If we sent them back, the Arab countries would just put them in their own refugee camps. As big a burden as they are for us, for their sake I'd rather we keep them here. At least they'll get better treatment."

Rick remembered the Haitian refugees and how they were received in America. How strange that the Maltese, with so little to share by comparison, should be so generous with their uninvited guests.

Josefina surprised him by leaning forward toward him. In a low voice she said, "You're very fond of Caterina, aren't you?"

"Even though I hardly know her, fond isn't strong enough a word."

"Good. She's interested in you, too, even if she won't admit it to herself. She has an *hrara* when she's around you."

"I beg your pardon?"

"An aura. She doesn't have one when she's with Andrew. You have one too. What's your birthday?"

"July 25th."

"You're a Leo. Good. If you want her, fight for her. I know you'll win."

Rick was happy for her support. "You may be right but she's made it clear my attentions aren't welcome."

"Don't let that stop you," Josefina said. "She's an Aries and can change her mind, even if she doesn't like to be wrong."

Caterina suddenly appeared in the doorway and frowned when she saw them sitting so closely together. "What are you two plotting?" she asked.

"He's telling me what I should make for supper tonight," Josefina chirped. "He says he likes lamb stew."

"That's strange," she said. "That's my favorite, too. Are you sure that's what you were talking about?"

"Of course, dear," Josefina said sweetly. "What else?"

Though she didn't say more, Caterina still gave Zija a suspicious look as Josefina got up and returned to the galley. Turning to Rick, Caterina said, "Sorry I took so long."

He smiled, thinking she looked unusually lovely and freshly scrubbed. "Think nothing of it. I found out some interesting facts from Stef's diary. For one thing, I was right that Cellini's work was called the *Aegis Dei*. Stef seems to think it must be magnificent."

"Why do you suppose no one has ever heard of it before?"

"Why indeed."

She buttered bread. "What's the agenda for today?"

"I want to meet George Bezzina. He probably knows Stef's kidnappers."

She smiled archly. "I can introduce you, but you'll need a disguise."

"What kind of disguise?" he asked.

"You'll see," she said.

They left the building through the front door and turned right to start up the hill. "Why are we going this way?" Rick asked.

"I want you to meet Father Modiglio. He's one of the priests in my church. He's a Franciscan and committed to helping the unfortunate, so we get along well."

"I can understand why."

When they knocked on the rectory door a tall man with sandy hair appeared wearing a tee shirt and jeans. Besides his light hair he was also surprisingly fair-skinned. "Caterina. What a pleasant surprise. Do you have another family who needs assistance?"

"Not this time, father. This is my American friend Richard Olsen."

As they shook hands, the priest looked at Caterina and asked, "How's Andrew?" Rick inadvertently squeezed harder.

"Very busy." She glanced at Rick. "Father Modiglio will be marrying us," she said.

Rick squeezed harder still and Modiglio had to pull on Rick's fingers with his free hand to loosen the grip. "What can I do for you?" the priest asked.

"Rick is in a play and we were wondering if he could borrow a cassock from you."

"A robe from Modiglio's Surplice Surplus?" the priest said with a grin.

Rick laughed, but Caterina didn't. "You'd get it if you saw it on paper," he said.

"Considering all you do for the parish," Modiglio said, rolling his eyes and wagging his eyebrows, "I guess I wouldn't mind giving your friend a shirt off my back."

After he disappeared, Rick said, "He must steal his material from Groucho Marx. I like him."

"I do too. But I'm afraid he has a crush on me."

"Doesn't everyone? I don't see how it's safe for you to walk the streets."

"That's why I drive everywhere," she said.

Modiglio returned carrying a cassock on a coathanger. "The pants are under-neath," he said. "I hope you can get into them."

"Thanks," she said. "We'd like to stay longer but we have to get to practice."

"Greet Andrew for me, Cat," Modiglio said. Rick made an unpleasant face and Caterina prodded him. "Nice to meet you," he said.

The *Qarnita* Pub was located a quarter of a mile south of the Promenade. A sign covering the entire side of the building depicted a giant octopus holding a tankard of ale in one of its tentacles and an assortment of unhappy-looking sailors in the other seven.

"Cute, isn't it?" Caterina said. "Who do you suppose gets the ale?"

"I think the octopus. It's saving it to wash down the sailors," Rick replied.

Caterina laughed. "You're probably right."

The street and the pub looked deserted. "Are you sure the pub is open this early in the morning?"

"*Sequ* has visitors at all hours. Now who are you and why are you with me?"

"I'm Father Segretti visiting from Naples. I'm working with Father Modiglio for a week. Do you think Bezzina will believe me?"

"Why not?" she said, straightening his collar. "He has no idea who you really are."

Though unconvinced, Rick followed Caterina into the tavern. He liked the décor with the pugnacious-looking rubber octopi and the large Davey Jones Locker on top of a rack over the bar. No one was around.

Caterina grabbed Rick's sleeve. "This way," she said. The walls were wood panels stained mahogany. Holding him by the arm she led him to a side room across from the bar. The door to the room was open, but she still knocked before entering. "*Iva?*" a voice said from within.

Caterina answered in Italian. "It's Caterina Borg. I want to talk to you."

"Come in. You're always welcome."

"I have Father Segretti with me."

"He's welcome, too." She pushed Rick inside and then stepped in herself.

Bezzina moved an expensive leather chair back and stood as they entered the room. Rick was surprised by what he saw. The crime kingpin looked to be little more than a foppish teen-ager even though he obviously went to great pains not to be taken as one. Every hair was in place and the deeply tanned face had no lines. Expertly tailored clothes showed off a well-trimmed body. Rick guessed the man worked out every day. "Good afternoon, Caterina. Father," Bezzina said in Italian. "What can I do for you?"

"The church needs a contribution to provide a home for one of our cases," Caterina said. "You probably heard that Ya'qub Qasem was killed in a drug deal the other night."

"I did. Shocking isn't it? He worked for me for a while, but I hardly knew him."

In an angry voice, Caterina said, "We have to find a home for his wife, Abra."

"I agree," Bezzina said, reaching for his coat pocket. "How much do you need?"

"Two hundred pounds should be enough," Caterina replied.

"Two hundred and fifty would be better," Rick interjected.

Bezzina looked him over with a bemused smile. "And who is Father Segretti?"

Rick started to answer but Caterina interrupted. With a glare she said, "He's visiting Father Modiglio from Naples. He'll be staying for a month or two to help with our refugee relief project."

"You mean the boat people, don't you." Bezzina said, making a face. "It's disgusting, isn't it? What makes them think they can come here and expect us to take care of them?" That said, he reached inside his jacket pocket and took out a leather checkbook. Besides checks it held a sizable wad of brown banknotes tucked inside.

"It's too bad what happened to Ya'qub," Bezzina said, laying the checkbook on the table. Caterina handed him a pen. "He seemed pleasant enough, but you just never know what type of person you'll run into nowadays, even when they provide references. He only worked a few hours a week."

Ignoring Caterina's worried looks, Rick asked, "What kind of work do you do?"

"I'm an independent contractor." Bezzina said coolly. He handed the pen back to Caterina then carefully tore the check out of the book and passed it to Rick. "Is there anything else I can do for you?"

Taking the check, Rick saw the black king chess piece logo at the left of the check. "Are you a chess player?" he asked.

Bezzina chuckled. "I've been involved in quite a few chess games, yes. Some of the people who know me call me The Black King."

Rick could understand why that would please him and wanted to find out more, but the dark look from Caterina stilled his tongue. "Muhammed Areef's brother Mustafa wants Muhammed to know that he'll be visiting him from Tripoli in a week or two," she said. "He apologizes for not having had the time to call."

Bezzina took a reminder book out of his suit pocket and wrote something in it with his pen. "I'll give him the message. You may also want to tell Father Modiglio that Seza Mousaden's brother's work permit came through. Seza was very worried about that. I was able to use my contacts with the government ministry to get him his papers."

"You must have forgotten," said Caterina coolly. "Seza left more than a week ago. If you're going to try to get work permits, you might try to get his brother one."

Rick chuckled to himself, enjoying watching Caterina put Bezzina in his place.

The man's smile faded. "You are of course correct," he said dryly. "My memory isn't what it should be, I'm afraid."

"I think your memory is just fine," Caterina said in a firm voice. "But I'll pass on the messages. We should be going, Father. Mr. Bezzina is a busy man."

"Never too busy to see your lovely face," Bezzina purred. As Rick and Caterina turned to leave, he called after them in English. "I understand you have taken custody of an American."

Rick turned and gave Bezzina a puzzled look. "Father Segretti doesn't understand English," Caterina said.

Bezzina grinned and repeated his statement in Italian.

"Richard Olsen?" she said. "I help people in trouble all the time."

"Though they're usually Arab. Where is this Mr. Olsen now?"

"He's with my aunt. He stays there when I'm working."

"Enjoy your stay and say hello to Father Modiglio for me," Bezzina said.

"I will," Rick replied.

When they were back in the street, Caterina gave Rick a stern look. "Do you realize how close you came to giving us away?"

"I do now. He's quite the young entrepreneur, isn't he?"

"He's a monster," she said disgustedly. "At least Fagan had some feeling for the boys who were working for him. Bezzina pays them pennies on the dollar and wastes thousands of liras throwing expensive parties for his friends on the weekends. Everyone on the island is dying to get on his invitation list. He has personal tailors and won't wear anything that costs less than a hundred pounds. What do we do now?"

"I need to check in with the embassy. I'll call you when I'm done."

11:05 AM

Carpenter was sitting at a computer terminal typing. He quickly switched screens when the sergeant brought Rick into the room. "Back so soon?"

"I've got some interesting news," Rick said. "I found Stef's room."

"Excellent. Did you find anything there?"

"His diary. He met Cornacchia at *Borgiswed*."

"Really," the agent said, eyes widening. "Does he say what happened?"

"Yes. Cornacchia told Stef that Alessandro hid Cellini's work, the Shield of God because he was afraid the Brits were going to arrest him and he didn't want them to confiscate it. Unfortunately for the family, he didn't tell anyone where he put it."

"I don't understand. If Cornacchia doesn't have the Shield, why would he care about the drawing?"

"The key question," Rick said. "Cornacchia also told Stef that Alessandro was obsessed with puzzles and he was sure his father must have left some cryptic clue to where he hid the Shield. Apparently he's always wanted to look for it, but his mother has discouraged him. He also told Stef that Agatha donated the family papers to the University. If Cornacchia intended to lead Stef into a trap, it worked. His last entry said that he was going to the archives the next day to investigate."

"Why didn't Cornacchia just grab him at *Borgiswed*?"

"He wouldn't do anything that blatant," Rick said. "How could he know Stef hadn't told someone where he was going?"

"Good point. Remember what I said about staying away from Cornacchia. I don't want you to do anything to spook him. I need to know what the Arab is up to."

Even though he was seething, Rick kept his anger in check. "Right. Can't you at least tell me who he is?"

"Sorry. No need to know. I can say that your help is greatly appreciated."

"Damn it, man, then at least tell me about Lorenzo Cornacchia's connection with the Arabs."

"Fair enough. Did you ever hear of the Zone of Death?"

"It sounds vaguely familiar."

"Back in the '80s Qadaffi wanted to extend Libyan territorial waters to 250 miles and declared a Zone of Death."

"That's essentially the same ploy the Barbary pirates used in the Nineteenth Century. Every ship had to pay tribute. They had a good thing going until the U.S. Marines put a stop to it."

"Right. Well Malta was the other side of Qadaffi's Zone. A lot of Arabs applauded him. They liked the idea that one of their own was standing up to the infidel. Cornacchia was one of Momar's biggest supporters here."

"Then Reagan spoiled their party by sending in the Sixth Fleet." He paused as he got to his feet. "Thanks for the info."

"Think nothing of it," Carpenter replied. With that he turned back to the computer screen, leaving Rick to find his way out. As he rode down in the elevator he decided to find out whom he had seen on Cornacchia's boat, one way or another. But first, he had an errand to take care of. Then he would call Kevin.

CHAPTER 14

▼

Monday
12:31 PM
Valletta

After leaving the Embassy, Rick walked to a shop on Republic Street in Valletta. He then returned to Triton Square to meet Caterina.

"Let's go back to the Bellestrado," he said. "After I call Kevin I'll have work to do on the computer."

Caterina nodded, glancing at the plastic bag in his lap. "I see you went to DeBono's. What did you buy there?"

"Just a CD. I'll play it later. You may like it."

After a moment of silence, she asked, "What's going on at the Embassy?"

"I wish I knew myself," Rick said. "All I know is that that Arab we saw on the *Fahal* must be important. The CIA is involved."

She made a face. "You'll never find anything out from them."

"No, but they IDed him using an on-line program, so there must be other law enforcement agencies that use it, too. My friend Kevin McIntyre can find a way into their files."

"He's a hacker?"

"He'd be insulted if he heard you say that. And it isn't called hacking anymore. It's cracking."

"Whatever it's called, what if this Arab is a terrorist?" Caterina asked in a worried voice. "We've only had two incidents of terrorism here so far. The first was back in the 'eighties when I was a little girl. Arabs hijacked an Egyptian jet here."

Rick nodded. "Yes. I remember because they shot a Minnesota woman and left her for dead on the tarmac. It was a miracle she survived. What's the other?"

"In 1995 a man and a woman on a motor scooter shot Fatqi Shqaqi in front of the Diplomat Hotel in Sliema. He was the head of Hamas and the Mossad tracked him here. It happened less than two kilometers from the Bellestrado. We were sure Malta would become a battleground, but neither side has done anything here since."

Traffic came to a stop. Several pickups passed them with tarp-covered loads. Rick wondered what was under them. "Did you ever hear why Cornacchia is putting up such a big building?" he asked.

"It's supposed to make Malta the trade center of the Mediterranean."

"A worthy goal, but that's an expensive building. It will take a century before they generate enough money to pay for it."

"Not quite that long. Some British and American telecommunication companies will be using it. It'll be the second tallest building between London and Singapore."

"It still seems like an extravagance to me."

"I think so, too," she replied. "Why don't you ask Marija Cornacchia why she's building it the next time you see her?"

"It's her idea?"

"Her idea, her company. Marija Cornacchia *is* Duchess Construction. Lorenzo doesn't have a thing to do with it."

They were soon back at the Bellestrado. Even though it wasn't yet one o'clock, the pub was busy. Anna sat alone at her table.

"Looks like she's between customers," Caterina whispered.

"If she is, they must be invisible," Rick replied with a leer. Unable to control herself, she laughed out loud before she could cover her mouth.

A klatch of four blacks in maritime uniforms were seated where the young Arab usually sat. Peter Grech stood behind the bar wearing an apron, with Manny O'Toole sitting on a stool in front of him. When Caterina noticed O'Toole she stopped short.

Rick chuckled under his breath. "I thought we straightened things out with Manny."

"I consider him one of my closest friends," she said. "But I'll still go in through the hotel door, thank you."

Still smiling, he walked into the bar alone. O'Toole was waiting to greet him. "Well, Richard Olsen," he said, "where's your gorgeous fiancée?"

"She's working," Rick said.

"Do you want something to drink?" Grech asked.

"Cisk," Rick said. He turned back to O'Toole. "What are you doing here at this time of day?"

"I've wondered the same thing myself. The old man cleared everyone out and told us to take the rest of the day off."

Grech set the beer on the counter, but Rick didn't notice. The Irishman's words had his heart racing. "Why did he do that?"

"I don't know. But it's fine with me. I'm getting paid by the hour," said O'Toole. He patted the stool next to him. "Sit down."

Rick grinned and moved the beer in front of O'Toole. "Sorry. I'd love to but I don't have time so it looks like its your lucky day again." That said he hurried back to the kitchen to gather up Caterina. Contacting Kevin could wait. He needed to find out what was happening at Black Dolphin Shipping.

Caterina took the binoculars from the car and they caught the bus on The Strand. After a short ride they got out in front of a very modern office building. Rick looked up and saw that it was at least six stories high. "This looks fine to me. We should be able to get a great view of the harbor and Black Dolphin from here."

Inside, a cement stairway took them up to the top level, but the door was locked. Caterina watched in bemused silence as he took the pick from his wallet and deftly opened the door. "You're a burglar, too, I see."

"Reformed," he replied. "A SEAL taught me how to do it."

"He must have had dexterous flippers," she replied.

The roof was flat and empty except for three intakes for air-conditioning. All were humming contentedly as he found a place to kneel. Below them, Marsamxett Creek and Manoel Island were clearly in view. Raising the glasses to his eyes he followed Manoel Island's shoreline to the quay for Black Dolphin Shipping, a wire-enclosed area that took up more than half the dock area. Barbed wire extended all around the building into the water. A wide gate was the only entrance. The doors were closed and no one was in sight.

"Waste of time," Rick said. "Let's go."

"Maybe not. Do you see that ship moored out in the harbor?"

Rick turned the glasses. A freighter lay quietly at anchor with a green flag hanging limply from one of its masts. "What about it?"

"It's a Libyan freighter. If it's the Da-iz-ref, it isn't supposed to arrive until tomorrow."

"And how do you know that?"

"I know the schedules for all the freighters," Caterina said. "They have a regular rotation and we get passengers at the hotel from them all the time."

Using the glasses Rick could easily see the name written in Arabic and Roman characters on the side of its hull. "You're right. It is the Da-iz-ref. Any idea why it's a day early?"

"None whatsoever. I've never heard of anything like that happening before. The only thing I can imagine is that something happened to one of the other ships and they switched their schedules for this week."

"This could be important," Rick said. "Let's take a ride on the Sliema ferry. I want to get a closer look at that ship."

2:05 PM

Rick kept the glasses trained on the freighter's deck as the ferry skimmed its way toward Valletta. Men wearing white caps were busily at work, but for all the activity he could see no cargo. Had they already unloaded her? Not likely. She sat too low in the water.

He turned to Black Dolphin Shipping. A heavy metal fence surrounded the building, extending out into the water. The company's shipping dock took up most of the quay and its massive gate was now open. Inside, barrels on pallets stood at the edges of the entrance. Oil drums? It would make sense since Libya was furnishing Malta with petroleum. As he watched, a man with steel gray hair suddenly appeared coming through the door from the warehouse.

Cornacchia! And deep in conversation with a second man dressed in work clothes. As he talked, Cornacchia pointed a finger at the pallets. The second man turned palms up and stared at the ground. It was an ass-chewing. Even at a distance, Rick knew one when he saw it. Cornacchia walked over to a barrel and summoned the chewee to join him. After some more gesticulating, the man nodded sharply, and Cornacchia went back into the warehouse. Rick could almost feel the worker's pain. He gestured to Caterina.

"Come take a look," he said.

She moved closer to him. An unexpected dip by the boat had her grabbing on to his arm for support. He hoped it wasn't just wishful thinking on his part but he did think she held on to it a tad longer than was absolutely necessary. "What?" she asked.

"Does it look to you as if Black Dolphin just got in a big shipment?"

She took the glasses. Seconds later she said, "Not really."

"I didn't think so, either. Maybe they're waiting until tonight to unload the freighter. We'll have to come back and take a look."

Rick kept watch on the ship until the ferry landed at the base of the wall in Valletta. The landing was a wide concrete apron with a ramp extending into the water. It also had a single kiosk, and several full-sized buildings. One of the buildings was a restaurant, and Rick could smell garlic through an open window. The other structures were smaller and looked like boathouses or garages. Most of the riders were already ascending by the narrow street that would take them up into the city. Some thirty yards away, a *carrozzin* driver splashed water on his horse and a pair of seagulls fought over a kernel of popcorn. The embarkation area would be very pleasant, except that it spent so much of the day in the shadows of the huge wall that soared behind it.

"Now that we're here," Caterina said, "what do we do?"

"Turn around and go back, I suppose," he said. "Unless you've got a better idea."

"Could we have an ice cream while we're waiting? I'm hungry."

After buying her a Good Humor bar, Rick found a place to sit and went back to examining the freighter through the binoculars. Except for two open portholes, the ship was tightly closed. Caterina sat beside him. "I just thought of something," he said. "Even if the ship is out of rotation, there must have been passengers. Would any of them have shown up at the Bellestrado?"

"I'd say the odds were better than fifty-fifty."

"Call Zija."

Caterina did. "Good news. One of the passengers from the ship is staying at the Bellestrado. Do you want to talk to Zija yourself?"

He fairly snatched the phone from her hand. "Hi, Zija. What's the story?"

"I have three passengers from the Da-iz-ref," Josefina said. "A mother and her two girls. They just finished eating a few minutes ago."

His eyes lit in excitement. "They haven't left the hotel yet, have they?"

"I don't think so. I'm almost certain they went back to their room."

"Good. Keep them there until we get back. See if you can find out why the boat was early. Get as much information as you can about how many other passengers there were and where they may have gone. Most important, ask her if she ever saw any of the cargo. If she did, try to find out if they were barrels or boxes and if there was anything strange about them. Got all that?"

Josefina hesitated. "I think so. But you should be the one asking the questions."

"You're right and we'll get back as soon as we can. Just try to stall her."

Ten minutes later the ferry attendant unhitched the chain barrier to let passengers board and they were the first in line. As the ferry chugged past Manoel

Island Rick got a good view of the open gate at Black Dolphin. Nothing had changed and activity on the freighter had nearly ceased. He spent the rest of the trip pacing the deck and took off on the fly when they landed.

Caterina soon dropped behind. "Do we have to go so fast?" she moaned. "These shoes aren't for running."

Rick slowed to let her catch up with him.

"You're a real bull when you're in a hurry," she said. "You're not terribly fast but you sure are determined. What's the big rush?"

"I don't want our Arab friend to leave before I have a chance to talk to her," Rick said extending his arm for her to hold on to as she slipped off her shoe and rubbed her instep.

"She won't go anywhere," Caterina said. "And I'll be the one to talk to her, anyway, so it won't do you any good if you get there before me."

"I've always been antsy. Tell me, with all the driving you do, how do you find time to work with the church?"

"The church always comes first with me," she said.

"Don't you ever do anything for yourself?"

She smiled wickedly. "All the time," she said with a low laugh. "I only sound like a saint if you don't know me."

When they got to the Bellestrado they found Josefina working at the desk. "They're in 308," she said. "Please be quiet. The girls are napping."

"We will," Rick said. "Were you able to learn anything from her?"

"She said she came to visit her husband and she got the schedule change last night."

"Did you tell her we'll be talking to her?" Caterina asked.

"Yes. She doesn't mind as long as you're done by the time her husband comes to pick her up."

They waited for the elevator until they gave up on it and took the stairs. "When you ask questions you want translated, be sure you use Italian," Caterina said. "She may be suspicious otherwise."

"Do you think she can tell the difference?"

"Yes. Italian is much more common in North Africa than English and it's considered less threatening. We don't want her to get the idea she's in trouble. That way there's less chance our conversation will get back to her husband, too."

Rick threw her an admiring look. "Smart girl. You'd make a first-rate interrogator in the military."

She turned to face him. "I know that's meant to be a compliment but I don't like that term at all. It makes me sound like I'm using her."

Rick was about to apologize but decided it was better to drop the subject entirely. 308 was on the same floor as Rick's room but in a different corridor. Caterina knocked on the door. A young woman opened the door, put her finger to her mouth and quietly shut the door before stepping out into the corridor.

"*Salaam,*" Rick whispered.

"*Salaam Aleichem,*" the woman replied. Caterina said something to her, then looked at Rick. "Ask her who called her about the schedule change," he said in Italian.

Caterina translated and the woman answered without hesitation. "She said someone from the shipping company called at her home. She was planning to come the next day but her husband was happy to have her arrive a day earlier."

"How many passengers were on the freighter?"

Caterina asked the woman. "She says there were only about twenty or so."

Rick shook his head. "Impossible. Are you sure that she understood the question? There should have been many more than that on board."

After another brief interchange, Caterina said firmly, "She understood what I was asking her. She thinks there were eighteen."

"Did she notice what kind of cargo they were carrying? Did she see any of the boxes or crates?"

The woman shook her head. "There wasn't any cargo," Caterina translated.

"That can't be," he said in a loud voice.

The woman looked frightened and Caterina glared at Rick. He put on the most ingratiating smile he could muster.

"*Ana Asif.*"

With his apology the frightened look disappeared and Caterina seemed impressed. "Ask her if anything unusual happened during the trip," Rick said.

Again the woman shook her head. There didn't seem to be anything more to be learned.

"*Shukran,*" Rick said, bowing his head. Both Caterina and the Arab woman look surprised. "*Alaafw,*" she replied.

Caterina thanked her, too. After the woman went back into her room, Caterina said, "I didn't know you knew Arabic."

"Not enough to carry on a conversation but enough that I can recognize some of the cognates in your language"

"At least you know the nice words. I know she appreciated your thanking her. You frightened her. What do we do now?"

"I have to make some calls. If you have anything to do, yourself, feel free."

"I need to go to the bank," Caterina said. "Zija likes long meals. I hope she won't be hurt when we tell her we have to be to the National Library at seven."

Rick returned to his room and flopped on the bed before taking out his cell phone. Kevin answered on the second ring.

"Good morning," Rick said. "I have an interesting problem for you. I identified someone using a Department of Defense face-recognition program. The station chief won't tell me who it is. Do you have any ideas about how I can find out for myself?"

"You won't be able to do it through DOD. Your best bet is Interpol or some country's police database. They all use the same identification system."

Rick nodded. "I know you're busy but would you have time to research it for me? It could help me find Stef."

"Finding someone who uses the system shouldn't take me very long. Getting into the data base is another story."

"See what you can do."

After Kevin hung up, Rick called Bob Carpenter. "I have something that may interest you. One of the freighters from Libya is a day early. It's the Da-iz-ref and it's at harbor just outside Black Dolphin Shipping."

"Thanks for the info. We must have missed that. I'll look into it. Oh, I just got the report on the cotton swabs. The blood-type is A negative."

Rick stood up in excitement. "That proves it," he said. "Stef was on that boat."

At five-thirty Rick and Caterina joined Josefina in the kitchen. She had traded the wide working outfit for a slimming floral-print dress and her smiling face was accentuated by perfectly applied makeup. A table was covered with a fine linen cloth with a lace pattern of a Maltese cross. It looked like she had used her best plates and silverware "Sit, please," Josefina said. She opened the refrigerator and took out a large green bottle. "I bought some wine. Would you like to open it?" Josefina asked.

"Of course," Rick said.

She carried the bottle to the table and handed it to him like a doctor presenting a newborn to its parents. He pulled the cork. "Pour some wine for Caterina and yourself while I get the stew," Josefina said.

Even though the wine shouldn't have been chilled, LaFitte Rothschild or Chateau la Tour couldn't have tasted better. "It's delicious," Rick said. "Will you marry me, Josefina?"

"I'm already married," she said sweetly. "Caterina isn't, though."

Caterina looked shocked. "Shame on you, Zija," she said in an angry voice. "I'm surprised at you. How do you think Andrew would feel?"

Josefina answered with an arch look and Rick wanted to kiss her. Zija had openly joined the fray on his behalf.

A delicious aroma filled the air as she laid her lamb stew on the table. "I can't tell you how happy I am to have you here," she said. "All I can do is pray for your safety and offer you my hospitality. Beyond that, God will provide."

"As he does for the other unfortunates who come here?" Rick asked.

"Yes. As he does for them."

"The people who come here aren't unfortunate," Caterina said. "They're lucky. They get a warm meal and a clean bed. And Zija will always do what she can for them. Sometimes she has no choice but to send them back."

"What happens to the unlucky ones?"

Caterina looked unhappy. "They usually end up joining gangs or becoming victims of crime. Joining a gang is an easy way to get money for papers."

"What about the ones who are legal?"

"If they're older they stay with relatives and work at menial jobs or just become another mouth to feed for the family."

"And the younger ones?" he asked.

Caterina pursed her lips. "They often join street gangs or get involved with crime bosses because they can make a lot of money at it. Every time they break into someone's house or rob someone, the locals take to the streets. Most of the time they find a car with Libyan plates and break the windows, but a few years ago there nearly was a full-fledged riot in Msida. The police had to break them up. The boat people have only made matters worse."

"So you're saying the natives don't like the Libyans."

"For the most part," Caterina said. "Some dislike them intensely, some think they're all right if they stay in their place. Most parents wouldn't want their daughters to marry one."

"It sounds racist," Rick said.

"It's actually more cultural and historical," Caterina said. "We've been enemies for centuries. Just about every Maltese knows that the Turks once came and carried the whole population of Gozo off into slavery."

"Why do you help them?" Rick asked, turning to Zija.

"I don't see a religion or a country, I see a person in need."

"How many refugees come here off the freighters?"

"Usually at least one or two a week. Recently it's been as many as twenty."

"And you feed them all?"

"I never turn anyone away hungry," Josefina said. "No matter how little food we have on hand, there's always enough to share. Some of them look as if they haven't eaten in weeks. Like that young man who tried to break into your room."

Rick's eyes widened. "Junior stayed here?"

"Yes. Back in June. I recognized him when the police took him away."

"I want to see the record," he said.

"It'll have to wait until another time," Caterina said. "We have to hurry if we want to catch the ferry."

They left by the back door. "Do you know Josefina spent fifteen pounds on that wine? That's more than thirty-five Euros. She really went overboard for us."

"That's my Zija," Caterina said with a sigh.

After walking about five minutes, they arrived at the top of a hill overlooking a scene that even Monet could never have envisioned. A cobbled street ran down the steep hill between balconied houses and glass-fronted shops to a pink sea under a baby-blue sky. Even Caterina seemed dumbfounded. "Have you ever see anything so beautiful?" she asked.

"Never. I just wish I had time to enjoy it."

"What are we going to do at the library?"

"The librarians are working with Cornacchia and I want to find out who they contacted," Rick said in a low voice. "You can come in with me or stay outside."

"I'm going in with you. They're old men. I won't let you hurt them."

"Whatever gave you the idea I would hurt them?"

He didn't like her laugh.

At the ferry dock, Rick paid the eighty cents for their fares.

"Do you promise to behave at the library?" Caterina asked.

Rick knew the tone. His mother used it when she dragged him off to Kelly Davis' third birthday party. "Absolutely. You have nothing to be concerned about."

"I don't believe you." Mother had said that, too.

Minutes later they were plowing through uneven water. Walleye chop is what the fishermen called it on Lake Minnetonka. It would be nearly sunset when they reached Valletta.

The freighter appeared, but darkness had already erased most of the details and it looked like a dark shadow resting on the water.

Before long, Caterina crossed her arms in front of her and grabbed her shoulders. "Are you cold?" Rick asked.

"A little."

"I'd say more than a little. You can sit closer if you want to."

"Absolutely not," she said firmly.

"Suit yourself." He didn't have long to wait. Seconds later she surreptitiously inched nearer until her hips and thighs touched his. "I guess I should have worn a sweater," she said in an embarrassed voice.

He put his arm around her.

"Don't," she said, pushing him away.

"Rub your arms with your hands, then. Your skin is like ice."

She pointed at a beacon to their right. "There's the quay at Manoel Island."

He could see it, outlined by the lights spaced evenly along the length of the structure. When he stood up to get a better look she let out a loud shiver. "Come back here. I'm freezing."

He did. When he pulled her toward him she didn't object. Teeth chattering, she nestled closer. He started to say something but kept his silence when he noticed the distressed look on her face.

As the dark settled in for its nightly stay, the lights of Valletta became more noticeable. From sea level, the bastions appeared even more daunting than in daylight. In other ages the black expanse that climbed so high against the night sky must have sent potential attackers off to find another, easier, target. Though forbidding, it also looked habitable. The random twinkle of yellow lights on the walls became regular and clearly defined at the top. "After the view from the street and this one, I can almost understand why you left Toronto," Rick said.

"Toronto is a beautiful city but it's too big and cold. I need the sun and heat."

"I don't. Heat makes me wilt. If this is fall, it's bad enough."

The boat slowed to dock at Valletta's landing. She disentangled herself and moved a safe distance away from him. Floodlights lit the docking area.

"I hope you have good climbing shoes," said Caterina.

"No problem," he said. He soon regretted the words. It was a strenuous ascent. Finally, with tendons aching, they reached the top.

"Where to now?" he asked, puffing.

"We've got another set of steps and we'll almost be there," said Caterina in an irritatingly cheerful voice.

Rick groaned. After two more set of steps, he was the one reaching for her hand to give him a lift. "For Pete's sake, slow down. I'm not a mountain goat."

Laughing wickedly, she went faster. At last they reached the top. When he saw they had even further to climb, he stopped and leaned against the side of a building.

"We haven't got time to rest. It's almost seven," she said.

They reached the stairs of the library just as the clock on St. John's Co-Cathedral began to strike. "What's your plan?" Caterina asked.

Puffing, Rick replied, "Beats me. Is the building still open?"

To find out, they climbed yet another flight of steps. The front door was ajar, but a quaky voice said, "Sorry but the library's closed," when they tried to enter.

"I just want to ask you a question," Rick said, stepping inside and shutting the door behind him.

"No time now. I have to lock up. Come back tomorrow."

"Don't you recognize me? I was in the day before yesterday. I asked you for the book about the Maltese nobility."

The man squinted at him. "Oh, yes."

Rick stepped toward him. "There's something else I need to know," he said.

"Keep away," the man said, inching away. "You're frightening me."

Rick grabbed one of the librarian's bony shoulders. "Tell me who you called when I asked about Cornacchia."

"I don't know what you mean," the man squawked. "You have no right..."

Fingers dug deeper into the old man's shoulder and he let out a weak cry.

"Stop!" Caterina said. "Let him go."

Eyes throwing daggers at her, he released his grip.

"Mr. Azzopardi is an old man, and he's worked here for years. How many years has it been?"

"F-Forty-five, miss."

"That's what I thought. You shouldn't be treated like this."

The old man threw her a grateful smile but it quickly disappeared when she spoke sharply to him in Maltese. As she continued, the man's eyes widened and he turned to look at Rick. At the word "Illuminati," the eyes widened further and he made the sign of the cross as she continued in an even angrier tone. Finally, uttering a little sound, he took off toward the front desk. Rick, thinking he was trying to escape, followed him. "No," the man said, turning to him and pleading with his hands. "Stay away. I have a phone number. I'll get it for you."

Hands quaking, he dug through a pile of notepapers. "Here it is."

As Rick took the paper, he again noticed the man's ring. Now he remembered why it looked familiar; Micallef wore one, too. A seven-pointed star with a large letter "A" surrounded by diamonds on a ruby setting.

As they stepped out the door he said, "I'm worried. How do you know he won't call Cornacchia?"

She whispered back. "He won't. He's too afraid the brotherhood will get him and his family if he does."

CHAPTER 15

▼

Monday 7:20 PM
Valletta

Once outside the library, Caterina hurried down the stairs and then broke into a full run. "This way," she called to him. "Hurry." He ended up on the same street he had taken to escape after his first visit to the library.

"What's the matter?" Rick asked, puffing.

"I didn't want him to see which way we went."

"So you *do* think he'll call Cornacchia."

"No. But I'm like you. I'm careful."

He impulsively pecked her on her cheek. "Don't get carried away," she said, taking a step away from him.

"Sorry. I just wanted to let you know I wouldn't have been able to do it alone."

"You're right, you wouldn't. You have to know something about us. If you forced it out of him, he would have called the police the second you were out the door. If he were still alive, that is."

"Don't be silly," he said. "I wouldn't have hurt him. How do you know he won't call them, anyway?"

"He's too afraid to do that. We're still a superstitious people, even if everyone wants to think we're not. Why do you think the fishermen still paint the eye of Horus on their boats? It's to protect them from the evil eye."

"But everyone must know by now that there's no such thing as Illuminati. Azzopardi must be an educated man. Why would he believe in such garbage?"

"Maybe he doesn't. But he can't be sure."

"I'm more worried he'll call Cornacchia. Let's get back to the boat."

"We took the last one. Do you want to take a cab or go back by bus?"

"Bus it is," he said. As they walked, the cobbled street, pitch black except for the lights from inside the buildings, still gave evidence of life. Echoes of laughter, the flash of headlights and glow of tail lights, the low voices of young people walking with arms about each other's waists gave sound and movement to la Valette's city. The air was heavy, with an odor that reminded Rick of fall days in Minnesota when farmers were burning cornhusks. Above everything, a heavy moon impaled itself on a television antenna. Sadly, in all the trips he had made to Italy, he had never visited this place just a few miles from Sicily. Some day he would have to come back again to enjoy it. With Stef.

*   *   *   *

Light blinded him. "Hello, my friend," *Pawlu said in a jovial voice slightly muffled by the mask he was wearing. He had had a visitor who called him 'Nerf.' Stef guessed it was Pawlu's boss.*

"Need food," Stef said, moving a hand toward his mouth to wipe it.

"You'll have food. And you'll be free soon," Pawlu said in a jovial voice. "Your brother is bringing us the drawing. When he does, you'll have your money and be on your way before the night is through."

The words tore into Stef's heart. Whatever Pawlu and his associate had planned, it didn't include freeing him. But Rick would never trust them enough to agree to a straight trade. But there was no reason to believe Pawlu anyway.

"Smile, my friend," Pawlu continued. "Your troubles are nearly over."

*   *   *   *

Back at the hotel, Josefina was waiting for them. "I tried to look up the record on the young Arab man you call 'Junior'," she said. "I can't find it. I must have been wrong about the date."

"Or someone deleted it from your records," Rick said. "Have you ever let any of your guests use your computer?"

"Occasionally. Why?"

"One of them may have planted the worm. It could have been downloaded from a floppy disk or CD."

"I had no idea," Zija said.

Rick handed Caterina the slip of paper the librarian had given him. She dialed, holding the phone away from her ear so they could both listen. After the first ring, a recorded message came on. "This is the Mosta Dome gift shop. We are open from 09:00 in the morning to 17:00 at night. Please call back or leave a message after the tone." After a pause the message repeated in German.

Rick snatched the phone out of her hand and hung up. "That's it!" he screamed. "That's where they have him. Stef told me he was being held in a church. Let's go!"

The street leading to Mosta Dome was filled with parked automobiles, and the enormous circular building stood out in the glare of floodlights. Caterina parked at a safe distance. "Now what?"

"I didn't realize it would be all lit up. Is there a back way into the building?"

"I have no idea." She turned on the ignition and slowly started forward. A white sedan appeared from an alleyway and abruptly pulled in front of them. Caterina shook her fist at them and muttered something under her breath as they sped away.

"Holy cow. Did you see that?" Rick asked.

"Yes," Caterina said angrily. "They ought to be reported."

"That's not what I meant. It's a Morris Princess. I bet there aren't a hundred left in the whole world."

"I've seen the one that belonged to Princess Elizabeth in a car show," said Caterina. "I think this one belongs to Cardinal Vella. The British consul gave it to him when he left in the late 'fifties."

The circuit of the building took several blocks and they wound up where they had started. "This is where the car came from."

"It looks like a private driveway," she said.

"Try it anyway."

She turned into the narrow lane. The rental car moved deftly between walls, then veered sharply to the left.

"Turn off the lights and stop," Rick said.

In the dark, the outline of a large wooden door stood in front of them. "Do you have a flashlight or some matches?" he whispered.

She handed him a flashlight. Rick covered the front with his hand and turned on the light. His hand glowed yellow in the darkness. The lock looked new and Rick couldn't get it open with his pick.

As they returned to the vehicle, Rick asked, "Did you get a look at any of the people in the car?"

"No. Do you think Stef could have been in it?"

"Why not?" He stepped back into the car. "We might as well go back to the Bellestrado. We can't get into the church tonight."

Tuesday
8:00 AM

Rick was in his priestly garb when Caterina knocked on his door the next morning. After a quick breakfast they were on their way to Mosta. The cassock was hot and Rick could hardly wait to get out of it.

"Why is your brother doing research on Benvenuto Cellini?" Caterina asked.

"The man is loads of fun. As Stef said, try saying Chill-lee-nee without smiling."

"Try being serious for once," she said.

"Cellini was one of our boyhood heroes. Did you ever read *The Autobiography?*"

"I did when I was living in Toronto. I don't remember much about it except that the man seemed to be a terrible rogue."

"That he was," Rick said. "And a drunkard, fornicator, and murderer as well. I hate to admit it, but he was just the kind of character every young boy loves to read about. We didn't even care that Cellini was an artist, even though we thought it made him sound like a sissy. It really blew my mind when I found out he didn't write it himself. He dictated it to a fourteen-year-old boy."

"Was he rich?"

"Not as rich as a noble or a merchant, but he made a good living. Goldsmiths were members of the silk-maker's guild so he would have been considered to be upper middle class in today's terms. Unfortunately he seems to have bought into just about every get-rich-quick scheme that ever came along, so he was always short of money."

"Did he really do all the terrible things he said he did?"

Rick laughed. "Who knows? He tended to exaggerate the bad as much as he did the good. He probably did break Michelangelo's nose. And he certainly killed at least two men. Whether or not he shot the Prince of Orange during the sack of Rome, no one can ever know one way or another. Murder aside, it was the way he mistreated women that was most reprehensible. One of his victims was named Caterina. He physically abused her and publicly humiliated her."

"If he had done it to me, I would have forgiven him and prayed for his soul."

"Why?" Rick asked. "You were castigating my father for the way he treated Stef."

"That's different. Your father should have loved Stef. He was his own flesh and blood."

"I see," Rick said. "Would you forgive me?"

"Of course not," she replied. "What did you do when you were boys?"

"The usual things. We both liked to fish and we used to shoot BBs at tin cans. He was a great shot. He could hit them just about every time."

"Did you ever think about how improbable all this is? I mean your brother finding the drawing and being kidnapped? Your winding up at the Bellestrado?"

"It never occurred to me. Have you ever seen an astronomical conjunction when three or more planets come together? It makes for a spectacular view. In fact, that's what the Star of Bethlehem may have been and the Three Wise Men Babylonian astrologers."

She frowned. "I have no idea what you're talking about."

"Things happen. Probability doesn't even enter into it."

Before he could say more, Caterina stopped. Across the street a mass of humanity was descending on Mosta Dome and there were no parking spaces in sight. Rick groaned. "Oh boy."

"Don't worry," she said. "I'll find us a place."

She did, a quarter of a mile away. When they reached the church, they saw a blue-capped tour guide talking to a group on the steps leading to the front door.

"He's probably explaining the miracle," Caterina whispered.

"What miracle? That they were able to find a place to park?"

"No," she said, laughing. "I'll tell you about it when we get inside."

Rick noted the church front with its tiers of statues. The dome itself made him think of Rachel's tomb in Jerusalem. As they passed through the door, a young priest standing next to a donation box blocked their path. "Good morning, father. Are you with a tour?" he asked.

"No. We're just visiting on our own," Rick said. As he said it, Caterina dropped a two-pound note into the box.

"God bless you, my child," the priest said. "Enjoy your visit."

Once out of earshot Rick whispered. "I didn't know they charged admission."

"They don't," Caterina said with a chuckle. "Or at least not exactly. If you're with a tour, the guide will suggest that you make a contribution. If you're not, you may as well throw something into the box. You'll feel like a cheapskate if you don't."

"I will not," said Rick indignantly. "I think it's outrageous. They should be reported to the tourism board."

"Relax," she said. "They already know about it. All the churches do the same thing. They couldn't pay the upkeep on the buildings if they didn't. The gift shop is this way. That's where they keep the miracle.

"During the Second World War, the Germans dropped a bomb on the church," she continued. "It was full and it would have killed a lot of people if it went off. But it went right through the roof and landed on the floor without exploding. Everyone considered it a miracle and the church keeps the bomb here as a holy relic." She stopped and whispered in his ear. "Actually it's a replica."

"Where does Cardinal Vella stay?" he asked watching for her reaction. She didn't skip a beat. "He lives next door."

"Why didn't you tell me that last night?"

She shrugged. "I assumed you already knew. And if you remember, I said the white car belonged to him."

Rick wasn't convinced but kept his doubts to himself as they entered the shop. Caterina led him to the far wall. The bomb sat in a plain display case, a cartoon caricature with a twisted metal tail. Rick nodded appreciatively, then pretended interest in the souvenir stand as he eyed the telephone hung against the back wall. It had to be the one they had called the night before.

"Let's take a look at the church," he said.

He was overwhelmed. Frescoed ceilings and oil paintings cried out to be looked at, making the interior a rival to any he had seen in Italy. Hundreds of flickering candles silhouetted ancient women standing in groups sending their mumbled recitals echoing quietly around the vaulted sacristy. The church was laid out with a central core of pews, a stairwayed pulpit, and a spectacular central altar and crucifix. Surrounding the sanctuary were several other smaller alcoves with altars. Rick could see at least three doors leading out of the sacristy. He also saw several priests scattered about through the building. Clerical security guards, no doubt.

"You don't suppose they'd leave the doors to the alcoves open, do you?" he asked.

Caterina snorted. "You're kidding, right?"

One actually was open. It led to a custodial area. The other two were locked. Both had large, old-fashioned keyholes. A priest approached him. "May I help you?"

"No. Just looking around."

The priest smiled but didn't move. Caterina took Rick by the arm and they started away. "I can't remember the church ever being so well-guarded before."

"I'm taking it to be a good sign." He pointed toward a small enclosure. "Can I hear your confession?"

"Not on your life," she said, taking him by his arm.

"Where are we going?" he asked.

"To find an iron monger. He should have a skeleton key that would fit."

As they rode, Rick unwrapped the Leontyne Price compact disk he bought and slid it into the car's CD player. The soprano's voice broke the silence at full volume. He made a quick grab at the buttons. After ejecting the disk and sending it back in to restart it, he closed his eyes and nestled contentedly against the seat cushion to listen.

"O mio babbino caro," Leontyne Price sang. Oh my beloved father. Was it because his own father was never around that the song so touched him? He mouthed the words, and again felt the heart-breaking sweetness as the song ended. He sat up straight as the player started on the next track. "Ah," he said. "I feel like a human being again." He glanced at Caterina, and was surprised at her furious look. "Is something wrong?" he asked.

"No," she snapped.

"I know it can't be anything I said. I haven't opened my mouth in the last ten minutes."

"I said no. Now drop it."

Rick was astonished to see tears welling in her eyes. "Damn you," she said, smashing her hand into the radio controls. Leontyne was cut off at mid-word.

"Take it easy," he said, throwing his hands up in defense. "I have no idea what's wrong but maybe you should stop somewhere and get a drink of water."

"Just leave me alone," she demanded. The pain in her voice nearly broke his heart. It also frightened him. Without her he was lost. At last she regained her composure. In a forceful voice she said, "I want you to tell me what you talked about when you and Josefina had your little tete-a-tete."

"You'll just get mad again if I tell you."

"TELL ME!"

"Okay! Mostly she said if I wanted you I shouldn't give up chasing you and she thought I would win."

Caterina sniffed and angrily swiped at her eyes. "She should mind her own business. What else did she say?"

"Just something about us having auras."

She tsked derisively. "That sounds like her, too. Stop playing games. She must have said something about Leontyne Price."

"Absolutely not. Why would she do that?"

"You know why. You bought the CD. You said you thought I would like it."

Bewildered, he said, "That's true, I did. But only because I absolutely adore Leontyne Price and I thought you would like her, too. Quite frankly, I have no idea why you're so angry."

"I don't believe you."

"Then don't. But it's true. You should have seen the CD that was in my player. It was almost worn out from being played so often. I know the words to *O Mio Babbino Caro* by heart."

"Prove it," she snapped.

"Do you want me to sing it or say the words."

"I don't care," she said impatiently. "Either way."

"English or Italian?"

"STOP STALLING," she screamed, banging her fists on the steering wheel.

"All right. Calm down." He cleared his throat and began to sing. *"O mio babbino caro, mi piace e' bello, bello; volandare ca' Porta Rossa, a comperar l'anello!"* It was a bit high for his range but he managed a reasonable falsetto on the high notes. As he sang, the look of anger on Caterina's face disappeared, replaced by one of amazement. When he finished she said, "You really do know it, don't you?"

He glared. "You're surprised I wasn't lying to you?"

"I guess I shouldn't be," she said with a sigh.

"It's Lauretta's aria from Puccini's *Gianni Schicchi*. If it weren't for this one song and Leontyne Price, only the buffs would know about the opera. Now the classical musical infomercials have popularized it so much that it's something of a standard."

She threw him a mirthless grin. "Amazing. Is there anything you don't know?"

"Try rock music. I don't know the first thing about that."

"All right. Who sang 'Ride Into the Sun?'"

He shook his head. "I have no idea. Def Leppard?"

"I hate you," she said, sounding as if she meant it.

"Sorry. I can't help it. If I hear it or see it, I remember it. I guess I'm just an infomaniac."

To his delight, Caterina snorted trying to suppress a laugh.

They drove to a dingy-looking shop with windows so dirty they didn't let in light. The monger was sullen and wouldn't help them, so it took them more than a half-hour to find three rusty keys hanging from a nail. "How much?" Rick asked.

The man pulled thoughtfully at the brim of his tweed cap and then made a sour face. "Seven pounds," he grunted.

"That's way too much," Caterina said. "Can't you see he's a priest?"

"That's the price."

Caterina took Rick's arm and started out of the store. "Okay," the monger called. "You can have them for five."

"Three," she countered. The man threw up his hands and growled. "All right, then. Three. Cheat a poor man."

10:50 AM

Returning to Mosta Dome, they followed the driveway to the rear door. The new lock was missing, but the door still wouldn't open. "Let's find a place to park," Rick said with a sigh.

The same priest greeted them at the door. "Welcome back. The Mass will start in ten minutes. Cardinal Vella is saying the service today."

Rick's pulse quickened. "*Si. Grazie*," he said. The man led them to a pew at the rear. Rick followed Caterina's lead, kneeling, crossing himself, and finding a seat. As the service began he watched her from the corner of his eye, kneeling at appropriate places, and moving his lips in sync with the others.

Vella's strong and confident voice rang out from the pulpit. The perfectly cadenced words and the closed book in his hand meant he still had a firm grip on the words of the canon. His self-assured step suggested he was robust despite his years. But the sagging red chasuble hanging from his shoulder blades and waist told another story, and so did the sallow skin that barely seemed sufficient to cover his large skull.

Watching closely, Rick noted the slight hesitation before each step as Vella climbed the stairs to the pulpit. Something pained him as he moved. But once he was in place he was once again in control. After greeting the parishioners and thanking them for attending, he said, "As we all know, we live in very dangerous times. We read in the book of Ecclesiastes, Woe to you, O land, when your king is a child, and your princes feast in the morning. Happy are you, O land, when your king is the son of free men, and your princes feast at the proper time, for strength and not for drunkenness. Through sloth the roof sinks in, and through indolence the house leaks."

Fascinated, Rick sat forward. The man was seething in anger.

"My children, our roof is sinking and our house doth leak. The promised benefits of our union with Europe have turned out to be naïve fantasies or willful lies. We first let our princes feast in the morning when they invited the European developers in the 1960s. Whole towns vanished overnight. Farms that were here before the arrival of the Knights became residences for people who already had houses but wanted a home in the country. The developers promised they would turn our islands into a haven for tourists and make us rich. But tourists would want to see pretty new buildings and be able to eat their own food. We believed them and the way of life that made us who we are began to disappear."

Rick looked at Caterina and was surprised to see anger on her face. The cardinal had struck a chord with her.

"We finally came to our senses when we realized that if we did not intervene, the whole island would be filled with their handiwork. When we put them in check they were offended and left. But then the construction trade took up the cudgel and continued to destroy our heritage to enrich themselves, saying it was necessary for the nation's wealth. And now the European Union promises us still more invaders—tourists. The Union says tourists will come because they will not have to convert their currencies and pay tariffs. Perhaps that is true, but our precious, ancient national identity will be swallowed up, and there will be still more development. We must not let this happen."

Rick wondered how Vella intended to stop it.

"We must look to our roots. Our language is a sister to Arabic. When the Saracens controlled our island, they taught us much and let us keep our religion. We must look to the East. If there can be a place where Arab, Christian and Jew can meet in peace, we can provide it. And the world will benefit if we do."

The impassioned plea was greeted with complete silence. It seemed like a strange sermon for a congregation that was mostly tourists, many undoubtedly from the EU countries. But other than the simplistic idea that closer ties with the Arabs would provide salvation, Rick could find little to disagree with in the Cardinal's homily.

The Eucharist began. At first Rick refused to move as Caterina tugged at his sleeve. Finally, heart in throat, he followed her to the altar. He watched in helpless desperation as Vella came over to him to offer a special welcome. When Rick looked up, he wondered if he had detected a look of suspicion on the cardinal's face. Not knowing what else to do, Rick merely nodded. Caterina whispered something to the cardinal, and he nodded with a sympathetic look. Rick's stomach churned.

When they were back in their pews, Rick whispered, "What did you tell him?"

Her breath warmed his skin as she whispered back. "I told him you had diarrhea."

He had to stifle a laugh. After what seemed an eternity, Vella finally said, "The Mass is over."

"Thank God!" Rick muttered.

After hiding out in the bathroom long enough to free himself of well-intentioned queries from Vella, Rick cautiously emerged and began his pilgrimage to the various altars. He kept a close watch for Vella, but apparently he had left. This time the other priests paid little attention to Rick. His tour soon brought him to the first of the locked doors. Looking around to make sure he wasn't being observed, he slipped a key into the lock opening. It didn't work, but the second key brought a satisfying clack. The room proved to be a storage area, with bins of candles, bags of communion wafers and bottles of wine on racks along the walls.

The second door was more difficult to open. The first key fit into the slot but refused to move. The second would have pushed through to the other side and he found himself cursing. Damn it all, Stef.

He heard a sound and turned to find an old woman watching him. Then she started toward him with upstretched hands. Withered lips mumbled something in Maltese. He shook his head and turned his back on her. Her shuffling steps got quicker and her mumbling louder. He rattled the key into the slot. To his relief the key caught and turned. Without a backward glance, he opened the door and hurried through.

Into a stinking pit.

Quickly retrieving the flashlight from his pocket he covered his face with his sleeve and followed the tiny tunnel of light through the darkness. He was in a hallway with another door beyond. A tall wastebasket stood along one of the walls filled with paper bags and plastic fast food containers. Not only was there a McDonald's on Malta, there was a Burger King, too. A bare army cot stood against the opposite wall.

After taking another breath through the sleeve, he continued forward. The beam rested on the handle of another door. As he opened it the sour odor turned into an overwhelming stench of urine, sweat and offal that made his eyes burn. Even so he recognized it immediately. "Stef?" he coughed.

His own voice was his only answer. The flashlight beam danced over bare stones and finally came to rest on a narrow crib that may have been made for a child. If possible, the stench seemed to get worse as he approached it. A flash of red inside the crib caught his eye. Stef's bandana. As he picked it up he got a distinct feeling that what had begun as a search for his brother had become a genuine quest. He was a catalyst for something even more important than saving Stef's life. They had both been swept into a game that had to be played to its end.

Wiping his eyes with his hands, Rick resumed his search. A double door awaited at the far wall, held in place by a swinging latch. Before brilliant sunlight blinded him he saw enough to realize he was standing in the alleyway they had found the night before.

He went back inside, resolved to continue the search until he found what fate had meant for him to discover. The trashcan was the place to start.

Leaving the storeroom, the air seemed easier to breathe. Amid the sandwich wrappers he discovered an empty plastic prescription bottle at the bottom of the bin. The name on the prescription was Pawlu Naxxar.

Rick's mouth pulled into a vindictive smile. I've got you now, you bastard.

CHAPTER 16

▼

Tuesday
12:34 PM
Floriana

Red and white banners spanned St. Anne Street, buckling and flapping in the light north wind. On Sunday, floats and uniformed men playing instruments would parade through Valletta by way of the breach in the north wall where goods from the custom area entered the city. A baby-faced Marine corporal came to attention when he saw Rick. Together they walked to the elevator.

Carpenter seemed surprised to see him. "Good morning," he said. "What can I do for you?"

"I found out the name of one of the men who's holding Stef." He took out the medicine bottle and showed it to the agent. "I want his address."

Carpenter nodded. "I can help you with that." He turned the bottle in his fingers. "Novasc 5 milligrams. It's blood pressure medicine. I take it myself. Let's see if we can find him in the phone directory."

He sat down at his computer terminal and typed in the name. A line of text appeared on the screen. "Naxxar lives in Hamrun. Should I have Margie call him?"

"You're not going to call him from here, are you? What if he has caller ID?"

The agent grinned unpleasantly. "If he does it will show the number from the pharmacy. We can make it look like the call came from any telephone in the world."

He pressed the intercom button. "Margie, make a call to Pawlu Nash-shar." He spelled it for her. "The number you're calling from is 9936285. Say that you're with the Gatt Pharmacy in Valletta and tell him his prescription is ready.

Do you have all that?" He paused. "Good. We'll listen in. If he asks any questions, put him on hold and we'll figure out what to say."

Carpenter pushed the loudspeaker button. The telephone rang several times before Margie hung up. "We'll try again later," the agent said. "I'll send someone to keep an eye on where he lives, too."

"Thanks," Rick said.

"Your tip about the Da-iz-ref was important. Two weeks ago a load of missile guidance components was hijacked on the way to Houston. It had all the earmarks of a coordinated terrorist act and the Homeland Security people put the country on orange alert."

"I must have been working in the fields and missed that. Two weeks would be enough time for the components to get here. My driver and I inspected the boat. It didn't look as if it had been unloaded. It lay too deep in the water."

"We're keeping our eyes on it," Carpenter said. "I've got a bonus for you. The weapon that killed Mario Agius is a sixteen-gauge made in the Czech Republic."

"Any significance to that?"

"It probably means it doesn't belong to a local. The police may be able to tell you if it's registered."

Once again, Carpenter's brusqueness puzzled Rick. "Great. Now if you would give me Naxxar's address, I'll let you get back to work."

1:19 PM

A five-minute drive brought them to their destination. "Hamrun's not one of our beauty spots," Caterina said, "but it's close enough to the University that many students live in apartments above the businesses."

"Where are we going?"

"To the old railway station. The boy scouts use part of it and the rest is a dairy." She parked next to an old building with three windows overlooking the thoroughfare.

"Where does Naxxar live?" Rick asked.

She pointed to one of the older buildings across the street. A wooden stairway led to the second floor. "It's a milliner's shop. He must live upstairs."

"Stef may be there. Why don't you go up and knock on his door? If Naxxar answers you can tell him you're looking for the apartment that's for rent."

"What will you do if he comes to the door?"

"I'll be up the stairs before you can blink an eye," Rick said grimly. "Just don't let him get past you."

With a dubious look, Caterina agreed. He watched her disappear from sight. When he heard a knock he tensed, ready to fly up the stairs. Seconds passed in silence; then he heard a second knock. After another short pause, Caterina came back down the stairs.

"Maybe we'll have better luck later," Rick said. "Next stop is the University."

2:00 PM

Building 218 was part of the Divinity School and one of the older structures on campus. From a distance it looked more like a cottage than an academic structure. Up close it resembled a monastery. Three large Mediterranean pines and a fence of white oleander surrounded it. The curator, who was dressed in a white cassock, had them sign a register. Rick paged back and found Stef's name.

They were on the right track.

"I see you don't have a briefcase with you. That's good. We don't allow them in the archives." The man's voice had a light tremor, like the beginning stages of Parkinson's Disease.

"What papers do you have on the Cornacchias?" Rick asked.

"All the papers from the family going back to Bartolomeo. The only ones missing are Alessandro's books of poetry and the rare books that are still in the estate library. Agatha Cornacchia donated all the others more than forty years ago."

"That was generous of her. Do you know why she did it?"

"The curator who was here before me said she told him she wanted to rid the family of its plague. He actually thought the papers were infected somehow and he didn't like to be around them."

Rick laughed.

"Where do you want to start?" the curator asked.

"The last papers you have for Alessandro Cornacchia, especially 1942."

After the man left Caterina asked, "What are we looking for?"

"Anything that will give us a clue to where Alessandro hid the Shield of God."

"If he left any clues, someone would have discovered the Shield a long time ago."

"Not necessarily. They may not have known what to do with the information."

The curator reappeared carrying a black binder and two pairs of white cotton gloves. Handing a pair to each of them he said, "Wear these."

Inside the binder was a large manila envelope with a small sheath of papers. He shook his head in disappointment. Besides announcements for *l'Ankara* and personal memos there was little else to be found.

"Wasted trip," he said. He was about to suggest they leave when the outside door opened. Looking up he felt a jolt so strong that he had to force himself to act naturally.

The Arab from the *Fahal* stood at the desk!

Caterina recognized him, too. The man wore a short-sleeved shirt and jeans and carried a leather briefcase.

"I'm sorry," the curator said. "You can't take your briefcase into the reading area."

"What would you have me do with it? I have some important papers with me." The English was quite good, Rick noticed.

"I have a safe under the counter. I'll put it away for you."

The Arab shrugged. "Let me get my notepad," he said. Undoing the leather straps, he opened the briefcase and took out a yellow legal pad.

The curator gestured at the registry and Rick's heart jumped to his throat. Would "Richard Olsen" mean anything to him? If he were privy to Stef's kidnapping, it might. And he might well recognize Caterina's name, too.

As they gripped each other's hands in fear, the Arab smoothly signed the register and sat down at the table next to them.

Rick's heart thumped. He nervously fingered Carpenter's card. How could he leave the building to contact him?

"What would you like to see?" the curator asked the Arab,

"Bartolomeo Cornacchia's papers. You can start with the earliest ones, please. I intend to read them all."

Rick relaxed. That could take days. He tensed again when the curator pointed at him. "The Cornacchia family is popular today. This gentleman asked about Alessandro."

Heart in throat, Rick turned to nod at the Arab. A faint, inscrutable smile crossed the man's face and he nodded back. Trying not to swallow visibly, Rick turned back to the pile of papers and pretended to read.

Caterina moved her chair closer to Rick and they watched the Arab out of the corners of their eyes until the archivist returned. Then the Arab started to read and never looked in Rick's direction.

Rick handed Carpenter's card to Caterina and took out his phone from his pocket. Covering his hand with hers she took it from him. As she attempted to slide it into her open purse it fell to the floor. Shuddering, Rick looked for a reaction. He didn't see one. The man sat placidly reading a document.

After sweating out another ten minutes, Caterina got up. In a low voice she said, "I have to get something from the car, <u>mahbub</u>. I'll be right back."

Ten seconds after she left, the Arab got to his feet. Without a word or even a look in Rick's direction, he opened the door and stepped out. Panic-stricken, Rick rushed out of the building.

Neither was in sight.

Oh my god, no. Hear pounding, he headed for the most likely hiding place. A quick look behind the oleander bush told him no one was there.

Feeling sicker by the second, he returned to the sidewalk and tried to map out other hiding places. Besides the oleander, the pine trees were the closest cover. He rushed toward them. No shot, and no sound of running feet.

Heart racing, he muttered a silent prayer as he strode to where they had parked. The sight of the empty car brought a low wail. "Nooo."

Reeling, he turned back toward the archive building and took off at full speed. A few steps away from the door he saw Caterina walking toward him. Overcome, he took her in his arms. "I've been out of mind worrying about you. Where did you go?"

She made no effort to push him away. "I stepped into the building next door. What's the matter?"

"The Arab left seconds after you did. When I couldn't see either of you I was sure he had grabbed you."

Her arms lightly embraced him. "Your heart is racing. You were really worried about me, weren't you?"

He wiped his eyes. "I thought I already told you once or twice that I'm crazy about you. Did you call Carpenter?"

She gently touched his cheek. "Yes. He's on his way."

CHAPTER 17

▼

Tuesday
2:50 PM
The University of Malta, Msida

Rick was sitting on a pylon at the edge of the faculty parking lot when a black Mercedes pulled up next to him. The rear window rolled down. "Get inside," Carpenter said.

Rick did. "You're about ten minutes too late," he said. "Our man took off."

Carpenter cursed. In an accusing voice he asked, "Did you do something to spook him?"

"We may have. Caterina accidentally dropped my cell phone when I tried to hand it to her. A normal person probably wouldn't have noticed, but a terrorist might. Twenty seconds after she went to call you he got up and left, too. He hasn't come back since."

"Then he won't be back," Carpenter said, slamming his fist into the car seat. "We had the bastard and lost him."

"His briefcase is still in the archives safe," Rick said.

"Holy shit!" Carpenter shouted. He grabbed his cell phone and hurried out of the car.

The driver, who was fortyish with flecks of gray in coal-black hair and swarthy features asked, "Do you have any idea what brought the Arab here?"

"He said he wanted to look at Bartolomeo Cornacchia's papers."

Carpenter returned. "Are you sure his briefcase is still in the building?" he asked.

"It has to be," Rick replied. "The curator locked it in a cabinet underneath the front counter."

Carpenter looked at the driver. "Probably a light metal door with a combination lock. The dials are usually stiff. It shouldn't be any problem getting in if we can keep the curator busy for a few minutes."

"I think I can do that," Rick volunteered. "I'll ask for some papers he might have trouble finding. Are you coming in with me?"

"No," Carpenter said. "I'll wait until he's out of the room."

"What if our man comes back for it while you're at work?"

"Then we may have to shoot our way out," Carpenter said, contemptuously. It sounded like a line from a '50s western.

"I'll get Caterina," Rick said. He entered the building and whispered into her ear. She got up and left.

Just then the curator reappeared. "Anything else I can get for you?"

"Yes. I would like to see the papers of Mandolfo Cornacchia," Rick said, remembering the name from the Balzan book. "He was Duke sometime in the Eighteenth Century."

"I'll see what I can find. Incidentally, do you know what happened to the other man who was here?"

"No. He just stepped out a few minutes ago. Maybe he went to get something to eat. I'm sure he'll be back before long."

"I'm glad he didn't try to leave with any documents. The noise from the alarm is dreadful. If he returns, tell him I'll be right back."

"I will," Rick said. He waited until the curator disappeared before opening the door for Carpenter. "Maybe we should reconsider," Rick said. "The curator says there's an alarm."

"I'm shaking," the man said. Rick gritted his teeth.

Finding the door locked, the agent nimbly climbed through the service window and disappeared. As the seconds ticked by, Rick's mouth got dry. A minute later he was pacing. "Any luck?" he asked in a stage whisper.

"I should be done in another minute or two," Carpenter replied.

The sound of a door opening somewhere in the bowels of the building sent Rick's heart to his throat. "Hurry up!" he said through clinched teeth.

He shivered as he heard footsteps approaching. Just when he was sure the curator would catch Carpenter in the act, the agent appeared with the Arab's briefcase in hand. "Here it is. I'll call you when we're done."

Rick sighed in relief then tensed again as Carpenter opened the door. No alarm sounded. Would the Arab return before the agent got back?

The curator reappeared seconds later with a large black three-ring binder. "This is all I was able to find," he said. "There's only a few letters inside."

Rick thanked him. When he shook the binder, four wads of paper fell out. The largest was on heavy paper, well-yellowed with age, with a broken red wax seal. It was a letter from Mandolfo's father written in Italian with a florid hand. Rick was amazed by the content and touched by its poignancy.

"21st February 1748, *Borgiswed*, Mdina, Malta.

My Dearest Mandolfo, Writing this letter to you is extremely difficult, but telling you in spoken words would be impossible. I am about to turn over a great responsibility to you and I know you will not take it lightly. You have known the Shield of God since the first time you reached out your hand to touch it while I held you in my arms. The fire of the gold and the cold twinkle of the jewels undoubtedly fascinated you as much as it did me when I was your age. Legend has it that it was fashioned from gold brought back by the Knights of St. John from the Holy Land. But the Shield is much more than a decoration and object of beauty. It is a touchstone, a talisman of such great power that it may be sufficient to save or destroy the world. The key to how to use it is hidden somewhere in that myriad of intriguing designs on the basin.

"I now know that finding this key cannot be accomplished by ordinary means. Prayer alone certainly is not sufficient. Were it so, the answer would have been discovered centuries ago. It may be that God's help isn't what is needed to solve its mystery. Seven generations have now passed since the fierce warriors adorning The Shield first took up their guard. Despite many lifetimes of work, the labyrinth remains uncharted, the puzzle unsolved. I can no longer continue the battle myself. My will and health fail me. The Shield and the quest now belong to you, my son. Use whatever means available to you in your search. If someone offers sorcery and the Black Arts as a means to its solution, do not be in haste to refuse. Surely magick was used to construct the Shield and magick may be necessary to tame it. If it be God's will, I know you will succeed. With my blessings and unbounded affection, Your Father, Donato."

Once again Rick felt that an invisible hand was guiding him. How else could he explain how a fool's errand intended to buy time would lead to such an important find? He hastily copied the entire note as he awaited Carpenter's call.

Ten minutes passed and he began to worry. As the seconds ticked by he cringed at every sound. He nearly passed out when the door opened and the Arab stepped in.

"I had to leave for a while," the man said. "Unfortunately I won't be able to stay any longer today. May I have my briefcase?"

"Of course," the curator said, disappearing from sight as he squatted. He reappeared, ashen-faced. "It's not here. I don't understand. It was locked."

The Arab threw a lethal glare in Rick's direction. "I'm afraid I do."

The curator picked up a phone receiver. "I'll call the police."

Before he could, the Arab left the building. While the curator was talking on the phone, Rick looked at the name on the registry. Abdullah Hassan. At last the foe had a name, even though probably made up.

"The police are coming. They want to speak to you and your lady friend."

*   *   *   *

Stef awoke. He had been dreaming that he was in a ristorante *in Florence with a huge plate of spaghetti and a whole bottle of wine in front of him. He had eaten too much and his stomach hurt. It still did, but not from overeating. He was starving.*

So was his mind. It needed nourishment, not the gruel it had been given the last few days. Instead of intellectual stimulation, it had fed on the few facts it had been able to garner.

Pawlu, who spent the most time with him, was clearly the boss. Kareem, the Arab, dropped in only on occasion and had little to say, although Stef got the impression that he was a student or young professional. He also spoke with a slight stammer.

What else did he remember? Stef tugged at his bonds. Oh yes, he had learned that Pawlu now knew how to tie a secure knot.

But most of all he remembered that he was no longer angry with Pawlu. Why was that? He had no idea but at least it was something to think about.

*   *   *   *

4:20 PM

The interview with the police was brief. Caterina and Rick testified that they didn't take the briefcase and hadn't seen anyone else do it. Each said that they had left for a short while to take a bathroom break in the next building and that was undoubtedly when the briefcase was stolen. The officer listened and nodded, undoubtedly puzzled about why the victim left without filing a complaint. Finally he said, "I'll need to know where to reach you."

"We're at the San Roque," Rick replied.

They arrived at the Bellestrado at twenty past five. The pub was crowded. Josefina was behind the bar talking to Manny O'Toole and Rick joined them. "I've been talking to your future mother-in-law," O'Toole said. "She speaks very highly of you. How's the groom-to-be?"

"Couldn't be better," Rick replied. "How are things at Black Dolphin?"

"Not good. The boss has been in a pissy mood and I haven't been able to get much work done. He's put the whole receiving area off-limits."

Rick's pulse nudged up a notch. "Have you ever seen any of the cargo?"

"No. He keeps everything under tarps. They gave me dirty looks when I first came to work so I make sure I never watch them move things around."

"Do you remember what they were moving those first days?"

"No, and I really shouldn't be talking about it, even though you're an okay guy."

"I understand," Rick replied. He noticed O'Toole's red and black picture identification badge. O'Toole flushed and hastily took it off. "Man, am I getting careless," he said, sliding the badge into his shirt pocket. "I'm not supposed to wear this in public."

Rick spoke to Caterina in a low voice. "See if you can take over for Josefina for half an hour or so."

O'Toole smiled and stretched out a welcoming hand when Caterina passed him on her way behind the bar. She smiled at him, then whispered something to Josefina.

"One of the guests needs something," Josefina said. "I'll be back in a little while. Make sure everyone gets enough to drink."

"We will," Rick said, slapping O'Toole amiably on the back. "Give this man another beer. I'm buying."

That brought a big grin from O'Toole. Rick made a circular gesture with his finger. Caterina set a foaming glass on the counter.

In the next hour, several more made their appearance filled and returned, empty. After about the fifth beer, O'Toole seemed to forget that Caterina was supposed to be engaged to Rick. She smiled and dodged his fingers when necessary while he babbled nonstop about the New Jersey Devils hockey team and the New York Jets. "I know you don't care," he told her in a slightly slurred voice, "but this year the Jets're gonna win the Super Bowl."

"You betcha," said Rick. As O'Toole blew foam off his seventh beer, Rick shook his head in wonder. How much more can this guy take? The Irishman stood. Grabbing the edge of the bar to keep his balance he asked, "Where's the pisser?"

"I'll take you there," Rick said.

They made their way to the bathroom with Rick helping him balance. A short time later O'Toole bumped twice and Rick opened the door for him. The Irishman had wet the bathroom floor.

With an apology to Josefina, Rick helped him back to the bar. O'Toole unsteadily climbed back on the stool, lay his head on his arms, and promptly fell asleep.

Rick waited for a minute. "Can you get his badge?" he asked Caterina.

"He's lying on it," she said.

Rick forced his hand in between O'Toole's chest and the bar and pushed his fingers forward. He patiently worked the badge out of O'Toole's shirt pocket. "Got it," he said. By the time he had pulled it free his fingers were numb. "Does Josefina have a scanner?"

"No, but she has a black and white copy machine."

"Darn. Well, it'll have to do," Rick said. "Be sure to copy both sides."

He kept a watchful eye on O'Toole, ready to foist another beer on him if he came to. But the man's heavy breathing continued to echo off the top of the wooden bar. He was still sound asleep when Caterina returned with the badge and photocopies. "Nice work," Rick said. O'Toole snored on as Rick slipped the badge under his chest.

Josefina returned ten minutes later. Pointing at O'Toole, she asked in a disgusted voice, "What's this?"

"A friend," Rick said. "Give him anything he wants except more to drink."

The Libyan archaeology student suddenly appeared and set an empty coffee cup on the bar.

"You better get along," Josefina said to Rick in an irritated voice. "Caterina wants you to go with her to the *Ta Karuna* for dinner even though she knew I had planned to make a big meal for us. Just don't buy any wine there. They charge way too much."

7:15 PM

The waterfront restaurant was clean but sparely decorated, with small glass vases of pink flowers sitting on blue and white oilcloth tablecloths. Rick savored the smells coming from the kitchen.

"So what's this lampuki pie that's supposed to be so good?" Rick asked.

"I can't explain it. Trust me, you'll like it." As she spoke she made brief eye contact, and then broke it to pick up her coffee cup. Rick was certain that their afternoon adventure had made a deep impression on her.

"I feel a little bit guilty about Manny," Rick said. "I hope we didn't do him any permanent damage."

"I'm sure he's fine. By the way, he told me that if I ever got tired of you, he would be happy to take your place."

"That's exciting," Rick said, reaching for her hand. "It implies I have a place to begin with."

She quickly put her hands in her lap. "Hold on, *habib*. He thinks we're engaged. I'm just telling you what he said."

She's calling me friend? Shit. "He might not be so bad, you know. You like muscles and he certainly has them."

"The ones between the ears don't count. I need some intelligent conversation once in a while."

"Speaking of which, what do you and Andrew talk about?" Rick asked.

She drew back in surprise. "The economy, Malta's future in the world. He's interested in theater and philosophy."

Rick thought that sounded like something Andrew himself might say to describe the interests of a business associate. "Does he ever let you pick the topic?"

"Of course," she replied.

When she didn't say more, Rick wondered why. Finally he asked, "What do you do on dates?"

"He takes me to company parties or we go to the movies. We both like ethnic food. Did you know we actually have a Ukrainian restaurant in Valletta?"

"With dancing Cossacks and balalaikas?"

She laughed. "No. But I think that's Russian, anyway."

"Do you have a picture of Prince Charming with you?"

"Yes. But I'm not going to show it to you. You'll tear it up."

"I promise I won't," he said.

She still hesitated before showing it to him.

A man lounged in a canvas-backed chair with Caterina in a bikini standing behind him. Rick wondered what she saw in him. Besides his money and great future he didn't seem any different from any other young Maltese men Rick had seen. It pleased Rick to see that his hair was thinning above the temples. Dark sunglasses obscured his eyes. Though Caterina smiled widely, Andrew looked only mildly bemused. He handed the picture back to her. "Where did you meet?"

"At a night club a few blocks away from here. I love to dance."

Rick didn't, but decided he wouldn't mind taking lessons from her. "Did you tell him you have a new suitor?"

"Absolutely not," she said quickly. "You don't have anything to do with him and he doesn't have anything to do with you."

Even though he had no idea what that meant, he took it as reason to be hopeful. "Do you realize you've stopped telling me to drop dead every time I try to get romantic?" he asked, reaching for her hand.

"You've worn me down. And if you try to touch me again, I'll break my chair over your head." The tone suggested that she meant it.

The waiter laid two steaming plates before them. Rick could detect a faint odor of fish in what looked like a potpie. "Try it," said Caterina, "and tell me what you think."

Cutting through the crust, he found strips of white meat amid carrots, potatoes, peas and broccoli in a white sauce. He scooped out a bit of the fish and vegetables, blew vigorously on it, then tasted. The meat was flaky and had a delicate, non-fishy, flavor. "Mmm. Very good."

"It's only available in the fall and we all wait for it. Lampuki is a Mediterranean variety of mahi-mahi."

They ate in silence. Once he briefly caught her watching him, but she quickly looked away. They spent the rest of the meal trying to make conversation and avoid looking at each other without succeeding at either. But whenever she met his gaze, Rick caught sight of Andrew's diamond and the mood ended with a crash. Soon his jealousy became poisonous.

"Why did you copy Manny's badge?" she asked.

"I may need to get into the shipyard or the construction site sometime," he snapped. "I just hope I can get the colors right. It would be easier if I had a color scan."

"You don't have to bite my head off," she retorted in an equally angry voice. "Josefina doesn't have a scanner. She doesn't need one."

"I'm not blaming her, I was just stating a fact."

Rick's wish for eye contact had suddenly been granted. Flashing eyes met flashing eyes.

After a short wordless truce, Caterina signaled for the waiter. He brought the check and set it on the table. As Rick reached for his wallet, she snatched the bill and handed it to the man along with two banknotes. "I'm treating," she said.

Darkness had fallen but Rick's anger could have lit the way back to the car. "You didn't have to pay, you know. I still have money."

"What makes you think this has anything to do with money? I asked you out to supper so I paid for it. I don't know what's so terrible about that."

"I don't like being patronized."

"Sorry. I didn't mean to prick your manhood."

It sounded to him as if she emphasized 'prick.' "Okay. If you're paying for the meal, at least let me buy you dessert. What do you want? Ice cream? Some cognac?"

"No thanks. Look. I don't know why you're so angry, but give it a rest. Please."

The pot boiled over. "Good idea. I'll walk back to the hotel. That will cool me off."

"Don't be an idiot," she said in a worried voice. "You know you can't be by yourself after what happened today. I buy you dinner and you act like I'm handing you your testicles in a box."

"Stop the car!" he shouted.

"Yes sir," she snapped, screeching to a halt. As he got out, she said, "Just stay on this road. The hotel's about three miles away from here. Don't expect me to come back to pick you up when you cool down."

He slammed the door shut and she took off with tires squealing.

Filthy bitch.

At the thought the extent of his foolishness hit him with the impact of a bucket of ice water to his face. *What the hell am I doing?*

His feet seemed leaden with shame as he started to walk in the direction of the hotel. He had only taken a few steps when his cell phone rang. Assuming it was Kevin, he answered quickly.

A familiar voice asked, "Did you enjoy your meal?"

"Very much," Rick said, feeling a chill of apprehension. "Who's this?"

"The one's who's looking after your brother, of course." Rick waited in silence. "You were at Mosta Dome. That wasn't a good idea. You know about curiosity and the cat. Take care, my friend. You have a long walk ahead of you."

Rick hung up and pushed the memory button for Caterina's number.

No answer.

After sliding the phone back into his pants pocket he cautiously looked around, trying to imagine where the call had come from. It had to be somewhere near. His heart picked up a beat. The first haven he saw was a large building across the street. He walked swiftly to the door.

A jolt of fear coursed through him when it didn't open. He felt another as a car stopped up the street from him and a man in a dark jacket got out and began to walk toward him. To his right, a corridor of cars parked bumper to bumper stretched off into the darkness. Somewhere down that street, a rock band was playing. Its bass beat thumped against his body. Should he seek refuge there? What would he do if his pursuers followed him in?

The man in the dark jacket slowed as he came closer. When he got within ten paces he unzipped the jacket and put his hand inside of it.

Rick bolted. *Even if the bastard has a gun, he won't be coming after me alone.*

Halfway back across the street toward the restaurant, he slowed to a walk, waiting to see if the man in the jacket was pursuing him. He was and Rick put his body into gear. Someone stepped out from behind a car and reached out his hand.

Rick hit his attacker in the solar plexus.

The assailant, who was also wearing a dark jacket, crumpled with a sound like a dying man's last gasp. Pursuer number one broke into a run towards him. Rick headed for the restaurant and was ready to make a dash for it when he saw the third man loping towards him from the same direction. In the space of a single breath he considered his options. Across the street to his left was a dark waterfront with boats at moor. Moving right sent him down a street without lights and nowhere to run if a car approached him from either direction.

Rick decided to risk the waterfront.

Without looking, he dashed into the thoroughfare. A motorist swerved and honked loudly, barely missing him. Number one pursuer matched him move for move, running at an angle to cut him off. Rick refused to give way and they collided. The impact bowled the pursuer over. The man got up, cursing, and started after him once more.

It was a game of hare and hounds and Rick was the hare.

Heels kicking high behind him, Rick dashed headlong toward a well-lighted area some two or three blocks distant. His heel caught in a mooring rope and he stumbled just as he heard a gunshot fired from behind him. Bleeding at the knees and hands, he got up and started forward.

Another shot rang out and a jagged hole appeared in the sign near his shoulder.

With guts burning and lungs gasping for air, his strides became shorter. In desperation, the hare looked back over his shoulder for the hound. It was now less than ten yards behind him and closing fast. Terrified, Rick darted into the street. The hound stayed on his heels all the way, gaining a step on him in the process.

Desperate, Rick dodged back into the street. With a car approaching he slowed until he felt a hand on his back then dashed forward.

A step behind him, the pursuer lurched after him. A horn blared as the left bumper grazed Rick's leg. The impact sent him flying.

Hurtled to the ground, Rick's forehead and chin bounced off limestone.

Brakes screeched. Rubber scorched against stone. Then, in the eternity of a heartbeat, metal collided with flesh. Glass shattered and a horn wailed.

Fighting off dizziness, Rick slowly got to his feet.

The car had stopped, its front end badly dented and the horn blaring. Beneath the bumper, head and torso protruded from beneath twisted metal. The driver of the car, a woman, had gotten out of the car and now stood covering her mouth with her hand. Motorists who stopped in the middle of the street paid no attention to Rick as he limped to the other side of the street.

Far away, a flashing blue light approached. He lunged forward, ignoring the loud sobs that were turning into agonized screams behind him. Surely the other would-be assassins were either scared off, or joining the crowd forming around the stricken gunman. Out of breath, he slowed to a walk. As he did, a police car passed him on the way to the accident scene.

CHAPTER 18

▼

Tuesday, 9:26 PM
St Julians

Rick pressed onward without a look back until he could no longer hear the crowd at the accident scene. His knees and face hurt, but he still gimped forward at a quick pace. With each step the dull ache in his head that started when the car struck him intensified. Finally, winded, he found a secluded place between two buildings and called Caterina.

"Well hello," she said in a hostile tone. "I hope you weren't expecting me to give you a ride. I said I wasn't coming back for you."

"I sure hope I can change your mind," he wheezed. "And if it will make you happy, you win. Big time. We're going to have to find another place to stay tonight and probably from now on. Josefina may even have to close the hotel."

"Good heavens, what happened?"

"Cornacchia's men were ten feet away and waiting for me when I got out of the car. I have no idea how I got away. We're going to need a new car and a different room. Preferably as far away from the Bellestrado as we can get."

"Then we'll stay at my farm. Where are you?" Caterina asked.

"I'm on the same road where you dropped me off but maybe a mile closer to the Bellestrado from where I got out. The harbor makes an arc and there's a dock with a lot of sailboats across the street from where I'm standing."

"I know where you mean. Don't move. I'll be there as soon as I can."

"Good. Just pull up and stop." As he said it he winced at a twinge of pain in his chin. "I'll be looking for you."

Twenty minutes later, Caterina arrived. She stared at him wide-eyed. "My God! What happened?"

"I had a run-in with a Mazda," he said, smiling weakly. "The guy who was chasing me didn't get off so easily. Where are we going?"

"To the hospital, of course. You're seriously injured."

"Then let's change automobiles first. We can tell the rental agency we need a bigger car."

"I better go in by myself. You look like Banquo's Ghost."

The trip to Msida took less than ten minutes. As he waited for Caterina to get a rental car, his left knee began to throb. He didn't mind it much because his headache was quickly giving way to a pleasant mind fog.

Soon, a dark Mitsubishi Lancer stopped by him. When he opened the passenger door to get in Caterina rushed around to help him. He was happy to let her. "I'm really feeling much better," he said. "Would you like to stop for a cognac somewhere?"

"You're delirious," she said. "We're going to St. Luke's Hospital."

"Where's that?"

"Just up a little ways farther down the road. It's on an island."

"Would you like to hear a poem?" he asked.

"Now?" she asked.

"Yes," he said. It's about you. Listen." He closed his eyes and began.

> "Thy black hair spread across thy cheeks, the roses
> O Liege, the garden's basil quite resembles.
> Beside thy lip oped wide its mouth, the rosebud;
> For shame it blushed, it blood outright resembles.
> Thy mouth, a casket fair of pearls and rubies,
> Thy teeth, pearls, thy lip coral bright resembles.
> Their diver I, each morning and each even."

"That's beautiful," Caterina said. "Did you write it?"

"No. It's by Suleiman the Magnificent. I ran across it on the Web."

"And you think that sounds like me?" she asked. "Thank you, but you're out of your head."

"Only since I met you," he said.

Conversation ended, but as they drove Caterina spent as much time looking at him as she did the road. Finally, in a quivering voice she asked, "How do you feel?"

"A little light-headed, but fine otherwise."

"I feel terrible," she said, her lip starting to tremble.

"Don't," he said, patting her knee, "It's my fault entirely. I was the one who let the green-eyed monster get out of hand."

She still looked unhappy. "I know. Until this afternoon, I didn't realize how much you cared for me, and after I found out, I felt helpless." She gave him an imploring look. "Do you have any idea what I'm trying to say?"

"Of course, but you should be used to men falling at your feet by now."

"Well, I'm not." She bit her lip, as if trying to decide whether to say more. "There's something else you should know. Remember how angry I got when you played that Leontyne Price CD?"

"How could I forget?"

"I was furious with you. And Josefina, too. I was sure you just bought the CD to impress me."

"Even if I did, I still can't imagine why you were so angry."

She flushed. "You don't know very much about women, do you? Didn't you ever see 'Groundhog Day?'"

"The movie with Bill Murray? I saw it on television."

"Don't you remember how he kept saying and doing things that he knew would impress the Andie MacDowell character and how mad she got when she finally figured out what he was up to?"

"Now that you mention it, I do? So what?"

"Ahh," she said, beating on the steering wheel in frustration. "How can you be so dense? He was trying to get her to love him by pretending to be someone he really wasn't, and she caught on to what he was up to. Do you understand now?"

The brain fog was on the creep again and Rick didn't fight it. Once in a while cloud-cuckoo land wasn't such a bad place. "Of course," he said.

"No, you don't," she said with a sigh. "I suppose I can't blame you for not being able to think straight under the circumstances. I haven't quite figured you out yet. But whatever you are, you're the real thing and I'm happy for it."

"So am I," he said.

St. Luke's Hospital was something of an anomaly. Since most of the buildings on the island were either very old or very new, one 70 years of age was an oddity. The painful process of binding up wounds and getting X-rays of his arms, legs, and skull took less than an hour. But the EEG and CT scans the doctor insisted on meant a much longer stay.

Finally, at 1:00 a.m., the x-ray results came back. Negative. The doctor on duty gave him a shot of Demerol and released him. He was floating by the time they got to the car and Caterina had to guide him in.

"We're going to my farm for tonight," said Caterina. "My horses need me. I've been away from them so long they won't even recognize me any more, the poor babies."

"Who takes care of them when you're gone?"

"A neighbor. I give her ten pounds a week but she would do it for nothing."

"Can I sleep in the same bed with you?"

"Absolutely not!" she said firmly. "We'll each have a bedroom."

"What if I need a glass of water during the night?"

"You'll just have to call me and I'll get it for you."

"I didn't know you had a farm," Rick said, dreamily. "I thought you lived at the Bellestrado."

"I might as well for all the time I spend there. I haven't been home for three days. I live in Qormi. It isn't very far from here."

As they drove, he noticed a building with an enormous moon painted on its side, and the words il Qamar Pub. Nice moon, he thought. Big. As they moved on, something stirred in the recesses of his mind, but the painkiller wouldn't allow him to process the information. He dozed off until Caterina shook him. "Here we are," she said gently.

She opened the passenger door and took his arm to help support him as they walked. He realized that they were in a driveway between two walls that led to a two-story building. The air was fresh, crickets chirped, and his nose identified the presence of horses.

She stopped at a gate and unlocked it. "Hold on to me," she said. "We have to climb some stairs. Hang on to the railing with your other hand. If you feel dizzy, tell me. Do you understand?"

"Yes," he said, not knowing if he did.

He clung tightly to the railing and Caterina's arm until they came to a patio where several flowerpots with a variety of cacti and flowering plants stood outlined against the moon. She stopped in front of a door and unlocked it. "This is the second floor," she said. "The bathroom is this way. I'll help you wash up."

He lurched unsteadily as she led him to the bathroom and sat him on the commode. Without a word she helped him strip down to his shorts. Then, using her left hand to prop him up, she used the other to wash his face.

"Are you as nice to everybody as you are to me?" he asked, having difficulty getting the words out with a washcloth over his mouth.

"Everybody," she said. "But I will have to say that you require more looking after than most. Usually they only need a meal or a place to stay." She slowly ran the washcloth over his arms and then his chest. When she was done she gently wiped him with a towel. Laying the towel down she took a sealed toothbrush box from the cabinet and opened it. She squeezed toothpaste on it and handed it to him. "Brush your teeth."

"Yes, Mommy." After he made a few desultory swipes at his molars, she helped him to the bedroom. It smelled of lemons and roses. Winnie-the-Pooh, sitting next to a laptop computer, eyed him suspiciously from the bed. Caterina moved aside the toy and computer and pulled the covers back.

"This is where I used to sleep when I was little," she said. He sat and she gently lifted his injured leg for him. When he was stretched out she pulled the sheet over him.

"Go to sleep," she said. "I have to tend to my other babies. They need an extra ration of sugar cubes and apples for being neglected for so long."

"Can I have a good night kiss?"

"Not tonight," she said.

"Okay," he said. "Night night." With that he collapsed on the pillow.

6:02 AM

He awoke in the morning, sore but with a clear head and the answer to why the moon he had seen on the side of the pub looked so familiar. Pulling the covers aside he sprang to his feet. "My God," he shouted, "That's where it is."

He made a dash for the bathroom. The door to Caterina's room was open. She sat up and stretched, looking delectable in a pink fluffy robe. "That's where what is?" she asked with a yawn.

"The drawing. I know where Stef hid the drawing!"

Rick flashed his key at the hotel clerk as he passed the front desk. Heart racing he took the stairs two at a time.

When he reached the landing, he moved straight to the door he wanted and eagerly turned the knob. It was locked. Then he heard water splashing. Was Queen Mab taking a bath? She wouldn't want to get her wings wet.

Amused by the thought, he took several steps back to wait. Minutes later the door opened and an older sprite with orange-blonde hair emerged in mules and robe. She colored and scurried past him without a word. Breathing a sigh of relief, he stepped inside and locked the door behind him.

And there she was. The queen, just as he had left her.

He sucked in a deep breath and took a step toward her. On second look, this Queen seemed a bit more benign than she should, considering what she did to unsuspecting lovers. Still, it wasn't a bad match. Stef liked Shakespeare and Rick could see how his brother could draw the comparison. Would the lovers in the poster be so intent on watching the moon if they knew they were themselves being watched? As he studied, he realized why the moon on the pub had brought such a strong memory. They were identical. The signature, Morgan, brought back another association. Queen Mab also was known as Morgan La Fay.

Heart pounding, he stepped forward and removed the frame from its nail in the wall. Carefully turning it over he laid it flat on the toilet seat. The poster was held in place by single nails top and bottom. He pried them out with a ten-cent piece.

The sight of a plastic bag lying on the reverse surface of the poster brought a gasp. There it was. The skin of a slaughtered lamb. How appropriate that seemed now.

Very carefully he set the frame on the sink and removed the parchment from its bag. He held the skin to the light and inspected the slightly uneven pen-strokes. There were holes at the top of the skin. Either something had been attached to it, or Cellini had hung it up so he could see it when he was working.

Benvenuto Cellini was anything but a saint, but his drawing was an object of reverence. Rick carefully rolled it up and set in on the sink before he reassembled the picture frame. Laying the back in place, he pushed the nails into their holes. Finished, Queen Mab took her customary place on the wall, her role as guardian completed. She had done the job well.

After straightening the picture, he gathered up the drawing and unlocked the door. As he left, he turned for a last look. "Take care," he said.

CHAPTER 19

▼

Wednesday 7:02 AM
Sliema

When she saw the rolled-up parchment, Caterina clapped her hands in excitement. "You found it!"

"In all its bloody glory, my sweet."

Without warning, she got out of her seat and kissed him on the mouth. It was a quick peck, and, like a butterfly on wing, she promptly flitted back behind the wheel. "In case you're wondering," she said, "that's a reward. From Stef."

His lips tingled. "You better tell my brother to stop doing that."

"Don't worry. It won't happen again. He knows how flustered you get."

"You have no idea how flustered I'd get if he actually did kiss me, and I'm no homophobe."

"Where do you want to go now?"

"Back to the Bellestrado. I want Josefina to see this, too." He paused. "You know I loved the kiss but you really shouldn't tease me like that. Having to deal with our situation is hard enough the way it is."

She looked him directly in the eye. "What makes you think I was teasing?"

The words tied his stomach in knots.

7:46 AM

A worried-looking Josefina unlocked the back door for them. Tears furrowed her rouge as she engulfed Rick in an embrace. "I heard what happened," she said. "And Caterina told me that you thought I should close the hotel. I can't do that."

"You probably won't need to," Rick said. "Just be a bit more watchful."

"I will," she said. Waddling into the galley she returned and laid a basket on the closest table.

"Take a look at this," Rick said, taking the drawing from the bag and laying it next to the bread. She took a step backward.

"It won't bite," he said. "Come here."

She blanched. Finally, at his insistent gestures, she took a step forward. "All right," she said, voice atremble.

"It's magnificent," Caterina said.

Josefina barely noticed. Instead of looking at the drawing, her brown eyes constantly darted from door to door as if making sure no one had picked a lock and was now sauntering in with gun in hand. Finally, she shivered and backed away. "I've seen enough."

With that, she left. Rick heard unsteady scratching as she locked them in.

Without a word Caterina moved close to his left shoulder and stood over him. He tried to ignore her but she bent forward to point at the drawing. "Why do you think it was called the Shield of God? It looks like a basin."

"That's what it is," he said, voice cracking. "The Knights of St. John Hospitalers were nurses, so it's appropriate, in an ironic way. It's roughly the same shape as a basin, but without handles. You would need both hands if you were using it for protection."

"What do you think the banners are for?" she asked, moving even closer.

"I was wondering the same thing myself. Especially the one with the runes."

She pulled out a chair and sat down next to him. Her body seemed to crackle with sensuality. "I've seen marks like that before but I can't remember where. I like the suits of armor." She pointed at a mark on the drawing. "Do you suppose the circular marks are supposed to be gems?"

"It wouldn't surprise me. Bartolomeo wouldn't have gone in for half measures with his soul at stake."

"What do you mean?"

"In order to be pardoned for practicing black magic he made a pact with the church that he would devote the rest of his life and his fortune to the service of Christ. Somehow I don't believe he did, though."

"I wish I could see the real basin," she said in a deep voice. "It must be breathtaking."

"Maybe you will. It's probably still buried where Alessandro put it, waiting to be dug up."

"How exciting," she said, her voice softer still. She slid over in her chair, moving closer to him until their thighs and shoulders touched. His heart pounded wildly. Emotionally their intimacy was entirely new territory for him. In a low voice he said, "Maybe I shouldn't be talking about this. You're not a spy, are you?"

She laughed deep in her throat. "Like Mata Hari?" Raising an eyebrow, she added, "What if I am?"

"Then you're supposed to go to bed with me to get more information," he said, barely able to get the words out.

"I am?" she whispered. Faces now inches apart, their eyes locked. "Are you sure about that?"

"Unh-huh," he said. She bent closer to him and he put his hand on her leg. Instead of moving it away, she bent closer still. As her face moved toward him he shut his eyes, shivering like a love-struck adolescent. Delicious anticipation ended with a jolt of electricity as their mouths met. Then he felt another, this one unpleasant, as his cell phone rang.

Caterina didn't move away but Rick quickly realized that the moment was over. Cursing, he pulled the phone out of his pocket. "Yeah," he said in an angry voice. "Who's this?"

"Hey, man," Kevin said. "Why so grouchy? It's after midnight here, so I'm the one with reason."

Rick cursed silently as Caterina removed his hand from her leg and backed away. Without a word, she got up and walked to the galley. "What are you doing up at this hour?" he asked.

"Having a ball," he said, sounding like a kid opening Christmas presents. "I've found a data base you can use to identify your Arab."

Rick sat up straighter. "Shoot."

"It's for the Principality of Luxembourg. It's a really crazy URL and I can't give it to you over the phone so I'll e-mail it to you. Just cut it and paste it in your browser. I'll send you the username and password to get in."

"Good work. You're forgiven, I guess."

"Forgiven? What were you doing when I called?"

"Nothing, unfortunately," Rick said, glancing up at Caterina. "You put a stop to things before they got started."

"Sorry."

"Forget it. I have some interesting information about the Shield. The legend in the Cornacchia family is that the Shield's a puzzle and solving it would unleash a power that was great enough to save or destroy the world."

"Way cool!" Kevin said.

"I knew you'd like that. You're the amateur physicist. What kind of power would that have been?"

"If the Shield was constructed in the Sixteenth Century, it could have been plasma."

"Huh?"

"You've heard of particles and waves. Plasma is the third state. It's like the Force in Star Wars. It's supposed to be everywhere."

"And people would have known about it in the Sixteenth Century?"

"Believe it or not, most scientists think the alchemists learned about it from the ancient Greeks, and the Greeks from the Chinese."

Kevin took a breath. "Actually, it's part of Stoic philosophy. According to the Greeks, every mind or soul is supposed to be a part of the whole called the *Noumena* that was shattered with the creation of the Universe. The Stoics believed that the whole Universe was in the process of rebuilding itself and would someday be complete."

"What's that got to do with plasma?" Rick asked.

"Plasma is the pure energy released when the *Noumena* exploded. It's neither a particle nor a wave and it's everywhere. Some people say Nicola Tesla tapped into it for his Death Ray."

"The electromagnetic pulse?" Rick said. "Child's play. Cops in England are using it to stop runaway cars."

"It's not the same thing. But speaking of the EMP, it was the Soviet threat our generals feared the most. Supposedly, once America had everything on computer, all the Russkis had to do was set off a thermonuclear airburst and the country would fall apart at the seams."

"Of course. And it's still a threat, even if it doesn't come directly from the Russians any more."

"That's right," Kevin said. "You remember Tunguska, don't you?"

"The place in Siberia where the meteorite came down?"

"Meteorite is the prevailing theory, but no one has ever found a trace of one at the site. They just call it that because they can't account for the crater any other way. An explosion equivalent to 10 to 15 megatons of TNT caused it. It was heard 600 miles away."

"And you're saying that was Tesla's work?"

"No one has been able to prove otherwise. And he was conducting an experiment with his magnifying transformer on the night it happened. The transformer concentrated a beam of energy into a thin beam so intense it wouldn't scatter and he bounced it off the ionosphere. After Tunguska he vowed he would never work on his invention again."

"I'm no expert, but I know that no ray could generate that much energy."

"That's what everyone says, but some scientists are saying it could have been a combination of plasma excitation in the ionosphere, and harmonics. You know what happens when soldiers cross a bridge. If they walk normally, there's no problem. But send them over in step and the harmonics created can cause the bridge to collapse. Reflecting the beam off the ionosphere intensified the energy on the rebound. The government has been doing the same thing for years. It's called the HAARP project."

"You need to go in for treatment," Rick said.

"Funny," Kevin said. "I never thought about it before but Malta is on one of Bucky Fuller's power grids. It's a crossroads for electromagnetic energy. Maybe Bartolomeo found a way to tap into the energy and wrote the formula on the Shield."

"Get real. Even if what you say about Tesla is true, no one would have had the equipment to make a death ray in the Sixteenth Century."

"Who knows what the alchemists came up with," Kevin said in an offended tone. "At the very least, they knew about electricity. You've heard the story about monks holding hands and touching a Bell jar. Anyone who controlled electricity at the time would have had the power of life and death in their hands."

"It may have been enough to impress Suleiman, but not our terrorist. There must be another answer."

"Then you got me, Bud. Sorry."

"Thanks for the help. Give Arthur an extra pet for me."

"I will. And I'll give him some of my whiskey when it arrives."

Rick hung up and looked for Caterina. Any hopes that he could pick up where he left off were dashed when he saw her pouring a cup of coffee. With a sigh, he returned to the table and rolled up the drawing. "I need to use Zija's computer," he said.

Kevin's e-mail appeared on the screen. Rick wrote down the username and password, then cut and pasted the URL, which was more than 30 characters long, into the browser. Caterina hung over his shoulder. Step by step he retraced his path through the screens until the all-too-familiar face finally appeared. An enticing button sat at the bottom of the screen. Heart pounding, he planted an anxious kiss on Caterina's nose and clicked.

She gasped. "That's him."

An enlarged picture and three-quarters of a page of text showed on the screen. After printing a copy, Rick learned forward to read the text. "Muhammed Bin-Said," he said. "He's a close friend of Osama Bin-Laden. Jeez. The son-of-a-bitch was the third highest ranking man on Khaliq Sheik Muhammed's VIP list."

"What's that?" Caterina asked.

"Muhammed was the one who got nailed in Pakistan with all the computers and cell phones." He read on. "That's interesting, Bin-Said has a doctorate in Islamic Studies from the University of Istanbul. He did his dissertation on Suleiman the Magnificent."

"Why is that important?"

"It could be a link to Bartolemeo and Cellini—and they're the only links we have to Lorenzo Cornacchia."

"I don't get it," Caterina said. "They all lived centuries ago."

"I know," Rick said, shutting down the computer. "It's time for me to have a heart-to-heart with Mr. Carpenter."

Rick dialed. Instead of a ring he got a recorded message saying that the number wasn't in service. "No go. Take me to the Embassy."

10:33 AM

Several guards had been added to the security force. When Rick approached the barrier, one of the newcomers came to meet him. "I've come to see Bob Carpenter," he said. "It's important."

"The embassy is closed," the guard, a Marine PFC, said. The young man couldn't have been more than nineteen and looked as if his uniform had been shrink-wrapped around his sinewy body. His icy look made Rick shudder.

"Is Sergeant White around?" Rick asked.

The PFC gestured and the sergeant appeared.

"I have to see Carpenter," Rick said.

"Sorry but I can't let you in. You shouldn't have come here. It may be dangerous for you."

"I'm sure the Arab has already connected me to US Intelligence. There's no reason for Bob to keep me away."

Under his breath the Sergeant said, "Leave quickly. Mr. Carpenter will contact you."

As he said it the PFC raised his rifle. The report of hand slapping the stock was startling. And effective. Rick beat a hasty retreat and stepped back into the car.

"Carpenter is covering his tracks," Rick said in a low voice. "We're on our own."

"Then we have to contact Inspector Micallef," said Caterina. "He'll see that the information gets to the Maltese government."

"I don't think telling Micallef is a good idea," Rick said. He told her about the rings that Micallef and the librarian wore.

She shook her head in disbelief. "You must be mistaken. I can't believe he would be involved with Cornacchia."

"I don't want to take the chance. We'll contact your government, but there are a few more things I want to do on my own first. Do you still have the photocopy of O'Toole's badge with you?"

"It's in my purse."

"Good. Do you know anyone who would make a badge for us without asking too many questions?"

"Hannibal Galea. He's in Sliema on Pius the V Street."

"I just hope we can get the color right."

"Don't worry," she said. "I know exactly what color it is. Grenadine. We use it in drinks."

"Good. I'll bring the drawing with, too."

The bogus Black Dolphin ID card was still warm when they finished 40 minutes later. It looked genuine.

"Don't you think the company uses security strips?" Caterina asked.

"I'm sure they do," he said, slipping the card into his wallet. "I just hope it can get me into the construction site."

"You're planning to go inside?" she said in a worried voice.

"Sooner or later. Right now I want to meet with Father Santorini."

"Is that why you made a copy of the drawing?"

"Yes. If the Shield really is some kind of riddle, he may be able to help us figure it out."

11:18 AM

Father Santorini was waiting for him by the door. "Come in, come in. Have a chair," the priest said, gesturing toward a wooden table with a bisque teapot and two cups. The man was aglow with excitement. "Would you like some tea?"

Tea sounded good.

Santorini filled a cup with a straw-colored liquid and handed it to him. "I wanted to tell you that you were right about the Polybius Square cipher. I decoded it. It was just a Maltese nursery rhyme."

"Bartolomeo may have been testing it to see if it worked."

"Yes. I suppose you're right." Rubbing his hands together in anticipation, he said, "Now where's the copy of the drawing? I can hardly wait to see it."

"It's right here and I'll be happy to show it to you, but you have to hold to your promise not to contact the Cornacchias."

"Yes. Yes. Of course. You have my word."

Rick handed it to him and waited for a reaction. The printer had scanned the original and enlarged it three times. Santorini unrolled it slowly as if savoring the redolence of a fine meal. Finally, in a distant voice he said, "How beautiful. It must have been a masterpiece."

"My thoughts, exactly," Rick said.

"*Aegis Dei* is ambiguous," Santorini mumbled. "Does that mean God's shield for man or man's shield for God? With Bartolomeo, one can't be quite sure, can one?" With a chuckle, he bent forward to take a closer look. "The figures are Knights, certainly. Yes. Did you notice the oboros on the first shield?"

Rick nodded. The snake devouring its own tail was a familiar alchemist's symbol.

"And there's the Lion of Judah," he said pointing at a figure. "It's a symbol for Ethiopia." Santorini's eyes suddenly widened. "Good heavens, did you see this?"

His finger shook as he pointed at the central figure holding a shield that showed a black cross between shepherd's crooks. "Yes," Rick said. "But I didn't pay much attention to it. Isn't it just one of the village's coat of arms?"

"Definitely not! That's the escutcheon of Prester John!"

"You can't be serious," Rick said.

"But I am. And look at the figure itself. Knights didn't wear robes and a crown. It's meant to represent a king. I'm sure the marks on the banner and inside the basin identify Prester John by name."

"I saw the marks but I didn't recognize them. Do you know what they are?"

"They're Amharic characters," Santorini said. "Ethiopian."

Rick felt a thrill of remembrance. "Of course. That's where I saw them before. They were on a stamp I used to have in my boyhood collection. Only the country was called Abyssinia. Can you read it?"

Santorini shook his head. "No, but I know someone who can. I have an Ethiopian friend at the University."

"Wonderful," Rick said, picking up his cup. "I'd appreciate the help. Assuming Bartolomeo had Cellini go forward with the work, I'm still wondering who was supposed to get it."

"I have a pretty good idea," Santorini said with a mischievous smile.

The teacup halted halfway to Rick's mouth. "Yes?" he said.

Santorini took two more paces with his hands behind his back before turning to reply. "Suleiman the Magnificent."

"You can't be serious," Rick said. But even as he said it, he felt an odd tingle.

"But I am. The drawing may explain what Bartolomeo was up to after the church seized his book."

"Go on."

"Let's start with the legend of Prester John since John is on the shield. Every Arab knew about him and feared him. According to legend, John lived in a golden city on a great river. The Arabs also knew he was a fierce warrior who had threatened to put every one of Allah's followers to the sword. Legend also had it that he had discovered the secret of eternal life. I wouldn't be surprised if Suleiman believed it, too."

"Eternal life is part of the quest of the alchemist," Rick said.

"So is being able to turn base metal into gold."

"But even if John were a real person, no one knew where he lived. It was supposed to have been somewhere in India, wasn't it?"

"Somewhere in the *Indias*," Santorini corrected. "At the time geographers thought there were three different Indias, one greater and two lesser. Europeans knew about Greater India because they had been looting it for centuries, but no one was exactly sure where the lesser Indias were located, only that they had to have been somewhere east of Constantinople."

"And since Bartolomeo had been to Ethiopia, he would have wanted everyone to think that the kingdom's great river was the Nile," Rick mused.

"Absolutely. Ethiopia was considered to be a magical place. Some natives still believe that King Solomon's mines are located there. And the Ark of the Covenant, as well."

Too excited to sit, Rick joined the priest on his feet. "Bartolomeo may have known about the legends," he said, "but I'm willing to bet that he didn't have the secrets of alchemy when he left Ethiopia."

Santorini smiled wisely. "You're right. But then, no one knew what he did have with him when he came home. As I already suggested, he first intended to use the trip to improve the credibility of the *Definitus Mallorum*. If potential buyers needed more convincing, he could resort to ancient magic tricks that would easily fool the greedy neophytes. I'm sure it never occurred to him that he would convince the church that the book contained forbidden knowledge, too."

Rick chuckled. "How true. But what has all this to do with Suleiman the Magnificent?"

Santorini took a deep breath. "I think the Aegis Dei was the *Definitus Mallorum* and Bartolemeo tried to sell it to him." He finished quickly and gave Rick an inquiring look.

Disappointed, Rick shook his head. "Sorry. I can believe he tried to sell the Shield to Suleiman, but I can't see how it could be the *Definitus Mallorum*. He could never have written a whole book inside the basin. There wouldn't be enough room."

"It wouldn't have to be the whole book. Just the important spells."

The air crackled. Was Father Santorini about to furnish the reason for Bin-Said's involvement with Cornacchia? "That's possible," Rick said. "So, how did Suleiman learn about the Aegis in the first place?"

"Well, here's my theory. I know from Bartolomeo's diary and shipping documents the Cornacchias had developed close ties with the Michiel family of Venice. The Michiels were important merchants, and Malta was a major stopover point on their route to Africa. Bartolemeo even married into the family. It was one of the best business moves he ever made.

"The Knights didn't mind, either. It gave them a way to spy on what the Turks were up to. In return, the Cornacchias gained access to ports in the Adriatic. That led to access to the former Byzantium, which was now part of the Ottoman Empire. I know from the diary that Bartolomeo was carrying on trade with the Turks."

"So, one step closer to Suleiman," Rick said. "What kind of trade was it?"

"He doesn't say, but my guess is that he sold back valuables the Knights had pirated."

"Donato Cornacchia said that The Shield was made from gold the Knights had brought back from the Holy Land. I found reference to it in a letter in the Cornacchia family archives."

"I never saw it but it sounds important. I do know that Bartolomeo probably had contacts within the royal palace that may have extended to Suleiman himself."

"Fair enough. But what makes you think he tried to sell the Aegis to him?"

"Patience," Santorini said. Once again the priest began to pace, but now in slow, contemplative steps. "For one thing, Bartolomeo hints at an important change that he expected to occur in 1565, even if he didn't say what it was.

"For another, he already had established some credibility with the Turks, but he needed to enhance his resume considerably to impress Suleiman. The best way to begin was to let him know that Bartolomeo was an alchemist. Suleiman was a goldsmith and would have been interested in alchemy."

Rick nodded.

"To do that he sent some of his alchemist's findings to a merchant in Constantinople knowing that it would ultimately reach Suleiman. Apparently it did."

"The next step was to publish a treatise about his travels. It includes a reference to Ethiopia that would help establish the connection with Prester John."

"When did it come out?'

"In February of 1565. It's extremely rare. He sent a copy to the same merchant. Bartolomeo especially wanted to make sure that Suleiman knew about Pius the Fourth's confiscation of the *Definitus Mallorum* and the heresy trial. Those two events alone would provide the strongest proof that he actually possessed forbidden knowledge."

Rick nodded. "It would also prove he had a strong motive for wanting to get back at the church, too."

"Perceptive as ever," Santorini said in admiration. "It all seemed to fit together nicely. Only someone as rich as the Sultan would have the money to buy the Shield and Bartolomeo would have his revenge."

"And how did he get all this to Suleiman?"

"He spread the word through some of his agents in the Levant. I'm sure it finally reached the right destination."

"I see," Rick said. After a moment's reflection he shook his head. "Sorry. Even if everything you say is true, I still can't buy the idea that Bartolomeo would think Suleiman would be naïve enough to believe that the talisman was authentic. The Duke must have known that he would want proof before paying an exorbitant price for it."

"You're right, so whatever money was involved would have been held in escrow by a third party that both sides trusted," Santorini said.

"Fine. Even so, sooner or later Suleiman would have found out that the Shield didn't really work. Then what?"

"Bartolomeo would have done everything he could to make sure Suleiman didn't feel duped. The classic excuses at the time were either that the ingredients were tainted or that the spell hadn't been performed correctly or under the proper conditions." Santorini stopped. "It just occurred to me why Bartolomeo went to so much expense to make the Shield."

"Shoot," Rick said eagerly.

"It could have been a way to palliate possible hard feelings when Suleiman found out the spells didn't work. I'm sure Bartolomeo wasn't expecting any money. The payment he wanted was something Suleiman would have been very happy to make even if the spell didn't work."

Rick waited as the priest moved closer. In a low voice Santorini said, "I think Bartolomeo asked Suleiman to drive the Knights off Malta so that he, Bartolomeo, could become ruler."

After taking a reflective swig of tepid tea, Rick nodded. "That would make sense from both their viewpoints. I can believe Bartolomeo wanted to rule Malta. And I know Suleiman would have been happy to eliminate the Knights. They were a thorn in his side and the only ones who could stop him from taking control of the Mediterranean. Once they were gone he had thousands of Moors waiting for him in Spain, to boot."

Santorini enthusiastically patted him on his back. "You have it."

Rick made fists. "Good work. I still think Suleiman would be angry, but then, as you say, he had that beautiful gold basin as a consolation prize and the Knights were out of his hair for good. Fair enough. That explains everything. Suleiman didn't win the Great Siege so Bartolomeo's plan didn't work. Brilliant."

A puckish smile appeared on Santorini's face. "Hold your applause, please. We haven't even come to the best part, yet."

"There can't be more," Rick said, giggling uncontrollably.

The smile grew larger. "But there is. After Suleiman and Bartolomeo came to terms, the question became how to get the shield into Suleiman's hands. As luck would have it, Kustir-Aga, the royal eunuch, had a ship returning from the Holy Land loaded with treasure for the Royal Harem's investment company. All of Suleiman's wives and daughters had shares in the company, and everyone had invested heavily in the project. Everyone was expecting big profits. The cargo was supposed to be worth 80,000 ducats."

Rick whistled. "That would be several millions of dollars in today's money."

"Indeed. Suleiman knew that the ship would be landing at Corfu, near Greece, at some time in early 1565. It was the last leg of the journey back to Constantinople and the crew needed to stop for water and provisions."

"I'm way ahead of you," Rick said. "Suleiman told Bartolomeo to send the basin to Corfu so they could take it home to Constantinople with the rest of the treasure."

"Exactly. Bartolomeo sent the Shield by his fastest ship to Nikos Villanopolis, who was his agent on the island of Cyprus, instructing him to sail on to Corfu and turn the basin over to Suleiman's representative. Apparently he did just that."

"Hold on," Rick said. "Why would Suleiman trust Bartolomeo enough to give him the location where a treasure ship could be found? That sounds foolhardy to me."

"I'm sure he didn't. All Bartolomeo knew is that one of sultan's ships would land at Corfu and that he was supposed to deliver the Shield there. Suleiman had also provided 300 Janniseries as a guard, in case the ship ran into pirates. All in all, he must have been very confident it would be a safe transaction."

"300 Janissaries? That's the same as saying 300 Green Berets. So what happened then? Get on with it."

"I will, but you'll never believe me. The treasure ship returned to sea. While it was still in sight of Corfu, pirates attacked. They defeated the Janissaries and sacked the ship, taking the Shield with the rest of the loot. Not just any pirate, mind you, but the infamous Romegas, the scourge of the Mediterranean."

"Yea!" Rick cheered. "Who's Romegas?"

"Suleiman's worst nightmare. Not only had the rogue looted millions of dollars of treasure and carried off thousands of loyal Muslims as galley slaves, he was a Knight of St. John to boot."

"Ohmygod," Rick said, barely able to breathe. "You're making this up, aren't you?"

Santorini crossed his heart. "Other than Bartolomeo's actions and Villanopolis' trip to Corfu, everything I've said is a matter of historical record."

"Are you saying Bartolomeo tipped off Romegas and caused the Great Siege?"

"Absolutely not," Santorini said emphatically. "In fact, that's the last thing Bartolomeo would have done. He needed Suleiman's help."

"So why did Suleiman invade Malta? To get back at Bartolomeo?" Rick asked.

"Heavens no. It was harem politics. His favorite daughter, Mirmah, asked him to. She lost a fortune when the treasure ship was pirated and she wanted her father to try to get the cargo back.

"As it happens, Suleiman had just been forced to kill his favorite son, Mustapha, because Mustapha was plotting to overthrow him, and I imagine he felt some familial responsibility towards Mirmah. He also may have thought it made good sense to attack the Knights before they completed fortifying the island. He failed and a year later, Bartolomeo took off for parts unknown, never to be heard from again. He must have been afraid that the sultan's agents would be looking for him to end his life."

By the time Santorini was finished, Rick was breathless. "Wonderful!" he wheezed. "Everything fits, except for one thing. If Romegas stole the basin, how did it get back into Bartolomeo's hands?"

"Bartolomeo must have bought it back from him. I'm sure he had to pay a big price for it, but Romegas would have had no idea how valuable it really was."

"How true," Rick said. "I haven't had this much fun since I was a kid. Bartolomeo was a terrible person and he couldn't have come to a more deserving end."

"It would have been a lot more funny if so many people hadn't died in the Siege," said Santorini. "Did you know that 30,000 Turks died and more than 500 Knights? Except for the Crusades it was one of the biggest holy wars of all times."

"We haven't learned much since, have we?" Rick said. "You just reminded me why the Sixteenth Century has always been my favorite era. Everyone was double-crossing each other. I would give anything to have been living then."

"Who knows? Maybe someone in another five hundred years will say the same thing about our times."

"I never thought of that," Rick said. As he got up to leave he decided Santorini was an important ally and that he needed to learn the full story about Lorenzo Cornacchia.

The priest listened, wide-eyed. When Rick finished Santorini could only say, "I'm shocked."

"I was sure you would be," Rick said.

"Then Agatha is right. There is a family curse. I'll do whatever I can to help end it."

CHAPTER 20

▼

Wednesday
?

Stef awoke from a light doze at the sound of Pawlu's voice. "Hello my friend," Pawlu said. "How are you today?"

"How do you think I am?" Stef growled.

"Such a sour disposition. Be of good cheer. Soon this all will be over for you."

"Yeah? Could I at least get something to eat before you kill me?"

Pawlu laughed. "Kill you?" he said. "Don't be ridiculous. I've brought you something to eat."

The aroma of a fresh orange made Stef's nose twitch.

"Open your mouth," Pawlu said.

Stef did and was rewarded by the delicious sting of acid on his tongue. As he chewed, he was sure he had never tasted anything better in his life. "More."

After dropping another section into Stef's mouth, Pawlu stared into Stef's eyes. In a somber tone he said, "I've been considering your proposition."

Though he didn't reply, Stef waited anxiously for him to continue.

"I accept it, but on one condition. You must tell me where you hid the drawing."

Stef barked in derision. "You can't be serious."

"But I am. I was careless and your brother may have found out my identity. If so, I'll never be able to stay here on Malta."

"What does that have to do with the drawing?"

"We have orders to kill you as soon as we have it. My associate intends to do just that so I will have to get you away from him. Once he finds out I've betrayed him he will come looking for me. Selling the drawing will give us money to escape whether we find the Shield of God or not."

Stef spat pulp as he broke out laughing. "So I'm supposed to trust you? You may have softened my brain with all the drugs you've given me, but I still have one."

"Of course you do," Pawlu said, taking off the mask. "It's time we start seeing each other as equals." He smiled, showing off a gold front tooth, then took a knife from his pocket and began to cut Stef's bonds. "Let's get the drawing."

*   *   *   *

1:25 PM

In the car, Rick told Caterina about his conversation.

"I'm glad he's decided to join us. While you were away, Josefina called. She said her church didn't bring enough food to feed the refugees and she wondered if we could watch the pub for an hour or so."

Josefina waved at them. "Thanks for coming. We didn't' bring enough food for Verdala camp and Father Modiglio asked if I could deliver some more."

Caterina looked at Rick. "Why don't we come with you. Can anyone else watch the bar for you?"

"I'll see what Peter is doing," Josefina said.

As they drove the chassis of the vintage Mercedes van overreacted to every irregularity in the stone road, making Zija groan with worry at every bump. "You're going too fast," she said. "You'll spill the soup."

"I have my foot on the brake," Caterina protested. "I can't go any slower. I told you two months ago you should let me put in new rocker arms for you."

Rick closed his eyes and inhaled the delicious aroma of lentil porridge and hoped there would be some left over after they fed the multitudes.

A man in uniform came forward to meet them. "More church ladies," he said. "You're late."

"We had to make more food," Caterina said.

"I'm not surprised," the guard said. He opened the gate and waved them through.

A Second World War barracks building loomed ahead. As they drove, a young boy wearing army fatigues came down the road toward them. One pants leg was dragging on the road and the other was folded under the knee with the bottom tucked in around his waist. He looked up and grinned at them. Caterina said something in Arabic, the boy shook his head and Josefina opened the back door for him.

"He hasn't eaten yet," Caterina said.

They drove past three barracks and pulled up next to a picnic table at the fourth. As if appearing out of nowhere, gaunt-faced men, women and children immediately surrounded the car. Not everyone, however. Several men stayed in the background. Rick wondered why most of the refugees looked malnourished while these men merely looked lean. Rick carried the heavy pots from the back of the van while Josefina balanced long tubes of coffee cups in one hand and individually wrapped plastic spoons in the other. Caterina struggled with two 10-liter milk containers.

After the food was on the table, the refugees politely lined up. Rick grabbed a handful of cups and began to hand them out. He tried to ignore the sore-looking bare feet and barley-sack clothing of the women and concentrated on their smiling eyes, instead. One wore a gold-colored bracelet, probably her only possession. An old man grinned toothlessly, nodding enthusiastically as he took Rick's offering. But still the younger men stayed next to the wall of the barracks and refused to come closer. When he was finished, he moved back to join Josefina. Getting down on all fours, he sent each child into screeching laughter by making monkey noises and staring into their cups.

As they ate, he turned roving magician, rolling a fifty-cent coin back and forth across his knuckles and pretending to pull it from their ears. Once he looked up and saw Caterina grinning at him.

When they finished eating, Rick got a large box out of the trunk of the van and set it by the table. The refugees passed by it and threw the cups away though most kept the plastic spoons, and a young girl retrieved the empty milk containers from the debris.

Each thanked him and each seemed very surprised when he answered in Arabic. Lavishing grateful smiles they disappeared back into the barracks as silently and mysteriously as they had appeared.

When they were alone, Caterina put her arms around him. Eyes sparkling she said, "I want you to know how much Josefina and I appreciate your help. You were the life of the party."

"Aw shucks," he said. "Has Andrew ever come with you?"

Her smile became reproachful. "No he hasn't. He's made several big contributions to our fund, though."

Rick nodded. Big surprise. His face became somber. "I'm puzzled. Who gets sent here?"

"Families. Why do you ask?"

"Some of the men seem a bit suspicious to me."

Caterina's brows furrowed. "They must be all right. We keep the dangerous ones locked up in Floriana."

"Good. Because I'm a little worried about the security, too."

She reached out her hand. "Let's pack up and get back to Sliema."

Back at the Bellestrado Josefina insisted that she reward Rick with a beer. Caterina joined him. When they had finished he said, "How can we contact Agatha Cornacchia"

"No problem," Caterina said with a wise smile. She took her phone out of her purse and dialed. After a pause she gestured wildly for Rick to hand her something to write with. "Would you please repeat that? Thank you." She scribbled a note and Rick took it. "Her number isn't published, but it is listed. She lives in Gwardamanga in an assisted living complex."

"Isn't Gwardamanga where you took me last night?"

"Yes, but she's up in the hills. Lord and Lady Montbatten had a villa there and Queen Elizabeth stayed with them for a year when she was still princess."

"Give her a call. Tell her I've been talking with Father Santorini about Bartolemeo and I had some questions. I'm sure she'll want an opportunity to refute him."

"I know what Santorini says and he's *mxiegher*," the old woman growled, tapping her forehead. She drew her shawl more tightly over her hair. "Bartolemeo was no charlatan. He was a devout Christian and he believed in what he was doing. The church had no right to censor his book. I've been trying to convince the old goat of that from the time he started writing his doctoral thesis but he won't listen."

"That's what he tells me," Rick said. He took a deep breath and smelled the tantalizingly sweet odor of mimosas. Of all the places he had been to on the island, this was most like a Mediterranean estate. The spectacular view of Grand Harbour alone was worth more than he could earn in several lifetimes. Agatha Cornacchia was every bit as impressive in her own right. Except for her diminutive size and her wheel chair, no one would believe she was nearly ninety years old. "What else did he tell you?" she demanded.

"For one thing he can't imagine why Bartolemeo disappeared after the Siege."

"He can imagine, all right," she spat. "He all but came out and told me that he thought Bartolemeo was a coward. He didn't dare put that in his book, of course, but I know that's what he thinks. We had a big argument when he suggested it and I didn't talk to him for months."

"What do you think happened to Bartolomeo?"

"I don't know. Maybe he didn't die." She said it quickly without smiling to end the questions. "Now what is it you wanted to ask me?"

Rick took a deep breath. "The curator at the archives said that you donated the Cornacchia family papers to the University because you wanted to be rid of the family plague. What did you mean by that?"

Her eyes flashed. "That's none of your business. It's a family matter and I won't discuss it."

"I don't want to cause you any discomfort, but I think I already know," Rick said in a soft voice. "I read the letter from Mandolfo to Donato referring to the Shield of God."

Agatha Cornacchia gasped.

"Is that the family curse?" he asked.

After a moment's hesitation, she answered in a resigned tone. "I don't know how you found out about it, but you're right. Not that it's any of your concern. I thought I removed everything that referred to the Shield."

"Why?"

"Because it's been bad luck for the Cornacchia family since Bartolomeo's time," she said angrily. "The men have been obsessed and the women frightened by it. It always gave me shivers so I made Alessandro keep it in the library under a cloth. No matter how valuable it was, I'm glad it's gone for Lorenzo's sake. He was still in the womb when it disappeared."

"Why did it frighten you?"

"I don't know," she said irritably. "I always felt that there was something imprisoned inside of it and I didn't want to be around it when it got out."

"That's the way Mandolfo describes it, too. And he called the Shield a riddle."

She made a sour face. "It's a riddle all right. Poor Alessandro spent his entire life trying to understand it. He had thousands of pages of notes. As brilliant as he was, he never succeeded. It finally broke his heart. Just as it did his father's and all the other Cornacchias who tried to figure it out. That's why I hated the foul thing."

"What happened to Alessandro's notes?" Rick asked. "Did you destroy them?"

"I didn't destroy anything," she said, eyes flashing. "I just didn't send them with the rest of his papers. They're still locked up in the library at *Borgiswed* where they belong."

Rick snapped to attention. If only he could see them! "I understand he thought the British were going to arrest him. Do you know why?"

"They considered him a traitor because he and his literary group were pro-Italian." She vented a spiteful sniff. "It was outrageous. Alessandro would never have done anything to help the Axis. He was just a poet. All the dangerous sympathizers were arrested in 1940 and deported."

Rick decided to run a bluff. "Was the Duke's Challenge supposed to tell where he hid the Shield?"

She sniffed again. "You *are* the nosy one," she said with glittering eyes, then pushed a lever on her wheelchair and started toward the door. "Why don't you ask Major Tomlinson at the Union Club? He's spent years trying to find that out."

✳   ✳   ✳   ✳

2:28 PM

He expected to find a simple stone building with stone lions and proud Britannias so he wasn't prepared for a sumptuous Baroque building with a balustraded front and gothic arches. The only hint of John Bull was the Union Jack hanging on the front door.

The doorknocker was in the shape of a lion's head. He lifted it and let it fall. Within seconds a young man in a shiny vest and bow tie answered. "Yes, sir?"

"Good afternoon. I'm doing research about Malta during the Second World War. I was told I might find Major Tomlinson here."

"Come in," the young man said.

Rick followed him into an oak-paneled room that smelled of cigar smoke and pipe dottle. Straight-backed chairs stood along two tables. Numerous easy chairs looked as if they had been flung into the room from the hallway, and the head of an unfortunate rhinoceros protruded from a superfluous chimney. It looked as if it had broken through the fireplace to be stopped in midcharge. At the opposite end of the room, Her Royal Highness Queen Victoria scowled imperiously in her widow weeds, following every movement with disapproving eyes.

"Remain here, please." With that the young man walked over to a table where a man was seated by a chessboard. The chessplayer stood, pulling a cardigan into place, and nodded at Rick.

"This is Major Tomlinson," the attendant said.

Rick took the introduction to mean he was given leave to join the major. "I'm Richard Olsen, a historian from Minnesota. I see you're a chessplayer."

"I am. I was just replaying the game between Capablanca and Niemzowich in '34. Cappy won in thirty moves. Pretty good for a Cuban, eh?"

Rick was offended by the implicit racism. "Pretty good for anyone of any nationality, I'd say."

"You're right. What can I do for you?"

"Agatha Cornacchia said I should see you. She says you have information about her husband Alessandro and the Duke's Challenge."

The major laughed mirthlessly. "She did, did she? I'm surprised. She doesn't like to talk about her family with strangers."

"You could say I forced it out of her."

"That sounds more likely," he muttered. "I got to know Agatha quite well over the years. She accused me of hounding her and finally refused to talk to me altogether. That was years ago."

"She thought you might have some ideas where Alessandro hid the Aegis Dei."

"She's wrong. I have no idea. I gave up trying to find it many years ago."

"How did you learn about it?"

"It's a long story. I was a mere lieutenant at the time," he said, his rheumy eyes puckering into a spiderweb smile. "I was a cryptographer and at the top of my class. I never did understand why I wasn't assigned to Bletchley Park."

Rick nodded in sympathy. Bletchley was the legendary cryptography center in the English Midlands where the immortal Turing and company broke the Nazi military codes. "I know a little bit about cryptography, too."

The spiderweb drew tighter. "Is that so? At any rate I was with the signal section. We kept our radio station going all through the war even though the Jerries did everything they could to put us out of business. One night I counted 60 bombs that fell where we were, alone. Then came Operation Pedestal and the *Ohio* arrived with food and petrol so we had new planes and gasoline to run them. We finally won but the whole island went through hell. You probably know that Alessandro Cornacchia was killed during one of the raids."

"Yes. I heard that."

A light glinted in the Major's eyes. "Did you also know he was involved in some asinine plot to turn Malta over to Mussolini in '37?"

Rick's eyes widened." No. What kind of plot?"

"Have you ever heard of the Sicilian Vespers, when the people of Sicily rose up and drove out the French?"

"Yes. But that was in the 13th Century."

"Right. Only in this case the uprising was organized by Alessandro and his literary society. He actually expected the population to rise up and throw us out.
He was sure he would succeed. After all, the Sicilians only had pitchforks to get
rid of the French. His army had shotguns."

The words sent a shock through Rick's whole body. Was that Cornacchia's
connection to the hunter's clubs? "Why did he think they would do that? You
had good relations with the Maltese people."

"For the most part," Tomlinson said. "And Alessandro had no complaint with
us, either. We approved his claim to his title when he applied for it in 1911. He
was even one of the leaders of the local governments."

"So what was supposed to happen after the peasants threw you Brits out?"

"The Italian army would take over. If Mussolini could take time out from
using poison gas on the Ethiopians, that is."

"Why didn't you arrest Alessandro then?"

"For strategic reasons, mostly. We were sure he had a dangerous saboteur in
his organization and we wanted to keep a lid on things until we found out who it
was."

"Did the saboteur do much damage?"

"Not at first. It was mostly harassment. Like finding an antenna knocked
down after a wind that wasn't strong enough to cause any real damage, or discov-
ering someone had put sugar in our petrol tanks. Then matters took a nasty turn.
A week before the insurrection was supposed to take place, one of our men found
dynamite under our headquarters at Fort St. Angelo. Everything was ready. All it
needed was a match. I wouldn't be surprised if that was meant to signal the
beginning of the insurrection."

"The Maltese version of Guy Fawkes, no less. Did you ever find out who the
saboteur was?"

"No. But in 1940 after the war started, we started to find hand grenades
strapped to the bottoms of our trucks. We decided that if we jailed or deported
Cornacchia, the real saboteur might take over. If he did, we could have had a genuine guerilla movement to worry about."

"I see," Rick said. "Then what?"

"After Duke Alessandro died, his organization seemed to die with him."

"Whose idea was it to leave Cornacchia free?"

"Governor-General Dobbie's." The major stood up and led Rick to a photograph of a man with a smallish round head with a military mustache and ears that
stuck out a bit under his cap. The strip under the photo read 'Sir William G. S.
Dobbie, Governor-General 1940–1942.'

"Fine gentleman, Dobbie. A Boer War Veteran, he was. A sapper."

"An engineer?"

"Exactly. We used to have a saying about sappers. They were all 'mad, married and Methodist.' Take a look at this," he said, moving to another picture. "She doesn't look like much, does she?" the major said. "She and two other planes like her were all that stood between us and the Axis when the war started."

"It looks like something out of the First World War."

"Almost. Mid-30s, though, actually. It's a Gloucester Gladiator. The planes were considered to be too old when the war started. They were used to pull targets for anti-aircraft gunnery practice. Everyone knows about Royal Air Force and the Battle of Britain, but those chaps in Faith, Hope, and Charity were every bit as important to this country. Hardly anyone else has even heard of them."

Rick nodded. "Getting back to Alessandro, did the police find anything in the car besides his body when he died?"

"The police didn't find him, actually. One of our bomb-damage-assessment parties did. They found a handwinch in the trunk."

"So he was probably planning to move something heavy. Do you have any idea why he was driving during a raid?"

"None. We were puzzled about that ourselves. It must have been important, the attack had been in progress for quite some time when the car crashed."

Rick felt a chill. Had Alessandro been dissatisfied with the place where he originally hid the Shield and moved it? If so, his chances to recover it were nil.

"You're sure the car was on its way to Valletta when it crashed?"

"That's the conclusion we came up with."

"How did they determine that?"

"I'm not sure. If you want, I'll look it up in Cornacchia's file."

Rick's ears pricked. "His file?"

"Yes. I kept all my personal files from my stint in the service. I've made arrangement for the war museum to get them after I'm gone."

Rick bent forward and gently put a hand on his shoulder. "If you have a file on him, for heaven's sake, please show it to me. I'm asking as one officer to another. I can't tell you anything more, but it's important."

The major stared, wide-eyed. "Well if that's the case, Capablanca can wait."

The major lived in a flat over a storefront on Manoel Dimich Street in Sliema. Rick paid for a carrozzin and the two men tried to make themselves comfortable in the horse-drawn carriage that was too cramped for one. They rolled into each other on the corners and flattened against the seatback as they started to climb.

Before long the carriage stopped in front of a building with an ornately carved front and a heavy wooden door with a dolphin-shaped doorknocker. "This was one of the buildings that didn't get bombed during the war," the major said as he fished a key ring from his pocket.

The door opened to a hallway with plasterboard walls. The Oriental rug in the hall was ancient, little more than gray and faded red thread. "My apartment is down this way." The hallway smelled of oregano and kerosene. When the major opened his apartment door, the blast of relatively cool air came as a refreshing slap in the face.

He pointed Rick to an overstuffed chair.

"Please sit down. I'll get the file for you. I keep them in the bedroom closet." Rick nodded and took a moment to appreciate his surroundings. Artillery shells arranged like organ pipes lined the windowsills, and the walls were covered with bookcases and black and white photographs.

The major returned, setting a large cardboard carton on the floor. "All alphabetical," he said. "C…CA…CI…CO. Yes. Here we are."

The dark brown file was fairly thick, filled with thin papers stapled or held in place by long metal clips. Rick wanted to go through the whole folder but decided it would take too much time. "Are the papers arranged chronologically?"

"Yes. What you want should be close to the top."

Rick flipped through the flimsy sheets until he found a typewritten memo dated 20/06/42. It was a report about the discovery of a burned automobile near the Porte Des Bombes. How appropriate, Rick thought. He had seen the Porte, which looked like the Arch de Triomphe, in his trips to and from Valletta. The report said that the automobile was lying upside down next to a bomb crater.

"All it says is that they found a body. Are you sure it was Cornacchia?"

"Quite. We identified him from dental records. He had two gold crowns."

Rick finished reading the report. "It doesn't say which way the car was travelling."

"Direction is a dicey thing to figure," said the Major. "But Valletta had been under heavy attack and it's not likely he would have been able to leave. We surmised he was coming from Notabile when his vehicle was hit."

Rick tried to imagine the Duke, head down, tearing down a blacked out street with bombs exploding around his car. What could have been *that* important?

"Do you have any information about Cornacchia's followers?"

"We had a partial list of the members of L'Ankra, his literary society. We were quite sure some, if not most of them, were fellow travelers in the conspiracy, but we couldn't prove anything. And they weren't actively anti-British. The ones we considered the most dangerous were rounded up in 1940. We deported them two years later."

"Do you have the L'Ankra membership list?"

"Let me see if I can find it for you." The Major licked his fingers as he turned the pages. "Ah. Here it is."

The list went on for three pages. Looking for familiar names, Rick recognized one immediately. Josef Vella, the Cardinal of Malta and Cornacchia's co-conspirator. Another had a familiar ring. Albert Micallef. A relation of the Inspector's? "Could I get photocopies of these pages?"

"Of course. There's a printer just down the street."

"How in earth did you hear about the Aegis Dei?" the major asked. "Agatha Cornacchia certainly would never have told you."

"I saw a clipping about it in the National Library."

"I see. Well, as Agatha says, it's a curse. So is the Challenge. I spent most of my life trying to figure it out. I finally gave up on it."

"What can you tell me about it?"

"Just a day or two before the Duke died he sent Commander Dobbie a manila envelope. The Duke challenged us to solve a puzzle and find his treasure. It was supposed to be extremely valuable."

"The Aegis Dei, I assume."

"Yes. Dobbie had already had more than enough of Cornacchia," the Major continued, "and with the bombings going on he didn't have time for any nonsense about solving puzzles. He threw the challenge into the wastebasket and didn't mind if I looked at it. It was a hand-written letter and a tearsheet from a newspaper that one of his literary society members published. I'll get it for you."

The major opened a desk drawer and handed Rick a 9x12" manila folder.

The folded newspaper page in it was brittle and beginning to split at the creases. "The Duke's Challenge," looked like a paid ad and took up the whole page. A parody of the Cornacchia coat of arms showed a diamond and a dolphin instead of a castle and a crow. At the bottom were the words: "If you search for a key, remove the city Malti." It was dated June 4th, the same date as the paper Rick saw in the library with the missing clipping.

"And you've looked for the Duke's treasure for most of your life?"

"I was originally interested because I was a cryptographer. I was young and feeling my oats. I figured there wasn't any code I couldn't break if I worked at it hard enough. I was wrong. Now that I'm old, I don't care anymore."

Rick turned to the letter itself. "It says the puzzle gives directions where to find the treasure and that it's hidden in a public place."

After looking through pages and pages of hand-written notes, Rick said, "Since you've given up looking, could I borrow this file for a while? I'll give it back to you."

"You're welcome to it. I hope you have better luck with it."

CHAPTER 21

▼

Wednesday
3:58 PM
Qormi

It was nearly 4:00 when they got back to the farmhouse. With the sun directly behind it, the building looked like a castle on a hill, standing in stark contrast to the golden autumn haze that hung in the air. As they drove up the driveway, a distant neigh told them that their presence had been noted.

They stopped and Rick expected Caterina to rush off to tend to the horses. To his surprise, she merely opened the door and went into the house. At the bottom of the staircase he nearly tripped over a laundry basket containing several skimpy bras and pairs of thong underwear. His eyes wrinkled at the sight. Did Malta have a Victoria's Secret?

Caterina rushed around him and picked up the basket, using her body to shield it from his view. "Sorry," she said, sounding flustered. "I didn't realize this was here. I'll just put these in the washer and be right back."

With a look of bemusement, he sat down at the kitchen table and opened the major's file.

His eyes went directly to the words. "If you search for a key, remove the city Malti." Which city did it refer to? Valletta? Mdina? Or some other city? And remove it from what? Notabile? Or Citta Vecchia, the Old City? Not likely. He was fairly sure it wouldn't be Italian terms. Mdina was the Maltese variant of Medina, important cities in Morocco and Saudi Arabia. It was the transliterated Arabic word for city.

Caterina returned. "They should be ready for the dryer in half an hour."

"Good. By the way, what does *Borgiswed* mean?"

"Black rock. I suppose it must have something to do with crows."

Stef's heart beat faster as he and Pawlu approached the door to the wc. He knocked on the door, listening for a response.

"So this is Queen Mab's castle," Pawlu said.

"Of course," Stef replied. "It even has a throne."

It was empty and they stepped inside. With pulse beating faster, Stef took the poster off the wall. "Here she is. If you were planning to stick a knife in my back, now's your chance."

"Having to carry your soul around with me for the rest of eternity would be too large a burden for me. You're safe as long as you do not try to trick me."

Stef turned the frame upside down and eagerly pried the nails loose using the file from Pawlu's fingernail clipper. "Here it is," he said, lifting the back away. His mouth opened in disbelief. "I put it here. I'm sure no one could have found it."

"Apparently someone did," Pawlu said in a dark voice.

Terrified by Pawlu's malevolent glare, Stef said, "My brother must have found it. I knew he could."

"Then let's get it back from him," Pawlu growled.

*   *   *   *

"Any luck with the challenge?" Caterina asked.

"No. But I've been thinking," Rick said. "Alessandro probably hid the Shield somewhere close to him and I'm almost certain it's in Mdina."

"There isn't anywhere to hide it there," Caterina said. "There's just streets and walls."

"They may have been in different places in 1942. No matter what else has changed, the geography must be the same. I'm going to take a balloon ride and find out. How would you like to come with me?"

Her eyes opened wide. "I'd love to!" The look of delight ended in suspicion. "Is this Josefina's idea?"

"Absolutely not," he said. "I'm capable of coming up with one or two without help. Why do you ask?"

"She knows how much I've always wanted to take a balloon ride. I've been waiting for Andrew to take me on one since I met him."

The words cut through him like a saber. "Sorry," he said, finding it difficult to keep from choking. "I should have realized. If you have an alarm clock I can get myself up. I'll take a cab to the site and you can pick me up when I'm done."

"Not on your life!" she said firmly. "You asked me, and I'm not going to let you wiggle out of the invitation. Andrew had his chance and blew it."

"Wonderful. Do you have any idea where we can rent a camera?"

"Yes. We can pick it up on the way to the Bellestrado tonight."

6:22 PM

Caterina parked behind the Chev and led Rick on foot to Tomaso's Gift Shop.

The tiny store had a rack of papers and magazines at the front and shelves along three walls. Besides a row of Italian candy and licorice-flavored chewing gum, most of the space was taken up by chintzy merchandise spilling on the floor from overflowing plain wooden bins. Rick was sure that even the half-price sign wouldn't entice anyone to dig through the mounds of key chains and miniature stuffed toys. The gentleman obviously had other sources of income or he couldn't stay in business. But how did Caterina know they could get a camera there?

Tomaso reached under the counter. Black hair on his chest showed through his flimsy tee shirt and he definitely needed to change the oil in his baseball cap.

"Here's your camera," he said with a New York accent. "You have forty exposures. It's super fast film and I've given you two more rolls. All you have to do is push this button," he pointed to one on the top, "and this will give you telephoto. The camera whirred and the lens extended. "This one," he said with another push, "is wide angle. Point and click."

He paused, then continued as Rick nodded. "When you're done, come back with the camera and leave the film. Your photos will be ready an hour later."

"Great. I'll bring in the film rolls first thing tomorrow morning."

Rick gestured to Caterina. She handed the shopkeeper a banknote for the *Elle* Magazine she had been reading and they left.

As they entered the back door of the hotel, Rick caught the scent of food cooking. It smelled delicious. "What are you making?" he asked Josefina.

"*Fenek*. It's rabbit stew. And it's ready, so wash up."

CHAPTER 22

▼

Wednesday
8:30 PM
Qormi

Rick was anxious to get back the Duke's Challenge so they left for the farm shortly after they finished their meal. Caterina turned onto the road that led to her farmhouse and made some fancy moves to straddle several piles of horse droppings. Pulling to a stop, she stretched and took a deep breath. "We'll have to get right to sleep to be up early in the morning. I'll make an English breakfast for you."

He had to keep from gagging. Grease and gristle. Mustering a smile, he said, "I can hardly wait."

Carpenter called at ten. "I hope you haven't gone to bed. I just wanted to tell you that the Da-iz-ref didn't sail tonight. Malta customs confiscated the entire cargo and arrested the captain."

"Missile Guidance components?"

"Yes. By the way, Qadaffi sent a contingent to the coordinates on the overlay you found. One of the radical groups had set up munitions dump and weapons storage area there. When the Maltese police boarded the freighter, they found the ship was headed for the same area."

"It looks like you've shut a big part of the plot down."

"Not really. We found charts for wind and current patterns in the Arab's briefcase. He's up to something else."

"Thanks for leaving me holding the bag, by the way" Rick said. "The police took us in. Luckily the SOB had already taken off or we could have been in some big trouble."

"That's too bad. Let me know if you find out anything else."

Rick sat open-mouthed. He had known cold characters before but Carpenter stood head and shoulders above them all. What in the hell was wrong with him?

Unable to sleep, at 11:30 Rick went down to the kitchen. The house was comfortably quiet and the tangy order of wood smoke hung in the air. The major's file sat on the table open to the Duke's Challenge. 'If you search for a key, remove the city Malti.' The faux coat of arms with the diamond and dolphin intrigued him, too.

He dug out his drawing of the actual shield and compared them. The black and red backgrounds were the same, but a diamond with the word 'diamante' beneath it replaced the crow in the left side, and a dolphin labeled 'delfino' replaced the tower in the right. The banner at the bottom of the original, reading *Cosi Forma il Signore*, was missing from the Duke's drawing, which had only a broken line to suggest that letters should be written in. He counted the dashes. Seventeen.

Opening the major's notes, Rick found several pages in which he had sketched the coat of arms and had written in "Diamond and Dolphin" with various letters crossed off.

Rick was sure the Major had taken the wrong path. The Cornacchia family motto was in Italian. Rick took out a new sheet of paper and drew the seventeen dashes, then wrote *Diamante e Delfino* into the spaces. Unfortunately, one dash remained unfilled. *Diamante e Delfino* was only sixteen letters long.

He took out the original sending from the Duke and laid all the contents on the table. The first was the letter itself addressed to Lt. General Dobbie.

> "Dearest Enemy, I hereby challenge you to solve a puzzle. An object of great worth has been hidden in a public place. The enclosed clipping and the other contents of this letter will tell you where to find it. If you succeed, I will surrender myself to you as well as all my knowledge of possible resistance. Cordially, Alessandro Cornacchia."

The second enclosure was a black and white copy of the family coat of arms that appeared to have been torn from a book. The third was a tiny Italian-English dictionary with time-yellowed pages. Rick opened the book to the English word 'diamond' and found *Diamante* underlined in red ink. Who had made the mark? The major or Cornacchia himself? *Delfino* was also underlined. Alessandro was being scrupulously honest. But if those were the words to write into the blanks, why the extra space?

At one time the Major had taken the words 'Diamante e Delfino' and anagrammed them into 'Toil and find a diem/dime?' His attempts to treat it as a substitution cipher were equally unsuccessful. Even if it were a cipher, the sample was too small to allow him to decode it and after several pages of attempts he had scribbled, Bugger Italian. Bugger Cornacchia.

Rick's eyes began to feel heavy but he labored on. Crossing off the letters of *Diamante e Delfino* didn't leave anything resembling intelligible words in English or Italian.

The pages blurred.

He came to with a start when he realized he was sliding off his chair to the floor. Determined to work on, he sat up straight and rubbed his eyes. But the words no longer made sense. He attempted to get to his feet, but before he could, he fell asleep at the table.

4:26 AM

A fully dressed Caterina woke him in the morning. "Have you been here all night?" she asked.

He took a moment to admire her appearance before answering. "I guess so," he said in a cheerful voice. "Is it morning already?"

"Yes," she said glumly. "Go get cleaned up."

"I'll be right back," he chirped. "You look absolutely gorgeous." Ten minutes later he was back in the kitchen and found her working over a cast-iron skillet. Still half-asleep she was browning potatoes and scraping them with a spatula to keep them from burning. It made his mouth water. She pointed at a mug. "If you want coffee, all I've got is instant. It's in the cabinet."

He made himself a cup using hot water from the kettle on the stove. "Do you want some, too?"

"No," she said.

"Did you have a good sleep?"

"No!"

The day was getting off to a great start. "Is this just the way you are at four-thirty in the morning or did I do something wrong again?"

"It's not your fault. Or actually it is, but it's not your fault."

He nudged her foot with his. "Why did you do that?" she demanded.

"Your tape is stuck. Is there anything I can do to help?"

"You can help out by sitting down," she grumbled. "I'm almost done."

He did. He had only finished half of the coffee when Caterina's version of an English breakfast appeared on the table. Beautifully browned sausage links, potatoes, fried eggs, and tomato slices in manageable proportions. It smelled as good as it looked. And tasted as good as well.

Caterina brightened noticeably in the car. "This is so exciting!" she said. "Andrew knows how much I've wanted to do this but he never made the time to take me."

"The dope. I'm glad I aced him out at something."

Once again his eyes were riveted on her. Her dark hair hung loosely next to her oval face and billowed when she moved. It would be blown around a lot when they were in the balloon. She wore green eye shadow and he could tell she had spent extra time on her mascara. He especially liked the sleek dress and Gucci sandals. She had obviously spent a lot of effort to look alluring. Did he dare hope it was for his sake?

"Take a picture," she said. "It'll last longer."

"I'm staring, aren't I?"

"Uh huh. I don't mind though. Middle-aged men have always interested me."

"Middle-aged?! For heaven's sake, I'm only thirty-two."

"And when I'm thirty-two, you'll be forty and really old. Did you realize that?"

"Are you trying to tell me I'm too old for you?"

She cocked her head. "No. I'm trying to tell you I like older men."

"How old is Andrew?"

"Twenty-seven, three years older than I am," she said. She sat up straighter as they approached a crossroads. "We've still got more than twenty minutes. If you want, I can give you a tour of Mdina before we fly over. It isn't far from where we meet the balloonist. Have you been there yet?"

"No. And it sounds like a great idea."

The parking lot was empty when they arrived. The entrance to the city looked like a medieval castle and moat with a pair of statues on either railing guarding the entrance. "It's kind of spooky, isn't it?" she said. "It's called the Silent City. Everything is behind walls."

Rick noticed the cross-shaped windows. "Do you know where the word 'cross-fire' comes from?" he asked.

"I thought I did. I suppose you know something I don't."

"It literally means fire from the cross. The archers could cross their arrows to fire so they could cover a wider area."

"Really," she said. For the first time she didn't seem to resent his knowledge of trivia. Pointing up at the top of the battlements she said, "In the old days, anytime pirates or the Turks arrived, everyone would come to Mdina and take their places on the walls. Each noble was in charge of defending his own section. It was called the desme system."

What was once a moat was now overgrown with trees and was being used as a place to park and play tennis. As they walked, Rick noticed an empty tuna fish can sitting on the railing of the bridge. Investigating, he heard a meow from the branches of a nearby Mediterranean pine. An orange and white tiger cat climbed on the railing and stretched. Then it butted its head against his hand and purred loudly. It seemed so starved for attention that he wondered if it was a homeless animal that someone had been feeding.

"He's adorable but we don't have much time," Caterina said. "By the way, about a thousand years ago the City was about three times as big as it is now. The Saracens built the moat around it and renamed the city Mdina. They also brought new plants and showed us how to irrigate the soil. Do you know, they never once tried to interfere with our religion. I wish we were half as well-treated by the Knights."

Inside the gate of the city, narrow streets cut between tall buildings that were shut off by locked doors and gated walls. As in other towns he had visited on the island, corner buildings had eyes of Horus and street names deeply etched into the stone. The whole town had an air of remoteness. If neighbors ever met, it would have to be entirely by accident. "Friendly place," he said.

"It actually is. There are a lot of gift shops and almost constant tours and the people who live here are very outgoing. Before it became a tourist stop they used to lock the front gate at night. Cars weren't allowed inside the city until twenty years ago. You still have to be a resident to drive in, though."

"Do you know which house is Cornacchia's?"

"It's on Magazine Street at the north end of the city. This way."

Rick looked at his watch. "It's five-fifteen. Are you sure we have time?"

"We could take in the whole city in half an hour. It's only two hundred yards long."

Borgiswed, Lorenzo Cornacchia's palace, stood by itself behind a thirty-foot wall. The now-familiar coat of arms with crow and dolphin marked the iron gate. The lion's-head doorknocker had no hammer, but Rick did see a white button discreetly hidden below it. The building faced the street. The garden with the human chessboard would be to the rear and abut the wall of the city.

"Not much to see from this side, is it?" Caterina said. "I've seen photos of the Palazzo and it's really spectacular. *Borgiswed* was one of the few places that wasn't destroyed by the Earthquake of 1693. The tremors almost leveled the rest of the city. The Knights essentially rebuilt Mdina from scratch."

"How did the Knights and the nobles get along?"

"They didn't. The Knights thought the nobles were dissolute and the nobles thought the Knights distant and self-absorbed. In three hundred years the Knights never accepted a native Maltese into their order." She broke into a wicked smile. "Now if you're talking about the Knights and the nobles' *wives*…"

Rick understood the look. "Let's hear it. I know you're dying to tell me."

"Don't be such a male chauvinist spoilsport. We women have giggled about the stories for centuries. In fact I have Spiteri blood in me so I may be related to a Knight of St. John, myself."

"Spiteri?"

"It comes from the word 'Hospitaler.' In case you haven't noticed, I'm not built like most Maltese women. I have longer limbs so I'm taller and slimmer."

"Vive la difference!" Rick said.

"Thanks. At any rate, the nobles' wives threw masked balls for years and the Knights were regular attendees. Everyone danced, ate and drank until they paired up and went off somewhere together. The idea was that if they kept their masks on, they didn't know whom they were sleeping with."

"It sounds like Venice."

"You're right. The parties got so much out of hand that the Grandmaster of the Order had to prohibit them."

"So what were the nobles doing while all this was going on?"

"Bowling?" she said. "Or maybe they were chasing the peasant girls. I really don't know. Anyway, I think we better get back to the car."

Rick watched for the cat as they left but it was nowhere to be found. When he came back he would have to bring a new can of tuna. He also wondered if Kevin had been feeding Arthur. "Thanks for the tour," he said. "But I bet it looks more interesting from the air."

They quickly arrived at their destination, an open field near Mosta. "Look!" Caterina said excitedly. "There's the balloon! This is so exciting, I can hardly wait!"

Even from their distance they could see the lopsided multi-colored sphere billowing and firming up. When they stopped, a young man who was arranging gear on the ground came over to meet them. "Good morning. You're right on time. I'm Tim Douglas."

Rick made the introductions and they shook hands. The young man was very light-skinned with a crop of red hair that was brighter than Rick's natural color. He pointed toward the sky. "It's a nice day but we may have some turbulence."

Rick patted defensively at the camera case resting on his hip. Turbulence? He hoped not. He needed a steady hand for the photos. Douglas plucked at the struts to make sure they were straight and taut.

"You're certainly not a native," Rick said. "Where are you from?"

"Ottawa. I married a Maltese woman. We decided to live here a while to see if we want to stay. I like it here, but sometimes there isn't very much to do."

"Caterina lived in Toronto. She went to Queen's College."

"I met Sophie in Toronto, too. There are a lot of Maltese families living there." The heater inflating the balloon hissed louder as he adjusted a valve. He continued in a louder voice. "We'll be ready to take off in just a few minutes."

When Rick rode in a balloon back home, he enjoyed floating over the fields at six hundred feet, but the noise was constant. "Are you sure the flight will take us directly over Mdina?" he shouted.

"Straight overhead. The wind hasn't changed course since I've been here. We'll have six knots at our back."

Rick nodded. A little faster than he hoped for, but it would still leave him plenty of time to get his pictures. He glanced with approval at the wicker basket. It had give and looked more authentic than the high-impact plastic models. "Want to help me stow the gear?" Douglas asked.

"Sure," Rick replied. "Let's have at it." He handed Douglas the 20-foot coil of rope. Next came a 10-foot pike used to push themselves away from or closer to objects. Then, the Styrofoam cooler, which contained a bottle of champagne nestled in ice cubes and a pair of inverted champagne flutes. Two heavy sandbags were the last items aboard.

Minutes later they were ready to go. "Are you two newlyweds?" asked Douglas.

"Engaged," Rick said. As he said it, he bent toward Caterina. She responded with a passionate, open-mouthed kiss. Astonished, Rick's head spun and he could hardly breathe, but she refused to let him go.

"Are you sure you want to go on your ride or do you want to get a room instead?" Douglas shouted.

"We'll be right there," Rick shouted back, feeling his head spin. He blushed. "Sorry to delay the flight. I guess we got carried away."

With Rick holding her hand, Caterina mounted the steps and climbed in. He followed. When their feet were firmly planted inside, Douglas dumped a sandbag over the edge. The balloon strained but didn't move. After he dropped the second one they began to rise.

"You haven't been together very long, have you? I could tell the moment I saw you."

"You're right," Rick replied. "We're celebrating our engagement."

"You certainly gave her a nice ring," Douglas offered. Rick responded with a skeleton's grin.

They climbed higher and Mosta Dome became clearly visible to their right. The hill that rose to Mdina lay straight ahead. Caterina sidled closer and reached for his arm, moving her fingers slowly across his rockhard bicep. As she did, Rick noticed she wasn't wearing Andrew's diamond.

The wind picked up, whistling around the struts and swinging the basket from side to side. Douglas pulled a lever suspended from the balloon and they started to descend. When they leveled off, the swinging stopped.

Mdina had come a great deal closer. In their on-land tour, he had only seen walls. Now he saw golden buildings stretching skyward to catch the first rays of the morning sun. Directly below, a man was riding a tractor between rows of squash. Retrieving his arm from Caterina's grasp, Rick took the camera out of its case.

The balloon held a tight course. Looking down, Rick saw the road that led to the city and the terraced fields that climbed gently up the hill. He extended the telephoto lens. Wh-ing went the camera as they passed over the south wall.

He saw a large building with a round roof, a church. *Wh-ing*. The camera advanced itself automatically in a steady cadence in intervals of less a second. They passed over a terraced roof with a pair of chaise lounges extended to full length. Far below, the narrow street crawled like a dark snake. Now a television antenna pointed at them. In the yard below it, a stone plaza surrounded a circular fountain.

Wh-ing, whi-ing. The camera continued its relentless staccato. His heart beat faster as they neared a large building that only had one house next to it. It had to be *Borgiswed*. The flat roof, covered with half-tiles, had a definite Spanish look. A garden of many colors surrounded the house. Near the wall, light and dark green grass formed a checkerboard of 64 squares. Wh-ing, Wh-ing. Then the camera suddenly went silent. It had come to the end of the film.

Seeing the city slip away, he frantically pushed the rewind button. Caterina had the fresh roll ready for him by the time he had the first roll out of the camera. He snapped the camera shut and turned around to catch the last few shots before Mdina receded irretrievably into the distance.

Once again, they floated over patchwork fields. "Don't forget the ice chest," Douglas shouted. "We'll be landing soon."

Holding up a hand in thanks, Rick squatted to open the chest. He straightened up with the champagne flutes in his hand, and held them out to Caterina.

Radiant, she took them from him, making sure to show off the bare finger in the process. He untwisted the wire and removed the restraint. The cork rocketed over his head and disappeared over the edge of the basket. Farmers on the balloon's route must have had a regular harvest of corks.

He took her hand to keep it steady as he poured the first glass. She lifted it to her mouth and dipped her tongue into the wine before taking a slow sip. Rick's stomach felt like it was back on the roller coaster again.

Still sipping, she held out the other glass for him, giggling as wine spilled on her fingers. She wiped them against his lips. After carefully setting the bottle back into the cooler he took his glass. Eyes locked, they entwined arms and drank. When the flutes were empty, they threw them over the edge of the basket. Another tradition and another bumper crop for the unfortunate farmers, shattered champagne glasses.

Bare seconds later, the balloon began its descent, relentlessly heading toward a dark blue SUV and trailer parked ahead. The earth rushed toward them. A round green object became a tree with branches, and then one with leaves. They hit the ground with a bump and the canopy collapsed on top of them. The heater went silent and Douglas pushed the red, green, and yellow fabric away from them.

"Did you enjoy your ride?" he asked.

"Fantastic," Rick said, happy not to have to shout. "How about you?" he asked Caterina.

"It was absolutely wonderful," she said in a breathy voice. "I'll never forget it."

Rick grabbed the champagne bottle out of the ice chest and handed it to her. "We don't want to forget the wine," he said. He wished now that he had been more careful in opening it. Without the cork, the champagne would go flat in a matter of hours—and they had most of the bottle left. It took less than fifteen minutes to pack up. Rick and Caterina sat in the rear seat while Douglas drove. She clung to Rick's arm with knuckles white from her grip.

Douglas dropped them off by their car. "Best of luck," he said. "I can tell you're going to be very happy together. By the way," he said, turning to Rick, "Maltese women make the best wives." With that, he shook their hands and got back into the SUV. They both waved as he left.

Caterina turned to face Rick. "Well?" she said, eyes sparkling.

"Well what?"

She stamped her foot. Her face and neck muscles stretched in anticipation. "Aren't you going to say something?"

"What a ride?" he said with a shrug.

"That's not what I meant," she said, stamping her foot again. Rick found the mannerism girlish and incredibly appealing. "You're not blind," she insisted. "You must have noticed."

When he said, "Noticed what?" she rolled her eyes in exasperation. "My finger, asshole. Didn't you see I'm not wearing Andrew's ring"

"I noticed. I just figured you put it away so you wouldn't lose it."

"Aaah!" she screamed. "Have I ever taken it off before?"

"How should I know?"

"Did you *have* to spoil this moment?" she asked, closing her eyes and making fists. She beat him on his chest with them, then stopped and hugged him. "You win, you filthy bastard. I love you." With that she reached up and kissed him.

"Filthy bastard? Is that supposed to be a term of endearment?"

"That's exactly what you are for messing up my life the way you did. Oooh, how I despise you. Everything was fine until you came along."

"But you realized you love me?" Rick said, barely able to breathe. "When was that?"

"When you put your arm around me on the ferry I was sure I wouldn't be able to hold you off for very long, but the kiss convinced me. It wasn't a peck on the cheek, in case you didn't notice."

"Was it like this?" he asked, pulling her to him. This time their kiss left them both breathless. Overcome with emotion, he opened the car door and reclined the seats.

"What do you think you're doing?" she asked in disgust.

"No one will notice us here. I haven't seen anyone else around."

She pushed him away. "You must be kidding. I want romance our first time. What do you think I am? Some cheap whore?"

"I..."

"Besides, I have to tell Andrew before we do anything, anyway."

Rick goggled. "What do you mean, you have to tell Andrew? I'm about ready to explode and so are you."

"I know," she said, running her hand lovingly over his chin. "And I want to. Really I do. But I can't yet. It wouldn't be right."

Rick could hardly believe what he was hearing. "Why on earth not? I hope you're not saying you're saving yourself until after we're married, because if you are, I'm the King of England."

"I'm not pretending I'm a virgin," she said, stroking his chest. "I just have to tell him first."

"Does Andrew have muscles there?" Rick asked.

"No, but he has hair."

Rick flinched. His chest was as bare as a newborn's. "You still haven't told me why you have to talk to Andrew first. As a famous Minnesotan once said, 'if you're not planning to go to Minneapolis, why get on the train?'"

She drew a circle on his chest with her forefinger. "I guess I must be a little old-fashioned because I think that until I do tell him, we're still engaged."

He grabbed for his cellular and held it out to her. "Then call him and tell him."

She pushed his hand away. "Not while he's getting ready to go to work. I want to be able to talk to him."

"All right, but if anything happens to me in the meantime, you're going to feel terrible. I'll be a male version of Catherine of Siena and die a virgin."

"And I'm the Queen of England," she said.

Caterina dropped off the camera at Tomaso's on their way and went on to the Bellestrado. Josefina was washing the counter in the pub when they arrived. Without a word, Rick walked behind the bar and kissed her on the cheek.

"Caterina isn't going to marry Andrew," he whispered. "There's a new man in her life."

"I noticed," she whispered back, "No ring. Congratulations. I knew it would happen when she realized she was only marrying Andrew for his money."

"Huh?"

"Not for herself. For the church."

"Oh. Suppose you could turn on the computer for me?" he asked.

"Of course," said Josefina, gesturing for Caterina.

Rick followed Zija to the desk. "Did you ever check through your files to see if any of your guest files have been tampered with?"

"I actually had planned to do that today," she said as she stepped through the gate to let him in. "One of my neighbors needs to make some extra money. She can tend the bar for me while I'm busy."

"Let me know how much you're paying her and I'll reimburse you."

She waved the palm of her hand at him. "Don't be silly. It'll only be a few pounds. Get to work. I'll send Caterina."

He logged on the Web and quickly found Cornacchia's page. It was arranged like a brochure with links to information about the services Black Dolphin provided. Colored arrows superimposed on a flattened globe showed routes. Some of the arrows were so dense that they obliterated parts of the Mediterranean Sea and the Atlantic Ocean. After thoroughly exploring the entire web page site map, Rick went back to the search engine and clicked on the next entry in the Black Dolphin hit list. This time a familiar box demanding username and password greeted him. As he did, Caterina appeared.

"Here's Black Dolphin's Website," he said. "What should we use for a user-name?"

Caterina shrugged. "Marija, I suppose."

"Okay," he said, typing in the letters. "How about a password?"

"I have no idea," she said.

"D-I-L-D-O," he said as he typed. Five stars appeared in the password box and he hit the 'enter' key. "Nope. Guess not."

"You've got a one-track mind," Caterina said without smiling. "It was a good guess, though."

"Maybe I should try again and use the Maltese word. What is it?"

"Go take a cold shower," she said.

"By the way, how do you say 'let's go to bed' in Maltese."

She colored. "*Imxi fis-sodda.*"

"Eemshee fiss soda. How do you spell that?" he asked.

She glared at him. With a sigh, he went back to Google and continued to search through the other references. He discovered twelve more pages with twenty entries per page, most of which dealt with tonnage and descriptions of the ships, cargo classifications, departure and arrival times, proposed new routes and bulk fees.

Finally Caterina said, "I never realized a Web page could be so boring."

He agreed and logged off. "What now?" she asked.

"We pick up the pictures, I guess. Then we'll need equipment to work on them. Scissors, rubber cement and an exacto knife."

"I'm sure we have them."

"Good. We'll also need two good loupes and some 1940s maps of Mdina."

"Those will have to wait 'til later."

"Then let's get to work."

CHAPTER 23

▼

Thursday
9:13 AM

Stef sat at Pawlu's bare wooden table with his working papers spread out in front of him and the seeds of a just-consumed apple in his left hand. They had gone to Valletta to retrieve Stef's papers from the public locker where he had stashed them. Seeing Pawlu's expression when he had to fork out the twenty-five pound lost key fee made up for a day of starvation.

The tattered newspaper clipping entitled "The Duke's Challenge" was glued fast to a piece of cardboard and stood at an angle propped up next to an empty cereal box.

Stef took a covert look at Pawlu who was sitting in a wicker chair with the gun in his lap. He never brandished it, but he didn't want Stef to forget that he had it, either. The words of the challenge echoed in his mind. How much longer would it be before Pawlu's patience came to an end? Some time soon Stef would have to catch him in an unguarded moment if he hoped to survive.

*　　　*　　　*　　　*

Armed with the proper tools, Rick spread the photographs out on a table. His original idea was to find photos of the wall and work inwards as if assembling a jigsaw puzzle, but it took less than five minutes to convince him they were in for a lot of work.

"The photographs have the time on them," Caterina said. "Why don't we match them that way?"

"Henh," he said, slapping his head. "Why didn't I think of that?"

Digging around through the pieces, he found a photo notated 6:14:15 and matched it to another with 6:14:16. After examining both photographs under his glass he found the common element, the edge of a flowerbed along a house.

"Watch this," he said as he trimmed off the excess paper with the scissors and laid one photograph on top of the other.

"A perfect match," she said.

After thinning the back of the top photo at the point at which it would overlap, he applied some rubber cement and carefully laid it flat. Caterina just as quickly connected three pieces. Within minutes, a photographic mosaic began to take shape on the tabletop. Ten minutes later they merged the pieces they were working on. Laying the loupe flat against the photo, Rick examined their progress in detail. The walls of *Borgiswed* and several more buildings were now clearly in view.

"We're doing great," he said. "What's the next photo in the sequence?"

She sifted through the remaining photos. "This one." Nearly half of the tiled roof of the estate showed up in the new piece and he added it to their montage.

"What do you think?" he asked.

"It looks good to me. Why don't you keep working and I'll try to get some maps."

"And see if you can find a couple of good rulers and loupes, too. Good luck."

The mosaic was half-finished when she returned with what they needed and they drove back to the farm. Working together it took them less than an hour to complete the project. It wasn't one hundred percent consistent because some of the shots were taken from a different angle when Rick changed film, but *Borgiswed* and most of the rest of Mdina were complete in all its glory.

"Now what?" Caterina asked.

"The rest is pure mathematics," he said. "Simple ratios. What we have, essentially, are two maps, a big one," he said pointing to one of the maps she had brought, "and a little one," he pointed to the mosaic. "The only real difference between the two is the scale. All we have to do is find an identifiable feature on the mosaic and compare it to the same feature on the map."

He looked over the mosaic with the loupe. "Here we go. Mesquita Street." Pointing to the short street on the map, he said, "You can see where it starts just before the wall, and where it intersects Villagaignon Street."

Carefully laying the ruler against the photo, he held the loupe to his eye and measured the distance on the mosaic. "Two centimeters or 200 millimeters. Take your ruler and measure the same distance on the map."

"It's 12 centimeters."

"That's 1200 millimeters," Rick said. "That means that the map is six times bigger than the photo. So, one centimeter six meters."

"All very interesting," she said. "So what?"

"So now I can start looking for where the Shield may be hidden."

Caterina got up. "I'll leave that up to you. Are you hungry?"

"Starving," he said, getting to his feet. "Come over here, I want to show you something." When she did he quickly moved behind her, caught her arms and wrapped them around her body.

"Stop that," she said, pulling away from him.

"What if I don't?"

"Big strong man," she hissed. Not knowing what else to do, he kissed her on the cheek. She responded by kissing him on his lips, passionately.

Surprised and slightly out of breath, he whispered, "Does this mean you like to be tied up?"

"I don't know," she said, making another weak attempt to escape. "Andrew never tried. But then he never tried lots of things."

"What did you expect?" Rick asked. "He's an accountant." As he said it he kissed her on the side of her neck.

"Don't," she pleaded. "You know we have to wait."

"I know," he said, gently running the tip of his tongue over her neck. "When are you going to tell him?"

She squirmed, then relaxed and leaned against him. In a breathy voice she said, "We're going to have dinner together if I can get away." When he brushed his lips against her neck just below the hairline, she shivered. "I...I hate to have to tell him," she said. "He'll be devastated."

"I know." As he began to nibble an ear she responded by backing up and rubbing her hips against him. He quickly let go of her and moved away. "He isn't a stalker, is he?"

"Of course not," she said, sounding surprised. She turned, flushed, and he got a strong impression she was sorry he had let her go. "I keep telling you, he's a very nice person. You two should meet sometime."

"Absolutely not!" Rick exclaimed. "You know how I feel about him and I'm sure he'll feel the same way about me once he finds out what's happened. And I don't blame him. If I were in his place, I'd want to tear me limb for limb, too."

"Forget Andrew," she said. Moving to him, she took his right hand placed it firmly on her butt. With her right she pulled his face to hers. She stared him in the eye. "*Imxi fis-sodda*," she said in a low voice.

"That's supposed to be my line," Rick said. "And besides, we can't do anything until you talk to you-know-who, remember?"

"You're right," she growled, pushing him away. "Give me your phone."

Excitement rose by the second as he handed her his cellular. How he wished he knew more Maltese and could listen in on the conversation. But just watching her was enough to get his blood perking. She stood with eyes closed, gesturing with her free hand. A short time later she wiped at her eyes and moved her free hand to her heart. When she finished she handed the phone back to him. In an angry voice she said, "I hope you're satisfied. I hate myself and it's all your fault."

"My fault? I'm okay with waiting."

"Well I'm not," she said.

"Have it your way," he said with a shrug. "I'll get the champagne."

He followed her up the stairway and found Winnie the Pooh on guard perched on a pillow. Before they reached the bed she stopped and turned to him. "I want you to know I'm absolutely furious at you," she said. Putting her hands on his shoulders, she pulled him to her and kissed him gently but earnestly, as if trying to reassure herself.

His heart pounded as she sat on the edge of the bed and his hands shook as he poured wine. Bubbles drifted languorously to the surface. A quick taste told him that it wasn't as peppy as it was on the balloon, but it wasn't bad, either. "Here you are, love," he said, handing a glass to her. "To us."

"It's warm," she said in a soft voice.

"I'll throw it away," he said, reaching for her glass.

She took his hand. "No. I don't mind warm."

He sat beside her. After they touched glasses she took a delicate taste. Rick downed his wine in a single swallow. Setting the glass on the nightstand, she grasped his hand and bent forward toward him. Her eyes were luminous and her breath sweet with champagne.

"I love you, Cat," he said softly.

"Oh Rick!" she said as their lips gently met.

11:40 PM

Though he found it hard to concentrate, Rick returned to the mosaic after Caterina fell asleep. Making tiny sweeps with the loupe he found the corresponding areas of the map and compared them. After an hour's work he had covered only a small portion of the mosaic and found nothing promising. As he bent forward, the ring of his cell phone startled him. He was greeted by Stef's voice.

"'Lo, bro. I have something I've been told to read to you," Stef cleared his throat. "'Tonight, you will deliver the drawing to a spot that will be described to you in exchange for my release. If you do not, you will receive a call an hour later to tell you where you can find my body. Please do what they say.' End quote. Did you get all that?"

"Yes," Rick said. "Are you being treated all right?"

"Much better than before, thank you. But I have to go. Someone's trying to break my wrist pulling the phone out of my hand."

A familiar voice came on. "Now that we understand each other, we will contact you later. You will have only enough time to get to the exchange stop when we do. Congratulations on finding the drawing, by the way."

"I'll be waiting for your call," Rick said.

Seconds later Caterina appeared in the doorway dressed only in a robe. She smiled sleepily, rubbed her eyes with her fists and yawned. "You had your wicked way and deserted me."

"Sorry, *Mahbub*, I just had too much to do."

"I forgive you. Who was on the phone?"

"Stef," he said. "Naxxar wants to make a trade. We only have a few hours and I've got a week's worth of work to do to get ready for tonight."

"I'll get dressed," she said.

"Where's Kirkop?" he whispered.

"Not very far away," Caterina said. "It's just a tiny village."

"Tiny or not, it has a leather shop." He turned back to the directory. "I just hope we can find the chemicals we need."

Caterina had a suggestion. After a short drive later they acquired a small bagful of bottles and Rick breathed easier. The hard part done they stopped at an art supply store before making a twenty-minute drive to Kirkop where she parked in front of a tiny shop next door to a pub. An oily smell greeted him as he stepped inside. Hides of various sizes and colors hanging suspended by clothespins from lines.

"You are in luck, my friend," the shopkeeper said. "The Masons haven't ordered lambskin for a while so I have two pieces in stock."

Rick picked one up and inspected it. Though slightly thicker than the vellum, it was surprisingly close to the size of the drawing. More importantly, the color was similar. "I'll take them both."

Grinning broadly he returned to the car. "That's it. We can go home."

*   *   *   *

Stef's stomach hurt, but not from lack of food. How could he willingly play a part in a conspiracy to deceive his own brother? He had little choice and the drawing was now of little consequence. Finding the Shield was all that mattered. And the solution to the Duke's Challenge was just a few tantalizing steps away.

*   *   *   *

"I don't know how much time we have," Rick said, "but I think we can come up with a copy that will fool them."

"What're all the chemicals for?"

"Aging the leather. We can use your friend's copier to make a counterfeit."

"Do you really think you can fool them with a copy?"

"If it will be good enough to take in some of the smaller auction houses in daylight it should be good enough to fool Pawlu in the dark."

Rick unpacked the bags on the kitchen table. When done he had three paint-brushes, two metal paint trays, a bottle of distilled water, a measuring cup, a set of metal measuring spoons and two brown bottles with glass stoppers.

"All right," he said, rubbing his hands together. He began by pouring one tea-spoon of lye into the tray and added a total of twenty cups of water. Taking a deep breath, he dipped one of the horsehair brushes into the solution. With a slow even motion he painted a strip along the left side of the lambskin, dipped the brush and started again. Two more strokes covered the entire surface.

He let the treated skin sit for three minutes, then examined the surface of the lambskin under the loupe. As hoped, the color of the skin hadn't changed, but the glossy patina of the surface had dulled significantly. Using a larger brush he painted the entire skin. When he was done he rinsed the surface liberally with a wet rag.

"So far so good," he muttered.

After a thorough drying with paper towels, he laid the skin back down on the table. In the second tray he made a 1 to 20 mixture of potassium bromate and water. The hoped-for light tan tinge appeared as soon as he touched the brush to the hide.

After a second coat, he repeated the process again on the edges where the aging process would be most obvious.

"What do you think?" he asked.

Caterina ran a loupe over the surface. "It looks authentic to me."

"Let's compare it to the original," said Rick.

It was a good match. No one would be able to tell the difference unless they saw the two together. "Let's find your printer friend," he said.

"Are you sure the copier can do the job?" Rick asked, giving the Toshiba eStudio 80 a nervous look.

"It's state of the art," Hannibal Galea responded. "I'll do a test run on a piece of heavy-stock paper. Let's see what it can do." He began by laying the drawing on the photographic tray. Rick shuddered to think of the delicate inked lines of the drawing being exposed to such an intense light, but there was no alternative. Galea pulled out a flat tray at the bottom of the copier and laid the cardstock on it. "We'll put it through at max resolution and print quality."

They both stood transfixed watching the bright light march across the length of the lambskin. Galea pulled out the lower tray. "Let's see what we have."

Viewed side by side, the results were astonishing. The printed image was an exact duplicate. Even the color of the ink seemed to be a perfect match.

"Ready to try the lambskin?"

"Go for it," Rick said. He held his breath as the printer pulled the tray out, then exhaled in relieved exultation when he saw the results. Except for the miniscule difference in the color of the lambskins, the two pieces were identical.

"A masterpiece," Rick said.

Once they were outside, Rick turned to Caterina. "We're on our way. Now all I have to do is put in the holes and add as many penstrokes as I can in the time we have left. I can tell already that it will be one hell of a fine forgery. I hope you can put your hands on some India ink."

Back at Caterina's table he looked at the original at an angle with a bright light, Rick could see the indentations Cellini's pen had made when he was drawing. After a few strokes of his own with a sharp point and ink, he realized what an enormous job duplicating the whole drawing would be. But it had to be done.

8:21 PM

Rick was still at work when his cell phone rang. The man he suspected was Pawlu Naxxar said, "Good evening, my friend. Do you have the drawing?"

"In my hand," Rick said.

"Very good. I'll give you the instructions where to bring it. Is Caterina Borg with you?"

Rick jumped, surprised Pawlu would use her name. "Yes."

"Tell her to drive you to the religious art museum at Zabbar. She will know where it is. Wait there for further instructions. You have forty minutes to get there. That is more than enough time."

"We'll be there. I'm sure you've picked out an open place to make the transfer."

"Yes, and you'll have a chance to look over the area when you get there," the caller said. "As you must realize, we will need to examine the drawing. Once we are sure it's genuine, no one will have the slightest interest in you or your brother."

The blank caller identification LED display turned off as Rick pushed the end-call button. "We're on," he said. "We've got our meeting place. It's a religious museum in Zabbar."

As they left the house to get into the car they discovered another car in their driveway. Rick's heart jumped. *Who the hell is that?*

Almost in answer the driver's door opened and a man got out. Rick recognized him immediately. It was the agent who was driving Carpenter to the archives. "What can I do for you?" Rick asked.

"Just making a social call. Were you planning to go somewhere?"

"As a matter of fact we were."

"Good," the agent said. "Take this with you." He handed Rick a Glock 9mm pistol.

"What's this for?" Rick asked.

"Just in case you need it. Have a nice night." With that he got into the car and backed out of the driveway.

Bewildered, Rick watched him until he was out of sight. "This is too strange for words," he said. "How did he know where we were? And how did he know I might need a gun?"

As he said it, a frightening thought crossed his mind. "You don't suppose..."

He took out his cell phone. "I took my phone to the embassy when I found the plastique in it. They may have fixed it so Naxxar couldn't trace or cause me trouble but it never occurred to me that they could have inserted a device of their own."

"If they did, why would they give themselves away by showing up here?"

"I don't know but we may have more problems than we realize," Rick said.

It was not quite nine when they arrived in Zabbar. As Caterina slowed, Rick's gut tightened. He fingered the rolled up lambskin in his hands and thought of the Glock in the glove compartment. The weapon was light and he liked the feel of it. When he met Stef's captors he would have the drawing in his hands. He would also have the gun tucked under his belt, covered by his shirt.

Caterina pulled to a stop next to a building with a stone angel standing in front of it. Rick got out of the car and looked around. The long lines of parked cars on either side of the street provided perfect cover for an ambush and he didn't like it at all. "I don't get it. He can't expect me to make an exchange here," he said.

His phone rang. "I see you've arrived, Mr. Olsen. Kindly hold the drawing up over the top of the car."

Covertly scanning the area for the caller's position, Rick reached into the car and took the lambskin. As instructed he held it as high above the top of the car as he could reach.

"Very good. Now if you will turn to your right and walk up the street you will see me."

Rick turned. Someone stood twenty yards away in the darkness. Even though the man was well away from any direct light, Rick could easily see the black mask he was wearing over his face. "I see you."

A large figure enswathed in a blanket stepped up next to the masked man. "This is your brother," the voice said. With that, the masked man removed the blanket from the figure's face. Even in the dark, Rick recognized him.

"Hi Stef," Rick called.

"Hey, bro. Thanks for coming."

"My colleague has a gun pointed at the back of your brother's head," the masked man said. "I assume you brought a weapon of your own."

Rick held up the Glock.

"You may find a place of cover and point it at me. Place the drawing on the hood of the car nearest you and I will come for it. Any attempt to break our agreement will cost your brother's life. Yours, too. The same goes if I find anything other than your brother's drawing."

"It's called a Mexican stand-off," Rick said. "Unfortunately I can't know if you have another person with you with a gun pointed at me. If anything does happen to me, the police will be here in less than a minute."

"I presume you're bluffing, but it makes no difference. You have nothing to fear as long as you aren't trying to trick me. You're close enough that we don't need the telephones any longer."

"Sorry," Rick said, making up a lie on the spot. "Both of our telephones have to remain on. That's part of my security system."

"Very well," the masked man said as he flicked on a powerful lantern. "Mr. Stefan Olsen, please describe the drawing to me. What kind of paper is it on?"

"It isn't paper," Stef said. "It's vellum. Lambskin."

"What does it say at the right side?"

"Cornacchia." Rick mouthed the word with Stef as he said them.

"What is the name of the artifact?"

"The Aegis Dei."

Every muscle in his body tensed as Rick waited for the next question. Instead, the masked man carried the lambskin to Stef. Turning the lantern onto it he asked, "Is this the drawing?"

Stef carefully looked it over before answering. "Yes."

The masked man began to walk toward Rick. "It appears we have a trade."

Rick sighed in relief. He turned, expecting to find Stef walking toward him, but no one was in sight. Jamming the phone back into his pocket he rabbited behind a car, expecting to be followed by a hail of bullets. Glock raised, he aimed in the direction he had last seen Stef's captor. All he saw was an empty street. The masked man had disappeared, too.

CHAPTER 24

▼

Thursday
10:00 PM
?

More ashamed of himself than he had ever been in his life, Stef sat silently as Pawlu parked in front of a darkened townhouse. The back car door opened and the man who had been with them at Zabbar got out. Pawlu rolled down his window and handed him a small bundle of banknotes.

"*Grazzi*," the man said, then quickly disappeared into the darkness.

"Where are you taking me now?" Stef asked as Pawlu started the engine.

"To our new quarters. We'll be safe there. Regrettably I'll have to tie you up again," Pawlu said. "But take heart, I'm sure it will be the last time it will be necessary."

"Why? You don't need me anymore now that you have the drawing."

Pawlu responded with a sigh of exasperation. "You are impossible, my friend," he said. "As we both know, what I'm being paid for the drawing is nothing compared to what we can get when we find the Shield. And, as I told you before, I'm not a murderer."

"Then how about stop starving me to death and giving me something to eat."

"Forgive me," Pawlu said, pointing at a bag on the floor. "You'll find apples and oranges in there."

After devouring an apple, core, stem and all, Stef finished the second one slowly, enjoying each bite. The juice was sweeter than anything he had ever tasted before. His fingers shook as he took the thin peel off an orange. It was small and he took the whole thing into his mouth, eagerly crushing it with his molars. Juice covered his whole palate. It wasn't until then that he realized that he was not so much hungry as dying of thirst. "Do you have any water?"

"There's a bottle on the floor next to you."

Groping about, Stef found a two-liter container of Evian water. He drank nearly half of it in three swallows. "Good," he said in appreciation. "Thank you."

"I have sandwiches for you at our new home, and goat's milk," said Pawlu. "I'll make sure you're well-fed before I go."

*   *   *   *

Rick flicked on his cell phone to call Kevin. The phone rang several times, then the answering machine came on. "Hey, Kevin," Rick said, "give me a call."

"What do you want?" Kevin interrupted in a gruff voice.

Nearly dropping the phone, Rick gasped, "Sweet Jesus, don't ever do that again. What's eating you?"

"Sorry. One of my servers is down. 'Sup?"

"I have another job for you. Black Dolphin Shipping has a web site. One of the pages has a username and password. I need to find out what they are."

"Really? And how soon would you like that done?"

"By tomorrow, hopefully," Rick said with a laugh. "ASAP."

"I'll see what I can do. Any luck finding Stef?"

"All bad. He was ten feet away from me," Rick said. After he finished relating what had happened at Zabbar he said, "What surprises me is that it looked to me as if Stef didn't even try to get away."

"Bummer. Okay. I'll take a look at the Cornacchia's web site and get back to you. I just hope I don't interrupt anything next time."

"That's all been worked out," Rick said. "As a matter of fact, so much so I may be living in Malta instead of Minnesota."

"Sounds serious. I'll talk to you later."

*   *   *   *

Stef woke up with Pawlu shaking him roughly. Opening his eyes, he looked into a face livid with rage "Your brother tricked us!" Pawlu shouted. "The drawing is a forgery."

Even though terrified, Stef was pleased to think that Rick had triumphed. "It can't be a forgery," he said with a yawn. "I recognized it immediately."

"It's a photocopy," Pawlu said. "All the buyer had to do was take a look with a loupe."

"I see," Stef said. "Would you please untie me and let me sit up?"

Free of his bonds, Stef swung his legs over the edge of the bed and stretched. "Continue."

"*He told me to take a look. I did and I could see what he meant. I was sure he would shove a knife in my ribs.*"

"*What happened then?*"

"*He offered me 5,000 lira for the copy. I was happy to accept it.*"

"*I don't understand why he gave you so much for a forgery. Are you sure it wasn't the real item and he wanted to buy it at a cheaper price?*"

"*Yes. He gave me a loupe and showed me how the printing didn't break the surface of the hide. He said he understood why I was fooled because the copy was of the real drawing. He also said there were more pages and that he wanted them.*"

"*He's mistaken. There are no other pages,*" *Stef said.* "*What else happened?*"

"*He asked me if I had returned you to your brother and he seemed pleased to hear I hadn't.*" *He stopped and put a hand on Stef's shoulder.* "*We are all alone, my friend, and in great danger. Now George Bezzina and his men as well as my former Arab associate will be looking for us. If any of them find us, we will both be murdered. We no longer have any options. We must find the basin.*"

Stef took a big breath. It was time to run a bluff. "*I'm almost sure I know where it is, but I need a map.*"

Pawlu grinned, showing off his gold tooth. "*Whatever you need I will get for you.*"

✳   ✳   ✳   ✳

11:33 PM

"Mr. Olsen?" said a raspy voice Rick had never heard before. "Forgive me for calling you so late but we didn't finish our transaction this evening."

Rick snapped to attention. "You're right. Maybe we both got what we deserved."

"Actually, my intent has always been honest. I would have seen that my end of the bargain was satisfied after I verified the authenticity of the drawing."

Rick was thrilled. Cornacchia!

The caller continued, "I wanted to tell you that I bear you no hard feelings and that we can still settle this matter amicably since no exchange was actually completed. Please join me for dinner at *Borgiswed* tomorrow night and bring the real drawing with you. Do you play chess?"

Rick was stunned. "You can't be serious."

"I didn't mean to insult your intelligence, my friend. We will have a referee of sorts. Do you know Inspector Rafael Micallef of the Malta police?"

Rick frowned. "We've met."

"He'll be with us. At some point you will hand me the drawing and let me take my time examining it. When I'm convinced the drawing is genuine, my manservant will go up to my houseguest's room to get his luggage. Does a million US dollars sound acceptable to you?"

"Very generous, if we're left alive to spend it."

Cornacchia laughed. "Despite what you may think, I'm an honorable man. Just be sure to bring the complete document."

Caught off guard, Rick nearly blurted out his surprise. Instead he caught his breath and answered, "Of course. What happens then?"

"You'll both be free to leave with the Inspector. He will have no idea what's going on."

"Too late, I'm afraid. He already does. I told him about the drawing when I was questioned about the attempted break-in at my hotel."

"Don't worry, I've already explained that to his satisfaction. The Inspector knows that it's all a misunderstanding and that your brother has been a guest at my palazzo since he arrived here."

"Good, but not quite good enough," Rick said. "He must still wonder why the men he found under my bathroom window were trying to break into my room."

"Ah yes," Cornacchia chuckled. "You apparently made the mistake of flashing a wallet full of banknotes at the airport and one of the cab drivers saw you. They sent some friends to rob you at the airport but you put up so much of a fight they settled on taking your luggage and valuables instead. They still wanted your wallet. When they attempted to burglarize your room you caught them in the act. It was a bad night for them all the way around, it seems."

"I see," Rick said. "And I imagine you didn't know that one of the burglars had a syringe with him that had enough sodium pentobarbital in it to kill a horse."

Cornacchia went silent. "I didn't," he said, sounding genuinely shocked. "I had no idea, believe me."

"Be that as it may, let's get back to the Inspector. He still knows about the drawing. I told him I didn't know where it was. How do I explain having it?"

"Your brother told you where you could find it. Your phone seems to have been out of order for several days. He was terribly upset because he knew how you would worry. And of course he had no idea of how else to reach you."

Another score. Whatever else Cornacchia was, he certainly was an inventive liar. "My missing phone was in the police report I filed."

"You had it in your pocket and didn't realize it."

"Very clever. Let's say I agree. What will happen after the transfer?"

"Inspector Micallef will give you and your brother a ride to wherever you want to go. As a matter of fact, if you're concerned about safety, as well we both should be, I suggest you contact Inspector Micallef and have him escort you to my home when you come."

"A good suggestion. What time?"

"Six-thirty," Cornacchia said. "We can eat and play chess afterwards. Later we can have a libation together. When we're done, you will both be free to take your payment and leave."

"That sounds agreeable. Let me speak to Stef," said Rick.

"He isn't here, but he's safe. He'll be there for the trade. The people who have him know what will happen to them if they try to harm him."

"I don't believe you," Rick said. "I want to talk to him."

"Unfortunately that isn't possible, but you can be sure I would never renege on our bargain with Inspector Micallef present. He will be coming to pick up my annual contribution to the policemen's association. If you think I'm desperate enough to try to harm him, too, he's already made his plans known to several other people and I also invited his wife to join us. Unfortunately she already made another commitment."

"Another point for you, but you still lose," Rick said. "You can't take the risk that we'll tell the Inspector about Stef's kidnapping after we leave. And we'll have the money to prove our claim."

Cornacchia's voice became less pleasant. "You can be sure I realize that. If you try to incriminate me, you will only succeed in getting yourself into trouble. Rest assured I am capable of doing it. But you bring up a good point. Right now there is risk associated with both our positions. Neither of us can afford a misstep."

"I've played many chess games like that," Rick said. "They're very enjoyable."

"I was sure you would see things that way," Cornacchia rasped. "Now please forgive me for interrupting your sleep."

Rick put the phone back into his pocket. Looking up, he saw Caterina standing by the door with eyes flashing. "What was that all about?" she demanded.

"I'm going to Borgiswed to exchange the drawing for Stef."

"You can't be serious!" Caterina said. "Cornacchia can't be trusted."

"Inspector Micallef will be with us."

"Even so, it's far too dangerous. Cornacchia knows you won't be willing to let everything drop. And you know Cornacchia won't call it quits, either. I can't believe you would even consider doing anything so foolish."

"I don't have any choice. Cheer up. I know enough not to go into a battle of wits unarmed. I'll just make sure that he doesn't see the weapons."

"Forget it," she said.

"You like to give orders, don't you."

"I don't give orders, I give lessons."

"Good. I intend to keep learning as long as Queen Mab lets me."

"What's that supposed to mean?" Caterina asked.

"I told you before, she tends to drive a hard bargain. She helps you find love but she charges a high price. Remember poor Romeo and Juliet."

"Don't say things like that," she said in a worried voice. "You frighten me."

"Don't worry. She's never been up against me before," he said with a grin. When he looked at Caterina he saw that she wasn't smiling.

CHAPTER 25

▼

Friday
6:00 AM
?

Stef took a deep breath. The mass of papers that once sat on the kitchen table had boiled down to one, a map, and he put the loupe to his eye and bent forward to look at it. His pulse raced.

There it was.

Pawlu hurried over to join him. "Did you find something?"

"Yes!" Stef shouted. "I know where Alessandro Cornacchia hid the Shield!"

✳   ✳   ✳   ✳

Rick got up at six and called Father Santorini then joined Caterina at the horse barn. In the stillness of the morning, horses and riders moved at a gentle trot. As they rode, Caterina pointed out the enclosed fields. Her farm had two, which made it unusually large.

"My father was the eldest son and inherited the land when my grandparents died," she said. "His brother, *Ziju* Giacomo lived with us and worked in the fields until my parents died. Josefina asked him to stay and tend the farm for me but he moved to Canada. I lived with him for a year when I was there."

"Who runs the farm for you now?"

"Uncle Michael, Giacomo's brother. He keeps 75 percent of what he gets for the crops and the rest goes to the church. Do you want to see where I rebuilt Tarbija?"

"Sure would," he said.

She got off her horse and led them to a large shed behind the farmhouse. "It used to be a blacksmith shop until Great-Grand-Uncle Dominic died in 1956. It wasn't used at all until I moved back. Wait until you see all the wonderful old tools."

Rick dismounted and followed her into the shed. Inside, a chain hung from the ceiling, and a socket wrench lay next to a dirty oil filter on a wooden workbench. "This is my workshop," said Caterina. "The blacksmith's tools are in the back."

It was a scene from the turn of a century past with a stone kiln at the farthest wall, a huge anvil sitting in front of it, and a variety of tongs, hammers, awls and double-handled knives hanging on the walls from nails. "This place is great," Rick said. He squatted, picked up a piece of charcoal from the floor and sniffed it. Even half a century later he could still smell the blacksmith's fire. "Did Great-Grand-Uncle Dominic live here?"

"No," said Caterina. "He and Great-Grand-Aunt Sara lived in Qormi. Sara had a dress shop there. She made the dresses she sold."

"Was she a fashion designer?"

"You could say that," Caterina said. "She made clothes for big women."

"My God! Why didn't I think of that before? You're a genius."

"I know. What did I say?"

"I think you just told me how to find Stef."

✳   ✳   ✳   ✳

Though it was still early, Mdina's narrow streets were already filled with tourists. Grammar school students stood lined up against the wall inside the gate waiting for instructions about where they were going and how they should behave. Many adults already were strolling through the streets, looking up at the buildings like rubes getting their first look at big-city skyscrapers. Stef quickly passed them, followed by Pawlu, who was casually strolling with a hand inside his suit jacket.

"What are we looking for?" Pawlu asked.

"A cul-de-sac between San Pawl and Villagaignon off of Mesquite. It should angle to the northeast."

They walked. As they did he became more concerned. All they found was a continuous wall. "I don't understand," Stef said. "It has to be here. It's on the map."

"That map is 75 years old," Pawlu said. Stef didn't like the trace of menace in the man's voice.

"Even so, it can't have disappeared without a trace. Let's take another look."

Pawlu pulled Stef to a stop and unrolled a yellowed paper. Stef pointed. "That's what we're looking for."

"Perhaps we can narrow down where the street used to be."

"Better than that. We can pace it off and pinpoint it."

"What do we do when we find it?" Pawlu asked. "We can't get behind the wall."

"We will have to use our ingenuity," Stef replied.

*   *   *   *

Father Santorini ran a questioning finger over the surface of the blank lamb-skin. Rick had prepared it as he had the one he used for the forgery. "Ibrahim said he was happy to help draw the inscriptions inside the basin," Santorini said, "but I don't know what he can do in the little time we have."

Rick handed him a two-inch piece of a feather that he had cut into a point. "Whatever he gets done will have to do. I tried to make a photocopy of the drawing and it didn't fool anyone. The inscriptions will have to be genuine this time."

Looking worried, Santorini shook his head. "I'm sure I'll have to do the work myself. I've worked on leather manuscripts before. It's terribly time-consuming."

"Write as many as you can, but a hundred characters should be enough."

Santorini still frowned. "I'll do my best."

Three bare upper story windows glinted in the sun above the milliner's shop. "That's the building," Caterina said. "Are you thinking of dropping down on the roof from a helicopter?"

"Why not?" He pointed at the carbon copy building next to it. "What's the building next to it?"

"A convenience store," she said. "They sell film and candy. I sometimes stop to get ice cream there when I'm driving the cab."

"With all the ice cream you eat, how do you keep your girlish figure?" Rick asked.

"I don't eat anything else," she replied.

Rick shielded his eyes to look at the sky. The sun beamed brilliantly. "It's a beautiful day. How would you like to do some sun-bathing?"

Twenty minutes later Caterina pulled up and parked at an angle behind the buildings. She got out of the car carrying a long cardboard carton in one hand and two large hardbound books in the other. Rick followed her with his eyes until she disappeared from view up the stairway. She was a picture of a college student returning from a class. No one would imagine she was wearing a bikini beneath the clothes and that she had a chaise lounge in the package.

A screen door slammed. As he waited for her to return, he squatted on his haunches to inspect the petals of a tiny blue flower growing out from under a wall in the building. It was an anemone, one of Malta's flowers that could live on a smidgen of dirt and a drop of water. Like desert nomads, they showed the rest of the animal kingdom how wasteful most creatures are with resources.

A short time later the screen door slammed again and he got to his feet. Caterina reappeared, now dressed in her tiniest bikini and carrying the folded lounge in one hand and a book in the other. He could imagine Carpenter's men's eyes bulging. With the Mitsubishi blocking the view of the stairway, no one would see him as he climbed the stairway. After gathering up the six-foot long aluminum channel he bought from a construction supplier he noiselessly started up the stairs in bare feet.

Reaching the landing, he found Caterina's jeans and tee shirt lying in a pile in front of the door. A roof overhang ran between the buildings and Pawlu's porch was some four feet away. Someone at a great enough distance might see him, but eluding surveillance no longer was his main problem. He had to cross a four-foot chasm that separated the two railings, and the aluminum channel was his bridge.

Angling the metal piece upward, he slid it across to the other railing. He spent several seconds moving it around to make sure it was straight and evenly distributed. Satisfied, he lashed the metal in place at his end using 3-mil electrical wire.

He climbed up on the railing and took a deep breath before stepping into the channel with his right foot. The bridge remained steady. Heart pounding, he planted his left foot in front of it. He exhaled loudly. The bridge held. When he got to the other porch, he rapped on the door. No one answered. It took him less time to open the door than it did to make the crossing.

Pawlu Naxxar's apartment reeked of tobacco. The floor was gritty under Rick's bare feet and the scurrying noise from the kitchen suggested the presence of mice. Despite the housekeeping problems, Naxxar had good taste in furniture and had obviously spent serious money on the black leather sofa and matching easy chair in the living room. The eight-foot plasma television on the opposite wall must have cost at least ten thousand dollars. Being one of George Bezzina's lieutenants had its benefits.

A roll-top desk was Rick's first destination, and he spent several minutes going through the many drawers and compartments before coming up empty. After searching through the kitchen cabinets and the shoes in the bedroom closet, he finally spotted what he was looking for beside the unmade bed. Tucked away in a corner was a black plastic file box. His heart beat faster as he opened the lid. Thumbing through the files, he found a folder of credit card statements and yellow customer receipts. He shoved his pockets full of paper and returned the box to where he found it.

It was time to go.

Retracing his steps, he returned to the other porch and gathered up the channel. When he reached the bottom of the stairs he stopped and made a megaphone with his hands. "Meow," he called softly.

*   *   *   *

Stef and Pawlu carefully paced the steps along the wall beginning at the intersection of Villagaignon and Mesquita Street. Both ended up at the same spot. "It must be right in back of this wall," said Stef as he wiped perspiration from his forehead.

"See if there's a name on the gate that's ahead," Pawlu replied.

After a careful look, Stef shook his head. "I don't see anything."

"This is not good. Other than climbing the wall, I don't see how we're going to get inside."

"If we do, you'll have to give me a boost," Stef said.

"This is no time for levity," said Pawlu in an angry voice.

"I think I can get us inside the gate. What we do when we get there is up to you. We're going to need to get some business cards made first, though."

Pawlu's face relaxed into a smile, showing off his gold tooth. "And what kind of ingenious plan do you have now?"

Stef's face was grim. "You'll see."

*   *   *   *

Caterina was fully clothed when he got into the car. "I sure hope you found something worthwhile," she said. "I almost froze to death."

Rick showed her the receipts. "I got to thinking that maybe Pawlu brought Stef some clothes. Then I thought credit card. You said Josefina has a credit card merchant number. What I'm hoping is that one of the credit card companies has another address on file. That's probably where Naxxar is keeping Stef."

*   *   *   *

Pawlu straightened his jacket as Stef pushed the button on the gate. "Iva," a tinny voice said.

"Good morning," Stef said. "I'm Professor Olsen from Columbia and Professor Naxxar is with the University of Malta and we're with Din L-Art Helwa. We were wondering if we could have a few minutes of your time."

"Of course. I'll be right with you."

Pawlu fingered his card nervously as a craggy-featured face topped by pure white hair peered through the gate. "You're with the national heritage group?"

Stef and Pawlu handed him their cards.

"I'm Chevalier Cremona," the man said. "Please step in. I'm pleased to meet you." He shut the gate after them. "What can I do for you?"

"I don't know if you realize it, but at one time there was a street that ran through part of your property."

"I know it well. My father bought the land and walled it off. It's been part of our garden for more than fifty years."

"We would like to examine the area," Stef said. "We think it may have some historical and ecological significance."

"You're certainly welcome to look. If you will kindly remove your shoes."

Cremona stepped out of his slippers at the door and waited for Stef and Naxxar to enter the house. "My wife isn't well, otherwise she would be here to greet you, too."

He led them across polished marble floors to the back door, which was heavy and double-locked. "We are very concerned about security," Cremona said. "We want no one in our house who hasn't been invited. Please put your shoes back on."

Passing an ornate gazebo and a flowerbed with gigantic chrysanthemums, the three arrived at the base of the wall. Cremona pointed to a spot on the ground. "This is where the street used to be."

Stef and Pawlu looked at each other. The area had become part of the lawn and looked very much the same as the rest of the yard. Pawlu's eyes narrowed.

"How far back did the street extend?" Stef asked.

"To here," Cremona said, walking to the edge of another flowerbed.

Stef's face lit up at the sign of a sizable moss-covered stone nearly completely covered with dirt. "Here it is!" Stef exclaimed.

Pawlu grinned. "If you don't mind," he said, speaking to Cremona, "we'll get our equipment so we can get to work."

Cremona's smile disappeared. "What kind of equipment?

"Just block and tackle, a triangular frame and a hand-operated winch," Stef said. "We'll be able to carry them by hand through the house without touching the floor."

"I told you, my wife is ill. I won't allow you to make noise and disturb her."

"She won't even know we're here," Stef promised.

*   *   *   *

"The bar is closed," Josefina announced. "Everyone is welcome to stay but no more drinks until I come back."

She met them at the desk. "I finished going through the files and you were right. Ten names have been removed from the computer records."

Rick took the yellow legal pad and held it so Caterina could read it with him. His eyes riveted on the second name. Ali Benaissa. Junior! Returning to the list, another name caught his eye. "Isn't Yusef Mansoor the archaeology student who's staying here?"

"Yes. And I haven't seen him for a day or two," Josefina replied.

"Come to think of it, he was in the pub when I first arrived Saturday night. He probably heard you mention that Caterina and I were going to eat at the *Ta Karuna* the night I wound up in the hospital."

Caterina looked shocked. "You think he's working with Stef's kidnappers?"

"If he isn't one of them himself."

"And all the other names are Arab men as well," Josefina said. "I don't think it's a coincidence."

"You're right," Rick said. "What do you know about Mansoor?"

"He has a student visa," Josefina said. "I saw it myself."

"Great work, Zija," said Rick enthusiastically. "Obviously young Mr. Mansoor isn't what he appears to be. Did you ever let him use your computer?"

"Yes. He needed to send some Emails about his enrollment."

"Did you stay with him while he did it?"

"No. I went back to work."

"That must have been when he put the virus in your computer."

She looked forlorn. Rick moved quickly to console her. "He's a charming person and there's no way you could have known. I've got another job for you."

Taking the telephone from its hiding place, she looked up a number in her Rolodex and dialed. "Hello," she said in a friendly voice. "This is merchant 62698J557 with the Bellestrado Hotel in Sliema. I have a chargeback from a credit card," she read off sixteen numbers. "Yes. It's a legitimate charge. The address doesn't match the one we have and I wonder if you have another one for

Mr. Naxxar besides the one in Hamrun. We haven't been able to reach him there."

Seconds later she looked up. "Yes. Oh, you do?"

Rick's heart beat faster as she wrote something on a pad. "How old is it?" she asked.

He danced excitedly in place until she finished writing, then literally snatched the note from her. After she hung up she said, "That's the address, but it's five years old."

"Just what we're looking for," he said, kissing her on the lips.

Her blush surprised him. "Before you go, I have something for you." She handed him an envelope. "Here's some money. Go with Caterina and buy some decent clothes so you look like a gentleman when you meet with Lorenzo Cornacchia tonight."

Rick flushed. "I can't take your money. You need it yourself."

"Don't be silly," Josefina said. "Let Caterina pick them out for you. Men never know how to shop for themselves."

"I'll do that a soon as we get back from Zejtun," Rick said.

1:30 PM

They parked in what must have been one of the oldest houses in the village, with a sun-bleached fence enclosing the yard and a gnarled apple tree visible alongside the house. Wrinkled fruit the size of prunes hung from its sagging branches. She knocked, waited and knocked again. At last she moved away from the door and ambled back to the car. "I don't think anyone is there," she said.

"Does he have a back door?" he asked.

"I would expect so. I'll look."

"No need to," he said. "I just don't want to have to go in the front door unless it's absolutely necessary. It doesn't look to me as if anyone has lived here for years."

"All the shades are drawn, too," Caterina said.

With a sigh, Rick said, "I guess it can't hurt to take a look."

She took his hand and gave it a squeeze. "For luck," she said.

The backyard garden had the sere stubble of long departed flowers; nearby was the decaying skeleton of a once black Citroen. Rick noticed that the wreck stood between the house and the back gate. At the house he easily opened the lock but the back door wouldn't open.

"It must be locked inside," he said. Without a second thought he made a run and threw himself against the door. It swung open with the sound of cracking wood.

"So much for Naxxar not realizing we're here," Caterina sighed.

He immediately went to work to hide the damage to the door. Although he had torn the hasp loose, he hadn't broken any of the wood and the damage didn't show.

"There's food in the refrigerator," Caterina called.

Beneath the sink he found a wastebasket. Inside was a shirt-bag marked XXXL. "That's Stef's size,"

They moved on to the bedrooms. "Someone's been sleeping in this bed," she said. "It isn't made."

He opened another door. "Someone's been sleeping in this one, too," he said. "And I don't think it was Goldilocks."

"Come here," she said.

He joined her in the bathroom where she was going through the cabinet. The smell of fresh soap hung in the air and water beads still clung to the walls of the shower. She showed him a yellow Bic razor and a nearly empty tube of shaving cream. Rick shook his head. "Pawlu must have known we were coming," he said sadly. "He didn't leave a thing. Take me to Mdina."

CHAPTER 26

▼

Friday
2:45 PM
Mdina

Boys dribbled soccer balls off their knees and girls in red school uniforms played hopscotch on the large clay court next to the old moat surrounding Mdina. It was recess at parochial school. But Rick was astonished at the crowds that were waiting to enter the city. "My God," he moaned. "Look at all the people."

As they crossed the bridge, he laid an open tuna fish can on the railing. A large branch rustled and the cat ran over to them. It ignored the food and headed straight for Rick to be petted. "Hello, sport. Have you seen Stef?"

The animal purred loudly but refused to answer. "Come on," Caterina said. "We can't waste time." The cat, fearing abandonment, moved to Caterina and brushed her with a question-mark tail.

"Do you think the horses would like him for company?" Rick asked. As if understanding the conversation, the cat tried to butter her up by licking her hand.

"If he's still here when we come back, I'll think about it," she replied. After giving the animal a quick pet, she tugged on Rick's arm. He looked back and saw the cat watching them as they crossed the moat. It still hadn't touched the food when they went through the city gate.

Inside, they were greeted by screams of terror coming from a door marked Dungeon Museum. "What was that?" Rick asked.

"One of Marija Cornacchia's victims," Caterina said, taking his arm.

"Funny," he said with a wan smile.

"Actually, that's where the Grandmaster of the Knights of St. John and the Inquisitor kept their prisoners. It has racks and gibbets and Iron Maidens and all kinds of spooky stuff. It even was supposed to have a secret passage that led to the Courts Building though no one has ever been able to find it."

"A secret passage? You must be kidding."

"I'm perfectly serious. Nearly all the pallazi have them. When invaders or pirates came, they needed a way to get out of the city."

Wheels turned in Rick's mind. "Does Borgiswed have one?"

"I'm sure it must. You'd never be able to find it, though."

He took a deep breath and inhaled the perfumed air. Even without chanting street vendors and snakecharmer's baskets, the area seemed like a Moorish town square. Rick caught the aromas of food and spices coming from the open shop doors. The main difference was the voices. English, German, and Slavic prevailed instead of Arabic.

They followed the square due north to where it ended in a high wall. A cross street jogged northeast and southwest.

"Which way?" Caterina asked. He stopped, remembering another large street that ran north and south. Villagaignon Street had to be a short distance to the left because he could see the walls of the city to the right. "There's a big church sort of in the middle of the city," he said. "Where's that?"

"You must mean St. Paul's Cathedral," she said. "It's to the right. And that's where the crowds will be thickest, too."

People moved out of their way as they trotted forward. "The Cathedral is on the site where St. Paul healed Publius' father. After he did, Publius converted to Christianity and Paul made him Archbishop. The earthquake of 1693 destroyed the original church and the Grandmaster had Lorenzo Gafa design the new building. It's every bit as impressive as the Co-Cathedral in Valletta."

"That's a good landmark," Rick said. "I have the whole city arranged in my head. I just want to see what it looks like from this perspective."

"I still think you're crazy. Do you know Cornacchia has a dog? A man tried to break into the estate last year and the animal nearly ripped him apart."

"That's good to know," Rick said in an even voice. "I'll have to provide for it."

An hour's walk covered all the routes Rick had seen on the map. The buildings themselves stayed hidden behind the walls. To his thinking, the most interesting find of the day was the Bonello's rental pickup truck in the parking lot near Verduta Gardens. He jotted down the telephone number on the door before following a worried Caterina back to the Mitsubishi.

When they returned to the car he found the green message light flashing on his cell phone.

"Good afternoon, Richard," Father Santorini's voice said. "The lambskin is going well and I wanted you to know I got the Amharic inscription translated for you. I'm sure you will be as puzzled as I am."

Rick eagerly hit the recall button. After exchanging greetings, he asked, "What does it say?"

"The banner reads, 'The true measure of a great man must be squared against what he eats. That which costs him most serves him best.'"

Rick finished writing the words and read them back.

"Do you have any idea what it means?" Santorini asked.

"Some. But if I'm right, it completely negates your theory that Bartelemeo tried to convince Suleiman that the Shield was made by Prester John. How many Amharic letters are there in the inscription?"

Rick heard mumbling in the background. "A hundred," Santorini answered.

"That's a square all right. In biblical terms the average man was 7 cubits in height, so 10 cubits would have literally been a great man, at least in size. If I'm right, Bartelemeo was using a ten-by-ten grid. All we need to do is figure out what we're supposed to square it against. Didn't you say that Bartelemeo had what looked like price lists in with his diaries?"

"Yes," Santorini said. "But I never copied them. I didn't consider them important to my dissertation."

"As I remember it, you decided that the prices were for various spices. Pepper would have been the most expensive, and you said it was the longest list. I wonder if any of the numbers in the pairs is greater than 10. If not, I would say we're on to something. The Manhattan Project used a 10 by 10 grid for their encryptions. A hundred characters is enough to encompass four Roman alphabets if you don't use the 'q' and 'z.'"

"Very good. After you pick up the lambskin I'll be happy to make a copy of the price lists for you. Do the letters from the inscription go into the grid?"

"Maybe, but I think it's more likely it's the letters inside the shield," Rick said.

"Which won't do us much good since the Shield is lost. I'll try the inscription anyway and see if I can make anything intelligible from it."

"Feel free. Without the price list, no one would have been able to decipher it."

"You're right," Santorini said, "and apparently no one ever was able to do it. That's the real mystery. The Cornacchias had more than four centuries to figure it out. Why didn't they?"

"I have no idea," Rick replied.

Hanging up, Rick made a second call to Bonello's. "One of my employees, Pawlu Naxxar, rented a pickup from you this morning," he said in Italian.

"*Si?*"

"Did he rent any equipment, too?"

"Just a moment, I'll get the invoice." He quickly returned. "It says block and tackle and heavy chain. Is there a problem?"

"No. I just wanted to make sure he picked everything up. I'm supposed to meet him in Mdina this afternoon. What time does it have to be returned?"

"We close at 7:00," the man said. "If you return it by then you won't be charged for the weekend."

"Did Pawlu have another man with him? Heavy-set with red hair?"

"Yes. He carried most of the equipment."

Rick hung up and turned excitedly to Caterina. "Pawlu and Stef are somewhere in Mdina. They're using block and tackle so they must be lifting something heavy. And since we didn't see them they must be inside one of the estates."

"Borgiswed?" Caterina asked.

"I doubt Pawlu would want to go anywhere near there," Rick said. "If you'll drop me off at the Bellestrado I'll go to work on the Duke's Challenge. I need a few things from Valletta."

"I want you to get your clothes first," she said. "I know a great men's shop on Tower Road. I brought Andrew there once but he didn't like what I picked out for him. I hope you have better taste."

Better sense, Rick thought.

Though he insisted on the color, for the most part he sat back and listened to Caterina and a female sales clerk cluck and preen over him. Like a schoolboy, he tried on various outfits. In the end they decided on tan trousers and a light green dress shirt topped off with a dun-colored knit sweater.

"You look very handsome," Caterina said when he modeled them.

"Good," he said as he ducked back into the fitting room to change. "Now if you'll make a shopping trip to Valletta, I'll walk back to the Bellestrado."

Rick was at work when Caterina arrived. "I found all the things you need," she said.

He gestured toward a chair. "Great. Do you want to see my arsenal?"

She sat next to him as he emptied the bag she had just brought him. Pointing to the bottle of Equanil and the pair of nougat candy, he said, "These are for Cornacchia's dog. One bar is for bait, the other will be loaded with enough sedative to put him to sleep for a week."

"Guard dogs don't accept food from strangers," Caterina said.

"You're right. But most dogs have a sweet tooth. Take a look at this."

Caterina had to lean across the table to see the foot-long piece of wire. "This is strong enough to hold my weight and it's deadly as a garrote. It will also be more than enough to take care of the dog if the Equanil doesn't. It's my most important weapon."

Caterina shuddered as he went on to his lockpick. "You know what this is," he said. "Now to hide all these goodies."

He took off his belt and laid it on the table. Using an exacto knife, he cut the seam to separate the halves of the leather then slipped the lockpick and wire inside. After he was done he Superglued the halves back together.

"Next comes the Equanil," he said. He took three capsules from the bottle. Opening them one by one, he poured the contents of each one into three small plastic bags. "This is in case I need to put someone besides the dog to sleep." After putting the three small bags into a larger one, he stood up and took off his shirt.

A faint smile tightened her lips and quickly disappeared as he taped the larger bag to his chest with crisscrossed pieces of surgical tape. "Are you done?" Caterina asked.

"Yes."

"Then bend forward so I can reach your head." He did and she slipped a thin silver chain over his head.

"What's this?" he asked.

"A St. Jude's medal," she said. "He's the patron saint of desperate causes."

Rick laughed. "I'm really not that desperate."

"You have no idea," Caterina said with an unhappy face. "Is there anything else I can do?"

"Yes. Just this side of the moat at Mdina there are some trees. About ten feet away from the kiosk toward the moat you'll find a tree with a big hole at the base. Hide my cell phone inside of it."

Caterina nodded. "How are you going to get away from Mdina?"

"You're going to drive me. That's why I need the phone. Otherwise I'll have to walk." He grinned and reached for Caterina's hand. She had tears in her eyes.

CHAPTER 27

▼

Friday
5:34 PM
Rabat

Father Santorini had the parchment ready when Rick arrived. "I didn't get very far. I was only able to copy a hundred and fifteen characters," he said.

"No need to apologize," Rick said. "You did a great job."

"Maybe so, but I don't think it will be good enough to fool Lorenzo."

"I don't think he'll be that concerned about it. He'll be far more interested in the drawing, and that will be the genuine article."

"God be with you," Santorini said.

Caterina delivered Rick at the police station just ten minutes late. Micallef, who didn't seem to notice Rick's tardiness, came out to meet him dressed in sweater and slacks. "Good afternoon," the Inspector said amiably. "Come along, I'm parked in the moat."

"Are we going by submarine?" Rick quipped.

The route to the car took them through city gate into Valletta. Once inside the city, they made an immediate right turn. Following a stairway downwards they emerged into the sunlight where the bastions of Valletta stretched halfway to heaven.

"I understand you're going to pick up Lorenzo's yearly contribution to the Police Officer's Benevolent Fund," Rick said.

"Yes. I have no idea how much it will be this year. Last year he donated fifty thousand pounds."

Something stirred in Rick's mind. "That's a lot of money. How much total has he given you over the years?"

"Several hundred thousand. He's been contributing since 1970. We have funds in New York and London. Our portfolio went down after September 11th and the collapse of Enron, but otherwise it's done very well. We all contribute but he's been the main source of the revenue. He makes donations to many organizations."

"Does that include the hunters' groups?"

"Oh yes. He's been giving them money for years and they're some of his strongest supporters."

Bingo, Rick thought with a smile. "Do you know why he makes such large donations to the police?"

"I think he feels guilty about what his father did during the war."

"Do you mean because Alessandro was pro-Italian?"

"That's part of it but he also knows that Alessandro indirectly caused the death of two of our officers in Mdina. A few nights before he was killed, the Duke's wife, Agatha, called the police station to say her husband was in a serious fight. Two officers responded and were killed in an air raid."

"Why should Lorenzo feel guilty about that?" Rick asked.

"There was a blackout on the island at the time. Everyone in Mdina had to be responsible for obeying the blackout because the wardens couldn't see over the walls. Allessandro had left his lights on at the palazzo. Ordinarily the infraction wouldn't have meant anything. The Germans seldom bombed Mdina. They concentrated on the harbor cities. It was overcast that night and one of the bombers must have strayed off target and saw the light at Borgiswed. The officers happened to be near the palazzo when the bombs exploded."

"Did the police ever find out what the fight was about?"

"No," Micallef said. "But Alessandro went to hospital to be treated for a bad cut. The report was it looked like a knife wound."

A short, tense silence hung in the air as Rick tried to decide whether he dared ask any leading questions. Finally he took a deep breath and said, "I've been watching the construction on the Mediterranean Trade Building. When is it supposed to be finished?"

"By June of next year. Every one of the Arab countries has already reserved office space. That only leaves thirty-five more stories to fill."

Rick snickered his appreciation. "For someone who doesn't like development, the Cornacchias are sure doing their part to support the building industry." Remembering Marija's cabin on the Stallion, he asked, "Do you know why they never had children?"

"That seems to be her choice," Micallef said. "She says she wants to finish her working career before she spends all her time in the home."

"There's no reason why she can't have children, too. Especially if she's running the business."

"She feels that when she has children, she should spend all her time with them."

Rick was unconvinced.

"Have you ever seen the statue of Melita in the government building?" Micallef continued.

"I certainly have. And I met her on the street. She could have her pick from just about anyone in this part of the world. Why did she marry Lorenzo Cornacchia?"

"Probably because he's almost unimaginably rich," Micallef said dryly. "But in her case, I think it's more because she wanted the title of Duchess. That's what she demands her employees call her and she's actually very good at running her fiefdoms, including Black Dolphin. What's better, Lorenzo is more than happy to let her be in control."

"Does she run the computers, too?" Rick asked.

"Yes. She seems amused by them."

Kevin would be interested to hear that. "What do you know about Cardinal Vella?"

Micallef frowned. "Why do you mention him?"

"I've read that he and Alessandro were very close. Is he as friendly with Lorenzo?"

"At one time Vella was almost like a father to him. He superintended Lorenzo's education. Things changed when Lorenzo married Marija. She doesn't like the Cardinal and the feeling is mutual."

Probably because they're too much alike, Rick mused. "Have you ever heard anything about why Alessandro was out driving during an air raid?"

"I have no idea. I've always suspected it had something to do with the fight he had the night when the officers got killed. Why do you ask?"

"I want to write a book about an important family no one has ever heard about."

"Is your brother helping you?"

The mention of Stef took Rick aback. "No. He's doing his doctoral dissertation on Benvenuto Cellini. Apparently Bartolomeo Cornacchia commissioned Cellini to do a work for the family."

"I see," Micallef said. Before he could say more, they arrived at the parking lot outside the gates of Mdina. Rick was surprised to see the Bonello's pickup was still in the nearly empty lot. "We'll have to walk from here," the Inspector said.

The last three players in a children's soccer game chased a ball and each other around the field beside the moat surrounding Mdina, and the last ice cream cones of the day changed hands at the concession stand. Rick looked for the tree where Caterina was to leave his cell phone. She would have no trouble identifying it.

"Some tourists think Mdina is the most beautiful place on the island," Micallef said. "I agree. It's actually one of the few truly medieval cities still left in the world."

When they reached the gate with the crow and castle, Micallef pushed the button beneath the lion's jaws. A voice that sounded like a parrot calling from the bottom of a well answered,

"Good evening, Lorenzo. It's Ray Micallef. Richard Olsen is with me."

"Excellent. I'll be right there to let you in."

Rick's eyes darted around as he tried to spot where Cornacchia's surveillance camera for the gate was located. He couldn't find it. It was too well hidden. Even more important, was Carpenter watching him now? What would his reaction be if he were? He shuddered, not wanting to think about it.

Lorenzo Cornacchia appeared with a German shepherd on a leash. "Welcome to Borgiswed," Cornacchia said in a raspy voice. The German Shepherd sat, silently taking Rick in with its tongue drooping over its bottom incisors.

"Hello, Ray," Cornacchia said, covering the Inspector's hand with his own.

"And you must be Richard Olsen," Cornacchia said, taking Rick's hand. "It's a pleasure to meet you after all your brother has told me about you."

Rick forced a smile. "Thank you. Where is Stef, by the way?" As he said it he reached with his left hand into his pocket for a piece of nougat.

"Getting ready," Cornacchia replied heartily. "He's very anxious to see you."

Rick wrapped the candy in the fold between his left thumb and forefinger and removed it from his pocket. The dog lowered its head and pricked its ears when he heard the candy hit the ground. Cornacchia pulled the dog back to him before it had a chance to investigate. "This is *Princep*," Cornacchia said to Rick. "That means Prince. Don't try to pet him. He'll bite you."

Rick nodded. "Where's the chessboard?" he asked.

"Around the back in the courtyard," came the strained response. "I'll show it to you later."

With that, Cornacchia turned his attention back to Inspector Micallef. Seeing them engaged in conversation, Rick dropped a second piece of nougat.

The dog didn't even notice. Heart tripping faster, Rick released the third just before they reached the door to the house. This time the dog's muzzle touched the ground and Rick was sure he heard sounds of chewing. Cornacchia unleashed the dog at the door and it ran ahead into the house. As interested as Rick was in the dog, the animal had already forgotten him. In its simplistic view of the world there were only three kinds of people: family, enemies, and nothings. Fortunately, Rick was still a nothing.

"You're in for a wonderful surprise," Inspector Micallef whispered to Rick as Cornacchia stood aside to let him go in first.

Rick quickly agreed. Stepping inside he entered another age when a wall was considered bare without an oil painting or tapestry and the furniture was expected to be heavy. A tan and black parquet floor stretched off in three directions. The path straight ahead led to a divided marble staircase, the one to the right to an enormous sixteenth century oak table. The one to the left meandered off to disappear out of sight around a corner. Rick was no stranger to antique furniture, but seldom did it seem to fit as well as it did in Borgiswed. If a man's home was his castle, this fortress belonged to Cornacchia.

"Welcome to my humble abode," Cornacchia said. "I would be deeply appreciative if you would remove your shoes."

As Rick did, he noticed the enormous floor-to-ceiling portrait in the parlor. A flinty-eyed giant stared out over what he guessed was the Cornacchia family nose, the beak of a bird of prey. Rick knew who it was long before he saw the metal identification plate at the bottom of the frame. Bartolomeo Cornacchia could have been Lorenzo's father, or his brother. The resemblance was obvious even though only the man's face and hands were visible. Although the smile tried to convey good will, his predatory eyes gave him away. His right arm was flexed with his hand next to his body. In it he held a long, thin book that looked like an account ledger.

Figures, Rick thought, smiling at his own pun. As he started to look away, another detail caught his attention. Well-hidden at the lower right corner of the canvas, Bartolomeo's left hand held another, much smaller, book. Though his fingers covered most of the title, the first three letters of the title were visible. DEF. Could it have been the Definitus Mallorum? If so, the man's audacity was stunning.

"I see you like Bartolomeo," Cornacchia rasped. "One of Michelangelo's students, Matteo d'Aleccio, painted the portrait. Bartolomeo asked Michelangelo himself to do the work but he couldn't so Michelangelo recommended d'Aleccio. Would you like some brandy? I know you will want some, Ray."

"Brandy sounds excellent," Rick said. "I look forward to our chess game."

"So do I," Cornacchia said, handing him a wafer-thin snifter. "I trust you'll like the brandy. It's more than a hundred and fifty years old. An English admiral left it with us when he was a houseguest during the Crimean War. Malta was a coaling station at the time. I only serve it on special occasions."

"Cheers," Rick said. Cold fire burned its way down his throat. "This is excellent, but it's out of my class. I know a bit more about wine."

"The wine comes later," Cornacchia said.

Rick set the glass down. "I expected Stef would be here by now."

"He wasn't finished dressing when you arrived," Cornacchia said. He eyed the rolled parchment under Rick's arm and pointed at it. "Is this the drawing?" he asked.

"Yes. I know you're anxious to look at it. Perhaps when my brother arrives. He'll want to take a look at it, too." Even as he said it, Rick was sure he would never see his brother that night. How did Cornacchia dare to pull such a blatant double-cross with Inspector Micallef present?

"Good afternoon," a female voice said.

Rick turned. Marija Cornacchia stood smiling directly at him, her beige caftan glistening like sleek fur and her voice a disarming purr. "I understand you play chess, Mr. Olsen. That's delightful. My husband hasn't had much opportunity to play lately. Are you...any good?"

Sure she wasn't asking about his chess-playing abilities, Rick said, "Good is a relative term. I once was considered to be an expert, but I haven't played for years."

She stepped forward and held out her hand for him. Not knowing what else to do, he kissed it. She quickly turned to Inspector Micallef. "Good afternoon, Rafael," she said, kissing him on both cheeks.

"Where's Stef?" Rick asked.

"I'll get him," Marija said. "Since you're both wearing sweaters, I'll tell him not to wear his suit jacket."

Rick snorted. Suit jacket! Stef didn't even own one. With a straight face he said, "Do that."

"Come with me to the garden," said Cornacchia, taking Rick by the arm. "Marija and your brother will join us there."

Cornacchia led him through a door that led to a veranda. As they stepped out, a young boy dressed as a black pawn waved a greeting. Where did he come from? Before he could ask, he heard Marija's voice behind him. Rick turned, and a very large man came over to embrace him. "Hello, brother," the impostor said, "It's been a long time."

Dumbfounded, Rick nearly laughed in spite of his rage. The impostor was several inches shorter, had brown hair rather than red, and was beardless. What was Cornacchia up to? At last he could speak. "I'm happy to see you. I've been worried about you."

Cornacchia smiled and pointed up towards a balcony visible through the open back door. "This is where we will play."

Children's voices chattered from somewhere under the building. He surreptitiously searched for a door or opening but couldn't see one.

"All the pieces should be here in an hour or so," Cornacchia continued. "Let's go back inside."

The Inspector went first, followed by Cornacchia. Rick gestured for Marija to follow. Her hand brushed Rick's thigh as she passed.

Princep was lying on the walk and sat up as Rick casually dropped another piece of candy. He was glad that Marija wasn't guarding the estate; at least he had a fighting chance against the dog. "Come inside," Cornacchia said.

As Rick did he dropped the rest of the bar.

"It's good to see you again," the impostor said, bravely taking Rick's arm and trying to start a conversation. Rick refused to even acknowledge his presence.

The balcony stood behind a pair of glass doors. Cornacchia opened them and pointed to three padded wooden chairs. Massive hanging pots swayed gently with a faint breeze, and a fly buzzed against one of the windows.

"What do you think?" Cornacchia asked in a voice so raspy that Rick had difficulty hearing him. "Has any general had a more imposing view of a battlefield?"

"Absolutely not. The view of city wall is beautiful from here," Rick said.

"The whole city is beautiful," Cornacchia replied. "Mdina is one of the few places on the island that still belongs to us exclusively. Everywhere else the real estate brokers have sold off the island to anyone who had the money to pay for it. Some day...." He broke off, red-faced. "Enough of that. I had Ibn prepare Bragioli for dinner. It's a beef stew."

CHAPTER 28

▼

7:03 PM
Borgiswed, Mdina

Dinner was served at an elegant Seventeenth Century Italian table, with Cornacchia at the head, Marija on his left, and the Inspector on the right. Rick sat next to Marija, with the impostor across from him. The rear windows were open, letting a light breeze in and their conversation out. Certainly someone was listening.

Marija Cornacchia put her hand on Rick's. "Pour some wine for me," she said in a deep voice.

After carefully laying the drawings between his feet he picked up the opened bottle. A glimpse at the label made his hands shake. Chateau LaTour 1969. He had never even seen a thousand-dollar bottle of wine before.

Marija's fingers wrapped around his as he handed the glass to her. Fearful it was a ploy to steal the drawing, he grasped it protectively as she did. Whatever else happened that night, the drawing would never leave his sight. Even so, he was sure Cornacchia would never willingly let him leave the house.

Rick watched attentively as Ibn ladled beef consommé into his bowl. With his first taste he realized how hungry he actually was. And though the rolls were excellent, he longed for Josefina's crusty bread. Once again the impostor tried to start a conversation but soon gave up. Marija watched him with a faint smile. He was sure he interested her, like a mouse interested a barn owl. Perhaps for the same reason.

Cornacchia tapped his spoon against his water glass and Ibn appeared to remove the soup bowls. The Arab's eyes never left Marija. Finished removing the dishes, he quickly disappeared and almost immediately returned with a large tray. Rick liked the fresh, slightly acidic, aroma coming from the plates. The rolled beef with mushrooms swimming in a white sauce was a delicious new experience for him.

As they were eating, Rick said, "Stef, tell everyone about Raynald the Third of Belgium. It's your favorite story."

The impostor looked puzzled. "I'm afraid I don't remember it."

"Of course you do. You know. Crassas. It's a variation on how to catch a monkey. Put a banana inside a cage. The opening to the cage is just big enough for the monkey to reach inside but he can't get his hand out while he's holding the banana."

Smiling widely, Rick continued. "Some of Stef's graduate school friends were worried about his health because he was so overweight, and they told him the story about Raynald.

"Raynald was a Duke in Fourteenth Century Belgium and he loved to eat. His brother Edward led a revolt against him and imprisoned him in a special room they built around him in the castle. The room had a door that was never locked, but Raynald was too big to get through it. To escape, all he had to do was lose enough weight to walk out. He never could. Edward made sure he was constantly given large portions of delicious foods.

"It wasn't until Edward was killed in battle ten years later that Raynald was rescued. After hearing the story Stef said to his friends, 'How did they get him out? Did they stop feeding him?' One of his friends said. 'No, they actually had to knock out part of the wall to let him out. But that's not the point, Raynald would have been able to escape without help if he had cut down in his eating." Then Stef said, 'That's not the point either. The moral is that if you wait long enough, sooner or later someone will come along to help you out of a tight spot.'"

Marija and the Inspector smiled politely. Cornacchia glowered and the impostor blushed.

"That's the joke Stef always likes to tell on himself when he's eating an especially good meal. My compliments to the chef."

"I agree," the impostor said with a weak smile. "I've never had anything like it before."

"I was telling the Inspector about your research about the Knights, Stef. Tell him your theory about why you think Bartolomeo Cornacchia got along with them so well."

After an electric silence, Stef's stand-in blanched and got to his feet. "Please forgive me," he said. "I don't feel well."

Glaring at Rick, Cornacchia stood and took the impostor by the arm. "Young Mr. Olsen doesn't seem to be himself at this moment. I know that will change later."

Rick threw him a defiant look. As he did he felt Marija's bare toes climb his calf. He crossed his legs away from her.

No one spoke until Cornacchia returned. "He's resting. It's too bad he wasn't able to enjoy the rest of his meal." As he said it he directed a sharp look in Rick's direction.

"It is," Rick agreed, finishing the Bragioli and a fresh green salad. Ibn brought in an enormous fruit trifle for dessert. Rick hoped Cornacchia would save some for the impostor. It was too good to miss.

While Ibn cleared away the dishes, Cornacchia passed around an ornate box. "Cigars?" Everyone declined but Marija hesitated when they came to her.

"It's time to play our game," Cornacchia said.

Children in tunics shushed each other as they made their way to their starting squares. Some were only five or six years old and looked like miniature English yeoman with wooden daggers tucked into their belts, caps covering their hair and ears, and miniature longbows strapped across their backs.

Teenagers were arranged by height. One boy wore what looked like an ermine cape and a crown with a jeweled cross. The white queen wasn't as tall, but appeared to be because she stood on a pedestal. The bishops wore mitres and bright red chasubles, and the knights' headgear had tall plumes. At the corners of the board stood uncomfortable-looking figures stuffed into wooden castles peering out from tiny slits near the teeth of the towers.

Finally, the last piece, a black knight, took his place. As he did, a powerful yardlight flashed on, illuminating the whole area in a yellow glow.

"How do the children get into the estate?" Rick asked.

"They come out of their box," Cornacchia said with an enigmatic smile.

From the vantagepoint of the balcony, the entire playing field was in view. The contestants and spectators sat at a semicircular garden table with Cornacchia opposite Rick and Marija between them. Inspector Micallef remained inside watching the playing field through a window. A small megaphone sat in the center of the table.

Rick flipped a coin to decide who got the white pieces. Cornacchia won and surprised him by choosing the black.

"Having the first move is a big advantage," Rick said. "I don't understand why you gave it away." Picking up the megaphone, he called, "White plays pawn to king four."

The king's pawn, a boy of about seven, bowed and took two strides forward. As he did, Rick felt strangely moved. He handed the megaphone to Cornacchia.

"Make no mistake," Cornacchia said in a dark voice. "I have the advantage." Raising the megaphone to his mouth he said, "Black plays pawn to queen bishop four."

Thumb in mouth, the child on the queen bishop's square stood immobile. The teenager behind her gave her a mild push. Her black robe rippled as she toddled forward to the next square, turned to look, then moved up to the next one.

The Sicilian Defense, Rick thought. How appropriate.

"You see, the first move isn't an advantage at all," Cornacchia said. "It's much better to see what your opponent is up to from the onset. It's like Oriental defense. Use your opponent's moves to defeat him."

Marija Cornacchia shifted in her chair. For an instant Rick could feel her thigh against his leg. Was Cornacchia trying to distract me? he wondered.

"White plays King's knight to bishop three." The knight broke ranks, backed off the playing field and reemerged in front of a wall of pawns.

Cornacchia quickly responded. "Black plays Queen's pawn to queen four."

Here we go, Rick thought. Of all the versions of the Sicilian, this was by the far the wildest. Cornacchia's move was dangerous, to himself as well as to Rick. So the man didn't mind taking risks, Rick thought.

"White plays pawn takes pawn." The boy stepped forward diagonally, raising his wooden dagger in mock attack. The boy on the attacked square left the field, pulling off his black cap on the way. It had to be hot in those costumes.

Suddenly Marija's knee was back. It was noticeably warm and this time she didn't pull away. Noticing the flush to her face, Rick thought she looked genuinely excited.

"Black plays queen takes pawn." The queen descended from her pedestal and moved forward. When she raised her mace over her head, the white pawn bowed and left the board.

"White plays knight to bishop three," Rick said without hesitation.

Cornacchia retreated his queen and Rick launched into an attack that led to the exchange of several pieces including the queens. As the pieces left the board, they strolled to the back and shed whatever parts of their costumes they could most easily put back on.

Soon only rooks, several pawns and a bishop and knight apiece remained. As the action became more intense, Marija's breath became shorter and she licked her lips nervously. Finally she put her hand on Rick's leg. He turned sideways and moved out of range.

Intent on the game, Cornacchia didn't seem to notice what was happening under his own eyes. He bent forward, scowling. Though he was an excellent player, he appeared to be a bit deficient in his knowledge of modern strategy and reluctant to take the offensive. But he met each of Rick's ploys with the proper counter-move. The game was potentially explosive. Neither player could survive a misplay.

After lengthy contemplation, Cornacchia called, "Rook to Bishop seven." The boy in the boxed castle slowly trudged across the board to Rick's second rank. Rick responded with a rook move of his own and Cornacchia yelled, "Black rook takes rook." Another wild sweep and Rick's rook left the board. Did the piece limp from the weight of the castle or was it only his imagination?

"Bishop takes rook," Rick said. The red-sashed bishop tightroped along the diagonal and touched Cornacchia's rook with his staff. Cornacchia's mouth twisted. As the man slumped forward with hands to his forehead Rick noticed several small burns and bandages on his fingers and wrists. Where did he get them?

Ten moves later, the bishops retired from the game. Rick had an unopposed pawn on the King's rook file, and Cornacchia had one on the Queen's knight file. Each of their kings were closer to the opposing pawns than they were to their own. They were locked in the non-nuclear version of mutually assured destruction. Neither man dared to try to win. To do so would mean almost certain victory for the other side.

Rick held out his hand. "I suggest a draw. Neither of us can afford to play on."

Cornacchia glared at the field for thirty seconds, then nodded and shook his hand without enthusiasm. "Agreed. Your attack was very impressive. I'll make sure you don't get such an opportunity again. You will, of course, play another." The tone made the statement a command and not a request.

Rick was about to answer when Marija said, "Oh, yes. Please do play another. I enjoy watching you."

Rick looked up to see her staring at him. He had no doubts who the 'you' was. He was Lancelot, and she was Guinevere. Only this Guinevere was a black widow spider and he was lunch.

Half an hour into the second game Rick sat stiffly on his stool, elbows on knees. Children stood head-to-head and toe-to-toe, forming a solid wall of pawns that stretched across the board. The second game was nearly an hour old and the strain showed on the pieces as much as it did on the players. The pawns whispered amongst themselves and the teenagers threw exasperated looks up at the contestants. Rick had never seen a more graphic example of a locked position. Neither side had any room to maneuver, and the Kings had already joined in the fray, something that rarely happened until the endgame. The bishops and the rooks stood immobilized behind the human chain in front of them. Knights made sorties toward the enemy's lines, only to return, disgruntled, when the other side counter-attacked.

At last, one young girl could take no more. She removed her white cap and sat in place on her square. Rick laughed, but Cornacchia stared out at the field with a grim expression. He made a few more impotent knight moves, apparently hoping for a mistake, but Rick parried each sortie. As he groped for a diplomatic way to suggest another draw, the suggestion came from Cornacchia himself. White-lipped, and in a voice barely louder than a whisper, he choked. "I offer you a draw."

Rick nodded acceptance.

"I would play another game but I find myself too tired."

"I've had enough, too," Rick said.

Rick and Cornacchia remained in place watching the pieces disappear into the shed to transform themselves back into mere boys and girls. Without being obvious, Rick bent forward to try to see where they went when they left, but all he could tell was that they seemed to disappear directly beneath him. Were they using a secret passage?

Cornacchia barely noticed Rick's attentions. By denying him victory, Rick had wounded him as severely as if he had defeated him. Seconds later, Cornacchia offered his hand. To his credit the color had returned to his face and he was smiling. "Congratulations on your fine play. You may be the best I have ever faced."

Rick managed a modest smile. "You're very good yourself. I'm sure you must win most of your games."

"I *never* lose an important one. In fact I'm playing my best when my opponent doesn't realize he's beaten."

"We're not talking about chess," Rick said with a smile.

"Of course we are," Cornacchia replied.

Before Rick could confront Cornacchia about Stef, Marija and Micallef entered the room. The Inspector held out a congratulatory hand in Rick's direction. The hand Marija offered him was hot. "I'm amazed," she said. "I wish I could play as well."

Rick took that as high praise. "Thank you."

"I think I better look in on our other guest," Cornacchia said. "Would you like to come with me, Mr. Olsen?"

"Of course," Rick replied.

As they climbed the stairway, Rick said in a low voice, "So what kind of game are we playing now?"

"It's the only one I can play, unfortunately. It's one you've made necessary."

"Not me. I brought the drawings with me tonight. Too bad I'll have to take them with me when I go."

"I'm afraid you will find you are mistaken, my friend," Cornacchia said in a low voice. "Your brother is on this floor."

He stopped in front of a door, knocked, and then opened it. Rick saw an unmade bed, but the room itself was empty. "He doesn't seem to be here," Cornacchia said.

"What a surprise," Rick said.

"Maybe he had to use the wc," Cornacchia said.

"That's probably it. By the way, your 'Stef' doesn't look anything like my brother."

Cornacchia threw him a cold look. "It doesn't really matter, does it? Inspector Micallef has never seen him. You told him that he was a large man. We found one."

"I also told him he had red hair."

"Apparently Ray must have forgotten that. By the way, your attempt to reveal my deception was ill-advised. If the Inspector suspects anything, neither you nor your brother will ever be seen or heard from again." He paused. "Or the Inspector, either for that matter."

"So Stef's stand-in is for the Inspector's sake," Rick said. "I wondered why you went to all the trouble. I imagine that if he found out something he wasn't supposed to know the two us will become victim's of a boating accident or a similar mishap."

Cornacchia threw Rick an appreciative smile but didn't answer.

"How long do we stand around waiting for 'Stef' to come back?"

"Just a while longer," Cornacchia replied.

"I'm not going to give you the drawings willingly."

"You don't have any choice. I have your money ready for you. Unfortunately I can't deliver your brother at this time. I wasn't able to contact the people who are detaining him."

"I don't want your money. No Stef, no drawings."

"Don't you understand? I fully intend to return him to you. Unfortunately that will be impossible tonight. And I'm sure you realize I can't let you leave."

"Then perhaps you should invite me to stay the night and we'll look for him in the morning. I assume you have an answer to the question of how you can let us live. You've done so well with answering all the other questions to this point."

Cornacchia smiled. "I can understand your skepticism but in a day or two no one will be able to touch me no matter what I've done. Now if you will kindly give me the drawings…"

"I have a better idea," Rick said. "Let's leave them to the Inspector's safekeeping. Not that I don't trust you."

"How do we explain why we're giving them to him?"

"We can say that we think they may be stolen property and that we wanted him to take charge until we decide who they belong to."

"The drawing belongs to me. It has my name on it," Cornacchia said.

"It has *Bartolomeo's* name on it. That makes a difference. There's no doubt it was stolen from someone at one time or another. Probably from Cellini himself."

"An interesting point. We'll have to discuss that further when we're alone."

"Since I won't be leaving with the Inspector, what will you tell him?"

"Leave that to me," Cornacchia said. "I suggest we go back downstairs. He must wonder what happened to us."

They found the Inspector waiting for them. In a concerned voice he asked, "Is Mr. Olsen's brother all right?"

"I assume he must be," Cornacchia said. "He wasn't in his room, but he may still be indisposed. I was a little puzzled that there was only one suitcase in the room. When he came, he had two. I'm sure one of the servants must have moved the other one."

Rick snorted noiselessly, impressed by Cornacchia's ingenuity. The statement not only explained the impostor's absence but it left open the possibility that Stef had left with a suitcase full of Cornacchia's valuables if such an accusation became necessary later.

"My friends," Cornacchia said. "It's time to have some of my fine white port. Its flavor is matched only by its rarity." He opened a cabinet in the living room and removed three long-stemmed goblets. After setting them down on a low table, he filled each of them three-quarters full from a cut-glass decanter. "*Alla vostre salute,*" he said.

The three gently touched glasses. Rick was intrigued by the flavor. "Excellent," he said. "To tell the truth, I've never even heard of white port before."

"An entertaining secret worth remembering," Cornacchia said. "This is also a good time for me to give you your check, Inspector." He walked to the mantel of the fireplace and returned with an envelope in his hand.

Inspector Micallef was taken aback when he saw what was inside. "But this is much more than you said."

"I'm just adding a deserved bonus. Our police are among the finest in the world."

The Inspector folded the check and put it in his billfold. "Once again, we are overwhelmed by your generosity. I can hardly wait to retire and get rich."

They all laughed. "I have something you can take with you, too," Rick said, handing the drawing to him. "Keep this for us until we decide who it belongs to. Put it away in your safe without looking at it. You can return it when we come to an agreement."

"Lorenzo?" Micallef said.

Cornacchia nodded. "Yes. Please. That's what I want, too."

"Then of course I'll be happy to," the Inspector said. "Are you ready to leave?" he asked Rick.

"Actually I've agreed to accept Duke Cornacchia's invitation to spend the night. We'll try to resolve our differences so we can get it back from you tomorrow."

"I see. You will have to call me on my cell phone. I'll be at the air show tomorrow. It's part of the Independence celebration."

"We'll remember that," Cornacchia said. He showed Micallef to the door. "Perhaps I'll see you tomorrow, then," he said.

"Thank you again for your hospitality and generosity," Micallef said. "I bid you both a good night."

Rick followed Cornacchia and Micallef to the gate and watched as Cornacchia pushed a button to let Micallef out. The dog briefly appeared from around the corner, then disappeared again as they started back.

"I wish you would explain why you had Stef kidnapped. I'm sure that Cellini's drawings must be worth quite a bit of money, but they aren't worth murder and kidnapping."

Cornacchia looked surprised. "What do you mean murder?"

"One of your kidnappers killed Mario Agius, the man who owned the car rental agency. Apparently he wouldn't tell them where Stef was staying."

"I had no idea. I've never had any intention for anyone to get hurt."

"You honestly have no idea where Stef is?" Rick asked.

"No. I'll have to talk to the man who hired his captors. I'm holding him responsible for your brother's return, and he won't dare to cross me."

Rick nodded. "Your father was a poet. Do you have any of his works?"

"The library is full of them," Cornacchia said. "Come and take a look."

Rick gasped when he saw the collection of Morocco-leather bound books. A first edition of *Orlando Furioso* stood cheek in jowl with first editions of Machiavelli's *Prince*, Francesco Giucciardin's *History of Italy* and Paolo Sarpi's *History of the Council of Trent*. His mind reeled. By the time he finished looking through the volumes of D'Annunzio's *il Fuoco* and *Laudi*, he was literally out of breath. He did take a second look at two books. One was entitled, *La Cifra del Signor Giovan Batista Belaso*. Belaso was an early master cryptographer who introduced the *tabula recta* to make the Venetian codes safer. The other was an Amharic-Italian dictionary. His heart thumped as he casually took the book from the shelf to check the publication date. 1899 clearly meant that a Twentieth Century Cornacchia, Alessandro most likely, had procured the book.

Rick turned to face Lorenzo Cornacchia. "You've got nearly every important Italian book from the Renaissance to the mid-Twentieth Century here," he said. "And every one is in mint condition. The collection must be worth millions of lira."

"I'm sure it is," Cornacchia said in a dry voice. "Unfortunately I seldom have time to read them. If you're interested, my father's poetry is over to the right."

Rick saw the one he desperately wanted to read, but decided to wait until he could view it without raising suspicion. "I think I'll pass on the book for now."

"Then I'll have Ibn show you to your room."

"Anytime. Just out of curiosity, what are you going to accuse Stef of stealing?"

"Probably a book or two from the library," Cornacchia replied with a bemused smile, "or maybe one of the paintings. I have a lovely little Titian on the wall in your brother's room."

Cornacchia followed Rick out of the library. As he reached to turn out the light, Rick noticed his ring. The sight gave him a chill. It was the same as the ones Micallef and the librarian were wearing, a seven-pointed star on a ruby background with the letter A on top. "That's a beautiful ring," Rick said. "What is it for?"

"L'Ankra. It means the Anchor. It's the society that Bartolomeo Cornacchia started in 1560. My father revived it in 1932. This is Bartolomeo's ring."

Rick suddenly wondered if he had put too much trust in Inspector Micallef. If he had, Cornacchia had already won.

Cornacchia turned off the light as they left the library. "Have a pleasant night," he said.

CHAPTER 29

▼

10:35 PM
Borgiswed, Mdina

The trip up the staircase was ominous. Ibn moved without a sound, staying two steps behind as they climbed. At the first landing, he tapped Rick on the right shoulder to indicate the direction he was supposed to move. Each step provided important geographical information for use when he escaped from the room.

The trip down the hallway took about 70 paces, with perhaps ten between the doors. At the last one, Ibn nudged him to stop and said, "Inside please." After turning on the light he said, "Have a pleasant night."

The room was out of the nineteenth century, replete with a canopied bed, unopened can of toothpowder and nightpot. The Cornacchias had been using this room for guests since Charlemagne.

Kicking off his shoes, Rick swung his feet up on the bed. As he stretched out, he felt a pull at the skin of his chest. For once he was happy it was hairless as he yanked the bag of Equanils free. After taking a moment to massage the instep of each foot, he stretched out full length. He found it to be a great pleasure. Nuzzling his face contentedly against the sleek bedspread, he closed his eyes. I'm glad only my feet are tired…

He woke with a start as he heard the door open. Marija Cornacchia stepped in dressed in a sheer green negligee and peignoir with low-heeled evening slippers. "You're frowning," she said. "Are you displeased to see me?"

"Not at all," he said. "In Eskimo culture it's common practice for the host to offer his wife to a guest. I didn't know you had a similar custom here."

She laughed a low feline sound as she climbed onto the far end of the bed. He watched in dumb fascination as the negligee and peignoir fell aside to reveal a very shapely tanned leg. Dustin Hoffman in *The Graduate* couldn't have felt more uncomfortable. "This isn't my husband's idea. It's mine."

Rick's neck felt clammy. "What do you want?"

"You are a very good chessplayer and you interest me," she said. "Very few people have ever played my husband as well. Lorenzo hates to lose and he seldom does."

"He didn't lose."

She looked at him through her lashes. "No. But he didn't win, either. To him that's the same as losing."

"You almost sound pleased."

"Not pleased," she said, drawing her leg further up towards her chin. "Impressed. I'm far more difficult to impress than to please."

He squirmed as she toyed with the ribbon that held her peignoir together. "Did you come here to play chess?" he asked.

She laughed deep in her throat. "No. I came to help you. Whatever Lorenzo is paying you for the drawing, it's not nearly enough. He's talked of nothing else since he found out about it."

"Then I suppose you didn't realize that the man he calls Stef isn't really my brother."

Again her eyes opened in what looked like surprise. "I had no idea."

"Your husband kidnapped my brother. I came here to trade the drawing for him."

A look of distress came into her eyes. "I'm sorry Lorenzo deceived you. But I may know where they're keeping him."

Rick sat up. "Where?"

"Mosta Dome. I overheard Lorenzo talking with Cardinal Vella."

He smiled at the harmless information. "They moved him. Do you know why your husband had him kidnapped?"

"No, but it may have something to do with whatever he's making in the basement. He locks himself in every night and sometimes the house is filled with smoke when he's at work. That's why he has such a hoarse voice."

Rick's eyebrows raised. "Is he making another statue?"

She shrugged her shoulders. "I really have no idea."

"Do you know anything about the *Aegis Dei*?" he asked.

He expected another show of innocence, but she answered straightforwardly. "Just what Lorenzo told me. Religious people get upset about the silliest things, don't they? Gold is just gold. What difference does it make where it came from or who took it from whom?"

The words left him breathless with excitement. *So that was what both Suleiman and Bin-Said were after! Stolen gold!* In a calm voice, he said, "You're right."

She cocked her head. "You're from America, aren't you? I'd love to go to New York, or to London, or Paris. Anywhere." She stopped and looked at him through her lashes. "But I wouldn't want to go alone."

"Take Lorenzo with you. The business can run without you for a few weeks, can't it?"

"Not Lorenzo. I was thinking of someone a little younger and better looking." Her eyelids closed slowly, then opened. "Someone like you."

Rick got the idea that she was halfway serious. "Sorry. I'm already taken, but I'm sure you can find any number of men to take you up on your offer."

"I don't want anyone else," she said. "You excite me. Let's have some brandy and see if I can't persuade you. I'm sure Ibn neglected to tell you, but it's in the stand next to you," she said. "You'll find four glasses in the bottom shelf."

"Four?" Rick said. "Are Ibn and your husband dropping in, too?"

Her plum-colored lips parted and she laughed a low, throaty laugh. "Neither one, I'm afraid. Ibn would be terribly jealous and I don't think Lorenzo would be interested." She pulled the negligee over her legs and he breathed a sigh of relief.

As he started to pour, he noticed the packets of Equanil on the nightstand. Surreptitiously emptying one of them into a glass, he covered it with brandy.

She smiled darkly as she handed her the glass, her fingers encircling his as she took the goblet. He watched in amazement as she downed half of it in one swallow. "You're staring at me," she said. "Why?"

"I was just wondering what your husband would say if he saw us."

Melita's pink tongue flicked over plum lips. "I'm sure he would be delighted. He would naturally assume I'm here to negotiate a better price for the drawing. I'm a far better bargainer than poor dear Lorenzo. Far more…creative. Don't you think so?" She paused, then continued. "Think about my offer," she said. "We could play a lot of chess together." Reaching out a finger she pressed it against his chest. "And many other games, too."

She stared at him, waiting for an answer. Realizing that one wasn't forthcoming, she swung her legs over the side of the bed and glared at him. "Perhaps I've misjudged you," she said, angrily downing the rest of the brandy. "Perhaps your interest runs to men. Like Lorenzo's. And Alessandro's."

Rick was stunned. "You can't be serious," he said.

"I'm very serious. I've caught him several times."

"Didn't you know that when you married him?"

"No. I was too impressed with his title and his money. And he actually seemed attracted to me when we first met."

Rick could think of many other reasons why his interest might have waned.

She sat down next to him and started to undo his shirt buttons. "I saw you at the Mall the other day. I hardly noticed your face but your body is absolutely delicious."

He caught her hand. "That's enough," he said. "I don't care why you're here. I want you to leave."

"No," she said firmly. "I hate to lose even more than Lorenzo does." With that she put his hand on her breast. Lips parted enough to show the biting edges of her remarkably white teeth as she pushed him backwards and climbed on his chest. Then, as she reached for his zipper, she yawned.

Surprised, she bent forward and kissed him. "Do you want some more brandy?" Rick asked.

She threw him a sleepy look. "Not yet, darling. There's enough there for the whole night. Lorenzo will never miss me."

"But Ibn might," he said.

She answered with a knowing smile. Bending forward once again, she was about to kiss him when her body unexpectedly relaxed. Struggling to keep awake, she pulled back, then, sighing, fell forward on him, full weight. He waited until her breathing slowed before moving out from under her. "It's going to be a wonderful evening, love," he whispered.

"Mmm," she said, without opening her eyes. Then she rolled onto her back. Soon she was sound asleep with her mouth drawn into a pout. He wondered if it was because she didn't get her way with him. He felt through the nightgown and peignoir for the key.

He found it, dangling from her neck over the pillow along with a small gold locket and silver cross. The reminders of her humanity surprised him. Asleep, she was almost supernaturally beautiful. Surely the houris of heaven couldn't be more alluring. Dark hair brushed against his hand as he pulled her head forward to undo the gold chain. Unable to open it, he gave the key a jerk. She didn't stir as it came loose in his hand.

He dressed quickly, then doused the lights. A tiny beacon of light marked the keyhole. Kneeling, he put his eye next to it and scanned the hallway. Nothing but white wallpaper. He got to his feet and slipped the key into the lock. Taking a deep breath, he gave the key a quick turn. The bolt fell back with barely a sound.

He counted to ten and opened the door. After taking a second to relock it, he skated across the marble floor on a slick direct course to the hall window. Despite Ibn's efforts to speed him along, he had glanced at it on his way to his room.

It was a single pane set in a wrought-iron frame and wasn't made to open.

Now what? Down the hall a black space indicated an open door. He remembered. It was the one with brocade curtains.

Stockings squeaking, he made a dash for it. Slick marble gave way to rich, warm wool pile. Another bedroom, he thought as he shut the door.

He could see a glow coming through the curtains from the outside. The yardlight was still on! The dog wasn't his only worry. He had to run the risk of being sighted from the house.

Maybe at least the window opens, he thought, turning the latch. The window swung out, letting in a cool breeze. All he could see below was a 50-foot drop with nothing between him and the ground.

An equally smooth expanse stretched in the other direction. And the roof was at least another 15 feet above him.

He jumped away from the window at the sounds of footsteps and labored breathing coming from the hall. Ibn!

Pulling the curtain closed, he inched further along the wall. A cone of light on the ceiling and a soft scraping against the carpet made him tremble. *The door was opening.*

It opened wider. "Marija?" Ibn whispered. Rick huddled impotently. If Ibn opened the door any further the light from the hall would put him in full view.

The door closed.

No time to congratulate himself on his good luck. If Ibn went into Rick's room, he would be back with the dog in an instant. And if he waited in the hall, Rick was stuck in the bedroom with only a window and a nasty drop as a way out.

What a fix.

The half-light from the yard illuminated two large beds. Tying sheets together might work, but he'd still have at least a 20-foot drop. Cellini had attempted a similar escape and had broken a leg in the process. And the dog would be waiting. There had to be a better way. Even if it risked a confrontation with Ibn.

Here goes.

He stuck his head into the hallway an inch at a time, all the while keeping a watchful eye for Ibn. At first he thought the Arab had left. Then he saw him two doors away sitting cross-armed on a chair, head resting against the wall. Rick bent around the doorway, flattening himself against the wall, then started toward the stairway in a sidestep.

Something in the air had his nose twitching. With each step the odor became stronger. It was hot and acrid, and so astringent he worried he'd sneeze. When he finally reached the top step it was enough to make his eyes water. Unpleasant, for certain. But familiar, too.

Halfway down the stairs, he remembered the stench of molten metal and flux from his metals class in high school.

Reaching the second landing he turned to the left, toward the library. After a quick look around, he slipped inside and shut the door. After wasting precious seconds he opened the door to the hallway to find the lightswitch. Then he made a beeline for Alessandro's books.

The first thing he looked for was the working papers on the Aegis Dei.

Several ledgers contained notes and Amharic characters in different combinations. There were far too many books to take with him and he picked one at random. Next he ran his fingers along the bindings of the books of poetry. Though unmarked, they were arranged chronologically. He stooped to pull out the last volume. The first notation was dated 13 di Settembre 1939.

The pages were penned with a delicate, almost feminine, hand. Faded ink left many pages nearly illegible. He turned to the last pages, found them blank, and then thumbed forward.

Nothing looked anything like the Duke's challenge.

In his confusion he turned past Cornacchia's last notations. Paging backward he found two stuck together, right and left, so a page after them appeared to be the last entry. Using the letter opener on the desk, he carefully separated them. What he found gave him a jolt comparable to finding the plastique in his cell phone.

The right page had the now-familiar parody of the Cornacchia coat of arms: left side, diamond, right side, dolphin rising from the sea. A scroll at the bottom spelled out, *"Diaman**tt**e* e Delfino."

Rick eyes opened wide. No wonder there was an extra space! Cornacchia had deliberately misspelled Diamante!

Just as intriguing was the banner stretched across the top of the shield proclaiming "Aegis Dei." Why had Alessandro copied the words from Cellini's basin onto a parody of his coat of arms?

The left-hand page was covered with scribblings in Italian, with Diamantte e Delfino written out many times, with various letters circled and scratched through. The Major had been on the right track. The Duke had just double-crossed him. Rick was about to make off with his treasure when he noticed another book that had been hidden behind the poetry book.

With an uneasy look around he took it out.

It was an old-fashioned accounts book with a hard leather cover, with corners fraying. At first he wondered if it was the one that Bartelemeo was holding in his portrait. The dated notation, Ottobre 1903, meant it belonged to Alessandro.

The first page was covered with familiar-looking runes. Were they from the basin? At the bottom, Alessandro had circled 100. One hundred characters? That was the number Father Santorini said, too.

The next page had a ten-by-ten grid with a character in each of the spaces. The pages that followed were filled with runes in combination and angry penned comments, *Sciocchezza*! *Assurdo*! Nonsense.

Alessandro's work filled half the book. The very last notation read, in Italian: *Will anyone ever solve the riddle of the basin?*

The words left him agape. What did that mean? Before he could puzzle over this, a noise from the hallway frightened him so much that he dropped the book. He waited in terror-struck silence, expecting the door to open and for someone to come into the library.

But the seconds passed with no sound audible other than his own stifled breathing. Even so, the noise was enough to convince him that he had spent too much time in the library. He tucked the book under his arm and turned off the light.

Opening the library door a crack, he listened for several seconds before stepping out.

He heard a soft padding sound and came face-to-face with *Princep*! The animal stood three feet away, staring. Rick stood unmoving in his tracks. So did the dog, obviously not knowing what to do about Rick's presence. If he were clearly out-of-bounds, it would have attacked without a moment's hesitation.

"Hi, *Princep*," he said, as quietly as he could. The dog's ears pricked at the sound of its name, but it stood its ground, neither advancing nor retreating. Afraid his lack of activity would make the dog even more suspicious, he moved his right hand toward his shirt pocket and took out the candy bar.

The dog growled.

He dropped to his knees and held out his hand, palm down. The dog ignored it and stared him the face. Left hand extended, Rick stuck the candy bar in his palm and used the right hand to undo the wrapper. The dog growled again, but didn't move.

Rick held out the unwrapped bar, palm up. For just a moment the dog looked away from Rick's face to the candy bar. Rick broke off a corner of the bar and tossed it at its feet. The dog never even looked at it. It just kept staring silently at him.

His heart thumped. How long would it be before Ibn or Cornacchia showed up? Or before the dog decided Rick didn't belong there and attacked?

He broke off another piece and tossed it, hitting the dog in the face. It flinched and backed up a step. But it never took its eyes off his face. Rick's hand found its way to one of the bags with the Equanil inside of it.

With minimum motion he tossed the bar at the dog's feet. It bent down to sniff, then straightened up. Ten agonizing seconds passed. Finally, determined to fend off the dog's attack by sticking his hand down the dog's throat if necessary, Rick took a normal step toward the staircase.

The animal still didn't move. But it didn't growl, either. Two more steps brought Rick to the doorway. After a few anxious seconds the dog moved out of the way. Walking backwards and facing the dog, Rick made his way to the staircase. Princep watched him a bit longer and then entered the library. Did he decide to go after the candy bar?

Still edging backwards, Rick climbed to the first landing. As he reached the second floor, he saw Princep walk past the stairway with its tail between its legs. Rick prayed that it had eaten the forbidden fruit and was feeling guilty. A sound from down the hall forced him to make a quick entry through the closest door. Was it Ibn? He didn't have time to ponder. The sound of approaching footsteps sent him scrambling under the bed.

Five minutes later he crawled out, assuming the dog was either asleep or in no condition to do him any harm and whoever had been in the hall was no longer around.

His luck held. As he reached the top step of the stairway he realized that the stench was many times stronger than it had been before.

The pathway remained clear as he descended the stairs.

When he reached the first floor he stopped. He had originally intended to head directly for the front door and exit through the front gate. The sound of voices coming from the area of the kitchen gave him pause. Though they were barely audible, he could clearly hear two. One belonged to Cornacchia. Who was the other?

As he listened, his curiosity became greater still. He could leave anytime he wanted to. He had to find out who Cornacchia was talking to and what they were saying.

As he approached the kitchen, he realized that the voices were coming from a more distant point. Tiptoeing toward the source of the sounds, he noticed that the door to the basement was slightly ajar, and that smoke streamed out around the door. The voices were still indistinct, often drowned out by the sounds of hammering.

Pulling on the knob and opening the door further, he was engulfed in a cloud of dense white smoke. An aspirant roar drowned out the voices only to be replaced by the sharp pings of metal beating against metal.

Overwhelmed by curiosity, he took a silent step down. It turned out to be a long, steep one. Just as he was about to take his second, he heard the gas torch go off.

A voice rang out and Rick caught his breath. Ohmygod. Micallef!

Cornacchia answered. Once again their voices were drowned out by the loud sibilance from the torch.

Even though aware of the danger, Rick took another step downward. Ahead and below, the stairs turned abruptly to the left instead of curving. The deeper he descended, the louder the sounds of activity. And the worse the stench. How could Cornacchia stand it?

Intense yellow light indicated the source was just a short distance away.

Rick stood at the bottom of the stairs for several seconds, listening. If Cornacchia had arranged his bench with his back toward the stairway, Rick was safest when he heard him at work.

Once again a hammer rang out.

As he started to take a step down he caught himself in mid-stride. There was a safer way. If he stretched out, actually lying on the stairs, he could keep his head low enough that Cornacchia or Micallef would have to be looking at the floor to see him.

Bracing himself against the wall and holding on to the handrail, he lowered his knees until they rested on the stone. Then he dragged himself on his wrists and forearms until his head reached the bottom stair. When he did he nearly broke out laughing. He still couldn't see around the bend at the bottom of the stairs.

A wiggle did the trick.

The hard-won view was disappointing. Micallef sat on a stool some ten feet away with his back to Rick, but Cornacchia was completely hidden by the smoke.

Little by little the smoke dissipated and he could make out Cornacchia's dark form vigorously at work at a bench that stood at waist-level. He was so engrossed in his work that Rick imagined he could walk up behind him and look over his shoulder without being noticed.

Spots danced in front of his eyes and Rick realized he had stayed too long. Unable to breathe, Rick pushed himself backward. The fumes became suffocating and black spots danced merrily before his eyes. The spots collided and he plunged irresistibly to the bottom of a lightless well. Before he struck bottom, someone grabbed him roughly by the shoulders.

Blackness covered him.

CHAPTER 30

▼

Saturday, 12:30 AM
Borgiswed, Mdina

He heard a buzz, an unintelligible droning of bees. And, as his head cleared, the droning turned into voices.

Lying motionless with his eyes closed, his other senses returned, each adding to his discomfort. His nose and throat burned and he could feel his eyes smarting behind swollen lids. A strange sensation at his left wrist made him wonder if he had lost his hand. But it was just asleep, jammed between his rump and the arm of the chair.

"I'll see," a voice said. Rick felt a hand on his shoulder and opened his eyes to find Cornacchia looking down at him with a benevolent smile. "You *are* awake. I'll have Ibn open the door. Fresh air will do you good."

Rick unfolded himself by wiggling upright, straightening his feet and pulling his hand free, all at the same time. Quite an accomplishment, considering the way he felt. "Your hobby is a real killer," he croaked.

"My hobby?" Cornacchia said. "Yes. I suppose it is a bit overwhelming, isn't it?

He handed Rick a tumbler of water. Fresh air and cold water assaulted his inflamed mucus membranes as he drank. The pain was almost pleasant.

"I'm afraid I've been unforgivably careless," Cornacchia mused. "I underestimated your resourcefulness. I won't be so careless twice." Knowing what was coming, Rick unbuttoned his sweater. Setting it on the table he started on the shirt. Ibn felt them and dropped them on the floor. "Now the trousers."

Rick climbed out of the pants, feigning unconcern as Ibn removed the belt and pulled it across the palm of his hand. The Arab was about to drop it on the rest of the clothes when Cornacchia stopped him. "Let me see that," he said.

What the bloody hell? Rick watched with saucer eyes as Cornacchia ran a finger along the tooled surface of the leather, then turned it over.

"There seems to be a loose thread," Cornacchia said. He pulled on it but the unglued part of the belt refused to separate. Sticking a knife blade in between the halves, he separated the pieces of leather. Rick's wire fell out first. Then the lock-pick bounced off the floor with a metallic clink.

"Your talents seem to be without limit," Cornacchia said. "You may wish you had your tools back before the night is over."

He watched impassively while Rick dressed, then pulled a kitchen chair around to face him, resting his chin on the back. "You should have stayed with Marija. Your room had a comfortable bed, and she would have seen that you were well-entertained for the rest of the night."

At the words, Ibn's eyes narrowed.

"I know she was with you," Cornacchia continued. "And I know why. She is a beautiful young woman, and I'm nearly twice her age. Ironic, isn't it? She married me for a title I can't use in a country that hasn't needed nobility since medieval times."

"Were the titles always meaningless?" Rick asked.

"No. At one time the church and the nobles ruled the island together. It was called the *Universita* system and the Cornacchias were the Keeper of the Rod. But getting back to Marija, I know she is quite taken with you. She's a good chess-player herself, but she has never come close to drawing with me. You drew twice and nearly won once. That makes you something special. By the way, as far as I know, Marija has never fallen asleep after an amorous adventure before. That is either a great compliment or an insult to your lovemaking abilities."

Rick's thin smile quickly disappeared as Ibn's evil look became darker.

"But enough about Marija," Cornacchia said. "What's the *real* reason you were spying on me?"

"I wanted to see why you were so intent on getting the drawing. Now I know why you want it so badly."

"And why is that?" Cornacchia asked. Rick could detect the note of bemused contempt in his voice.

"Because you're making a replica of the Aegis Dei and you're afraid that whoever you're making it for will find out it's a forgery."

Cornacchia looked alarmed. "Whatever gave you that idea?"

"I watched you at work. I'd love to get a closer look at what you're making."

Cornacchia regarded Rick thoughtfully, then nodded. "Why not? There's no reason you can't know now. Would you get it for me, please, Rafael?"

"Do that, Inspector," Rick growled. "I'm sure it's in as safe place as my drawing."

Micallef disappeared without a word. He returned carrying a heavy object with both hands. "Where do you want me to put it?"

"On the kitchen table, please. We'll all take a look at it together."

The table was in front of a window and Rick was certain that at least one of Carpenter's men was watching. As Rick got up, Ibn took several steps closer to stand directly behind him. The Arab's labored breathing fumed with jealousy.

The shield amazed him. It could have been the original. At least sixteen inches in diameter, it must have weighed close to the fifteen pounds of metal that Cellini had used to make Francis' legendary saltcellar. And some of Cellini's craftsmanship was evident in the heavy embossments of the shields and the knight's armor. Cornacchia had also done an excellent job detailing the expressions on the knight's faces and the texture of the chain mail they wore.

The banner with "Aegis Dei" was present, too, but quite different from the one on Cellini's drawing. The best work was done with the precious stones used to embellish the work. The large number of rubies, garnets, sapphires and emeralds must have cost more than the gold. But the work also had an obvious defect based on what Rick had learned about the original. There were no Amharic inscriptions. Also the patina was too clean and sharp, a result of chemical treatment rather than years of aging.

Nodding in approval, Rick said, "Excellent. A work of a master craftsman. Your forgery would fool nearly anyone."

"Forgery? It's my own work. Forgery implies criminal intent."

"You forget I've seen Cellini's drawing. This is an obvious attempt to replicate the Aegis Dei. I also know that your father hid the original during the Second World War and as far as anyone knows it's never been found. Someone wants it and you're making another to replace it."

"I have no idea what you're talking about," Cornacchia said testily.

"Of course you do. I watched you work. You even used Cellini's tools. For one thing, you use a *rasoio*. Cellini used them to plane gold work."

Cornacchia didn't respond and Rick continued. "And there's the hare's foot. Goldsmiths use them to gather up filings because the dust doesn't stick to the fur. You've been careful, but there's still some on your pants."

"That hardly proves I'm trying to forge Cellini's work."

"Maybe not, but you'll have to admit that my theory provides a very good motive for your being so desperate to get the drawing back. You're afraid it could be used to prove your work was a counterfeit."

"But why would I make a counterfeit?" Cornacchia asked, genially. "To sell? A few million pounds more or less wouldn't mean a thing to me. I already have more money than I could ever need."

Taking a deep breath, Rick said, "Someone who frightens you wants the Shield. And you are very anxious to please or you wouldn't take such an enormous risk."

Cornacchia laughed. "And who would that be?"

"I don't know." Rick lied.

"My family has an old story. I don't tell it to many people, but I think you'll appreciate it.

"Many hundreds of years ago a wise and benevolent king ruled our island. He tended his kingdom with a loaf of bread in one hand to feed his subjects and a sword in the other to protect the bread.

"This went on for many years. Unfortunately, bands of robbers began to show up trying to steal the bread. As time went by the king had to resort to holding a larger sword to keep them away. As the swords became larger, it also became more difficult to hold the bread so the loaves got smaller. Finally there wasn't enough food to go around and some of the people went hungry. The bands of thieves got even larger. Finally the King had to use both hands to hold the sword. Once again the people were starving."

"Sounds like the history of civilization," Rick said.

"Precisely. At any rate, so many people came to petition the king he became frightened and locked himself in his castle. The people finally decided they had no choice but to rebel and they sent out their wisest man to travel around the world to find the bravest and best warrior to unseat the king and take over the throne. The envoy traveled the world for many months until he finally found a warrior he was sure could do the job. After a fierce battle the warrior slew the king and took the throne. For many months he ruled with his sword and his loaf, but once again thieves began to show up. All too soon, the new king was alone in his castle with his sword. Finally the wise man again offered to go search the lands for another warrior.

"'Don't,' everyone said. 'You know what happened the last time. And it will take an even fiercer warrior to defeat our new king.'

"'Fear not,' the wise man said. 'This time I won't come back until I find someone with three hands.'"

Rick laughed. "Very good. And have you found a warrior with three hands?"

"I do hope so," Cornacchia replied. "Once again, good night. Ibn will take you to your new room. I want you to know you have nothing to fear from me. I fully intend to return your brother to you and let you both go."

"I believe you do. But before I go, why are you so frightened of the European Union?" Rick asked.

"We've worked for centuries to get our Independence. I can't allow us to blithely give it away."

"I have one last question for you. Your father wrote in his book 'Who will solve the Shield's riddle?' Do you know what that means?"

Cornacchia sighed. "Before Bartolomeo disappeared he told his son that the basin was a puzzle to be solved and that whoever did would someday rule Malta. Three hundred years of Cornacchias have tried to discover what he meant and my father spent his entire life trying to solve it, but couldn't. Since the basin is gone, I'm sure no one ever will. Now please forgive me. I wish I could spend more time talking to you, but I am tired. Escort Mr. Olsen to his new room, Ibn."

With that, Cornacchia and Micallef left. Now alone with his prey, Ibn grinned obscenely and thrust a pistol into Rick's back as hard as he could. "Move," he said.

They started up the staircase. When they reached the third landing, Ibn gave Rick a vicious jab in his left kidney, leaving him dizzy with pain. They turned left and walked down a corridor until Ibn assaulted him again. "Stop."

Another thrust was meant to be an order to open the door. Nauseous, Rick stumbled inside. Even without a light he knew that his new room was a mirror image of his first. And windowless.

Ibn's hatred generated energy like a dynamo. Though it made him extremely dangerous, it also made him vulnerable.

Properly meek, Rick stood aside as Ibn strode into the room. Keeping a wary eye on his captive, the Arab poked and pushed at the bare bed. Finished, he struck Rick in the solar plexus, doubling him over. Then he left the room and locked the door.

The bolt was barely in place before Rick was planning his escape. There were plenty of weapons available at hand: the cord from the lamp, the lamp itself and the bedslats. All he needed to do was to lure Ibn into the room, and, given the man's state of mind, that wouldn't be difficult at all.

Rick beat a tattoo on the wall, hammering until Ibn ordered him to stop. When he started on the door Ibn broke into scornful laughter. "Beat until your hands are raw. I will not open the door."

Not to be discouraged, Rick grabbed a bedslat and stationed himself next to the door. "Lorenzo is right," he said in a loud voice. "I should have stayed with Marija. I can still feel her beneath my belly."

Even though there was no response Rick could feel electricity gathering in the air outside the room.

"I bet you heard her scream in pleasure. She told me that she hasn't had much to excite her lately."

Rick pressed his ear against the door. No click of the lock, but he was sure Ibn was breathing harder. "She said even the dog was better."

The door swung open without warning, and Rick toppled to the floor. An outlined form flew at him from the lighted hallway, right arm raised.

"*Zebbar!*" Ibn shouted, throwing himself at Rick with knife in hand.

Rick rolled and a knife buried itself in the carpet. Just as quickly he rolled back and swung the bedslat as hard as he could with his left hand, hitting Ibn squarely on his shoulder.

"*Shitan,*" Ibn hissed, seizing Rick's throat with one hand and reaching for the knife with the other. Rick slammed his knee into Ibn's groin. Yelping with pain, Ibn grabbed Rick's neck with both hands. And with Ibn's knees on his shoulders, all Rick could do was buck and weakly flail at the man's back and arms with the bedslat. He rapidly lost the battle. Ibn's hands were too strong and he had enough bulk to resist Rick's desperate attempts to get free.

Rick's breath quickly became short rasping gasps. With his last flickerings of consciousness, he stopped struggling.

Ibn refused to move but finally released his grip on Rick's throat. As he started to back away to stand, Rick acted. With his last ounce of strength, he swung the bedslat at Ibn's head. This time it connected. With a nasty sounding crack, he caught the man on the back of his head. Screaming with pain, Ibn reached for the knife. Before he could reach it, Rick struck again, slamming the bedslat sharply into his forehead. Ibn fell backward to lie on the floor. Breathing shallowly, he lay motionlessly as blood trickled from a long cut on his scalp. A quick run-through of the man's pockets produced Rick's lockpick. He was happy to get it back.

Using Ibn's knife, Rick sliced several narrow strips of cloth from the mattress cover. He wrapped them together for a serviceable cord to tie Ibn's hand behind him. Flipping the mattress over, he started on the other side. A short while later, Ibn was bound hand and foot, lying between the boxspring and what was left of the mattress, a ridiculous pea to Marija's princess.

"*Salaam,*" Rick said as he opened the door and stepped into the hallway. He looked for Ibn's gun but couldn't see it. Finally, after stopping for a moment to listen for Cornacchia, he found the staircase and slowly started down to the library.

At the bottom step, he heard voices. Cornacchia and the Inspector were arguing.

Rick continued forward, toes before heels. The voices got louder. As suspected, the front door was locked and none of the windows opened. With a sigh he crossed to the staircase and started up. Before long, Cornacchia would come up to check on his houseguest and would find Ibn. If Rick were still around then, he would have no choice but to kill or incapacitate Cornacchia and perhaps Micallef, too.

One possible way out was through the garden, as the children had entered the estate. But even if he could find the entrance, certainly Cornacchia wouldn't have left it open.

The second possibility was to fashion a rope and climb to the roof, then jump from roof to roof until he could get down to ground level. He knew from the mosaic that there was a parapet running around the top of the house. All he needed was a hook. He had seen one somewhere in the house, but couldn't remember where.

Reaching the landing for the third story, he remembered. One of the enormous hanging pots in the balcony over the checkerboard had a hook. No sure thing, but it might be strong enough to support his weight.

The hanging pot turned out to be even more of a bonus than he suspected. A sturdy cord ran through the hook. Though he could barely lift the pot, he hoisted it free and set it on the balcony. The knots were tight but he finally undid them, leaving him with a serviceable rope and hook.

Maybe he could get to the roof from the balcony.

After several unsuccessful throws, the hook caught. He gave the rope several good yanks, then started to climb. Three feet up, the hook came loose and he landed on the balcony in a heap.

He heard a sound below and jumped back inside at the sight of Inspector Micallef on the ground. Without a thought, he ran through the door and across the hall to the room directly opposite. This room had a window but no balcony. Cornacchia was calling to Micallef, and he wasn't far away.

Without a second thought, he braced his butt on the edge of the windowsill, bent out backwards, and swung the hook and rope upwards.

He couldn't get the rope to grip the roof. The sound of Cornacchia's voice but a few feet away made his skin crawl. "Did you see where he went?" he called in English. The Duke was in the hall just outside the door.

Teeth chattering, Rick swung again. Again the hook fell back, this time nearly hitting him on the head. Someone turned a doorknob behind him.

Shutting his eyes he threw once again. To his amazement, the rope hung straight down. He pulled and it stayed fast. The door opened as he stepped out.

"Stop!" the Duke shouted. Rick planted a foot and started upward.

"He's over here," Cornacchia called. Micallef answered.

Swallowing, Rick put his whole weight against the rope. The hook and rope held steady. Taking his first step out, he did his best to keep from spinning sideways. His next step brought him to the top of the window. It would be the last horizontal surface until he reached the roof. After a brief rest he was off again, tugging himself hand over hand.

He was still five feet from the top when Cornacchia's head appeared out of the window beneath him. "Come back," Cornacchia demanded. "I meant it when I said I wouldn't hurt you. Please don't leave me with no choice."

Rick's hand reached the parapet just as he heard an explosion. The bullet struck between his legs. Micallef shouted just as Rick planted his feet on the side of the building and pulled himself up over the top of the parapet.

Panting and with heart racing, he took a deep breath and got to his feet. As he retrieved the rope, he realized someone had grabbed it. Rick yanked it free.

Without a second's hesitation, he started running south toward Mdina gate. The buildings on his route were only four to six feet apart, and he had broad-jumped much farther before.

With more than half a moon shining brightly overhead, he had a clear path ahead. He heard footsteps behind him. Someone had climbed to the roof and was following him. Even so, when he came to the end of the first roof his knees turned to water.

Jump, damn it! Steeling himself, he backed up and landed on the next roof, clearing the parapet by several inches.

He looked back for his pursuer. He could hear staccato footsteps of someone running. When he came to the edge of the next building he didn't hesitate. He jumped and landed cleanly, feeling only a tingle in his ankles. In the background the footsteps still kept time with his. At the Cathedral, Rick stopped for a moment to look down at the black street but found he couldn't see a thing.

Three more rooftops brought him to the square. His pursuer had gained on him. As Rick got to his hands and knees to look over the edge, he heard a gunshot. The bullet glanced off the roof three feet away from him. He scrabbled over the side. Hanging full length, he still had at least a fourteen-foot drop below him. He took a deep breath and let go. His right leg glanced off something as he fell, but he landed on both feet with his knees bent. The force of the impact still sent him sprawling.

Quickly getting to his feet, he headed for the gate. As his feet touched the bridge he saw the glare of headlights and heard an automobile bearing down on him. He ran toward the tree where the cat had come from and jumped up on the railing. The car slowed and the driver's window came down. A pair of arms reached for him. Before they could close on him, he leaped.

CHAPTER 31

▼

2:12 AM
Mdina, Malta

He hurtled forward in a powerful arc. Nearing the branch, Rick threw one arm up to protect his face and the other out to grab for the tree trunk. Needles punctured his hands as he crashed through and continued to hurtle headfirst toward the ground. Too terrified to scream, he stretched out his arms to grab for a large branch beneath him. It broke with a loud crack. Wrapping his arms around the trunk, he finally came to a stop with bleeding hands and a thumping heart.

As he hung gasping for breath a powerful searchlight hit him in the face. Someone called from the bridge and other voices gibbered in reply. When a second car pulled up and stopped, he was sure he would be captured. Then the light moved away. He exhaled, hugged the trunk and started down.

He had but one route to escape: Up the side of the moat. And he had but seconds to do it. A car parked ten feet away would give him concealment. But to get to it, he would have to dare the searchlight and cross an open expanse.

As if drawn by his fears, the searchlight began to crawl back toward him. He flattened himself face forward against the inner wall of the moat. The powerful beam slowly crept across him, and stopped. He held his breath. Just as his legs began to quiver, it moved on. Belly flat against the wall, he inched forward. Headlights appeared some forty feet away. Dizzy with adrenaline, he dropped to his knees. The searchlight crept back toward him as he crawled forward. Just as it was about to overtake him he sprawled to safety underneath a car.

Lungs screamed for air but he didn't dare breathe as he heard the scratch of approaching footsteps. A voice called from the distance and another, this one much closer, answered. Rick recognized it and grimaced. Inspector Micallef was only five feet away.

Rick reacted by pulling himself into a tight ball. The footsteps grew louder and a flashlight beam splashed on the ground beside him. He heard a soft grunt as Micallef got to his knees. The beam lit up his backside and he waited for the Inspector to shout out his discovery. Instead he was plunged into darkness. Micallef got to his feet, called out something in Maltese, and walked away.

Though puzzled, Rick had no time to wonder what the Inspector was up to. He worked his way to the front of the car and darted forward on all fours to safety around the curvature of the moat.

One thought consumed him. Like Rick, his pursuers knew there was only way out of the moat. Why weren't they patrolling above with flashlights? Were they lying in wait? Whatever the answer, he would soon find out. He had come to the end of the trench.

Moving away from the wall he made his first toss up the side. He cursed as the hook fell harmlessly at his feet.

"*Hawn*," a voice called from very close by.

He threw again and the hook grabbed on to something. Planting his left foot firmly against the wall, he leaned back to test his weight. The cord tightened and remained firm. The shouts got louder as planted his right foot and started up. The rope held but he uttered a noiseless groan as a stray bit of illumination showed how far it was to the top.

On his next step, the hook slipped and dirt sprinkled into his face. He stopped, gritted his teeth and took another step up.

The top of the moat was only ten feet away.

"*Hemm*," someone shouted from directly below him. Suddenly caught in the light of a powerful lantern he vowed he would not be captured or die meekly.

As he was about to jump a muted voice called from above him. "Rick?"

It was Caterina!

"Yes!" he gasped. The rope moved in his hands and he grasped it more tightly. A shot rang out and he heard the thud of a bullet imbedding itself in the lime-stone rock next to his ear.

"Don't shoot," Micallef shouted. "We'll capture him on top of the moat."

He flinched but ignored the burn in his palms as the rope slid through. Bathed in light, he reached the top and Caterina stretched out her hand to him.

"Hurry," she said. *Tarbija* stood five feet away with a heavy cable attached to its bumper.

"Get in the car," she said taking the cable in her hands. Seconds later she jumped in next to him. The Chev started smoothly. As she turned on the head-lights, Rick saw two men running toward them, trying to get into the path of the car. She stomped on the accelerator. At the last second they leaped out of the way.

With rubber burning and their teeth rattling, they careened forward. The road curved and the men reappeared, this time with weapons. Caterina cursed and floored the gas pedal as a bullet struck the hood of the car. A second shot passed harmlessly over the top of the Chev. Neither man made a move to get out of the way.

"Hang on!" Caterina shouted as she swung to the right. The car lurched and nearly tipped over, but suddenly they were in the clear. *Tarbija* plunged forward, nobly sacrificing its suspension system to the will of its driver. Screeching a plea, it rounded another corner and they were on a thoroughfare.

Tears in eyes, Caterina patted the dashboard and uttered, "Sorry, baby."

Rick turned to look for headlights behind them. All he saw was the rooster-tail of dust they were leaving. He breathed a sigh of relief. "How did you find me?"

"I was watching from the park. That was quite a dive you made."

"I'm glad you came, but you were supposed to wait for me to call you," Rick said.

"I don't recall that being a direct order, sir. So I used my own discretion. It's a good thing I did. Otherwise it would have been the two men who were watching for you who would have been waiting for you when you came out of the moat."

When he asked what happened to them, she answered with a smile. "You're an amazing woman," Rick said.

He sniffed and didn't like what he smelled. The moist odor of steam and burning rubber meant the ancient Chev was overexerting itself. With all its new parts, it was the automotive equivalent of Frankenstein's monster. But it was a genial one and didn't deserve to be tortured.

"How was your evening with Cornacchia?" asked Caterina, eyes riveted on the rearview mirror.

"Lovely," he said. "I had a great meal, saw the basin Cornacchia is working on, and I found out Micallef is one of his accomplices. I also found out why I couldn't solve the Duke's Challenge. Not bad for a night's work."

She frowned. "What makes you think Micallef is in with Cornacchia?"

"He was in the basement while Lorenzo was working on his phony basin. And he led the posse after me, too."

"Then I guess you must be right," she said with a sigh. "By the way, Father Santorini wants you to call him tomorrow."

"You must have picked up my cell phone," he said.

"Yes," Caterina said. "I saw the green message light flashing while it was hidden in the tree and I was afraid someone else might notice it, too."

"Smart girl," he said. "I'll call him first thing in the morning."

Rick was startled as a large orange cat jumped up next to him on the seat.

"Surprise," she said. "I found him while I was waiting for you."

The animal settled in Rick's lap. "Where are we going?" he asked, scratching under its chin.

"The Royal George in St. Julians," she said. Smiling wickedly she continued, "They've got a nice big bed. Unless Marija already wore you out, that is."

"How did you know? Cornacchia had no more than locked me in my room for the night when she came in dressed in a negligee."

"Oh my," she said in a shocked voice. "Then what happened?"

"She sat down on the bed and exposed her private parts to me."

She giggled. "How disgusting. Tell me more."

"I don't dare. You'll be terribly jealous."

"Tell me anyway," she purred, resting her hand on his leg. "And I want the whole story."

"All right. But remember you're forcing me. First she told me that she wanted me to go on a world tour with her, then she pushed me on the bed and tore off my clothes. We spent hours making wild, passionate love. I finally exhausted her and she fell asleep. That's when I made my escape."

"It must have been quite a night," she said. "Are her breasts bigger than mine?"

Rick chuckled. "Maybe a bit, but they aren't as nice."

"Hmm. Does she have any tattoos?"

"None that I noticed."

"How about piercing? Does she have a pearl in her nipples or her, you know?"

"She's too old for that," Rick said. "And I'll answer your next question for you. She's a regular tiger in bed. She bites and scratches. And screams. She sounds just like an animal. My hair stood on end."

"Not just your hair, I bet," she said. Her smile disappeared and her grip on his leg tightened. "You better be making this up."

When he said, "A gentleman never tells," she dug her fingernails deeply into his flesh. "Ow. Stop," he said. "I gave her some Equanil. She fell asleep sitting on my chest."

"That's better," she purred. "You can tell me more in bed."

"We haven't got time," said Rick. "We have to find Stef and we have to find him soon."

CHAPTER 32

▼

Saturday, 3:18 AM
St. Julians

Though barely able to keep his eyes open, Rick eagerly took out the Major's file and laid it on the couch. As he did, Caterina curled up next to him and began to gently massage his neck. The cat settled into her lap.

"Now let's see what we have here," he said. With a look of triumph he drew seventeen dashes on his legal pad and filled in the letters of 'Diamantte e Delfino.'

Caterina looked at the clipping and said, "If the Duke misspelled Diamante, why was it correctly spelled in the newspaper?"

"The key question. An editor must have noticed the misspelling and corrected it before it got into print. Apparently Alessandro didn't realize what happened."

Once again Rick read the words of the challenge. "'If you search for a key, remove the city Malti.' At least we know what we're supposed to remove it from, now."

"The Maltese word for city is 'belt,'" Caterina said. "But there's no 'b.' in Diamantte e Delfino."

"And it can't be 'Valletta' because there's no 'v.'"

"We Maltese call Mdina 'The City,'" she said. "Did you try crossing out 'Mdina' from 'Diamantte e Delfino.'"

"Let's give it a try," he said. He did, working from left to right, and came up with 'atte e Delfino.' Then he drew a line between the Ts.

"'At tee Delfino'?" Caterina asked. "What is that supposed to mean?"

"I don't know, but at least the words make sense." He pointed at the words 'Aegis Dei' at the top of the page. "I always wondered why Alessandro mentions the Shield in the challenge. It wouldn't mean anything to the Brits."

Caterina sat up straighter. "No, but what if the entire clue was supposed to read, 'The Shield of God at tee Delfino?'"

His scalp prickled. "You may be right!"

Caterina beamed. "I'm almost sure I am. There's no way you could have known, but at one time almost all the street names were chiseled on stone shields on the corner buildings in the villages. You can still find quite a few of them. They used the eye of Horus on them, too."

"And Horus certainly was a god to the Egyptians, whether or not he needed a shield. Brava, *qalbi*," he said, remembering the word that she had called him. "Is there a Dolphin Street in Mdina?"

"Not that I know of. There may have been at one time."

"Let's take a look at the 1940s maps."

Cheek to cheek they scoured the first. The 1:1000 scale map listed the names and locations of the street names for the whole island. Rick shook his head. "I don't see any Dolphin Street in Mdina."

"Maybe it wasn't important enough to make the list," she said. "Try another map."

Caterina clung to his shoulder as he unrolled the 1:200 of Mdina City. When he had unfurled she knelt on the floor to help him look. After a five-minute examination, Rick found a small offshoot from Mesquite Street. "This could be something. Let's take a look at what's on the other maps."

He eagerly shuffled through the maps and laid it on the table. Taking a deep breath he said, "This is the 1:100. If it isn't on here, it wasn't in Mdina."

Caterina pressed closer as he looked for the spot. Rick's heart began to pound. A tiny circle at the end of an unnamed cul-de-sac caught his eye, as did the faint perpendicular line next to it. "Where's the mosaic?" he cried. "I need a loupe, too."

She jumped to her feet. When she returned, they crouched together expectantly as he laid the glass against the table. The loupe came to rest on what appeared to be a small mound a few feet from the city wall. "That's it," he shouted. "Stef must have found it, too. If I'm right, Stef doesn't have much time left. Every second counts."

The streets leading to Mdina were quiet and lifeless but Rick didn't want to take any chances of running into Inspector Micallef. "We can go in Greek Gate," she whispered. A sallyport lay nearly invisible amid the dark stones. Inside he found a wide avenue where several cars were parked.

She took his hand. "This way."

They moved slowly, following the walls with their hands until they came to a turn. "This must be it," Rick said.

He took another step forward, and then turned right. "One...two...three..." At sixty paces he stopped. "This is it."

Caterina stared at the blank wall in puzzlement. "Now what do we do?" she asked.

Rick backtracked and called to her. "This must be the gate here."

"Chevalier R. Cremona," she said. "Chevalier means he's a Knight." With a sigh she pushed the button. Fifteen seconds later she pressed it again.

"*Iva?*" an angry male voice said.

Caterina spoke. The voice remained angry but became less so as she explained why they were there. Finally the man said, "I'll be right down."

A light on the second floor turned on and Chevalier Cremona soon appeared in a robe in slippers. Though older, he still had the lean body of an athlete. "I apologize for the way I talked to you before. My experience with my earlier visitors infuriated me. They claimed to be members of the National Heritage Society and I believed them. They seemed to be colleagues. Especially when the younger man caught the tripod before it landed on the other man. It never occurred to me that they would merely abandon the equipment here."

"You say the younger one caught a tripod?" Rick said.

"Yes. It was part of the block and tackle. The older man slipped and it would have landed on his chest if the younger one hadn't caught it."

Rick spoke excitedly. "The younger one was my brother. The other man kidnapped him. He may have left the equipment because he couldn't carry it by himself."

"Then we had better hurry," Cremona said. "Your brother may still be in the bin."

They removed their shoes and noiselessly sped through the house. A sodium lamp filled the yard with yellow light and they sat on the steps to put their shoes back on. In the garden they found a dun-colored bag sitting next to a heavy metal tripod that stood over a heavy stone.

One look at the stone was all it took for Rick to recognize what it was. "I knew it," he exclaimed," It's a lid for a storage bin! The map was right. This used to be the end of a street." He turned to Cremona. "Do you happen to remember its name?"

"It was called Strada Delfino on the surveyor's maps," Cremona said. "From what I understand the name went all the way back to the days of the Knights."

"Why was it walled off?" Rick asked.

"The street hadn't been used for years and was turning into an eyesore so in 1946 my father got permission to wall it in."

"Did your father ever move the stone?"

"No. It was securely sealed and he didn't have the equipment to move it. Your brother and the other man were the first ones to investigate it. They said it was a grain storage bin and that they wanted to explore inside it because they hoped to be able to reintroduce some older strains of cereal grasses to the island. I have no idea what they really wanted, and I didn't watch them while they were working."

Rick knelt and turned on his flashlight. A heavy chain lay trapped beneath the massive stone. After several turns of the tackle wheel he used the bar to move the stone away completely. As he did, he caught a whiff of fetid air coming from below. It frightened him.

"Do you need my assistance?" Cremona asked.

"I appreciate the offer, but no thanks," Rick replied.

"Then please try to keep the noise to a minimum and let me know when you're done," Cremona said. "If you'll excuse me I'll go back into the house. I must tend to my wife. She isn't well and was very frightened to be awakened in the middle of the night by the bell."

Caterina apologized once more and Cremona returned to the house.

Rick dropped to his knees, then lay on his stomach. Holding the electric lantern in his hand he lowered his head as far down as he could reach. "Stef?" he shouted as he moved the light about, "are you down there?"

He was greeted with silence. After calling again he got to his feet. "I'm going down. We have to hurry."

"Here's some cable," Caterina said, "but it's all tangled up."

Five minutes' work straightened it out. Rick removed the chain from the tripod and secured the end of the cable to the drum. Caterina's hands were covered with grease by the time they were done feeding it back on the winch. "It reminds me of when I'm working on Tarbija," she said with rueful grin.

Rick fashioned a loop in the end of the cable and stepped into it with one foot. "Lower me," he said. With that, he slowly began his descent into utter blackness. At last his leading foot landed on something soft. "Stop!" he shouted. He didn't need light to know what was underneath of him. "Stef! Wake up. It's Rick."

No answer. Rick turned on the light and called out again. Turning it downward he saw his brother's body below. "He's here," Rick shouted.

At last he reached the bottom and straddled the motionless figure. The air at the bottom of the pit was unbreatheable. Panic rising, Rick took Stef by the shoulders and shook. Still no response. Fear and lack of oxygen had Rick gasping for air.

"Stef!" he shouted.

Feeling woozy and certain he would pass out, Rick took one slow, measured breath in the carbon dioxide-laden atmosphere before yanking once on the cable. A foot more of cable dropped on Stef's inert body. Lungs burning for oxygen, Rick held his breath as he slipped the cable over Stef's head and under his arms. When it was secure, he yanked twice.

The cable tightened and Stef's massive body began its slow ascent to the top of the shaft. Rick exhaled loudly and took another breath. He spat it out, retching. The light from the lantern swam in his vision but he refused to exhale. Barely able to stand, he heard a noise, then saw the cable descending. Exhaling explosively, he climbed feet first into the loop and pulled twice. The bottom dropped out from under him making him nauseous. Colored lights danced in front of his eyes. At last he could stand it no longer and he took a breath. Though thin, the air was breathable. When he reached the top he was too weak to climb out and lay with his head resting on his arm for several seconds gasping for breath.

Caterina futilely pulled at him, then cried out. "What can I do?" At last he could breathe normally. "I'm fine. How's Stef?"

"He's still unconscious."

"We have to wake him up," Rick said. Stumbling forward three steps, he fell to his knees beside Stef. "Wake up," he gasped, shaking his brother roughly.

But Stef didn't respond. Without a second thought Rick cradled Stef's head and tilted it back. Then, taking a deep breath, he blew into his brother's mouth. Pressing his cheek against Stef's, he listened for the air to come out. Then he blew again.

Two breaths later, Stef coughed and Rick backed away. Stef opened his eyes. "Where am I?" he asked.

"In Chevalier Cremona's garden," Rick said.

Stef pulled himself up to a sitting position. When he saw Caterina he asked, "Who's she?"

"I'll explain later," Rick said. "Can you stand?"

"Maybe, if you give me a hand."

They each took an arm. When he was on his feet, Caterina surprised them both by throwing her arms around Stef. Bewildered, Stef stood immobilized for several seconds. Then he returned her embrace.

"This is Caterina, Stef," Rick said. "The most wonderful person in the world."

"She certainly is," Stef said in an admiring voice. After they untangled he stepped back to take a closer look at her. He shook his head. "You must have made her out of a kit. Nothing this lovely exists in nature."

Before she could respond, Rick said, "You're right, but we have to get out of here. Let's clean this up."

"We can use Pawlu's rental truck if he didn't take it," Stef said.

"It's still in the parking lot," Rick replied. "Do you have a key?"

Stef took one from his pocket. "I worked it off the key ring when Pawlu wasn't watching."

"Well done," Rick said. "Maybe we can get some use out of it ourselves."

It took the three of them nearly twenty minutes to move the equipment through the house to the street. As they left, Cremona sighed in relief and locked his gate.

"I'll get the truck," Caterina said.

"It's a good thing I showed up," Rick said. "Pawlu must have intended that you have air because he left the lid partially open. I don't think he realized how little air there was at the bottom and how soon the poisonous gases would return. How did you figure out the Duke's Challenge?"

"I just kept at it. When I came up with 'a tee Delfino' I was sure I had the right answer."

Rick told him about the Major. "At some point he must have made the same attempt and concluded that it was an incorrect solution. Even if he knew there was a Dolphin Street in Mdina, the bin wasn't *at* the tee with Mesquita Street; it was at the *base* of the tee. You just made a lucky guess."

"Wrong," Stef said triumphantly. "It didn't mean the basin was at the tee, it meant the *street sign* was. All the street signs are on shields."

"Why didn't I think of that?" Rick asked in a disgusted voice.

Headlights appeared in the distance. For a moment Rick feared it was Cornacchia, but when the truck stopped beside them he saw Caterina behind the wheel.

A short time later the equipment was loaded on the truck. Stef rode inside and Rick stayed in the back clinging to the edge of the bed as it crawled through the streets. When they reached the Mitsubishi, Caterina said, "I'll drive the car. We'll have to drop kitty off with Josefina because animals aren't allowed in the King George. You can follow me."

"Lead the way," Stef said moving into the driver's seat.

Once on the road, Rick said, "Fill me in on what happened to you after you called me back in Minnesota. Were you still in Florence?"

"No. I called you after I arrived here on the hydrofoil from Sicily. I had just rented a car from Mario Agius. He's the one who suggested the San Roque, too."

"Mario Agius is dead. Someone shot him with a shotgun."

Stef shook his head. "Too bad. He was a nice person."

"Do you think this Pawlu did it?"

"No. It must have been one of the people working with him. I don't think Pawlu would do anything that violent."

"Do you have any idea how the kidnappers found out about Agius?"

"His name was on a business card in my pocket when they kidnapped me. What happened to the car?"

"It was towed away," Rick said. "And it's a good thing, too. We found it in an impound lot. Your receipt was in it. That's how I found out you were staying at the San Roque."

"Why did Cornacchia have me kidnapped?"

"I'm not sure. At first I thought he wanted to protect the forgery he's making of the Shield. But he seemed to think there was a second page."

Stef nodded. "He mentioned that to me when he saw the holes at the edge of the drawing."

"Apparently the Cornacchias actually believed the Shield had some sort of supernatural power," Rick said.

"Really. Why is Cornacchia making a forgery?"

"It's a long story," Rick said. "I think he's involved in a plot to take over the government and he got in over his head. Unfortunately for us, he's got the drawing."

Stef cursed. "And he's probably got the real Shield, too. Pawlu said he was selling it to him."

"The Shield and the drawing no longer matter," Rick mused. "What Bin-Said intends to do with the Shield is what's important. Cornacchia is just a parlor revolutionary."

Stef nodded. "You say the Shield is supposed to have supernatural powers? Did you know Cellini was involved in alchemy"

"No, but it wouldn't surprise me. Nearly all the metalsmiths at the time studied it."

"It wasn't just a fad with him. He actually believed in it."

"How do you know that?" Rick asked.

"For one thing, he made a special trip to Germany to meet with an alchemist in hopes of curing his syphilis. Have you ever heard of Brother Konstanz of Sponheim Abbey?"

"No," Rick said. "Who's he?"

"I don't really know but he had the same master as Paracelsus and Cornelius Agrippa. They were all students of Trithemius."

Rick was startled to hear the name.

Trithemius was a prodigy. The head of an abbey at twenty, he was also an important theologian who made magic respectable with the Church. Magic was nothing more than work of the Magi, and hadn't they been present in the manger with Jesus? The Church later changed its mind about his interpretation, but not before he had mentored two of the most important alchemists in the Sixteenth Century. Paracelsus was said to have succeeded in turning base metal into gold and allegedly discovered the secret of eternal life; Agrippa was world-renown and also an important astrologer. Even more important than his alchemical skills, Trithemius was considered to be the father of cryptography and his *Polygraphiae* was one of the foundations of the science.

"Even so, sooner or later he must have realized the good brother Konstanz was a snake-oil salesman."

Stef snorted a reproof. "You know yourself they weren't all charlatans. Alchemy was an honorable profession that went back to the Egyptians. And the good brother must have fooled him for quite a while even if Cellini didn't like him. I found several references to 'that damnable alchemist' living on one of Cellini's farms. Apparently the miscreant stayed there for years without paying a cent. Cellini absolutely despised him."

Rick laughed. "He never liked any of his tenants. He was always complaining that they were trying to cheat him out of rent or steal his crops. It's hard to believe he would let a freeloader take advantage of him, though."

"That's what I thought, too," Stef said.

They continued on to the Bellestrado, where Caterina opened the front door to let the cat go in. The next stop was inside the hotel-parking ramp. When they got to their room, Caterina immediately went to bed leaving them alone to talk.

"You say that Cornacchia thinks the Shield is a message?" Stef asked.

"Apparently so," Rick said. "And it's written in Ethiopian, no less. Father Santorini thinks Bartolomeo had the shield made as window-dressing to impress Suleiman. If so, he was lying to his own family. I already told you they seem to have been convinced it actually contains some sort of mystical power."

"Sorry," Stef said. "But mystical power is out. If this Bin-Said is as interested in the Shield as you say he is, he wouldn't be taken in by some Sixteenth Century hoax Suleiman may have fallen for."

"Maybe it wasn't a hoax. Marija let slip that the gold had a religious significance."

"What do you mean?"

"According to legend, the Shield was supposed to have been made from gold from the Holy Land."

"Then there's your answer," Stef said. "Suleiman and Bin-Said both must have realized the Shield's potential to unite the Arabs against the infidel. The rank and file Muslim in the Sixteenth Century probably didn't like their Islamic brothers being expelled from Spain, but it wasn't a hot issue that would put them on the warpath. But gold stolen from one of Islam's holiest shrines and made into a symbol to mock their religion would have been an affront that every Muslim would react to."

"The proverbial bloody shirt," Rick said."

"Absolutely! Every Muslim knew about the atrocities that the Crusaders committed against Islam when they invaded the Holy Land. And I bet Bartolomeo knew exactly how to bait Suleiman. He knew Suleiman was desperate to win at Vienna and that he was also champing at the bit to return to Spain. Moreover, Bartolomeo also knew that the Turks alone couldn't supply the manpower to wage all the battles that were necessary for Suleiman's plan to be successful. The Pasha needed the help of the entire Islamic population and the best way to get it was to provide a common enemy. The Shield must have been exactly what Suleiman was looking for. No matter what it cost Bartolomeo, exchanging it for Malta had to be one of the biggest bargains ever."

"I see what you mean," Rick said. "How did Bartolomeo convince Suleiman he had the bloody shirt?"

"The gold came from the Knights. The Knights of St. John Hospitalers and their brothers the Knights Templars were among the first Crusaders to enter Jerusalem. They helped sack Al Aksa Mosque and slaughtered hundreds of Arabs who had taken refuge there."

Smiling, Rick nodded. It was always fun to listen to Stef when he was on a roll.

"Al Aksa Mosque is one of the three most holy sites in Islam," Stef continued "The Mosque was the location where Muhammed did his Night Journey and his ascent into heaven. Anything associated with the sack of the Mosque would have great meaning to a Muslim of any time. Anyone as clever as Bartolomeo could have come up with the provenance he needed that the gold came from Al-Aksa. His biography says he traveled in Palestine."

"Yes. And if Bin-Said had run across a reference to it, he would want it for the same reason," Rick said. After a moment's reflection he shook his head. "This doesn't make sense. Bartolomeo never would have spent the money to have Cellini make such an elaborate piece of art if all he intended to do was to sell it to Suleiman as gold stolen from a mosque. And why the codes and references to Prester John?"

Stef shrugged. "You got me. At least my theory would provide an explanation of why both Suleiman and this Bin-Said would be interested in it."

"You're right," Rick said. He closed his eyes and massaged his forehead with his fingertips. "Is it possible the basin was originally made for someone other than Suleiman?"

"I don't see why not. Who are you thinking of?"

"Charles the Fifth, maybe. The drawing isn't dated. What year did Charles give Malta to the Knights?"

"1530," Rick said.

"Cellini would have only been thirty years old then. I suppose it's possible Cornacchia could have contacted him even then."

"But why would he have done it?" Rick asked.

"We both know that Bartolomeo was a master con artist. He might have thought that Charles would have considered Prester John's secrets in exchange for Malta to be a good trade."

"But Charles was worried about the Turks. Francis the First of France had given Suleiman access to his ports. That's why Charles gave Malta to the Knights."

"Right," Rick said in reflective voice. "It wouldn't surprise me if you were right, but I don't see how we can prove it one way or the other. Maybe Father Santorini found out something useful. Wash up and take the other bed. I'll stretch out on the couch."

CHAPTER 33

▼

Saturday, 5:00 AM
St Julians

Rick awoke before the sun came up. After tossing fitfully for an hour, he finally got up from the couch where he spent the night and quietly crawled in with Caterina. When he kissed her on the cheek, she muttered something that sounded like 'go away' and turned on her stomach.

With a sigh he got up and took a shower. After he finished he called Father Santorini.

The priest answered immediately. "I'm glad you remembered I was an early riser," he said. "You were correct about the price list for pepper. There was nothing greater than ten for quantity or price. And the list is more than ten pages long. I'm sure there must be at least twenty-five thousand entries."

"That would be more than enough to cover the recipes for a spell or two," Rick mused. "Did you try transferring the letters from the banner and translate them?"

"Yes, but my Ethiopian friend says it's gibberish."

"Then I suspect I was right and the right characters are carved inside of the basin. Do you have any way to date the price list?"

"From the entries before and after, it would have been late August of 1565."

"Just before the Siege," Rick said. "Thanks for your help. I'll talk to you later."

Five minutes later his phone rang and he was greeted by Kevin's excited yell. "I've got great news. I've broken into Cornacchia's files! You've got a year's worth of reading to do, but he doesn't have any secrets anymore."

"Fantastic!" Rick said. "Are you sure you weren't detected?"

"Absolutely. Their operating system has its own file transfer protocol. I found out a way to use it and no one will ever know I was there."

"How many disks are we talking about?"

"Probably at least a dozen," Kevin said.

"Marija Cornacchia isn't as invincible as she thinks," Rick said, remembering what Inspector Micallef had said about her liking computers. "Hold on." He returned to the bed and gently nudged Caterina awake. She moaned softly and finally turned over to open her eyes. "What?"

"Sorry to have to wake you, kitten," he said. "Do you know if this hotel has Internet access?"

She sat up. "I think so. What's going on?"

Rick passed on what Kevin had said and she shrugged. "I'll have to get back to you," Rick said into the phone.

"Do that," Kevin said. "Better still, see if you can find somewhere that has a static IP address. I can send Cornacchia's whole library using my file transfer protocol."

"Say that again. In English," Rick said.

"You've sent scans so you know how to send them as an attachment to an E-mail. It's like sending a letter and putting a picture inside. If we use a file transfer protocol, it would be like sending a whole album. It takes a lot less time."

"How do I find someone with a static IP address?"

"Easy. Any Internet provider would have one. By the way, I found out the password that unlocks Cornacchia's files. Four-four-six-eight. The username is Duchess. If you have to, you can get into the company files through the Web-site."

"Just for that I'll send you an extra case of Bush." When Kevin groaned, Rick said, "Cheer up. I'll talk to you later."

Caterina lay back on the pillow. "Come over here," she whispered. When he did she pulled him down on top of her. "Kiss me."

For a moment, Rick thought he was with Marija. "Are you crazy? What if Stef wakes up?" he asked.

"That's what makes it exciting. Get out of those clothes."

"The way you like to throw orders around you should be wearing black leather and carrying a whip," Rick said.

"Take a look in the middle drawer," she whispered.

"You're kidding aren't you? Ow."

Miraculously, Stef was still asleep when they were done. "Now what were you trying to tell me?" Caterina asked, stroking Rick's head.

"Kevin said we need to find an Internet provider. Do you know where we can find one at this time of day?"

"Zija uses Alex Mizzi," she said. "I can call her and get his number. Is it all right if I take a shower first?"

Half an hour later they left Stef asleep and drove the 2 miles to Alex Mizzi's apartment. Mizzi was a bristly-faced Gen-Y and Rick didn't like the smiles Caterina traded with the man. A brace of computer screens that looked like oscilloscopes with lines down the middle sat on an assortment of tables. Rick told him what he wanted done and Mizzi took the laptop from him. After a quick call to Kevin, the files were loading directly into Caterina's computer.

"Would it be possible to put them on CD, too?" Rick asked.

"No problem," Mizzi said. "I'll make the copies as soon as the files finish loading."

Everything was done in less than fifteen minutes. Instead of a dozen disks, Rick had all the information on three bronze-colored CDs. "Let's get something to eat," he said.

The restaurant in the hotel was open and while they breakfasted on sausage and eggs, he pondered how to get the CDs to the embassy. "I sure don't want to deliver them myself," Rick said. "Carpenter would have my hide if he thought I was interfering."

"We can send them by cab," Caterina said. "I know all the drivers."

"I don't want to get anyone into trouble," he replied.

"Don't worry. We make deliveries all the time."

They found a cab sitting outside the hotel with driver asleep behind the wheel. Caterina tapped on the window to wake him up. "Hello, Dom," she said.

He answered with a snaggle-toothed grin. "Hi, Cat. Where have you been? I haven't seen you for days."

"I've been working as a private chauffeur," she said. "I need you to make a delivery." She handed him a package wrapped in brown paper. "Take this to the American Embassy and give it to the guard. The name is written on the parcel." As he took it from her hand, she gave him a ten-lira note. "And take Giulia out to dinner."

8:34 AM

Even though it was early morning, large numbers of people had already gathered on the street when they returned to the hotel. The air show was still several hours away, but natives and tourists alike had greedily preempted all the vantagepoints overlooking the sea. A continuous line of beach chairs stretched in front of the hotel. Across the street, every table was occupied. As they stepped inside the hotel, Rick got his first real look at the lobby and its genuine French Provincial furniture. That, with the marble floor and the expensive-looking oil paintings on the walls suggested they weren't staying in a Motel 6. If Caterina had any faults, extravagance could be counted among them. And yet he knew he could never deny her anything she asked for and he was already desperately trying to think of a way to replace Andrew's ring. Joining the Josefina and Caterina matriarchy would suit him just fine.

Stef was still asleep and the couple took off their shoes before stepping into the room. Rick turned on the computer. When he clicked on an icon called 'Rick's Files' the computer screen lit up in a shower of yellow folders. "Good heavens," she whispered. "There must be a million of them."

"Let's open one and see what's inside."

She did and an Excel spreadsheet for the cargo ship *Eleganza* appeared. "What should we be looking for?"

"Start with the ones for Dukessa Construction," Rick said. "I have a hunch that's where we'll find the most interesting material."

She scrolled through the file folders. "There are a lot of them."

"I know," he said.

Ten minutes later she threw up her hands in frustration. "I give up."

"Easy, love," he said in a gentle voice. "Let's see if we can find the profit and loss statement for the whole corporation. That should give us an idea where the money is coming from and what they're spending their funds on."

Using the find function he came up with twelve files named Proffit u Telf. The second one was what he was looking for. "Here's the companies Black Dolphin owns," he said. "London BDS, Ltd.; BDS Inc; BDS Pty Ltd, Australia; BDS et Cie, Paris; BD Gloucester & Liverpool Overland Carriage…" his voice trailed off as he read. "Here's *Dukessa Construzzjone*. Look at this. Melita International. Sounds like Marija is spreading herself all over the world."

Once again the find function produced results. Under the rubric of Black Diamond Honey Products Cornacchia had spent two million Maltese lira on barrels, hives, and apiary equipment to produce gross sales of less than 350 thousand lire in transactions that went back two years. "Cornacchia is selling honey and losing his shirt," Rick said. He stopped and his eyes widened. "My God," he said.

"What's the matter?" asked Caterina.

"Almost a month to a day after September 11th President Bush uncovered one of Bin-Laden's networks that dealt in honey. Some businessman in Yemen was involved."

"Now that you mention it, I guess I do remember. It was on CNN. Honey is a big product in the Middle East. It was a good way to launder money, too, because almost all the transactions were in cash."

"Some of the news analysts said the terrorists even shipped their people around the world in the barrels." His eyes grew big. "My God, why didn't I think of this before." He took out his wallet and removed the printout on Bin-Said. His eyes quickly scanned it. "There it is," he said, gesturing at the paper. "One of Bin-Said's covers was selling honey."

They worked on for another hour and a half. Rick occasionally wrote down some figures, but Caterina was clearly overwhelmed by the mass of files. "I hate to have to say this," she said, scratching Rick's ankle with her toenails, "but I don't see how I can be of much use to you. You've been running a business so this must be familiar to you. All I see is words and numbers."

"So do I," he said.

"We need an accountant."

"True, but not a good idea. Even a beginner would know in a minute that we shouldn't have this information."

Her voice became cajoling. "Not if it was someone we could trust."

Rick began to see the light. "You don't mean Andrew, do you? We can't get him involved in this. Even if he wanted to help us, he could lose his license or go to jail."

"It wouldn't matter to him. He'd do it for me because he'd know I wouldn't ask him to do something unless it was important," Caterina said quietly.

"Yeah?" said Rick in a suspicious voice. "And why is that?"

"Because he's helped me before. Some of the things he did were technically against the law."

"Does this have anything to do with your rescue operation?"

"Yes. But I can't tell you any more."

"I'll admit I haven't been one of his biggest fans, but he doesn't deserve to be taken advantage of." He stopped and continued in a slow voice. "Unless you're not really taking advantage of him because you still have feelings for him."

"Of course I still have feelings for him," Caterina said, averting her eyes. "They just aren't the same ones as before. I see now we were more like friends."

"Maybe that's how you feel about him, but are you sure that's the way he feels about you? I don't think I would feel we were just friends if anything ever ended our relationship."

"Of course not. But things have always been different with Andrew. If you can imagine what it would be like having a sister you slept with, you might get an idea of what I'm trying to say."

Rick shrugged. "Love is love. All I know is that he's going to be mighty pissed when he sees me."

"He's not going to see you," Caterina said decisively. "That will have to wait until another time."

"What are Stef and I supposed to do while you're here with Andrew?"

"Why don't you go to the Esplanade and have a cappuccino? There are plenty of seaside snack bars."

"The tables are already taken up. Besides, what if Andrew wants you to do your sister act again while I'm gone?"

"You'll just have to trust me, won't you?" she said archly. "Just like I had to trust you when you said that you didn't do anything with Marija."

"Right," he grumbled. Somehow he didn't find the words very reassuring.

Even though Rick understood little Maltese, he knew enough that he couldn't stand to listen to Caterina's end of the conversation, and he retreated to the bathroom. Shortly, she knocked on the door. "He says he'll do it."

"When will he be here?"

"He said twenty minutes. He's at home in Paceville and he's taking a cab because there isn't anywhere to park. You're not really jealous, are you?"

"If I were, I wouldn't admit it. As much as I hate to say it, having him help may be a good idea. If you're sure we can trust him, that is."

"We can."

Rick opened the door. After giving Caterina a goodbye peck, he walked to the bed to wake up Stef. It took some heavy shakes to do it but Stef finally opened his eyes. "What's the matter?"

"Get dressed. We're being evicted."

Across the street from the hotel Rick found a vacant table behind a kiosk and ordered a cappuccino. The table didn't have a view to the sea, but he didn't mind. The only view he cared about was the one to the hotel.

"Is it okay if I take a walk?" Stef asked. "The sun never looked so good to me."

"Have a ball," Rick said. "Just don't go too far away. I don't want Pawlu grabbing you again."

"Next time I'll be the one doing the grabbing," Stef growled.

Rick went back to his watch and he didn't have long to wait. Even though he had only seen Andrew's picture once, he easily recognized the balding man wearing a baseball visor who was quickly climbing the stairs to enter the hotel.

Was he in a hurry to meet Caterina? Of all the strange twists of fate, Andrew's arrival was the most bizarre by far. Rick's musings ended as a gust of wind nearly tipped his table over. Then he heard an explosion over his head and dived for cover under the roof of the kiosk.

The frightful din continued as a Harrier jet with British bullseye insignia slowly flew out over the bay, dropped straight down and hovered bare inches above the water. Spectators, lined up on the waterfront, broke into applause and far out in the harbor a freighter tooted in approval. The Harrier was always the big attraction at air shows. Today it kicked off the event.

The young man attending the refreshment kiosk cranked his arms over his head in approval. "What do you think of that?" he yelled at Rick.

"Exciting, isn't it?" Rick said. "I've seen them perform quite a few times."

"That guy came from *Hal Far*," the teenager said.

"What's a *Hal Far*?"

"It's an airfield. It's been closed for years until Dukessa got a permit to use it six months ago. There's going to be more than fifty aircraft today, so the Minister of Tourism talked the company into allowing them to use the airfield for the show."

Rick froze as his intelligence analyst alarm bell rang out sharply in his head. "Where is *Hal Far*, anyway?"

"Near Luqa on the southeast coast and not far from Kalafrana. Do you know where Marsaxlokk Bay is?"

"I sure do," Rick said, remembering Mario Agius. "Why does Dukessa have its own airfield?"

"They didn't want to interfere with normal operations at the airport with their construction. I read an article about it about a month ago in the *Malta Times*. Have you been by the construction site yet?"

"A couple of times. The Trade Building will be quite a structure."

"I drive by it every day. I can hardly wait until they cut some holes in the fence so we can watch."

Rick laid a pound coin on top of the ice cream cooler. "Have a Kinnie on me," he said. Quickly crossing the street, he rushed up the steps into the hotel. The house phones were located at the left. He dialed the number on his room key.

Caterina answered.

"How much longer do you have to stay with Andrew?" Rick asked.

"He knows what to do so I can leave anytime. Why?"

"I don't want to spoil your family reunion but I need a lift to *Hal Far* Airfield. Meet me in the lobby when you can break away. And bring the Black Dolphin identification badge with you when you come."

Minutes later, Caterina arrived in the lobby wearing a freshly pressed dress and a dubious look. "Now what's so important about Hal Far that couldn't wait? Or are you so worried about Andrew and me that you don't dare let me out of your sight for ten minutes?"

"Jealousy doesn't enter into it. I just found out that Dukessa Construction has been using Hal Far Airfield to fly in construction materials."

"So what's so earth-shattering about that, if I may ask?"

"Maybe nothing. I just know I want to take a look."

"I don't care what you say," she said in a feline tone. "I still think you don't trust me with Andrew."

"Would it make you happier if I said I didn't?"

"Yes."

"Then I admit it. I've been sick with worry ever since I saw his stubby little legs take him into the hotel."

"You were watching?" she asked with a giggle.

"How else would I know he that he's got knobby knees and was wearing one of those silly baseball caps that doesn't have anything but the visor to it? Of course I was watching. Wouldn't you under the same circumstances?"

"No, and shame on you," she said with a big smile. "Where's Stef?"

"He went for a walk."

After a ten-minute search they found him on a dock wandering among a line of fishing boats. Without sunscreen, his light skin was already turning pink. Rick could tell he was reveling in the sun.

"We're going to take a drive. Do you want to come with us?" Caterina asked.

"Would you mind if I stay here? I've been in the dark for so long, I hate to be away from the sun for a minute."

"Suit yourself," Rick said. "Just don't get burned. Go back to the hotel when you're done and wait in the lobby."

Stef nodded in agreement. "What does 'Nerf' mean?" he asked.

Caterina frowned. "It's like a whip, only it's a solid piece of leather with a ball on the end of it."

"The Russians call it a gnout," Rick said. "Where did you hear the word?"

"One of Pawlu's friends called him that. Pawlu called him *sequ*. What does that mean?"

"Eagle," Caterina said, looking at Rick. "That's George Bezzina. On Malta, men in the towns actually inherit their nicknames."

"Keep out of trouble," Rick said. "I don't want to have to look for you again."

"Count on it," Stef said. "See you later."

"And get some sunblock," Caterina said. "You're starting to look like an *awwista* already."

"I assume that means a lobster?" Stef said. "I'll do that."

The route to Hal Far took them past Malta International Airport. As they passed, Rick watched an F-16 Fighting Falcon fly over them. Earlier a B1 bomber had circled high in the sky over the sea. Uncle Sam was taking an opportunity to display his fighting muscle.

"Didn't Andrew say anything when he realized we had Black Dolphin's files?" asked Rick.

"No. He didn't react at all. I told him we suspected some misdealings in the company but he has no idea where the files came from. I didn't explain who the 'we' were, either. I think he may have the idea that Father Modiglio is involved."

"And he didn't act hurt or angry that you had dumped him?"

"No. He just seemed like the same old Andrew to me."

Rick shook his head. "The man must be made out of granite. Did you kiss?"

"Yes," she said testily. "Not that it's any of your business. And I told him I wanted the three of us to get together for dinner some time. He said he'd like that. So would I."

"I always knew accountants were androids," Rick said. "But I'm still worried he's going to be suspicious about how we got the files."

"I told him that an employee in the company gave them to us. I'm sure he believed me."

"I suppose I shouldn't generalize too much, but it appears to me that you Maltese seem to have loose boundaries on what's right or wrong, or at least what's legal and what's illegal."

"You're right. It's part of our national heritage. How do you think we survived all the years of foreign domination? Except for the French we never fought anyone. And we never joined anyone, either. Someone once said that when we learn that someone got cheated we shake our heads. Everyone thinks we're sympathizing but in reality we're cursing ourselves for not having thought of it first."

Rick broke out laughing. "Is that the way the police operate, too?"

"I don't think so," Caterina said. "Why do you ask?"

"I'm still trying to figure out how Inspector Micallef could have got himself into Cornacchia's cabal."

Caterina looked puzzled. "It's really hard for me to believe, too. Looking the other way is one thing. Aiding and abetting is a different matter entirely. Especially if Cornacchia is involved in treason. To tell you the truth, I really am amazed. From all the flags he has around his office I would say the Inspector was unusually patriotic."

"Looks can be deceiving," Rick said with a shrug.

The brilliant sunlight made their southeasterly drive painful. Caterina wore sunglasses but he had to hold his hands in front of his eyes to cut out the glare. A jet with French insignia passed over them, but Rick couldn't identify it. Five minutes later they arrived at the entrance to the Hal Far airfield. A guard stepped out and held up his hand. Caterina stopped.

"Good afternoon," the guard said. "What can I do for you?"

Rick held up his Black Dolphin identification card. "I need to get into the hangar."

The guard glanced at the badge. "You're way too early. The shipment doesn't get here until ten tonight. And the air show won't even be over for another hour."

Shipment? Rick shivered in excitement. "I just wanted to make sure we have enough space to handle all the cargo. Can't I come in and look?"

"Not until the air show is over. The government put the airfield off-limits to everyone except the air-traffic controllers and we still have six flights left to take off from here."

"How much longer will it be?"

The guard looked at his watch. "Maybe an hour. If you're looking for somewhere to pass the time, there's a restaurant in Birzebbugia where you can get something to eat."

"Good idea," Rick said. "Thanks."

Before he turned to leave he looked through the fence and saw an enormous vehicle standing outside the hangar. Even from a distance it appeared gargantuan, with its four tall wheels and chassis resting on what appeared to be a hydraulic lifting system. It looked like a machine called a Lull that was used to move construction materials.

The guard waved as Caterina backed up to turn around. "What do you want to do now?" she asked.

"I'll buy you a pea cake for lunch. I still have twenty cents. That should be just enough to pay for one."

The Cachia Pub was open, but Rick and Caterina were the only customers. Did the Hal Far Hunters Club meet there? Cachia was the Maltese word for hunter. The bartender seemed grateful for the company, and sat down with them as he waited for their food to heat. He was in his forties and very stocky with curly hair. He was also wearing a purple and gold Minnesota Viking tee shirt, which immediately endeared him to Rick.

"Why aren't you people at the air show?" the man asked.

Rick flashed his badge at him.

"Oh, you're with the construction company." He took a closer look at Rick. "I don't think I've ever seen you before."

"I just got in from Canada," Rick said. "This is my wife, Catherine. Her parents came from Qormi."

The man nodded at her before turning back to Rick. "You must be an engineer."

"You're right, I are one." As Rick said it he wondered if the man had heard the old joke.

The bartender didn't react. "I didn't realize Dukessa had any Canadians working for them. Most of the ones I see are Arabs. Are you replacing one of the Libyans who left?"

Rick's ears pricked. "Yes. I didn't hear what happened to them. Do you know?"

"No. All I know is that there were two of them. They were around for maybe two months. The first month they were smiling and happy all the time and had tans like your wife. They didn't drink any alcohol but they were good-natured and laughed a lot. And they came in every day for lunch so I started to make dishes especially for them like lamb kebab and couscous and they really seemed to appreciate it."

"I imagine they did," Rick said. "That was generous of you."

"Thanks. That was the first few weeks. Then things started to change. The second month they didn't laugh much and then they commenced to look pale. Then they stopped coming in every day. When they did come in one of them looked like he lost quite a bit of hair. One of their friends told me that he had alopecia. That's some kind of problem that makes your hair fall out. About a week ago they stopped coming in entirely. One of their friends told me they went back to Tripoli."

"I never heard anything about that," Rick said, feeling wheels turn in his mind. He didn't dare to think too hard about it because a terrifying specter was turning the crank.

"Did you forget your hardhat?" the bartender asked.

Rick looked surprised, then touched his head. "Oh, no. I didn't forget it. It gives me a headache. Must be from too much noise." As he said it, the building began to shake. Somewhere a very noisy aircraft was taking off. When the rattling stopped they heard the microwave oven buzzer. "I'll get you your food," the bartender said.

He returned with two plates of shepherd's pie and set them down. "You'll like it. I just made it last night," the man said.

"Any bread?" Rick asked.

"That's yesterday's, too. But I have almost a whole loaf. I might as well give it to you. It'll just get stale otherwise. Does the lady want another Kinnie?"

"Sure. Bring another one for her," Rick said. "And bring me another Cisk." Once again the bartender took off toward the bar.

"You're being awfully free with my money, aren't you?" Caterina asked.

He tried to smile but couldn't. All he could manage was an embarrassed "Henh."

"Sorry. I hope I didn't hurt your feelings."

"I'm getting used to it. Being broke, I mean."

The bartender returned with a breadbasket tucked under his right arm and the drinks in his hands. Rick took the basket from him with a scowl. The bread didn't need any moistening. Didn't the guy know about trays?

Setting the drinks on the table, the bartender sat down with them again. "Will you be working tonight?"

Rick stared at him. "Yes. How did you know that?"

"I overheard the Arabs talking. They didn't know I understand the language. I hear you'll be using a special crane."

"Have you ever seen it?"

"No. What do they use it for?"

"Sorry. I'm not supposed to talk about it."

The bartender looked disappointed. "Oh. Sure. I understand."

Once again the building shook as another aircraft took off. "When did the government close the airfield here?" Rick asked.

"It must have been the 'fifties, some ten years before I was born. I know the Brits used it during World War II and they used to hang out here in the pub until the government shut the field down. They made Luqa the airport because the runways were longer. What kind of engineer are you, anyway?"

"Mechanical. I keep the machinery working."

"Tell me, why do they need so much concrete to build the Trade Building? The whole island is rock."

"Even so, you have to anchor a structure that size. That gives the building something to stand on. After you've done that you can use its own weight to keep it from falling over or collapsing."

"Why are they building it so tall?"

"It's supposed to be a trade and communications center for the entire Mediterranean."

"I heard that when the building is done, they'll be able to see it on Gozo and Sicily."

"That is pretty exciting, isn't it? Have you ever been to New York?"

"No. Why?"

"I was just wondering if you ever saw the World Trade Center towers. They were twice as tall as the building we're constructing. They had to build the towers like a teeter-totter so they could balance each others' weight."

"That was terrible what happened to the World Trade Center. At least we don't have to worry about anything like that happening to our building."

"Why do you say that?"

"The Arabs are our friends."

Rick and Caterina were back at Hal Far Airfield as the last aircraft took off. When it was airborne, the guard motioned for them to come over. "Does the lady have a badge?"

"No," Rick said. "She doesn't work for the company."

"Then she'll have to wait here. How long do you think you'll be?"

"Just a few minutes. I just want to make sure everything is ready for the shipment."

The guard tapped himself on his head.

"Oh. My helmet. I left it in the hotel room. All the noise was giving me a splitting headache and I forgot it."

The guard handed Rick a red hardhat. "Put this on. I can't let you in without it."

Rick mumbled thanks. It didn't fit. Even after adjusting the band it still rattled. "Thanks."

Heat rose in shimmering waves off the faded tarmac. It had a gritty smell and the whole area was covered with a layer of dust. The hangar building was nearly a quarter of a mile away. It and the control tower were the only two buildings at the field. Over the years, grass had sprouted through the surface and now the once black surface was a motley gray riddled with brown tufts of dead vegetation. He also could see tiny shards of broken glass twinkling in the sun. If this part of the airfield were ever to be used again, it would have to be gone over carefully. Any debris lying on the ground could be sucked up by the intake of jet engines with potentially disastrous results.

His first destination was the over-sized vehicle he had seen. The closer he got to it, the more overwhelming it became. The wheels dwarfed him, standing at least ten feet tall, and the chassis twice that. Even at rest it was a display of testosterone run amok. Hydraulic lifters showed off their stainless steel sinews. Powerful mechanical arms on the side of the machine poised waiting for a command. The sight of the behemoth gave Rick a cold feeling in the pit of his stomach. What would it be used for?

His feeling of dread grew as he approached the hangar.

A heavy padlock guarded the hangar doors. The main entrance, next to them, was locked, too, but it took longer for his eyes to get used to the darkness inside the building than it did to get the door open. He found the light switch by touch, and the hangar leaped to life.

He breathed a sigh of relief at the sight of the forklifts and pallets of construction materials. The hangar was a storage area for the building site. Having spent two summers as a hod carrier in college made him feel right at home. It was a makeshift warehouse with aisles and piles, sacks and stacks. Nearly every hardhat knew the rhymes. Ten-foot high mountain ranges of pallets lay beside wide lanes. On the pallets lay bags of concrete and an assortment of huge bolts and nuts inside plastic-sealed containers.

And everything covered with dust. With his first step, he covered his nose with his right arm to keep from breathing the gray powder that puffed off the floor.

Feeling like a stock villain from an operetta he kept his arm in place as he moved along the aisle inspecting the pallets. His skin again began to crawl when he came to a special room made out of what appeared to be stainless steel. Giving one of the walls a thump, he was answered with an echo indicating that it was heavily lined. The roof was, too. Yellow stickers on the door warned of chemical, biological, and radiation hazards. A storage cabinet for hydrochloric or sulfuric acid, he wondered? Or maybe a few containers of anthrax spores? Or worse? The whole area reminded him of the secure space at the embassy, including the touch pad lock.

Curious about what else he would find, he decided to follow the wall back to the door rather than take the route through the center of the hangar. As he went he discovered three gas driven generators and several more stacks of pallets. He also passed another locked door that he couldn't open.

His feeling of dread refused to go away. But now he was puzzled, too. All the bits of information pointed in one direction, but the location of the room pointed in another.

Whatever was coming in that night would have to be handled outside. There was little room to maneuver inside the hangar unless they moved several tons of material out of the way.

It all made sense: The Zone of Death, the Trade building with its massive footings to support a building and tower, the mammoth transporter with the over-sized wheels. Each discrete piece fit together into a whole; a whole that terrified him.

One thing was certain. He had to get out of there as fast as he could. Once again throwing his arm in front of his face, he ran back to the hangar entrance.

He stood panting, wondering if he already had been in the building too long. Was there a way to seal off the building to keep others safe from the hazards that lay inside? The desolation of the gray tarmac matched his own. When he reached the car, he was greeted with Caterina's voice. "I just heard from Andrew," she said brightly. "He wants to talk to you."

On the drive back to the hotel, his cell phone rang. "This is Bob Carpenter. I understand you've tried to contact me."

"Yes. Did you get the CDs I sent you?"

"I did. Where did you get them?"

"A lucky guess at the Black Dolphin Website," Rick said. "I also wanted to tell you that Cornacchia has a big shipment coming into Hal Far airfield tonight. I broke into the hangar. I'm sure they've stored radioactive material there."

"Really. What time is the shipment coming in?"

"It's scheduled at 10 PM."

"We'll have someone there to meet it."

"So will the Maltese Government. We're contacting them."

"There's no need," Carpenter said, quickly. "The Ambassador will do it. Thanks for the information."

After Rick hung up, Caterina lit into him. "Radioactive material?"

"It would explain why the Libyan engineers got sick. They may already have brought some on the island and the concrete is shielding the radiation."

"So what's supposed to happen tonight?"

"I think Bin-Said intends to bring a nuclear weapon onto the island."

"Oh my god," said Caterina.

"I also am sure Bob Carpenter already figured it out before I talked to him. If so the US military and the CIA will be swarming over the island with everything they've got. And believe me, they're not going to worry that your government is playing second or third fiddle or even if you're in the same orchestra for that matter."

"Sounds like old times, doesn't it?" Caterina said with undisguised sarcasm. "We've always been at the mercy of whoever is running the world at any particular moment. Greeks, Romans, Brits, or the good old US of A. The Arabs treated us pretty well compared to most. Well, screw your friend Bob Carpenter. And you, too. I'll contact the government myself. They have to know. We're the one who will have to live with the consequences."

"You're absolutely right but there's a hell of a lot more involved in this than you realize. If I'm right, this scenario is every bit as brilliant and devious as nine-eleven, and much more scary."

"What do you mean?" she asked.

"Everyone's been worried about nuclear weapons getting into the wrong hands since Hiroshima. Building the bomb is easy. You can get a plan for it off the Internet. Getting the nuclear material and controlling the radiation is the hard part. And even if you have the knowledge and technology and materials to make one, you can't hide it. The radiation will give you away every time."

"But if you're as rich as Cornacchia, you wouldn't need to try to make one," Caterina said. "Why wouldn't he just buy one from the Russians?"

"That's another scenario. And we know there's a number of nuclear weapons unaccounted for from the former Soviet Union's nuclear arsenal. But moving money around to pay for them is an enormous problem in itself. And even assuming they can get the money into the right hands, there's always the difficulty of moving the weapons without being detected. Besides that, once you have it, where do you keep it? You can't hide all the emissions."

Still holding his face in her hands, she kissed him on his lips. "It sounds like you're telling me that we have nothing to worry about because it can't be done."

He gently covered her hands and moved them away from his face. With an anguished look he said, "That's the whole problem, love. It *can* be done, given enough money and ingenuity. The world is too big and no matter how careful we are, we can't be everywhere all the time. It's like the drug trade. Stuff always slips in between the cracks. Only this shit will give the whole world a hangover."

Caterina buried her head into his chest. "And you think Cornacchia is behind this?"

"I'm sure of it."

"But why?" she asked. "What can he do with a nuclear weapon?"

"Did you ever hear the one about the Slobbovian who walks into a bank pointing a gun at his head? 'If anyone makes a false move the poor dumb Slobbovian gets it in the head.'"

"You mean he would use it on us?"

"That's part of the beauty of the plan. It's a one-sided use of Mutually-Assured-Destruction. Once Cornacchia takes over, no one will dare to try to oust him."

"Doesn't he realize everyone will leave?"

"Not if he does things correctly," said Rick. "He'll spread the information to the right people in the foreign governments. That way if word ever did get out, he would only have to deny it and call it propaganda."

"What…what would happen if he ever set the bomb off?"

"A nuclear blast would wipe out most of the population and radiation would take care of the rest. But Malta is just a small part of the scenario. It would immediately contaminate parts of Sicily and North Africa. It would kill hundreds of thousands of people, but that's nothing compared to what would happen in Greece and Turkey. Water currents and the winds would make them dead zones, just like Malta."

Caterina stared him in the eye. "Dead zones. What are you talking about?"

"Just that. No life of any kind. Nearly all the land animals will die immediately, others in a few months. And most of the sea creatures that ingest the contaminants will, too. The ones that don't will suffer genetic mutation. Imagine a fifty-foot octopus."

"How long would the contamination last?" Caterina asked in a small voice.

"If the nuclear material is Tritium, thirty or forty years at least. That's based on a half-life of twenty-years. If it's Plutonium…" He stopped, unable to go on.

"And if it's Plutonium?" she said in a firm voice.

"We're talking a half-life of five hundred years. It could be a whole millennium before this place will be habitable again if anyone ever wanted to come back."

Caterina shuddered. "Even Cornacchia can't be that ruthless."

"He may not have much say in the matter. Once the bomb is in place, it may be entirely out of his hands."

"That Arab is behind it, isn't he?" she said. "Doesn't he realize all of North Africa will be affected by the radiation, too?"

"Yes, but he also knows that the threat is much more effective than the actual act. It will be an enormous feather in their cap if the radical Muslims can say they took back the Mediterranean right under the infidel's nose. Even better, it will make the US look like cowards for not trying to do something about it."

"I've heard enough," Caterina said, sobbing. "We have to tell the government."

"You're right, but remember Bob Carpenter will have the full resources of the US military behind him. The government may not be able to do very much."

"Where would this Bin-Said put the bomb?"

"The easiest place would be somewhere off the north coast of the island," Rick said. "He could case it in concrete and sink it to the bottom of the sea. What's so scary is that they may already have done it while they've been laying cable. If so…"

"Don't even think of it," Caterina said with a sniff. "We have to assume he hasn't."

"You're right and I have reason to hope that they're bringing the weapon into Hal Far tonight. There's a huge machine they can use to move it. Let's just pray I'm right. Otherwise we're toast."

"Where do you think they'll take it?"

"If they're not going to sink it offshore, they'll put it somewhere that offers the most shielding. Lead and concrete are great shields. Can you think of any place that would fit?"

After a moment's reflection Caterina's eyes grew wide. "The Trade Building?"

"You've got it. They've already got the concrete footings. They can put in lead shields when they erect the superstructure."

She didn't say anything, but he could feel her heart beat faster. Without warning she kissed him again. It was passionate but not sensual. How he wished she were on a jet to Hawaii putting as much distance between her and ground zero as possible. But he needed her. More than ever they were a team. Their fates were bound up inextricably together like the bars of metal in a Damascus blade. And now Stef had joined them.

Unaccountably his mind turned to alchemy. A nuke was the ultimate example of the alchemist's art, transforming matter into pure energy. How ironic it would be if a Cornacchia finally succeeded in bringing it about.

CHAPTER 34

▼

Saturday
3:04 PM
St. Julians

Rick shivered as they approached the door to the hotel room. Having to meet Andrew was bad enough. But if what he suspected about Cornacchia were true, the accountant would soon provide proof of the expenditure of the vast sums of money necessary to buy Bin-Said's bomb. Caterina squeezed his hand to reassure him before she knocked on the door. He fidgeted when he heard sounds inside the room. Then the door opened.

"Come in," Andrew said. The Bantam Rooster stood aside to let Caterina in. Rick hesitated, then stepped in, too. Did accountants pack guns?

"So you're Rick Olsen," Andrew said glowering. If the man wanted to throw a punch, he would have to jump to connect with Rick's chin.

"You are correct," Rick said. "I am Rick Olsen. You must be Andrew Xuereb. I've heard a lot about you."

"Unfortunately Caterina didn't tell me anything about you until it was too late."

Once again the two men eyed each other like two tomcats before a fight. Caterina, who may have been secretly enjoying the confrontation, stepped in. "What was it you wanted to tell us, Andrew?"

"Not a thing except that you have illegal copies of Black Dolphin's and Duchess Construction financial files and I intend to inform the Cornacchias about it."

"Andrew," Caterina said in alarm. "You can't mean that."

His eyes glittered. "But I do, my dear."

"You have no idea what you'll be doing," she said. "If you do, you'll get me into trouble, too."

"Not you," he said, smirking at Rick. "Just your new infatuation."

Rick glared back. "What makes you think the files came from me?"

"The folder is named 'Rick's files.' How much more obvious can it be?"

Rick decided it was time to bluff. "I guess we can't very well stop you, but aren't you curious about where all the money Duchess Construction is spending is going?"

"I have no idea what you're talking about," Andrew said with a contemptuous smile.

"Of course you do. Even though they're a privately owned corporation, they can't hide the huge sums they've spent in the last year. What kind of capital improvements would cost that much?"

Andrew's smile faded a bit. "I don't know, but it's none of my concern."

"Does your bank have dealings with Black Dolphin or Duchess Construction? If so, I'll bet your president and board of directors would like to know about their expenditures. What if Cornacchia can't pay his debts? And what would your bank think if they found out you knew about it and didn't tell them?"

A note of hesitation crept into Andrew's voice. "These records are privileged information. I can't tell the bank what I know."

"But you can," Rick said. "Especially if the source is a whistle-blower within the organization. You can even come off being a hero. Do you realize that?"

The words obviously took the accountant by surprise and he broke eye contact.

"Tell the Cornacchias if you must," Rick continued. "But when you do you had better also tell them what you're going to tell your own bank, too. If you don't, they'll want to know where you got the information, how much you know and who else knows about it."

Fine beads of perspiration appeared on Andrew's head. "You can't frighten me."

"Don't you realize that the records are as dangerous to you as they are to them? If I were Lorenzo Cornacchia I would worry about what *you* could do with the information."

The accountant's eyes opened wider. "They know me better than that. And they know they have nothing to be concerned about. Their cash flow will take care of their debts and increased revenues will pay off the debt in a few years."

"How much debt and how many years are we talking about?" Rick asked.

"You seem to know so much. Why don't you tell me?"

"With a company like Black Dolphin, what's a few billion lira, right?"

Andrew's eyes widened momentarily and then a look of understanding came to his face. "I have no idea what you're talking about," he said. "Just out of curiosity, if you already knew so much about their books, why did you have Caterina call me in?"

"It was her idea. I wanted to turn the disks over to your bank without your knowledge. I told her I didn't think you'd even want to know what was going on, but she insisted that I tell you. She wanted to make sure that you got the credit."

Andrew turned to Caterina and then looked back at Rick. "You're lying," he said. "Stealing Caterina isn't enough. You have to humiliate me with my bank, too."

Rick tried to lay a consoling hand on Andrew's shoulder but the man batted it away. "I understand how you must feel about me," Rick said, "but I had no intention to humiliate you. When I saw the files, Caterina told me we should contact you because we could trust you. You must realize yourself that the Cornacchias are up to something suspicious with all the spending. We were hoping you'd help us find out what."

Defeated, Andrew sighed. "The main expenditures seem to be related to construction. They also have purchased several new large ships. Nearly one and a half billion lira's worth."

"Do you mean Black Dolphin actually owns their own ships?" Rick asked.

"They always have. Most companies lease equipment so they don't have to maintain it. But Black Dolphin has made it a practice to own their ships for as long as they've been in business."

"Who did Black Dolphin buy the tankers from?"

"A company in Bahrain. Petranco."

"That could be Petroleum Transfer Company, I suppose," Rick said.

Andrew nodded. "Now where did you get these files?"

"They came from an employee at Black Dolphin," Caterina said. "She was worried about her retirement funds."

"I see. Then the first thing I suggest you do is to change the name of the folder. Does your laptop have a CD burner?"

"No. We'll have to copy them onto disks. I have several in the carrying case."

"I'll stay and help Andrew," Caterina said. "I think you should find Stef."

Ten minutes later he found Stef walking along the Promenade. "Sorry to spoil your afternoon but we have work to do." He took out the cell phone and called Caterina. "Any chance your friend Nibblu from the print shop will be around?"

"It's possible. I'll call you back." Minutes later she did. "He says he'll meet you at the shop."

Forty minutes later they were on their way to the Trade Center. Armed with a bogus equipment rental agreement and a freshly made ID card for Stef, Rick's heart beat faster as they approached the entrance to the construction site. The odor of ozone from the welders and diesel oil from the generators perked him up and he confidently got out of the truck to approach the gate. It was locked from the inside. Stef honked. Several seconds later it swung open and a burly man wearing a hardhat, short-sleeved shirt and dusty jeans walked out to meet them. After eyeing the identification badges, he asked, "What's going on, gentlemen? I wasn't expecting any deliveries until tonight."

Rick held his breath as he handed him the phony rental form. "We got a call from Gilbert Falzon half an hour ago to pick up some equipment and deliver it here. We have to hurry because we're supposed to return the truck when we're done."

"I've never heard of Gilbert Falzon," the guard said.

"He's one of the new foremen. We'll be coming back with him tonight. Ten o'clock, right?"

"Yes," the guard said, handing him the paper. "I hope it won't take too long. I want to be in bed by midnight."

"So do I," Rick said. "Where will they be bringing the delivery?"

To Rick's surprise the man pointed directly across the huge excavation to a temporary steel bridge resting on top of the footings.

"They're planning to take it across that bridge to the hydraulic elevator. I don't know why they don't just bring it down the hill. The transporter has a low center of gravity so it should make it down all right. They could come back up by the elevator."

Rick's eyebrows raised. "I didn't realize the elevator was ready. When did they finish it?"

"Yesterday morning," the guard said. "It took them more than three weeks working 24 hours a day to get it done. How long will you be?"

"Just long enough to drop off the equipment and inspect the delivery area. It shouldn't be more than ten minutes."

"Proceed," the guard said.

Before getting back into the truck, Rick took a practiced look at what lay before him. Far below, the footings were arranged in the shape of a semicircle with a third of it missing. The layout conformed to the architectural drawing for the completed building he had seen in a magazine: a curved structure with a C-shaped base that rose forty stories with a series of microwave dishes on the roof. Looking down to the center of the "C," Rick could see a concrete cylinder, which he took to be the elevator shaft.

He got into the truck and Stef shifted into low gear to begin inching their way down the steep road. Rick had watched truck drivers with loads charging forward from the street at twenty miles an hour and he wondered how they could be so cavalier. Even in low gear the truck had to grind its gears to restrain its urge to dash downward. Rick worried that the brakes would give out and send them plummeting down the incline. As Stef drove down, Rick noticed a few men at work, one of whom seemed to be taking core samples of the footings using an electric auger. Another drove a small Bobcat-sized tractor between the trees of the concrete forest that had sprung up in the last few weeks. Several others stood idly in various places around the footings. The next stage would require tower-sized cranes to lower the metal framework onto the footings.

They reached the bottom and Stef shifted into second gear. He stopped a few feet away from the forest of concrete towers, ten feet to the left of the opening.

At first glance, it wasn't much different from the site where Rick had worked as a hod carrier back home. "Things look pretty tame here," he said. "I'm surprised."

"What did you expect to find?" asked Stef.

"Something that doesn't belong here. Let's take a look at the elevator shaft."

The truck pulled forward. With the temporary bridge overhead, the whole area was dark. "Turn on your headlights," Rick said.

The headlights flared on to illuminate a concrete cylinder that looked to be approximately fifteen feet in diameter. Rick got out of the truck and walked to the doors. They were made of thick metal and securely locked. They also were so solid that they didn't echo when Rick rapped on them with his knuckles. He guessed that when the building was completed, the entire basement could be used as subterranean storage area, perhaps as a secure area for the telephone link equipment. Foot before foot, he began to pace off the circumference of the shaft. Not far from the doors he came across a locked metal panel set into the wall. The elevator controls, he decided. And right now, they might be the only ones working.

He returned to the elevator doors to conclude the walk. The outside circumference was about 32 feet. So the inside circumference would probably be slightly more than 27. If Bin-Said were delivering a nuclear weapon, he had picked the ideal place to hide it. The bowels of the construction had more than enough concrete to shield the radiation of a dozen bombs.

That thought stopped him in his tracks. Was that part of the plan? Was it meant to be a storehouse for terrorists' nuclear weapons? If so, wouldn't it negate the threat Cornacchia needed to support his coup?

With a shake of his head, he walked back to the truck. "Okay, Bud. Let's unload the block and tackle and move our fannies out of here," he said.

With Stef holding one of the sides of the tripod and Rick the other, they quickly unloaded the gear and got into the truck. "Main floor," Rick said.

The trip up wasn't as easy as the trip down. The truck whined incessantly about the climb, but steadily clawed its way upward. As they neared the top, Rick caught sight of the guard standing in the middle of the road staring down at them. "I don't like the looks of this," he said.

When they closed within ten yards, the man raised his hands to stop them.

"Slow down," Rick whispered, "but be ready to gun it when I tell you to."

The guard moved aside and made a motion for Stef to roll down his window. Stef did. "Anything wrong" Stef asked in Italian.

"What were you doing by the elevator?" the man asked.

Rick swallowed. "We've got a big shipment coming in," he said. "I was just making sure it will fit on the elevator floor."

"It will," the guard said. He held a clipboard. "I need your signature. I put in the time you arrived and when you leave."

Stef took the clipboard and scrawled a signature before handing it back. "See you later," Rick said.

"I'll be here," the guard said. With that he shut the gate.

Stef sat idling outside the gate as motorists passed. "That was fun," he said. "What do we do now?"

"Let's find the surface entrance to the elevator," Rick replied.

The side entrance to the construction site was easy to find. It branched off a large street that intersected the Strand. A Lull would be able carry the payload to the bridge, but the makeshift structure could never handle the immense weight of a nuclear weapon.

Something was wrong.

Swinging down from the truck, Rick walked to the gate. It was locked with a heavy-duty padlock, but easily picked open. Why hadn't Cornacchia stationed a guard at the gate? Certainly he wouldn't be that careless if a nuclear weapon were on the way. "Find a place to park," Rick said. "I'll be right back."

Even though the bridge was constructed of heavy steel, it could support only a few tons at most. If Cornacchia had a nuke, he wasn't going to get it into the elevator that way.

The burden on Rick's mind seemed considerably lighter as he reached the doors to the elevator. The two heavy doors were padlocked shut. Once again the security seemed criminally lax, as he easily opened the lock. The doors were heavy, but he was able to lift them open. Under them he found a fifteen foot circular metal platform.

Where were the controls? Were the ones he saw in the excavation the only ones? Maybe they would install another set at the top when construction was completed. It was an expensive set-up. A hydraulic lift with a platform of that size and height would cost several millions of dollars to build.

The engineering was first rate. The shaft certainly was strong enough to support the equipment, and Malta was dry enough that they would never have to worry about water seeping into the mechanism. But if not a nuke, what were they bringing in tonight?

His reverie ended with the sound of Stef honking his horn. Hastily he shut the doors and replaced the lock. Then he ran back to the gate. Cautiously opening it a crack to look out, he saw a police car with its blue dome light flashing. Stef had the truck window rolled down. A black-uniformed officer stood bent over talking to him.

Rick couldn't hear what they were saying, but he could see the officer gesturing and Stef nodding at times. A minute or two later the officer got into his car and drove off. After it turned left onto the Strand, Rick shut and relocked the gate before returning to the truck. "What was that about?" Rick asked.

"Something about trucks not being allowed to use this street until two o'clock tomorrow morning. Did you find anything interesting?"

"More puzzling than interesting," Rick said. He was interrupted by the sound of his cell phone. "Hello?"

"Don't come back to the hotel," Caterina said. "Zija just called. George Bezzina contacted her."

CHAPTER 35

▼

5:05 PM
Sliema

At Stef's knock, Josefina opened the door and peered out. "Come in and be quick about it," she said reaching out and grabbing him by his lapels. After hastily locking the door, she held him at arm's length to look him over. Aglow, she planted two large lip-glossed kisses on his cheeks and said, "I'm so happy you're safe. I'm your Auntie Josefina."

Then she turned to Rick and her cheery façade crumbled and she began to tremble. "Easy, Auntie," Rick said, gently. "When did Bezzina call?"

"About an hour and a half ago while I was working in the bar. He said he was looking for Pawlu Naxxar. I told him I didn't know who he was but that I would give Caterina the message. That terrible Sequ wouldn't dare show up here, would he?"

Caterina appeared. "No. He wouldn't leave his party. He'll send someone else."

"It might be the young Arab man Pawlu had working with him," Stef said. "Kareem il-Tariq. I never saw him but I heard him several times. He has a speech impediment."

"Yusef Mansoor!" Rick said excitedly. "If George Bezzina is that anxious to find Pawlu it would be a good idea for us to find him first." He turned to Stef. "Was this il-Tariq ever at Pawlu's house in Zejtun?"

"No," Stef said. "In fact Pawlu told me he brought me there because he was sure it was safe."

"Then he could be there now," Rick said. "Let's find out. Cat, stay here with Zija. Does she have a gun around here?"

"I think Ziju has a shotgun somewhere," Caterina replied.

- 312 -

"Find it. Josefina, close the pub and lock all the doors. If il-Tariq shows up here, don't be afraid to use the gun if you have to."

7:15 PM

Nervous about driving on the left, Stef sat stiffly in his seat and followed the signs through the towns of Marsa and Paola in the general direction of Marsaxlokk. At last they arrived in Zejtun. The town was an early battle site during the Great Siege. This would be the opening foray of the most modern battle for Malta.

Rick kept a sharp eye on the streets. "Take the next right. It'll take us where we want to go." They stopped a short distance from the house.

"Are you sure you can get in the back door?" Stef asked.

"As sure as I can be of anything. I had to break the back door to get into the house when Caterina and I came here. Luckily I just pulled the hasp of the safety lock out of the wall and I fixed it so it wouldn't be obvious it was broken. If Pawlu hasn't tried to use the door, the house will be wide open."

"And if he has, he's taken off for parts unknown," Stef said.

Rick sighed. "Let's keep our fingers crossed."

"Even if he is here, do you really think Pawlu still has the Shield? He's had more than a day to sell it to Cornacchia."

"I didn't get the impression Cornacchia had the basin when I was at Borgiswed. Pawlu is under a lot of pressure and he may have been edgy about contacting Cornacchia, especially if he's worried about George Bezzina finding out. He may even have taken time to try to find another buyer."

Stef scoffed. "And get pennies on the hundreds of dollars. I don't think so."

"I didn't say he'd find anyone, I'm just saying he might look."

"Right. Whatever, I sure hope your plan works."

The back gate was locked, but a twist of a screwdriver opened it and he crawled to the gutted Citroen for concealment. The Glock poked him uncomfortably in the stomach and he took it out and laid it beside him. Next he removed his shoes.

Eyes glued to his watch, he waited until the countdown reached a minute before he readied himself. A grim smile formed on his face as he rose to a crouch. If Pawlu Naxxar were in the house, in forty seconds he would get the surprise of his life.

He fingered the Glock. Five, four, three…Now.

With heart pounding he inhaled deeply and got to his feet. As he reached the back entrance he heard the sound of someone knocking on the front door.

Grasping the 9mm tightly, he gently turned the door handle and gave the door a push. It opened without a sound. The kitchen was empty. Sighing in relief he stepped inside.

He heard Stef's voice. "Open the door, Pawlu. I know you're in there."

Total silence. Stef called again. Ten seconds passed in a silence so complete that all he could hear was the refrigerator hum.

Stef's voice rang out once more. "Open the door, Pawlu, or I'm coming in after you." Rick heard the sound of Stef's body slamming against the front door. "Let me in or I'll break the door down."

Still no sounds and Rick began to fear Pawlu wasn't there. Stef slammed again. This time Rick heard a sound from the living room. Seconds later a man stood framed in the open kitchen door with a large suitcase in hand. Wide-eyed, he dropped it when he saw Rick. When he tried to duck back, Rick fired a warning shot that struck the doorframe. Pawlu stopped in his tracks. Grinning, he raised his hands.

"Put your hands behind your head and move forward," Rick said.

The man complied, his gold tooth standing out against his white teeth. Rick patted him down and quickly found a Sig Sauer automatic in a holster under the man's jacket. "Now let's answer the door."

Pawlu's smile grew wider when he opened the door and saw Stef standing outside. Ignoring the dark look on Stef's face he said, "Come in my friend," in a quavering voice.

Stef did, rushing forward and grabbing him by the throat.

Terrified, Pawlu grabbed at Stef's hands. "Please don't hurt me."

"I wouldn't hurt you, Stef said in a menacing voice. "I'm too happy to see you again." He moved an inch away from Pawlu's cheek. "I didn't expect to after you abandoned me in the grain bin. You surprised me. It didn't occur to me that you would do that after I just saved your life."

"I left you food and water."

"But not enough air. If my brother hadn't arrived, I would be dead."

"I...I didn't know what else to do," Pawlu spouted. "I wanted you to be safe. I knew if I kept you with me, your life would be in danger. That's why I left you there. I knew that someone would get you out."

"And what about the money we were supposed to share for finding the Shield?"

Pawlu's gold tooth seemed to glow especially brightly as he grinned a deprecation. "I would have made sure it got to you later."

"Of course," Stef snorted, tightening his grip on his former captor's throat.

The man uttered a strangled cry.

"That's enough, Stef," Rick said.

With a glare, Stef backed away. Pawlu threw Rick a grateful look.

"You should be happy we found you," Rick said. "George Bezzina is looking for you."

"I know," Pawlu said in a quiet voice. "He wants his money."

"The money you got for bringing the Shield to Cornacchia?" Rick asked.

"Yes. We made the exchange this morning."

"What's in the suitcase?" Rick asked, pointing.

"Take a look for yourself," Pawlu said.

Stef got the suitcase and laid it on the couch. Rick motioned with his gun and Pawlu moved over to join him. "Open it," he said.

Pawlu undid the snaps and lifted the top. Under a single layer of clothes the suitcase was filled with wrapped stacks of 500 Eurodollar banknotes.

Rick's eyes opened wide. "Just how much did Cornacchia pay you?"

"Three quarters of a million Euros. That's half a million, Maltese. I know the Shield is worth many times that and he offered to pay me another three million Maltese pounds, but I didn't dare to wait around to get paid."

"Do you have any idea why Cornacchia had that much money in cash?" Rick asked.

Pawlu nodded. In an angry voice he said, "It was meant to be his payoff to Bezzina for finding the drawing. Bezzina demanded Euros instead of Maltese Lira because Euros are much easier to dispose of."

"I'm sure they are," Rick said. "What's wrong with that?"

Pawlu spat in disgust. "Nothing except that when he hired us he said he would give us half of what he was paid. He told us that the four of us would divide twenty-five thousand lira when we found the drawing."

Rick laughed. "That's two-hundred-and-fifty thousand Euros. He was holding out on you."

Pawlu responded with a rueful grin. "Not only that, George lied to me. Cornacchia didn't insist we kill Stef after we got the drawing. That was Bezzina's idea. He was sure that the police would find out he was involved in the kidnapping and he wanted to cover up any connection."

"Leaving you to kill Stef or to have to face kidnapping charges," Rick said. "You did the right thing when you spared Stef's life. I'm sure it will have some effect on your sentence even though you're wanted for kidnapping and murder."

"I didn't kill Mario Agius. il-Tariq did. He shot him three times with a shotgun as calmly as if he were tying his shoe."

"You'll have to convince the police about that," Rick said.

"No!" Pawlu said earnestly. "Please don't turn me over to the police. Some of them are working for Bezzina. If I'm arrested, no one will ever see me again. No matter what I've done I don't deserve that. I'd rather that your brother would strangle me."

"What else can we do with you?" Rick asked.

"If it's George Bezzina you want, I can help you."

"He's not that important now that Cornacchia has the Shield."

"You don't understand. There's a secret passage that goes into Cornacchia's house and George knows where it is."

Rick's heart beat faster. "How do you know that?"

"He told me himself. He learned about it when he was one of Cornacchia's chess pieces. He was the black king for years."

Rick was barely able to control his excitement. He remembered seeing the chess piece logo on the check Bezzina wrote to Caterina. The man had even called himself the black king when Rick asked him if he played chess. And Pawlu had just confirmed that there was a secret passage. That explained how the children got into Cornacchia's garden without going through the front gate.

"Even if Bezzina knows where the entrance is, Cornacchia must keep it locked."

"Yes, but George discovered the mechanism that unlocks the outside door, too. He told me the passage has two branches. One goes to the garden and the other into the house. He said he found the way to unlock the door to the house."

"And how do you know all this?" Rick asked.

Pawlu's voice became anxious. "George told me. He said he followed the passage into the house one night and ended up in the library. He gave some thought to stealing some of Cornacchia's rare books but he gave up on the idea because he didn't know where to sell them. I think he was worried Cornacchia might be able to figure out who stole them, too."

"Even if you're telling the truth why do you think that being able to get into the passage will help us get the Shield back?"

"I met Cornacchia in the library when I brought the basin to him. I had to use the wc. When I got back The Shield was gone."

"So you think he may have put it in the passage for safe-keeping," Stef said.

"Yes," Pawlu said. "I can help you capture him. He'll be at the Qarnita Pub."

"Why should we trust you?" Stef asked.

"*Vendetta*," Pawlu said. "He must pay for his lies."

CHAPTER 36

▼

Saturday, 8:48 PM
Sliema

Stef found the entrance to the alley and crawled the pickup forward until Tarbija's taillights lit up in front of them. Coming to a halt with a rattle and squeak, he turned off the headlamps. They were thrown into utter darkness.

Startled, Rick grasped the 9-millimeter more tightly, intending to fire if Pawlu made the slightest movement. "Go knock on the door, bro," he whispered.

Seconds later Caterina's form appeared, silhouetted against the light from the kitchen. She motioned to them. "Move," Rick said, pushing Pawlu out the door.

Pawlu dashed for the door with Rick a step behind him. "Hello, love," Rick said. "Meet Pawlu Naxxar."

She answered Naxxar's grin with a glare. "Come in," she said. "Josefina Grech welcomes everyone to her house. Even torturers."

Rick shoved him through the door. "Hurry up, Stef," he called over his shoulder.

Stef scurried in with the suitcase in hand. Rick sat Pawlu at a table and unobtrusively gave the 9mm to Stef. "Find some way to tie him up," Rick said.

"I'll get some rope," Caterina replied.

After Pawlu was safely bound with his hands behind his back Rick asked, "What do we do with him? We can't take him with us or leave him here. And he's afraid of the police."

"I know someone in the police we can trust," Caterina said. "He'll make sure that Mr. Naxxar is safe." With that she took out her cell phone and stepped out of the kitchen.

"I think I know how we can stop Cornacchia," Rick said.

Stef liked Rick's plan. He especially liked being with Caterina while Rick gathered the pieces for the device. Josefina had readied a room for him and he found all his clothes freshly laundered and hanging in the wardrobe. He was about to pick out an outfit when Caterina pushed him aside. Thumbing through the clothes, she laid out dark pants and a dress shirt he hadn't worn in years.

"Use the shower first," she said. "Be sure to put some conditioner in your beard."

It was good advice. When he combed it, it relaxed into neat rows instead of its usual rampant disorderly curls. With his long hair pulled back and his beard under control, he looked nattier than he had in at least ten years. Caterina disappeared into the bathroom to shower and change clothes. When she emerged she was wearing a sleek black dress with a string of pearls and shoes with transparent soles and heels. By the time she was done with her makeup, Stef was insanely jealous of Rick. She grabbed an enormous black leather bag and they were on their way to the kitchen to pick up Rick's device.

10:15

The police arrived to take Pawlu away. Rick started at the sound of the phone.

He hesitated, wondering who could be calling. Had Stef and Caterina run into a problem?

"This is Tom Scicluna," the voice said. "I work at the embassy with Bob Carpenter. I'm the one who gave you the gun."

"Yes," Rick said, surprised. "How did you know how to reach me?"

"I'm the one who debugged your cell phone and put one of our own in its place."

The man sounded frightened. "What's going on?" Rick asked.

"I'm on the road from Hal Far. The shipment arrived safely and the Lull is on its way to the Trade Building right now. We tried to stop it on the road near Hal Far but there was a company of men in uniform guarding it. There're not carrying a bomb, it's a god damned box and it's hotter than hell. My God. They might as well have used a paper bag."

"Then they're spreading contamination all over the place," Rick said.

"Yes. But it gets worse, there's an antenna sticking out from the box."

"It must be rigged for remote detonation," Rick said. "I think I know whose finger is on the button. We're not dealing with ordinary nukes here. In some ways it's much worse. Bin-Said is putting together a dirty bomb."

"You're right," Scicluna said. "It achieves the same purpose as a nuke without the dangers of detection. The way they're doing it, they can use a conventional bomb as a propellant. All they would have to do is lay the radioactive waste on top of it."

"And just shield the radiation from detection," said Rick. "The elevator shaft at the Trade Building would be perfect for that. It would act like a Roman candle and shoot the radioactivity straight up into the air."

"Yes," Scicluna said. "But that would also require a special explosive, or they'd lose a lot of the propellant power in back blast."

Rick shook his head. "That wouldn't be hard to do at all. They'd just need a few bombs rigged together in a shaped charge."

"You're right!" Scicluna said in a hollow shout. "Bin-Said must have been buying radioactive material anywhere he could find it. And dividing the dust up into three different packages is smart, too. If one of the shipments gets detected, they always have two others to fall back on."

"How much dust are we talking about?" Rick asked.

"I'd guess that around 700 to 800 pounds on top of the explosive would do the trick. The island would be wiped out in a generation or two if the victims don't get enough radiation to kill them immediately. And then we have the radioactive material getting into the water. Every life form in contact with it will either die within days or months. The ones that don't die immediately will ingest the contaminants and spread it."

Finding a place to park took ten minutes longer than the drive to Qarnita Pub. "Do you think we're close enough here?" he asked.

"This will be just fine," Caterina said. "We don't want anyone to see us drive Bezzina away."

A stream of well-dressed young people queued outside the pub and they fell in behind them.

"Are you sure Bezzina won't have bodyguards?" Stef whispered.

"Absolutely," Caterina said, taking his arm. "He honestly believes everyone loves him."

Inside, a bartender dressed in a pirate outfit replete with a patch over one eye pointed toward an open door. "The party's in there," he said.

The sound of loud music and laughter echoed through the pub. Young men and women good-naturedly jostled each other, trying not to spill their drinks as they attempted to make room to move their arms. They were barely inside when newcomers engulfed them. Directly in front of them a young couple holding plastic glasses in their hands was attempting to move to the music. The woman was wearing a very short black leather skirt and black nylons and Caterina seemed to be especially interested in her shoes.

Shoved from behind, Caterina bumped into her. The woman turned her head.

"Sorry," Caterina said.

"No harm done," the other woman said amiably. "You'll never be able to get in. There isn't any champagne left, anyway. George ordered more. You may be able to get some when they come with it."

"Then I guess we'll come back," Caterina said. "I have to use the wc, Jimmy." As she said it, she playfully kissed Stef on the cheek.

His heart beat uncontrollably. Even though it was only for show, he nearly passed out from the excitement. "W...where are the loos?"

"Back there," the young woman said, pointing to the left. "At the end of the bar. I sure hope you're not in a hurry."

"I'm not," Caterina said. "Thanks."

With Stef running interference, they barreled through the crowd to the back of the bar. When they were safely out of earshot, Caterina giggled. "Did you see her shoes? They're Anne Klein. They cost enough to feed our refugees for a year."

At the other end of the bar two long lines queued back to the door to Bezzina's office. Another door lay straight ahead. Stef moved around through the lines to stand next to Caterina.

"It's going to be forever," she said. "Would you hold my purse, honey? It's heavy."

He took it from her. After waiting with her for a while, he wiped at his head. "It's too hot," he said, turning his back and walking several steps away from the queue. Keeping his back to the crowd, he took out Rick's invention from her purse. Sucking in his stomach, he slipped it beneath his belt and pulled his shirt over it. It was uncomfortable but well covered. He turned around and walked back to Caterina.

"You'll need to hold this yourself, love," he said, handing the purse back to her. "I have to go myself."

With that he went to the end of the queue to the men's room.

The line moved slowly as the done-pissing stepped out and needing-to-piss stepped in, but at last he reached the door to the lavatory. After locking the door he sighed in relief. He took the contraption out from beneath his belt and stepped into the stall. After laying it on top of the commode tank, he left and closed the door. A quick turn of a coin in the slot in the lock secured it.

He got a dirty look from the next person in line as he left.

I wasn't in there that long, he thought. With a nod to the man, he went back to rejoin Caterina. As he took the purse from her he wondered how long would it take until someone discovered the commode door was locked. Would the man behind him be able to get the door open himself or would he have to get one of the bartenders to help? Either way someone was in for quite a surprise.

He didn't have long to wait for an answer. The man who was second in line after Stef ran excitedly out of the wc and headed for the bar. The bartender cum pirate returned with him and pushed his way to the front of the line. The man's uncovered eye squinted evilly as he pounded on the door. A frightened patron opened the door and stepped out. The bartender entered and soon came back out. Scurrying back to the bar, he rang the ship's bell several times until the noise abated. "Everyone has to leave," he shouted.

The noise level dropped but he still had to repeat the announcement. He was greeted with groans and cries of surprise. Stef and Caterina exchanged secret smiles. So far their plan was working perfectly. Stef watched as the bartender whispered something into his colleague's ear. The second bartender summoned his colleagues and they talked in whispers. As the men conferred, Stef moved to a strategic point at the front exit and Caterina took a position outside.

One of the bartenders rang the ship's bell and the noise in the bar stopped. "Everyone, please listen to me. You will have to leave the pub. Two at a time, line up and exit through the door."

"What's happening?" someone called.

"We have to leave the bar. The police will be coming. There may be a bomb in the men's wc."

Instead of the expected gasps of fear and a general rush for the door, everyone looked dumbfounded. "Bomb?"

"No questions. Please line up and leave the building."

Stef waited, determined to be the regulator to see that no more than two left the building at one time. Caterina stood where she could see each face as it appeared. He also was praying that no one would panic.

His prayers appeared to be answered as the first pair calmly walked out of the pub and passed through. He glanced at Caterina, but she made no signal. "Keep moving," he said in Italian. "There are a lot of people to get out of here."

At last Caterina nodded and Stef took Bezzina by the arm. "Come with me."

When Bezzina resisted, Stef showed him the 9mm.

No one noticed. Apparently more concerned with their own safety than his, Bezzina's guests passed by without a second look at their host. Stef's hand held the 9mm against the man's stomach. Then Caterina took him by one arm and Stef by the other. When they reached the car, Caterina sat in the driver's seat. Stef pushed Bezzina next to her and got into the back seat. He bent forward and pressed the gun to the man's neck before settling back.

"What's going on, Caterina?" he asked.
"You'll find out soon enough," she said as she slipped a blindfold over his eyes.

CHAPTER 37

▼

Saturday
11:00 PM
Sliema

Stef and Caterina arrived at the Bellestrado five minutes later. She was in the back seat with George Bezzina so Rick got into the front seat with Stef.

"Why Father Segretti," Bezzina said affably. "What a pleasant surprise."

"Sorry to ruin your party," Rick said. "You're needed elsewhere tonight."

"I'm at your service," the mobster said in an unconcerned voice. Why was he so cool?

"There was a news report on the radio," Caterina said. "Someone released the refugees at Qrendi. The army was able to stop them before the ones responsible could do the same thing at Verdala Barracks."

"Ben-Said's work," Rick said. "He's moved up the timetable."

Half an hour later, they were on the road that circled the south wall of Mdina. The structure showed as a black expanse against a dark sky.

"Are you sure you know where the entrance to the passage is?" Rick asked.

"I've been there often enough," Bezzina replied. "Stop here. It's in this field."

Stef stopped. Some twenty yards farther up the road, a red Mercedes was parked next to a wall.

"Why do you suppose that's parked here?" Rick asked.

"I have no idea," Bezzina said.

Rick got out and Bezzina followed. Once out, Bezzina confidently strode to the gate and turned the handle.

The rest followed. The field was barren and dusty. It would stay that way for several more weeks before the next growing season would start. Mdina wall loomed as a sheer cliff.

"Does anyone have a flashlight?" asked Bezzina.

Stef turned one on. "There are two latches," Bezzina said. "One unlocks the entrance and the other opens the door. If I may borrow the light from you."

Rick held the Glock tighter as Bezzina took the flashlight. Light skittered over the stones until it came to rest on two rocks that resembled a duck's bill. He pulled on the lower one and it moved up. They heard a distinct clack behind the wall when he put his hand into the crevice.

Bezzina replaced the stone and moved a short distance farther down the wall. After a short search he removed another stone. A grinding noise sounded. "If you gentlemen will help me, we can move the door away."

Seconds later a section of the wall pulled back to reveal a stygian passage. "Here you are," Bezzina said. "Follow me."

Caterina pulled on Rick's arm. "I'm worried," she whispered. "Something isn't right."

"I agree," Rick said. "Stay close to Stef. I'll keep a close eye on Bezzina."

Once inside, they could easily tell that young people had passed this way. A charred heart and arrow and the words 'Ayden loves Kelly' stood surrounded by chalk-drawn innocent faces wearing spiky hairdos and similar-looking suns. Bezzina plowed forward with a confident step. They came to a cut to the right. "That's the passage to the garden," Bezzina said. "The one to the house is straight ahead."

Borgiswed was almost a hundred-feet directly above the bottom of the wall and it took twice as many steps to traverse the distance. At last the stairway leveled off. After a short distance a new flight took off to the left and another rose straight-ahead. Bezzina slowed.

Three steps from the top, Bezzina stopped and knelt. "Hold the flashlight, please," he said.

Stef cautiously moved closer and took the flashlight from him.

"The release is here on the step," Bezzina said.

As he said it, the ceiling opened up. Stef blinked as the passage was flooded with light. Lorenzo Cornacchia beamed down at them from above. "Hello, George. It was nice of you to bring guests."

11:45 AM

Rick cast a worried look at Caterina but her eyes were on the large cloth bag sitting on the kitchen table. Muhammed Bin-Said watched them with a malevolent eye. Completing the cast were Micallef, Cardinal Vella, two armed guards, Ibn, and Marija.

"George must have neglected to tell you that I installed a detection unit in the passage," Cornacchia said amiably. "A while ago I found out someone had been in my library. I knew there was only one way the intruder could have got in."

With a triumphant smile, Bezzina moved away from Caterina to stand by Cornacchia. Rick watched him through half-open eyes. No wonder the bastard was so cooperative. He knew he didn't have anything to worry about.

Muhammed Bin-Said angrily approached the group. As he came nearer Rick noticed he was carrying something the size of a cell phone in his hand. "Ah yes," the man said in a venomous tone, "The young safe-crackers. Did you find anything interesting in my briefcase?"

"I never saw it," Rick said.

"I don't believe you, but even if it's true, it wouldn't have interested you, anyway. Just some flow-charts and weather data."

"Dispersal vectors," Rick said in a low voice.

Bin-Said gave him a hard look. "How would you know that if you didn't see them? It appears that my secret is out. No matter. Even if you've told the world you can't stop me. This little device," he held out the black box he was holding in his hand, "makes me invulnerable. If anyone tries to interfere, all I have to do is push this button. Such a tiny action to end the world as we know it."

He was greeted by total silence. The Arab sauntered over to Caterina. "And who is this young woman?"

"Caterina Borg is her name," Bezzina said. "She and her church have been helping immigrant Arabs. She's been working with this man who calls himself Father Segretti. His real name is Rick Olsen."

Bin-Said glared at Caterina. "This is all very confusing. What is your involvement in this?"

"I've been helping Rick find his brother. George Bezzina kidnapped Stef."

Bin-Said grabbed Caterina's hair and Rick tensed, wanting to throw himself at the man. "Why were you at the archives with this man?" he asked, jabbing a finger in Rick's direction.

"He was in my custody. I had to go wherever he did."

Cornacchia spoke up. "Ray?"

"It's true. He was released into her custody last Sunday."

Bin-Said turned back to Bezzina. "Is it true you kidnapped this man's brother."

A look of fear briefly flitted across Bezzina's face. "Lorenzo Cornacchia hired me. We're old friends and I did it as a favor."

Bin-Said turned to face Cornacchia with terrifying look. "Why did you do that? Didn't you realize you could be endangering our plans?"

Though smiling, Cornacchia shifted his feet uncomfortably. "I felt I didn't have a choice. He had a drawing of the Shield."

"I don't understand. Why was that reason to kidnap him?"

"I was afraid it would expose the Shield as Cellini's creation. It was supposed to have been made by Prester John."

"It wouldn't have made a bit of difference who made it," said Bin-Said in a contemptuous voice. "But then you could never have figured that out by yourself." The Arab turned back to Rick.

"If you were trying to find your brother, why were you reading Alessandro Cornacchia's papers at the archives?"

"I hoped to learn something to help me get my brother freed," Rick replied. "Did you find out what you wanted to know about Bartolomeo?"

"Yes. He was an interesting man. Unfortunately for him, he tried to trick the great Suleiman into believing that he had discovered a powerful alchemical spell. The blessed Sultan was far too wise to be taken in by the infidel's foolish claims. In fact this Bartolomeo never even realized why the so-called Shield of God actually was so valuable."

"Was it because it was made from gold that the Knights of St. John stole from Aksa Mosque in Jerusalem?" Rick asked.

Rick didn't like the expression on Bin-Said's face. "How did you know that?"

"I ran across a reference to it in a letter by Donato Cornacchia in the archives."

"Did it say specifically that Mosque?" Bin-Said asked excitedly.

"No. It simply referred to gold brought back by the Knights from the Holy Land."

"I see," said Bin-Said. "The extent of your knowledge surprises me. But I still don't understand why you and your brother are here now."

"Lorenzo has been deceiving you," Marija broke in. "He didn't have the basin and he made one himself. This man's brother found the original. They must have come to Borgiswed to steal it."

Lorenzo Cornacchia looked thunderstruck by Marija's betrayal and Rick actually felt sorry for him. "It was your idea to make the counterfeit," Cornacchia said, pointing at Marija. "Just as it was your idea to involve Muhammed in the first place."

Eyes glowering in rage, Bin-Said took three threatening steps in Cornacchia's direction. "You were going to deceive me? Where is this counterfeit?"

"It was in the basement," Marija said.

"See if you can find it, Ibn," Bin-Said ordered.

Ibn nodded and opened the basement door.

Bin-Said took Cornacchia by the shoulders. "You have no idea how foolish it is to try to trick me," the Arab growled.

"I didn't want to. I never would have involved you at all if Marija hadn't insisted you were so indispensable to the takeover. She told me that you could get support from the Arab countries and that you had a weapon that could prevent anyone from trying to depose me."

After a glare at Marija, Bin-Said asked, "Did she tell you what the weapon is?"

"No. But I believed her. I wasn't trying to cheat you. You would never have known it wasn't the original if Marija didn't tell you."

"What happened to the original?" Bin-Said asked.

Cornacchia collapsed. "My father hid it during the Second World War and no one had been able to find it until now."

"Tell me more about this meddler," the Arab said, gesturing toward Rick.

"His brother Stefan found the original drawing Cellini had made for the basin. Bartolomeo's name was on the drawing and Stefan Olsen contacted me. I told him I wanted to buy the drawing but he refused. He said he wanted to include a photo of it in his doctoral dissertation. He also wanted to know if Cellini had completed the work and I told him that he had. Mr. Olsen was very excited and said he wanted to see it. I was so worried that the drawing would expose Cellini's work that I felt I had to stop him."

"You weren't worried about that," Marija said. "You were afraid the drawing would expose your forgery."

"I see," said Bin-Said in an ominous voice. "So after you had Stefan kidnapped, brother Richard came looking for him."

"Yes," said Cornacchia. "I hadn't counted on his resourcefulness. He found the drawing and offered to exchange it for his brother. When he came here he caught me working on my copy. He told me he had guessed that I was planning to overthrow the government. He escaped. You'll have to ask him why he came back."

Ibn returned carrying a heavy object. "Put it on the table," Bin-Said ordered. As he set it down, Marija and Caterina ooed at the size. Even George Bezzina caught his breath. Turning to Marija, Bin-Said asked, "Are you sure this is the copy?"

"I don't know," she responded. "I've never seen either one. Cardinal Vella will know. He's the only one who ever saw it before it disappeared."

All eyes turned to Vella.

"I know it well. Alessandro and I spent years trying to decode the message written in the runes. It hypnotized us."

"Do you know why Alessandro was out driving during an air raid?" Rick asked.

"I was with him that night and I forced him to go. When the car hit the crater and overturned, I was able to escape. Alessandro was trapped behind the wheel."

Cornacchia moved to him. "Why didn't you ever tell me about what happened?"

"You only would have blamed me for your father's death. He had been attempting to decode the runes for years and he never succeeded. When the war started and the Italians couldn't take over the island he must have given up. He devised some absurd plan to make it a prize in a game with the British and would have let them keep it if they found it. It was a priceless relic and belonged to our people. The night he died, I came to Borgiswed with a gun. I told him to drive me where he had hidden the Shield. He drove me to Valletta. I realized he never intended to give it to me."

"Which one is the original?" Bin-Said asked.

"I won't tell you.

Bin-Said laughed derisively. "Fool. We'll take them both."

"No," Vella shouted. Infuriated, he made a movement to his pocket.

Rick shouted an alarm. His voice was drowned out by the sound of gunfire from one of the sentries. As Vella fell to the floor, an ancient short-barreled pistol fell from his hands.

Bin-Said, seemingly offended that the cleric had meant to make such a feeble attempt on his life, kicked the body. "You stupid old man," he muttered. Then he turned to Rick with an evil smile. In a mock genial voice he said, "We seem to have a problem. Can you tell which is the original?"

Rick glanced toward Caterina as he saw her hand quickly move away from Marija Cornacchia's handbag. Turning his attention back to Bin-Said, he said, "I'm sure I can."

Everyone but the guards followed him to the kitchen table.

The basin Ibn had retrieved sat on the table. "This one is Lorenzo's forgery. He showed it to me."

"Which means the original is in the black velvet bag," said Bin-Said. "Show us, Lorenzo."

All eyes were riveted on Cornacchia as he slid the bag off from its contents. As the basin came into view it was greeted with a collective gasp from the onlookers. Even by the light in the kitchen, the work was breathtaking, and impossible to take in at a single glance.

Its gargantuan size alone boggled the mind. Rick guessed it was more than twenty-five inches in diameter. The metal gleamed like molten sunshine and the garnets, rubies, sapphires and emeralds looked like embers burning at the bottom of a crucible of flame. In a never-ending moment of birth, the figures stood ready to step out into the world for the first time. The centuries had played an important role, too, adding a deep patina that added greater depth to the figures and the other delicately raised areas. Altogether, Rick couldn't remember ever seeing anything that combined birth and fulfillment in such a remarkable way. For a magical instant, being and becoming were one.

He wasn't the only one to be impressed.

Marija's ever-present look of sensuality was gone, and she looked as if she were genuinely startled. Rick guessed it was one of the few moments of true surprise she had ever experienced in her adult life. Bin-Said became silent. Micallef shook his head, perhaps in disbelief. And Lorenzo Cornacchia stood with his eyes closed, gently running his hand over the basin's textured surface. For the moment, at least, no one was a friend or an enemy. They were all participants.

At last Stef broke the spell. Overcome with curiosity, he tried to move closer but the guard restrained him.

Rick took a deep breath to clear his head. As impressed as he was by the work, he was also more puzzled than ever. Cellini could never have resisted the urge to crow over such a masterpiece; he should have mentioned it in many of his papers. By comparison, Francis' salt cellar was merely impressive. The basin he created for Bartolomeo Cornacchia was awe-inspiring.

Something was seriously wrong, somewhere. "Do you mind if I take a closer look at it?" he asked.

"Why?" Bin-Said asked suspiciously.

"I need to get a better view of the details. There's something I don't understand."

Ibn pressed the point of his blade deeply against Rick's back as Rick knelt on the floor and bent as close to the basin as he could. He examined the surface inch by inch, occasionally reaching out a finger to touch it. The finely etched lines meant that the gold had been poured into a painstakingly crafted sandcast at exactly the right temperature. The twenty-five odd gems scattered at strategic places all had perfectly cut cabochon facets that were set flush with the surrounding surface. He guessed that the Amharic characters on the ribbon that wound around the inside surface were hand-carved.

"It's magnificent," Rick said. "It could be the most important work Cellini ever crafted."

"I agree," Cornacchia said.

"Enough!" Bin-Said shouted, pushing Cornacchia aside. "I should kill you for trying to deceive me."

"As I said before," Cornacchia said, "what else was I to do? I used more than sixteen pounds of pure gold and several hundreds of thousands of Maltese lira in gems. In totality, it probably cost me more than a million Maltese pounds to make it. That is probably close to what the original cost. You can sell my shield for at least double that. The original is worth even more."

"You're wrong," Bin-Said said. "It's priceless. It was made from gold stolen from one of our holiest temples. Every true believer will be outraged when they find out what the infidel did with it."

"And rightly so," Rick said. "Do you have a magnifying glass?"

Bin-Said looked suspicious. "What do you want that for?"

"I thought I noticed something. I want to take a closer look. I think you'll be interested, too."

"There's one in the living room," Cornacchia said. "You know where it is, Ibn."

The Arab disappeared and quickly returned with a loupe glass.

Rick took it and bent forward for another look. With magnification, the details in the facial features and the chain mail of the warriors stood out clearly. He painstakingly went over every inch, taking in the minute asymmetries in the banners that would be caused by the furls. Examining the basin made it difficult for him to keep notice of his watch, but after five minutes, Bin-Said began to get impatient. "You've had long enough," he said. "What did you see?"

"I haven't been able to find it yet." He went back to his inspection. "How did you learn about the basin?"

"Marija contacted me and asked me if I had ever heard of an artifact made from gold stolen by the Knights of St. John from the Holy Land. I told her that I hadn't, but if such a thing existed, I would be very interested in it. Now enough. I've grown weary of you."

"I'm almost done," Rick said. "Yes, here it is."

Putting the glass to his eye, he bent closer to the basin to examine a deep pit in the surface beside one of the figures. Under the glass it appeared that a small stone, perhaps a diamond representing a star, had fallen out. As he looked closer, his suspicions were confirmed. All the questions about why the basin had escaped detection for so long seemed to be answered at once and he broke out laughing. "Stolen gold or not, I'm sure Suleiman wouldn't have bought it."

"What do you mean?" Bin-Said asked in an angry voice.

"Take a look where I have my finger."

Looking puzzled, the Arab picked the loupe up from the table. He bent closer, gasped, then slowly straightened up, his face ablaze. He turned it to Cornacchia. "You have tried to deceive me again."

"I have no idea what you're talking about," Cornacchia said.

"Take a look for yourself," Rick said. "The color of the metal at the bottom isn't the same color as the surface. The surface is gold but it's only a few millimeters thick. The rest is lead. Cellini used lead because it's about the same weight as gold. He must have used the rest of the gold to pay off his debts. And with the sizable fee he received for making the basin, he even had enough left over to purchase two farms."

Obviously terrified, Cornacchia took the glass.

"That would explain why he doesn't mention the work in any of his papers," Stef said. "He must have been too ashamed. Or afraid."

"How wonderful!" said Rick. "You have a solid-gold copy of a gold-plated original!"

Cornacchia looked crestfallen. "Bartolomeo must have found out what Cellini did after he paid him," he said.

"None of this matters," Bin-Said raged. "The relic is worthless."

Rick shuddered as the Arab held up the detonator.

"Don't be a fool, Muhammed," Marija said. "It doesn't matter if it's pure gold or not. The gold Cellini used was still stolen from a mosque in Jerusalem. If you replace the stone, no one will know the difference. And you can sell Lorenzo's forgery for enough to fund your operations for years to come. No one will know the difference."

"But I will," Bin-Said growled, raising a pistol.

"Muhammed, don't," Cornacchia said, putting his hands up to protect his face. Bin-Said fired and Cornacchia dropped to the floor.

Then the Arab waved the 9mm at Marija. "I should kill you, too. You are as guilty as he is." He gestured to Ibn to pick up one of the basins. "Get the other one, Mustafa," he said addressing one of the guards. "It's time for us to leave. You're coming with, Marija."

Just then, something shattered the kitchen window. Bin-Said grabbed for his shoulder and dived for the floor. "Snipers!" he shouted, crawling for cover. "Kill everyone."

The guards opened fire.

George Bezzina was the first one to fall. He grabbed for his chest with an astonished look, covering the two red spots on his tailored suit with a hand.

Rick dove for safety. As Rick hit the floor he saw Stef push Caterina down and try to shield her with his own body. Micallef rushed the guard closest to him, hitting him on the side of the leg and knocking his feet out from under him.

The other guard opened another burst just as the lights went out and the kitchen was plunged into darkness.

After a flurry of footsteps everything went quiet.

In the silence, fresh air coming through the window mingled with the odor of cordite from the weapons. Rick listened for signs of movement from outside, but nothing stirred. As he started to get to his feet, someone turned on the lights.

CHAPTER 38

▼

Saturday
12:16 AM
Mdina

Rick called out, "Is everyone in one piece?"

"Nearly," Stef said, cupping his hand over a two-inch cut above his left eye.

Caterina handed him her handkerchief. "Put this over it," she said.

A man knelt beside Inspector Micallef, who was lying motionless on the floor with his shirtfront soaked in blood. Caterina ran to them. "Is he still alive?" she asked.

The officer put his ear next to Micallef's nose. He nodded and unbuttoned the Inspector's collar. "The bullets must have missed his heart. An ambulance is coming for him."

"Why do you care about Micallef?" Rick asked. "He was helping Cornacchia with his plot."

"Didn't you see him attack Bin-Said's guard?" she asked. "He's been spying on Lorenzo for months to try to uncover what he's been up to."

"How do you know that?" Rick asked.

Her face turned deep red. "Because I'm with the police, too. I've been trying to put George Bezzina out of business for more than a year."

Rick was too shocked to say anything more. It all made sense, but he was still unpleasantly surprised to find out about Caterina's true identity. The thought that she was anything other than the wonderful creature he had fallen so madly in love with made him heartsick.

He forgot about his disappointment in a hurry. Outside, men shouted. Police forces had surrounded the house and were now gathering up any of Bin-Said's men who still remained on the premises. Rick snatched up the dead guard's automatic from the floor and started toward the hallway that led to the library.

"Where are you going?" Caterina called.

"After Bin-Said. Everyone stay here." He stopped when he reached the door. As he flung it open he dropped and rolled through the opening, keeping the rifle in front of him. Bullets buried themselves in the wall several inches above his head. He immediately fired back at the point where he saw the gun-flashes. The sentry, who was standing braced against the wall with his feet planted apart, slowly crumpled and dropped to the floor.

Rick scrambled to his feet and flattened himself against the right hand wall to continue onward until he came to the closed library door. After standing to the side and putting his ear to the door, he pulled his head backward and slowly turned the doorknob to unlatch it. Taking a deep breath, he kicked the door open. He was greeted with silence. Still cautious, he counted to three before moving sideways through the door.

Empty.

Caterina and Stef appeared behind him. "They're in the secret passage," Rick said. "The mechanism that opens the door must be in the books."

Gently but quickly he pulled several of them at a time and laid them on the floor. One of them, the *Orlando Furioso*, refused to move. Pulling back on it he was greeted with the sound of clockwork and scraping. A portion of the floor slid open to reveal a stairway.

"Wait," Caterina said as she left the room. Seconds later she reappeared carrying the dead guard's rifle. "Let's go," she said.

Rick started down the stairway tightly gripping the Kalashnikov as he went. A few steps down he stopped to light a match. A tarry-looking torch rested in a sconce above their heads. A second match flared as he lit it. Flickering light revealed the staircase. Holding tightly to the metal railing, they took the steps two at a time. Seconds later they puffed to a stop in front of a heavy door. "Stand aside," Rick whispered. Using the butt of the rifle he pushed against it.

The door slid open. A tongue of orange fire greeted him as bullets ricocheted off the steps behind them. Rick's Kalashnikov rattled to the ground and he fell to the floor with a groan. Seconds passed in silence, then the barrel of a rifle appeared. The door rattled open and a figure in uniform holding his weapon at waist-level jumped into view. Caterina fired and the man fell backward.

Rick got to his feet. "Good work."

Stef pointed down the field at a gate some 25 meters away. "That's where we came in," he said.

As they hurried forward, Rick asked Caterina, "What were you doing with Marija's purse?"

"I dropped my tracking device into it," she replied. "It's the one I used to find you at Mdina. You didn't even know you had it until it fell out of your sweater when I rescued you from the moat." She stopped to point at a small black sedan. "This is Inspector Micallef's car. Do you think you can get the doors open?"

Rick answered with a derisive snort. The pick had the driver's door open in a matter of seconds. "For your information, I know how to hot-wire, too."

The sedan jumped to life. Caterina turned on a radio. Garbled sounds ended with the voices of Marija and Bin-Said, talking in Arabic. When there was a break in their conversation, Rick asked, "What's going on?"

"Nothing good," Caterina said. "Bin-Said wants to set off the charges, but Marija says that they still could go on with their plan for a takeover with her at the head of government. She's trying to convince him that he can still reestablish the Zone of Death."

"I didn't think she would be anxious to be a martyr," Rick said. "Unfortunately there isn't much we can do unless we can come up with a way to keep him from setting the charges off."

"What's wrong with using a signal blocker?" Caterina asked.

Rick smiled wanly. He had given up on that idea a long time ago. A blocker works by interfering with the electronic signal from the transmitter. It required knowing the frequency. Suddenly Bin-Said's and Marija's voices became louder.

"What's that?" Stef asked.

Rick looked toward Caterina. "She still hasn't talked him out of it," she said.

After a glance at the locator she said, "They must be headed to the construction site. Bin-Said wants to make sure the first delivery is still there. I don't know if the material has been taken off the ship yet."

"How can we stop them if Bin-Said has a detonator?" Stef asked.

"Our only chance is to find some safe way to knock it out," Rick said.

"What else is there besides a blocker?" asked Caterina.

"I don't know," Rick said. As he said it he had a brief inkling that he did know of another way. If only he could remember how. "We've got another problem, too," Rick said. "Bob Carpenter is still on the loose."

"Is he the one who shot at Bin-Said?" Stef asked.

"Yes. My guess is that he'll try again at Golden Bay. Either he doesn't know about the detonator or he doesn't care, so he's as dangerous as Bin-Said is himself. We have to stop both of them."

As he said it, a vague recollection tugged at the back of his mind. There was a safe way to nullify the detonator. Think!

His mind was still working desperately as they approached the construction site. Police had blocked off the streets surrounding it in tacit admission of Bin-Said's victory. Caterina found a seldom-used delivery passage that brought them to within a block of the Trade Building. As they were about to get out of the car, a man with a rifle stepped out of the shadows. "Don't move."

Rick recognized the man from the embassy who had furnished him with a gun before his meeting with Pawlu.

"You must be Tom Scicluna."

"Yes. Bin-Said is coming here and he has a detonator."

"Bob Carpenter tried to kill Bin-Said at Borgiswed," Rick said. "If he tries again, Bin-Said will push the button and contaminate the entire Mediterranean."

"I know. Bob may not even care. He hasn't been thinking straight since his daughter was killed at the World Trade Center on 9-11. He's been intent on revenge ever since."

"That explains a lot of things," Rick said. "I always wondered what was eating him. Do you think he'll take a shot at him here?" Rick asked.

"No. He'll be waiting at Golden Harbor. Bin-Said issued an ultimatum to the Maltese government. He's demanding that they deliver the payload from Golden Harbor to the construction site."

"Then the elevator must literally be the bomb," Rick said. "All they would need is a shaped charge. We must let the Maltese Army know. They should be able to send in a demolition expert."

"That's not going to solve the problem. Unless they can disable the detonator, they won't have any choice but to comply with Bin-Said's demands."

The coin dropped.

"There is a way," Rick said excitedly. "How quickly could an aircraft get here from England?"

"An F-111 could make it in an hour. Why?"

"The London police are testing an auto-disabler. If we can get it here in time, we can fry the detonator. I'm sure they would let us use it if they understood the crisis."

"I'll get the ambassador to arrange for the transportation. The Maltese Prime Minister can contact Scotland Yard."

CHAPTER 39

▼

Sunday 1:36
Sliema

Caterina listened as Bin-Said spoke, then breathed a sigh of relief. "Bin-Said is leaving for Golden Bay."

"Good," Rick said.

"The Army is sending in a demolition team dressed as construction workers," Scicluna said. "We have radiation readings coming from somewhere near the elevator."

"I thought so," Rick said. "And that's where the nuclear material is probably locked away. If it's some kind of combination lock, tell them that Marija uses 4-4-6-8 to unlock Black Dolphin's computerized financial files. It's her birthday She could be using the same numbers."

"I'll pass that on," Scicluna said. "If they can defuse the bomb at the Trade Center, part of the problem will be solved."

"Just a small part, unfortunately," Rick said. "We still have to knock out the detonator. Let's hope the EMP generator gets here in time."

"I don't understand how we can use that," Scicluna said. "It would be far too dangerous."

"We're not talking about a nuclear blast. The automobile disabler sends out a much smaller pulse, and it's far more localized. EMP is really just a form of static electricity. It's like a lightning bolt, but without the heat."

"And you say police officers in Britain are using it to stop automobiles?" Stef said.

"At least a few of them. When the police aim the disabler at a car, the pulse travels along the welds in the chassis and attacks the electrical system. It never touches the driver, and it isn't supposed to short-out anyone else's car."

"And just how do you know so much about the subject?" Caterina asked.

"I heard about it on CNN in the Leprechaun Pub the first night I came to Malta. I was interested because it reminded me of how much Kevin likes Nicola Tesla. Then Kevin reminded me of Tunguska. It just occurred to me that if the disabler can knock out the electronics in an automobile, it certainly can do the same thing to Bin-Said's detonator. The only question is whether or not they can get the machine here in time. We haven't had much luck so far."

Conversation ended with Bin-Said's voice. As they listened, Rick became more frustrated. Finally he could control himself no longer. "What's going on now?"

"The Prime Minister agreed to meet Bin-Said at Golden Bay," Caterina replied. As she said it, her cell phone rang. "Good news. The Prime Minister likes your plan. He and the commandant of the Maltese military want to meet you."

1:48 AM

Ten minutes later they were on a lane between fields on a road a short distance from the outskirts of Ghain-Tuffieha.

Scicluna, who was driving Micallef's car, slowed as they came to a large moving-van rig parked along the road. It appeared to be abandoned. "Here's where you get out," he said.

"They won't let Stef come in," Rick said. "Why don't you take him with you? We used to shoot tin cans with a twenty-two. He's a better shot than I am and I scored Expert when I was in the army."

Scicluna looked at Stef and Stef nodded. "Then we'll meet you at Golden Bay."

As Rick and Caterina started toward the van the crunch of their shoes against the road sounded like cannonfire. Startled, Caterina's grip on Rick's arm tightened. He patted her hand reassuringly. Grabbing a handle on the side of the van, he swung himself up. Caterina gave him her hand and he pulled her up beside him. After a few light raps the door moved slightly and he put his mouth close to the door. "It's Rick Olsen and Caterina Borg," he said.

No one spoke. The air coming through the door had a hot, dusty smell and he couldn't hear a sound. Centuries later the door opened wide enough for them to turn sideways and slip inside. The door closed with a quiet thump. As it did, a camp lantern came to life to reveal five men sitting around a table.

One stood. He was short and wore evening clothes with a red sash extending over his left shoulder. Even in the poorest of light, his white teeth glowed when he smiled. Rick liked him immediately.

"Good evening," the man said. "I'm Prime Minister Antony Farrugia. I understand you're the one who gave us the keypad combination that opened the vault where the radioactive material was stored at the construction site. We were able to disable the charges."

"Excellent. Why did the Lull have a military escort from Hal Far?"

"I didn't know it did," Farrugia said. "Perhaps Brigadier Borg-Oliver can explain."

A second man stood. His shadowy profile showed not an ounce of body fat, and his uniform looked as though it had been riveted to his body. He was nearly bald; his few hairs stood rigidly at military attention. Rick guessed that the blue epaulets on his lapels meant he was with the army.

"They weren't ours," the Brigadier said. "Earlier this evening men in military uniforms broke into the camp at Qrendi and freed more than 300 of the refugees. Fortunately we were able to prevent them from doing the same thing at Verdala Barracks."

"Then Bin-Said has moved the takeover up," Rick said. "He's broken cover."

"How can we stop him," the Prime Minister asked.

"We can't do it by force while his detonator is working," the Brigadier replied. "Using an EMP generator to disable it is a good idea but we don't have much time to make our plans. Bin-Said is impatient and wants an answer."

"I'm sure he does," Rick said, moving to the table. Circles and squiggles in red and blue grease pencil decorated the acetate covering a 1:50 scale map of Golden-Bay and Il-Karraba. Cornacchia's beachhouse and dock as well as the bluffs surrounding the area were circled in red. Bin-Said's defensive perimeter was huge, and for that reason, porous. An even larger one in blue engulfed the red circle. "As soon as we have all our information we'll give him one."

After a quick assessment of the map he asked, "Is this a representation of the present situation at Golden Bay?"

"Yes," Borg-Oliver said. "We're faced by at least two hundred men, most of them from the refugee camps. They've set up accordion wire in some places, but generally they're hidden behind the walls and are keeping in contact using walkie-talkies. We're using IF-sensors to locate them, then a special stealth squad wearing special footwear moves in. After they listen to their messages for a while, they know how to respond to calls and they can take over. Bin-Said must have fifty outposts and we own six of them."

"Good work," Rick said. "The important ones are the bluffs so we can use the automobile-disabler when it comes."

"That's what we're working on," the Brigadier said. "We do control the bleachers."

"What are Bin-Said's demands?" Rick asked.

"Essentially that we escort the entire payload to the Trade Building," the Prime Minister said. "It's being transported to the dock at Golden Bay now."

"Did he specify any particular way he wanted the payload delivered?"

"No."

"What do you have for air assets?" Rick asked.

A man in an Air Force blue sweater got to his feet. Younger and heavier than the Brigadier, he also had considerably more hair. "Major Facciol of Number 2 Regiment, Air Squadron. Sir, we have five SA 316B Alouette III Eurocopters at Malta International airport. The load would be too heavy for them, but the Mi-8 inter-island shuttle 'copter may be able to handle it."

"Have you contacted the shuttle service yet?" Rick asked.

"Yes," the PM replied. "It's a concession run by Russians. They were reluctant to get involved but I hinted that it might not be so easy to get their licenses renewed if they didn't cooperate. We'll need them. They're excellent pilots."

That brought a brief collective chuckle from the men seated around the table.

"Anything else?"

A woman stood. "I'm Captain St. Martin with Number One Regiment. We're using parabolic listening devices against the three main positions. As far as I know, no major communications have been intercepted. Bin-Said's men seem to be waiting for orders."

"Anything happening aboard the *Stallion*?" asked Rick.

"There are people on the boat," St. Martin replied. "We can hear their voices. Unfortunately that's about all I can tell you."

Rick nodded. "What about the disabler?"

"I contacted Downing Street," Farrugia said. "The machine and the police officer who operates it are on the way here. It will be coming by way of an F-111 Fighter from Heathrow. It should take a little more than an hour to get here once it takes off."

"Then it's crucial we be able to convince Bin-Said that we need time. That will be up to you, Mr. Prime Minister."

Farrugia nodded. "Oh yes. For one thing he's going to have to produce proof of his claims about the radioactive material. There's really no reason for him to expect me to believe him."

"Excellent idea," Rick said. "Make the SOB produce bills of sale and dates where he bought all the material. We have to buy at least an hour. That should be enough time for the fighter to make it here from Heathrow. Will we have a place to put it when it arrives, Brigadier?"

"You can be sure of that. Our prime objective is to take over the rest of the area around where the bleachers are located. It will give us a base of operations and if worst comes to worst we can hide the equipment behind them."

"I'll do everything I can," the Prime Minister said. "This briefing is over. Everyone get to work and good luck."

*   *   *   *

Three uniformed men suddenly appeared on the road with their rifles leveled on Tom Scicluna. Stef felt a shiver of fear as Scicluna screeched to a halt. One soldier cautiously approached the automobile. "This area is off-limits," he said.

Scicluna stepped out of the car. A second soldier appeared and gestured for Stef to get out, too.

"I'm with the CIA," Scicluna said. "My ID is inside my jacket pocket."

The third soldier moved behind Scicluna with a 9mm pistol in hand. He held it against the agent's head as he used the other hand to reach around to remove the wallet from Scicluna's pocket. He handed it to the first soldier, who examined it with a penlight.

The tension eased. "What are you doing here?" the first soldier asked. "Don't you know the terrorists control the whole area surrounding the bay?"

"No. We were sent ahead to help with the disabler when it arrives."

The soldiers looked at each other. Apparently Scicluna had said the magic word. "We've got a lot of work to do before then. We control the road and after we clear three more posts, we'll have the bleachers, but whoever operates the machine will still be in danger if anyone sees them."

"Where do you want us to park?" Scicluna asked.

"Over there," the soldier said, pointing toward a lane leading between the fences to a field.

After they stopped, Scicluna went to the trunk and returned with two M-16 rifles. He handed one to Stef. "They're loaded with armor-piercing bullets. We may need them."

Stef took a look through the scope. Everything turned incandescent green. "I've never shot at anything living before."

Scicluna nodded. "Let's hope you don't have to use it."

*   *   *   *

The wind whistled around the bleachers as Rick looked through the pair of Canon 15X50 IS binoculars the Brigadier had supplied. The view was so clear that he could count the number of non-slip dimples on Cornacchia's metal dock. He also got an excellent perspective of the fougasse. The pile of rocks that would be thrown into the air was carefully massed at the front of the excavation behind a barrier so they would be thrown forward rather than backwards or to the sides. Shaped charges weren't new. The idea had been around for centuries.

As he slowly scanned the area he saw a small tent at the neck of the outcropping with a light on inside of it. A guard. Probably stationed there to keep juvenile thrill-seekers away, as difficult as it would be for anyone to pass the overhang in the ten-foot climb to the top of il-Karraba.

He handed the binoculars to the Brigadier and turned to look at the bleachers behind them. They were well constructed and afforded a wonderful view of the ancient weapon. But would the Independence Day celebration still go on with Marija Cornacchia in control? Would anyone dare to leave their houses if Bin-Said set off the charges? Hiding would do no good because there was no escape. If the radiation didn't kill them immediately, it would be inhaled or ingested and finish the job later.

All such options nauseated him. Somehow they had to stop both plans cold.

The Brigadier, who was wearing an earpiece, interrupted his musings. In a low voice he said, "The Prime Minister is talking to Bin-Said. He's demanding proof that there is radioactive material."

"I bet Bin-Said loves that," Rick chortled. "He hates being challenged. Do you know he once said that if he were the commander at the Siege of Malta instead of Mustafa Pasha, the Turks would have won?"

"No, but it doesn't surprise me. He's a megalomaniac, if I have the term correct."

"That describes him perfectly."

"Whose idea was the dirty bomb?"

"That probably was his. Marija just provided the opportunity to set his idea in motion. Apparently they were business associates for several years before they became partners in the cabal."

Rick looked at his watch. If all had gone as planned, the F-111 would now be halfway to Malta. What would the situation be when it arrived here? "Do you have any idea where Bin-Said is now?" he asked.

"No," said the Brigadier, "but he demanded that the Prime Minister meet him at the beachhouse for the inspection."

"Isn't the Prime Minister worried he'll be kidnapped?"

"Of course. But he's too intent on preventing a disaster to worry about his personal safety."

Caterina sat next to Rick on the bleacher seat shivering. Rick put his arm around her. "Scared or cold?" he asked.

"Both," she said, teeth-chattering. She took his hand. "Are you disappointed to find out that I'm a cop?"

"A little. It's hard for me to think you're anything other than what you seemed."

"You know the real me. I'm actually just a reservist," she said. "Inspector Micallef saw my work with the church as a perfect cover to go after George Bezzina. I intend to resign when this is over. You're not angry at me for not telling you, are you?"

"No," Rick said. "I've always liked your tough side, too. Do you want to take a look through the binoculars to pass the time?"

"Why not?" she replied. Rick handed them to her. She slowly scanned the area controlled by Bin-Said's troops. Then she stopped. "What are you looking at?" he asked.

"The summer house. Strange. No one seems to be there and nothing's happening."

"How about the dock?" asked Rick.

"Just three soldiers standing around and smoking. They're not even talking to each other. They look bored stiff."

"What's happening at the top of the hill?"

She turned. "Nothing. Wait. I see headlights. Someone must be coming."

Rick could see the headlights without the binoculars.

"It's a Mercedes," said Caterina.

"The villains have arrived on the set."

After a series of switchbacks the auto reached the bottom of the hill. Rick saw three soldiers come out of the summerhouse to meet them. Bin-Said embraced all three of them, then started toward the house leaving Marija and Ibn to fend for themselves.

"Half the cast is on the stage. I wonder how long it will be until PM Farrugia arrives."

They were both thoroughly chilled when a limousine flying gold-bordered governmental flags arrived fifteen minutes later. Rick handed Caterina the binoculars. "I'll keep you warm while you look through the glasses," he said.

She took them from him. "Someone rolled down a window in the limousine, and one of the soldiers is talking."

"To the driver or the PM?"

"To the driver," Caterina replied. Even without binoculars Rick could clearly see the soldier start forward, his body outlined by the headlights of the limo just a few feet behind him. Another soldier followed the vehicle, holding his weapon at firing position at his waist. Men and machine traced the tortuous route Marija had used, and soon they were at the bottom of the hill.

"It looks like it's time for Bin-Said and the PM to have a chat," Rick said.

Once again a window in the rear of the car rolled down. A soldier approached the window, then nodded. Rick and Caterina watched as he walked off the dock and up to the door of the summerhouse.

"Now things start to get interesting," Rick said.

Brigadier Borg-Oliver was waiting for them inside his makeshift headquarters underneath the bleachers overlooking il-Karraba. The army had covered a section with a tarp and surrounded the space inside with acoustic foam. Even though the enemy was only seventy meters away, they had no idea the Brigadier was there in a soundproof and lightproof shelter. Despite its rude appearance, the tiny cavity under the stand was crammed with sophisticated electronic equipment. The Brigadier sat at a table that was little more than a camp cot with a piece of red cloth on top of it. "Sit down," he said pointing at two stools. "I have extra headsets."

A short-wave radio sat on the table with a split extension plug leading from it. Rick plugged the earphones into one of the sockets. Voices speaking in English came from the receiver.

"Is the Prime Minister wearing a bug?" Rick asked.

"Yes, but Bin-Said knows about it and he doesn't mind," the Brigadier replied. "He says he wants as many people as possible to listen. In fact he has someone videotaping the conference and he wants CNN to rebroadcast the entire meeting."

"Why doesn't that surprise me?" Rick said in disgust.

"Hello, Mr. Prime-Minister. Thank you for coming." Bin-Said's voice was urbane and friendly. Rick snorted.

"You didn't leave me much choice," Farrugia replied in a cold voice.

"We're sorry to have to resort to blackmail, but reestablishing Islamic control of this part of the Mediterranean is of utmost importance to all of our people. We only do what is necessary."

"You don't represent Islam," Farrugia said firmly. "And what you're doing isn't necessary."

Rick smiled as he imagined Bin-Said struggling to keep his composure. "Don't you understand? The only way to accomplish great deeds in the face of a stronger enemy is to present a threat that he cannot overcome."

"I'm not interested in hearing your justification for your actions," the PM said angrily. "You have a dirty bomb on *my* island and all I care about is finding out what I have to do to prevent you from setting it off."

Bin-Said's voice was no longer friendly. "The materials for our defensive weapon came in three shipments. The first was already at the assembly point and the second came in by aircraft. The third is being delivered to the dock at Golden Bay. When it arrives the Islamic people demand safe passage to the site. If you do not comply we will be forced into an action that will have a dire effect on your island and the entire Mediterranean."

"And all the Islamic countries in Africa and the Middle East, too, sooner or later," Farrugia added dryly.

"There is no danger. No one will dare to confront us."

"What if there's an accident? You can't control all situations."

When Bin-Said didn't answer, Farrugia continued. "Since I have no choice, you have your guarantee of safe passage."

"Then we understand each other," said Bin-Said. "You are responsible for getting the payload to the construction site. The payload will be on the dock in half-an-hour. Your conveyance must be there to pick it up and deliver it to the construction site when it arrives."

"That's impossible," said the Prime Minister. "Your transporter would never get here in time and the helicopter shuttle that runs between the islands is the only conveyance that could carry that much weight. It will take at least an hour to get here."

"Too long," said Bin-Said.

"It can't be helped," the Prime Minister said firmly.

Bin-Said snarled in frustration. "Then you have forty-five minutes to complete the delivery,"

"It sounds like the Russians agreed to help," Rick said.

"The PM says they're very willing to do whatever they can," said the Brigadier. "They didn't like the idea of carrying radioactive material around but they were sure the 'copter will be able to handle the load."

Rick looked at his watch. According to Bin-Said's timetable, they had only forty-five minutes left. "We're cutting this way too close," he said, shaking his head.

"I know," the Brigadier said. He took his headset off and got to his feet. "It sounds like they're done. Let's go outside and make sure that the PM is allowed to leave."

As he said it, Farrugia emerged from Cornacchia's summerhouse. The doors of the limousine opened, then the headlights turned on. Once again the vehicle started its torturous back-and-forth run to the top of the hill following the soldier who led it.

"The Prime Minister is safe," the Brigadier said. "Let's hope everything else runs as smoothly."

*   *   *   *

Stef stayed a step behind Scicluna as they cautiously moved forward through the dry scrub. Neither had spoken for several minutes and speech seemed unnecessary. They were alone except for an occasional rustle of a small animal. Once Stef heard the flap of wings coming from a tree above them and guessed it must have been an owl angry with humans disturbing its hunting ground.

Scicluna stopped suddenly and held out a hand to stop Stef. The agent took several steps forward, then returned. Cupping his hand over Stef's ear, he whispered. "There's someone up ahead."

CHAPTER 40

▼

Sunday
2:31 AM
Golden Bay

Bin-Said's helicopter arrived in a tantrum of noise. The racket brought Rick, Caterina and the Brigadier scurrying from the bleachers. Rick caught a look at the craft as it was outlined against the night sky above the dock. "It's what we called a Hind," he said to Caterina. "The Soviets used them as war planes."

The craft moved slowly straining to support a heavy weight dangling beneath it. Then a light from its belly turned on to illuminate the dock.

Two men in uniform came running to meet it. When the chopper was directly over the dock the load slowly descended until it landed heavily on the planking. One of the men undid the chains and the craft pulled free. Rick watched it as it swung about and headed back to sea.

"The payload is here," Rick said. "Now where's the shuttle?"

They didn't have long to wait. They heard rotor noise coming from behind them. Another, larger, helicopter appeared and slowly moved toward a soldier on the dock who was waving a powerful flashlight.

The 'copter moved above him, hovered for an instant, then dropped a heavy cable with a hook attached to it. The two soldiers worked together to fasten the cable to the pallet. Then, wraithlike, the chopper rose a few feet higher. The cables tightened. When the soldier who had been securing the load gestured, the helicopter slowly lifted the pallet off the ground. It dangled without swinging. The engine noise changed and the craft started away.

"There they go," Rick said.

Within seconds craft and cargo passed over the sentries at the top of the hill. "Now we have to hold our breath until it arrives at the Trade Building," Rick said. "I still can't figure why the F-111 hasn't arrived yet."

"I'll contact the airport," the Brigadier said. "It must have been delayed."

Rick and Caterina watched until the red and white lights on the chopper disappeared, then huddled together for warmth. Everything suddenly seemed very cold and dark. The mood didn't improve when the Brigadier returned with bad news. "The plane was delayed in leaving Heathrow. It's supposed to be here in ten minutes."

Rick sighed. "We'll have to arrange for a helicopter to carry the equipment somewhere near here. Tell your pilots to find a place to land. I have an idea how we can flush Bin-Said and his detonator out of hiding."

Bin-Said sounded livid as he repeated Prime Minister Farrugia's statement. "What do you mean you ordered the helicopter to land because you can't be sure I won't detonate the explosives while your helicopter is in the air?"

"I'm only stating a fact. An air burst would give you maximum dissemination."

"If I intended to do that, I could have done it when I was bringing the cargo here."

"Perhaps you want everyone to be watching when you set it off," Farrugia replied.

"That's ridiculous," the Arab steamed. "I've given you my word."

"And I've given you mine. But we both have to have a way to ensure that the agreement is carried out. There's no more reason for you to trust me than there is for me to trust you."

Rick smiled. Beautifully put. Distrust was a two-way street.

"You have offended me deeply and it would cost a lesser man his life, but I understand your concern. How do you suggest we go about ensuring mutual compliance?"

"The only way I can see to do it is if you keep the detonator somewhere in my view but within your reach until the mission is completed."

"So your sniper can kill me before I can press the button?" Bin-Said scoffed. "I won't be that careless again."

"We'll be out of sight inside the summerhouse or on the boat," Ferrugia said coolly. "Any place you feel safe. It will be more difficult for me to stop you from pushing the button than it will be for you to incapacitate me."

Again, Rick had to applaud. The PM was a masterful negotiator.

"By your logic, how do you know I won't incapacitate you and do it anyway?" asked Bin-Said.

"I don't," the Prime Minister replied. "But I'm willing to take that chance."

After what must have been a thoughtful silence, Bin-Said replied. "I see your point. Then perhaps adjourning to the Stallion would be the best course. How quickly can you return?"

"I'm only ten minutes away," Farrugia replied.

After another cold and nerve-wracking delay, Rick and Caterina saw the headlights of the Prime Minister's limousine glowing some two hundred yards from them. After zigzagging its way down the hill, it stopped in back of the summerhouse and Farrugia stepped out.

Two men emerged from the house. A fourth man dressed in a dark-colored suit—Rick guessed the Prime Minister's bodyguard—got out of the limousine and the four of them walked to the dock and got into a waiting dinghy. A small outboard motor coughed into life and the boat was on its way to the *Stallion*. After the men disappeared into the cabin, Rick lowered the glasses. They felt like a lodestone around his neck.

Minutes later Brigadier Borg-Oliver appeared from under the bleachers. "Good news. The F-111 arrived at Malta International Airport. One of my 'copters is bringing it here."

They waited in silence. An eternity later they heard the flail of helicopter rotors a distance away behind the bleachers. Rick trained the binoculars at the top of the hill overlooking the summerhouse and watched the huge rotors slow and then stop.

"It's Bin-Said's chopper," Rick said.

"Why did it come back here?" Caterina asked.

"It's probably waiting to take him back to the freighter when the meeting is done."

"No danger of that," the Brigadier said grimly. "You can rest assured it will not fly again tonight."

A young soldier emerged from the darkness. After coming to attention and saluting, he said, "Your equipment is here from the airport, sir. We landed at the same time as the other chopper so the enemy wouldn't hear us coming."

"Give my congratulations to the pilot, young man," the Brigadier said.

A Hum-V with lights off approached them and stopped. A man dressed in a raincoat and galoshes emerged. He was nearly Rick's height.

"You must be the operator," Rick said in a whisper. "Was it raining when you left London?"

"No," the man whispered back. "I don't like to operate the disabler without protection. That bleeding machine scares me, it does. I'm Police-Sergeant Guilfoyle."

A second man got out of the car. "I'm Lieutenant Sciortino, 2nd Division," the pilot said in a low voice.

"Where's this death ray we've been waiting for?" Rick asked.

"In the back seat," Guilfoyle said. "But I wouldn't joke that way, sir. It really is spooky. I've only used it twice against vehicles. It's like poof! and it kills the engine immediately. Why are we whispering?"

"The enemy is less than 50 meters away," the Brigadier said.

Rick, Caterina and the Brigadier gathered around as two young men moved into the backseat of the Hum-V. It took both of them to move something that looked to be just slightly larger than an over-sized suitcase. "We generally set the disabler on the fender of a car and run it off the battery," Guilfoyle said.

"All you need is a twelve-volt battery?" Rick asked in astonishment.

"It doesn't take much to build up a charge. It operates on a laser. Have you ever heard of an en-dee Yag?"

No one had.

"You don't want to know the technical rot," Guilfoyle said in a disgusted voice. "Someone explained it to me, but I have no idea what it all means." He gestured for the soldiers to put the disabler on the hood of the Hum-V.

"How does it work?" Rick asked.

"What happens is the laser ionizes the air and the current follows it. Where is this detonator I'm supposed to short out?"

"It's on a boat," the Brigadier said. "You'll be able to see it when you move further forward. If we keep the bleachers between us and the enemy, we should be able to move it into position without being seen."

"If it's on a boat, we're going to knock out the entire electrical system, too," Guilfoyle said.

"The Prime Minister will be in danger if Bin-Said finds out," said Caterina.

"We don't have any choice," the Brigadier said. "What do we do with the machine?"

"We'll mount it on the fender and aim it by line-of-sight," Guilfoyle said. "It's supposed to work on Global Positioning but as far as I'm concerned it's point and shoot. The rear end of a car is a fairly sizable target. The boat should be even bigger."

The police sergeant and the driver lifted the case onto the fender of the HumV and Guilfoyle opened it. Rick had guessed it would look like a terminal of a Jacob's ladder and it did, somewhat. Several inches of tubing sat on top of a rectangular box. The front end of the tubing had a pointed nose. Guilfoyle connected two wires to the back of the machine. "We have to ground it," he said, clamping an alligator clip connector to the fender. The second cable he fastened to the vehicle's battery.

As he did, Rick thought he heard a low hum. "It runs on 12 volts?" he asked.

"It does, and it only takes a few seconds to warm up," the sergeant said. Tension grew as they waited for the next pronouncement.

Finally he said, "Let's move it into place."

The Hum-V crept forward and everyone else walked alongside it. Everyone held his or her breath as it ran over a branch producing a large snap. When they reached the edge of the hill, Guilfoyle moved forward. Seconds later he said, "This won't work."

"What do you mean?" asked the Brigadier.

"The angle is wrong. We need to position this thing so it's aimed at the boat."

"How do we do that?"

"There's only one way to do it," Guilfoyle replied. "We have to drive the vehicle into position and use a rifle scope to target it."

Rick snorted. The futility of using line-of-sight targeting at a boat that was more than 700 meters away made him ill. Twenty-Second Century technology or not, Guilfoyle's auto disabler was a dud.

One of the soldiers left and returned with a night scope. Rick nearly laughed as he watched him strap it on top of the disabler with duct tape. When the scope was firmly attached to the front of the disabler, Rick bent forward to look through it. "We're still aiming too high. We'll have to get a lower angle."

"We only have a few feet to the edge of the cliff," Caterina said.

"If we move it ahead that far we'll be in plain sight," the Brigadier said.

"What choice do we have?" Rick asked.

"You're right," said the Brigadier.

The driver pulled ahead. As it reached the ledge, a rock pulled loose and clattered over the side of the cliff. Rick sighted again. "Still too high. Can you pull ahead a bit more?"

Just then several rifle shots coming from below and the positions on top of the bluff interrupted him. One bullet whizzed over the top of Rick's head. "We've been spotted," he cried. "Hit the ground."

"We're not going to have much time to use the disabler," the Brigadier shouted. "Bin-Said must have heard the shooting by now."

"I'll pull forward another few inches," the young soldier in the driver's seat said. Bending low, he reached for the brake. Before he could reach it they were the targets of another fusillade of gunfire. The driver cried out and slumped against the wheel.

"Help me get him out," Caterina cried as she tugged at the soldier's arm. Rick stood on the edge of the floorboard and pulled him away from the wheel. A second later a bullet passed through the windshield where the soldier was sitting.

Caterina coolly got into the driver's seat.

"Get out," Rick shouted. "I'll move the Hummer."

She wasn't listening. She disengaged the emergency brake and the vehicle rolled forward. A shower of rocks dropped over the edge to the ground below.

"Get out," he shouted. "I'll take it from here." Without regard for his own safety, Rick looked through the gun scope.

The lights of another Hum-V lit them up as it started to climb the hill below them, followed by several uniformed men who were following it, firing as they moved.

More frightened for Caterina than himself, Rick doggedly stood his ground. "We're still aiming too high," he said in desperation. On cue, the vehicle took another baby-step forward. Another hail of bullets and Caterina gasped.

"Are you hit?" he screamed.

"Forget me," Caterina replied. "Shoot."

Wiping his eyes with his upper arm, he bent forward. The scope was directly on the Stallion's middle. Turning to Guilfoyle, he shouted, "Fire!"

Guilfoyle pushed a button. The machine made a buzz but nothing seemed to happen although Rick caught a whiff of ozone. "The damned thing didn't work," Rick said. "Try it again."

"It worked," Guilfoyle said simply.

Rick braced himself and opened the door of the vehicle. Outlined against the sky, he presented a perfect target. Reaching out his hand, he pulled Caterina out of the Hum-V. He barely had a hold of her when the vehicle slid forward.

"Watch out!" Rick shouted. The vehicle rolled forward another foot, then toppled forward down the side of the steep hill toward the on-coming men. It hit the ground and burst into flames. The enemy Hum-V caught fire. The men near it scattered, some with uniforms ablaze.

Rick helped Caterina to her feet. "Are you hurt?"

"Not very," she said lifting her hand away from her left shoulder. Rick could see blood. "It's just a flesh wound."

Below, the handful of men had now turned into a large company and another contingent moved toward them from their left flank. Before they could get any closer, they were greeted by gunfire from the Brigadier's men. Rick and company turned at the sound of a loud explosion and one of the Brigadier's men dropped. Then a second report and a second soldier fell to the ground. The other soldiers turned to fire behind them.

"That sounded like a shotgun," Rick said. "Who's shooting?"

"I have no idea," the Brigadier said. Several of his soldiers rushed forward. One fired at a position behind where the troops had been standing when they were shot.

"I think I have a pretty good idea who it is," Caterina said.

"Il-Tariq?" Rick asked. She nodded.

Someone appeared on deck of the Stallion then quickly ducked back inside. Why hadn't the yacht taken off? The Brigadier ducked inside his headquarters and quickly returned. "We did it. We're not getting any radio signals from the Stallion."

"Maybe Bin-Said doesn't need a radio. Look."

Far out to sea in the darkness, a light flashed intermittently. With binoculars, Rick saw a man on top of the Stallion with his back to the shore. Probably signaling using an electric lantern.

The light flashes from sea ended.

Ben-Said's minions took cover as the Brigadier's men began to fire. "I've called for a Navy boat to board The Stallion," the Brigadier said.

"I hope it gets here in time," Rick replied. He pointed at a silver streak in the water moving in the direction of Cornacchia's yacht from where the light flashes had originated. "If they're coming for Bin-Said, we have to stop them. That's a speedboat and it's probably from the freighter. They must have sent it because they can't contact the helicopter."

"How do we stop them?" the Brigadier asked.

"It won't be with the disabler," Guilfoyle said.

"We don't need it," Rick replied. He turned to the Brigadier. "Do you have any hand grenades?"

"No, but all my men carry one with them."

"Then let's gather up a few," Rick said. Turning to the helicopter pilot, he said, "Lieutenant, you and I have some work to do."

After requisitioning three grenades, the two of them hurried to the 'copter. With a sound of whirring metal, the blades began to turn above their heads. "We're going to have to hurry," said Rick.

The Alouette lifted off the ground.

"Can you scan to see if you can pick up radio signals from the speedboat?" Rick asked.

"Yes," the Lieutenant said. As they climbed higher, Rick caught a view of Bin-Said's escape craft mooring next to the Stallion. He also saw lights coming from the other side of Golden Bay. A powerful light searched the water ahead of them as a dark craft sped onward. The harbor patrol boat was moving toward the Stallion, but was still a long way away from it.

The scanner stopped at the sound of an Arabic voice. "That must be from the speedboat," the pilot said.

Rick returned his attention to the Stallion. The first person to board the speedboat was Marija Cornacchia. Then Ibn, carrying what must have been one of the basins. The next person out appeared to be Prime Minister Farrugia. A flash of light inside the Stallion meant gunfire. Rick and Caterina gasped as Farrugia dove headlong into the sea. Bin-Said emerged with the second basin and made his way over to the waiting seacraft.

The boat moved away slowly without lights, keeping to the shadows of il-Karraba. The patrol boat continued on a straight course for the *Stallion*.

The radio came alive with the sound of Bin-Said's voice.

"Your ship doesn't see Bin-Said's boat," Rick said. "We'll have to be the ones to stop him. If he gets away with the Shield there will be hell to pay."

Below them, il-Karraba jutted boldly into the sea.

Bin-Said's boat picked up speed and the terrorist's voice came on the radio. Rick prayed that they would be able to stop him. The red lights of the fougasse glowed scant meters ahead. "Break off to the left," Rick said. "We don't want to spook them."

As they did, Rick felt something-cold press against the back of his head. "Hand me a grenade," said a familiar voice.

"Hello, Bob," Rick said staring at the automatic in Carpenter's hand. "I wondered where you were." He passed a grenade over the back of the seat. The helicopter lost altitude, and Rick pitched forward.

Carpenter was unaffected. "I don't recommend you do that again," he said. "Or we'll all be dead. Does this window open?"

"No," the Lieutenant replied.

Below, Bin-Said's boat was now nearly to the end of il-Karraba. "Back over the peninsula," Carpenter shouted. Without warning, he opened the door.

Wind blasted Rick in the face. "Are you crazy?" he shouted.

Carpenter pulled the pin on the grenade. The 'copter passed over the red light marking the fougasse's location. Although Carpenter waited until they were directly over the pit, the grenade dropped and exploded without setting off the charge.

"We'll have to make another pass," Rick said. Bin-Said's voice still came through over the wind coming through the open door.

"Give me another grenade," Carpenter shouted. "I'll make sure the son-of-a-bitch goes where's it's supposed to."

"Get back in here, Bob," Rick said. "We'll make another pass, but come in lower this time."

"Don't argue. Just give me the grenade."

Rick was about to hand it to him when Carpenter said, "Pull the pin first."

He did, feeling a moment of terror as he held it out. Carpenter deftly wrapped his fingers around the trigger plate. "Take us down," the agent shouted.

The helicopter moved downwards. The pit of the fougasse was but yards ahead of them. A form below tried to wave them away, then, apparently understanding what was happening, ran headlong toward the neck of the peninsula. Rick hoped the man would be all right when the fougasse went off.

"Come ahead more," Carpenter screamed. Holding on to the doorframe with one hand, he bent backwards, clutching the grenade with the other hand.

The Alouette hit an air pocket and made an unexpected dip. Rick reacted immediately by grabbing for Carpenter's hand. His fingers brushed against the agent's wrist but he couldn't get a hold. Caught by surprise and holding on with only one hand, Carpenter swung away from the 'copter then silently dropped toward the pit.

"Ohmygod!" Rick said in a choked voice. Then, realizing the danger they were in, shouted, "Get us out of here, quick! We've got three seconds."

The Alouette veered off in a sharp turn, fighting to gain altitude. Two. The pilot pointed the nose toward the ground, intending to take the shock waves of the blast in the fuselage rather than in the blades. One.

The fougasse erupted into an orange inferno and a powerful invisible hand shoved them forward, shaking the machine so violently that Rick was certain they would be knocked out of the air. Unconsciously he grabbed for his St. Jude medal.

The chopper dipped. But the blades continued to turn. An instant later they were again moving forward. He fingered the medal, remembering the sight of Carpenter's body hurtling into the pit. Was it a foretaste of what lay ahead of him in the afterlife? Or did God have the compassion to forgive the actions of the heartbroken?

"Great flying," Rick said. "Let's go back and see what happened."

As they emerged over the point of the peninsula a thick cloud of smoke hung over the water and Rick could see nothing. "Can we go lower?"

The craft eased downwards.

The first thing Rick saw was the patrol boat coming in their direction with its searchlight on. Below them, flotsam bobbed on the surface, but he saw no signs of survivors. "I think we did it," he said. "Let's go back."

As the chopper made a lazy arc and started back to the mainland, Rick realized that the circle was now complete. The story begun with Bartelemeo Cornacchia and Benvenuto Cellini had ended with the detonation of a weapon as ancient as gunpowder itself. Marija, Ibn, Bin-Said and Bob Carpenter as well had left the earth to face their ultimate destinies. It wasn't until he realized that he was still fingering the medal that he realized how much he had changed since coming to Malta.

The Alouette returned to the field and set down. Caterina and the Brigadier were waiting for them. Tears streamed down Caterina's face as they emerged. Rick reached for her. Brigadier Borg-Oliver seemed speechless. As they neared the gate a voice cried out, "Stop." Rick squinted and saw a dark form standing in front of the gate.

"Who's that?" the Brigadier asked.

"Kareem il-Tariq," Rick whispered. "He's one of the men who kidnapped Stef."

"Y-you m-murdered M-Muhammed Bin-Said," the young man said in a choked voice. "He was A-Allah's an-anointed."

"He was a murderer," Caterina said. "He was deceived by Satan."

"Are you crazy?" Rick asked, catching her arm. But she yanked free and took another step forward. Il-Tariq raised the shotgun. "S-stay where y-you are."

Rick inched forward, trying to catch hold of Caterina's waist but she continued to inch forward. As he stared at il-Tariq he could swear he saw Stef on the road behind the Arab. But it was such a brief glimpse that Rick was sure he was imagining things.

"My Aunt Josefina and I gave you a room," Caterina said. "You know from your friends we do Allah's will by tending to the needy, as it says we should do in the Koran."

Rick caught her by the waist and pulled her to a stop.

"You d-do not do Al-Allah's will. You are assassins." He raised the shotgun.

Rick pulled Caterina's feet from under her and she fell to the ground. Frightened, il-Tariq turned the shotgun toward him. With what he knew would be his last breath Rick saw il-Tariq's finger tighten on the trigger. Then an explosion and something slammed against his chest.

Falling, he heard Caterina shouting his name. As he drifted off into oblivion, his last thought was "Who's going to look after Stef now?"

EPILOGUE

▼

Though his eyes were closed he saw light, and he wondered what he would find in the afterlife.

He also heard sounds. Voices?

Then he realized he was breathing, though it was difficult, and the sharp odor of disinfectant hurt when he drew a breath. Surprising, but not impossible.

Unable to control himself any longer he opened his eyes. Caterina bent forward and kissed him on the forehead. "You're awake," she cried.

"What are you doing here?" Rick asked. "Did il-Tariq kill you, too?"

"No. You're alive but you have two badly broken ribs. The doctors wanted you to stay still so they kept you sedated."

As he opened his eyes farther he noticed that not only was Caterina with him, but Stef, and Josefina. It was too much. "I don't understand," Rick gasped. "Il-Tariq had a shotgun. I heard it go off and I felt the shot hit my chest. I should be lying around in a hundred pieces."

"That wasn't the shotgun that hit you," Stef's voice said. "I shot il-Tariq before he had a chance to shoot you. The bullet went right through him and hit you."

"If your heart were on the other side of your chest, you'd be dead now," Caterina said.

"Isn't today Independence Day?"

"That was yesterday," Caterina said. "You slept through it. We had a wonderful parade and publicly mourned the deaths of Lorenzo Cornacchia and Cardinal Vella at the hands of an assassin. Everyone was extremely disappointed they couldn't watch the firing of the fougasse, but since some vandal set it off, it couldn't be helped." She paused. "You also have a long message from Father Santorini. Do you want to hear it?"

"Of course," Rick said.

"'Dear Richard, After our last conversation I transcribed the letters on the banner above the Prester John figure on the outside of The Shield to a ten by ten Polybius Square and wrote out the characters from all the price lists and showed them to my Ethiopian friend. Believe it or not, the cinnamon price list contained this message, apparently intended for Bartolomeo's family. "28 September 1566. The damnable Cellini betrayed me twice. Not only did he steal my gold but he inscribed the characters on the inside of the Shield incorrectly so the message cannot be read. He will pay. Travelling to Florence to exact my revenge.'"

"It looked like he failed," Stef said. "Cellini lived for another twelve years."

Rick started to laugh but with his chest taped up he could hardly breathe. After much coughing he was finally able to talk. "You're wrong," he gasped. "He did get his revenge. You told me about finding reference to some 'damnable alchemist' living on his farm for years without paying. You thought it referred to Brother Konstanz. It was Bartelemeo Cornacchia."

"You're kidding," Stef said. After a moment's thought, he broke into laughter, too. "But he was a noble. He would never stand for living like a peasant on a farm."

"Of course not. So Cellini had to keep him in the manner he was accustomed. Bartolomeo must have been afraid the Knights or Suleiman would come after him. I hope the son of a gun soaked Cellini bigtime. This is wonderful. If ever two men deserved each other, they did. They were two of the biggest scalawags in history."

Caterina took charge. "That's enough fun for now," she said. "Any more last minute revelations to make? If not, I think Mr. Olsen can use some rest."

"What happened to the Prime Minister?" Rick asked.

"He swam to shore safely. The only ones that didn't make it were in the boat."

"Great."

Stef, who looked as if he were groping for words, finally bent forward and kissed Rick on the forehead. "I bet if we went snorkeling we could find the basins," he said. "But it's going to have to wait until I'm done with my dissertation. I hope I can still get it published. It was a sure thing when I had the drawing."

"It still is," Rick said. "All you need to do is get the documentation from Bartolomeo's journal. Father Santorini has a copy of the drawing."

"When will you leave for home?" Stef asked.

"In a week or two. I'll have to pack the household goods and put the house up for sale. Caterina and I will be living here."

"You're not living with her unless you marry her," Josefina said, hands on hips.

"The wedding will be in April at Ta Pinu Church in Gozo. It's a holy site of many miracles and she has already planned the date."

Caterina lay her head on his shoulder. "And guess who's not driving on the honeymoon," she murmured.

THE END

0-595-66688-4

Printed in the United States
96848LV00008B/14/A